Contents

SUMMER

Kerry Profitt's diary, August 11

Once again I woke up screaming. Drenched in sweat, wet sheets tangled around my legs as if I'd been flailing them for hours. Brandy even came into our room and told me she could tell the instant I snapped out of it. My mouth was open like a gasping fish, she said, and then it closed, and my eyes opened. And I had let out a real ear-piercer, because, after all, there was this face in front of me, looking at me like I was some kind of sideshow freak.

Which, you know, if the shoe fits . . .

When my heart stopped trying to tear through my rib cage, and I could breathe again, she asked me what I'd been dreaming about. Hell if I know, I told her. Whenever I wake up, I can never remember anything more than an overpowering sense of dread. Doom on wheels.

Maybe it's the weird hours I've been keeping. I worked till eleven last night, same as the night before, but had the breakfast-and-lunch shift for three days before that. Today it's the late shift again, so I slept in probably longer than I should have. My head is throbbing so hard I can barely see the computer screen, and who knows if I'll be able to read this later?

But that's why Einstein invented ibuprofen, right? And spell check. And Scott's brewing fresh coffee. Nectar of the gods.

More later.

K.

1

She couldn't see the ocean from where she stood on a grease-caked cement step just outside the kitchen's back door. A row of bungalows—identical dark boxes, some with glowing windows—blocked her view. She could hear the water, though—the steady, dull thunder of the surf reminding her that it was close, at the edge of both the Seaside Resort and the continent. And she could smell it, a sharp tang that battled for supremacy over the smells of steak, seafood, and smoke that blew out from the kitchen. Towering above the bungalows, underlit by the resort's floodlights, incredibly tall palm trees swayed on their skinny trunks in the evening breeze, looking like skyrocket bursts frozen in time at the ends of their own contrails. A sliver of crescent moon dangled above them, high and distant.

Kerry Profitt was a daughter of the Great Plains, born and raised near the confluence of two great rivers in Cairo, Illinois. But the Mississippi and Ohio, powerful as they were, had nothing on the Pacific Ocean. The ocean was magical to her, its depths and mysteries were boundless, its call irresistible. She had made a point, since hitting La Jolla, California, for her summer job, of keeping it in sight whenever possible. Bad for the skin, all that sun and salt air, and she, with her complexion like fresh snow ("whitest white girl I've ever seen" was what Brandy said) knew better. But she couldn't deny the ocean's magnetic pull.

Lost in thought, she didn't see the shadowed figure slip into the alley, didn't know she wasn't alone until the voice startled her. "Hey, Kerr, where is it the swallows go back to?"

Startled, she managed to keep her cool, and she smiled when she recognized the voice. She knew it belonged to Josh Quinn, one of her housemates, but it took her a moment to refocus her gaze and pick him out in the dark alley. His skin was every bit as pale as hers, but by choice, not genetics, and the black of his hair came from a bottle, unlike hers. He looked as out-of-place in the valet's uniform—white shirt, maroon vest, black pants—as a lion on a kindergarten playground.

"Umm . . . Capistrano, I think," Kerry replied after a moment's consideration. She was used to this kind of thing from Josh, king of the nonsequitur. *If his middle name isn't Random, it should be.*

"Yeah, that's right," he agreed.

Since it didn't seem like he was going to take the discussion any further, she decided to press the point. "Why?"

He struck a match in the darkness and shielded it with cupped hands to a cigarette held between his lips. "These tourists, man," he said around the butt. Then, blowing out a plume of smoke—away from Kerry, because she would have killed him if he hadn't—he continued with an exasperated tone. "They're like those swallows."

"The ones in Capistrano?"

"Yeah, those."

"In what way?" *You had to ask,* she immediately chastised herself, bracing for the answer.

"Some of them seem to come here every summer, like clockwork."

She had noticed the same thing, though without the bird metaphor. "Good for business, I guess," she pointed out.

"I guess. But this one guy—you know the kind, enormous gut, Texas accent, gold watch that cost more than everything I've owned in my life put together—yelled at me just now because I didn't turn on the heat in his Mercedes."

"The heat?" Kerry asked with surprise. It was a fairly cool night. They all were here, close to the water, and balmy eves, she had learned, were not so much a southern California thing. Once the sun went down, the day's heat fled fast. But even so, far from wintry cold.

"That's what I said. Only it was more like, 'Dude, are you

freaking crazy? It's August!' And he was like, 'I told you last year, if it's after dark, I like the heat on when you bring the car around. It takes time to warm up.'"

"But you didn't work here last year," Kerry pointed out.

Josh jabbed the glowing end of his cigarette at her to emphasize his point. "Exactly," he said. "But you think reality matters to this guy? Like I'm the first Goth valet in California history or something, so it couldn't have been someone else he told last year. He's so convinced it was me, he stiffed me on the tip."

Kerry pushed aside the hand that held the cigarette. She had made clear, plenty of times, what she thought of that habit and couldn't understand how he managed to reconcile it with his vegan lifestyle. "Hey," he had said when she'd raised the question once, "who said life was free of contradiction? Anyway, it's a vegetable. If tobacco had a face, I wouldn't smoke it." Sympathetically, in spite of the noxious weed, she rubbed Josh's bony shoulder. "There are always a few pains," she said. "But most of the guests are pretty nice."

"Maybe to you," Josh countered. "You can spit in their food. All I can do is adjust their seat backs wrong, and the potential threat level just isn't the same."

Kerry laughed then and punched the shoulder she had just been rubbing. "I'll tell you what," she offered. "I'll trade places with you for a day. You deal with complaints about food being too hot or too cold or too spicy or too bland, and guys grabbing your ass and winking at you like you're going to go, 'Oh, you're just so handsome. I'll put this tray of food down and meet you in the alley.'"

"I guess it depends on the guy," Josh suggested with a smile she could see in the glow of his cigarette embers as he inhaled. "Hey, my principles are nothing if not situational. And believe me, I'm not under any illusions that you have an easy job either."

"Summer jobs aren't supposed to be easy," Kerry replied, ignoring his jokes. "They're supposed to be brutal and demeaning and ill-paying. Toughens you up for the rest of your life."

Josh nodded. "I guess you're right." He flipped his smoke to the sidewalk and crushed it out with his shoe. "So, you ready to jet? Waiting on Mace?"

"Waiting on Mace," Kerry confirmed. It had become a house motto over the summer. Mace Winston was never ready on time for anything—he was the only person she had ever known who was perpetually late *leaving* work. She was more than ready to go—her headache from that morning had never really gone away, and working in the noise of the crowded dining room had just made it worse.

Before Josh could reply, Mace came through the kitchen door. He was a dishwasher, and the hairs on his muscular forearms were plastered to his skin by the water that had leaked into his rubber gloves. Even the sleeves of his T-shirt were wet. His broad, handsome face was flushed from the hot water he'd been working in, a line of sweat sitting on his upper lip.

He tossed Kerry a lopsided grin, as if something hurt

in a place too embarrassing to mention. "You've got to start encouraging those folks to eat less," he told her. "Fewer side dishes. Better for their hearts, and better for me."

"I'll see what I can do," she said with a laugh. Neither of these guys were people she'd have been likely to hang out with under other circumstances, but over the course of the summer, they'd become close friends. Whenever she was talking with them, Kerry felt an easy, pleasant sense of comfort envelop her like a warm blanket on a cold night. It almost—but not quite—overwhelmed the sense of impending disaster her dreams had left her with and the headache that accompanied them. "Now can we go home?"

The others offered consent, as if either of them would be likely to argue in favor of staying and working awhile longer. Kerry took one last glimpse toward the water she couldn't see, breathed in a final lungful of ocean air, and headed for the parking lot with the others.

The Seaside Resort at La Jolla, to use its full name, was as soulless and impersonal as most large corporations. But it was also a corporation that recognized the fact that its business was largely seasonal, and to help it through the busy summer season, it hired a lot of temporary workers. Summer help came from all over the world—Prague, Sydney, Heidelberg, Minsk, and even the exotic climes of King of Prussia, Pennsylvania. So the resort offered, as one of its worker-friendly perks, a roommate-matching service. Kerry had signed up, filling out the requisite forms and answering a slew of questions about things she wouldn't even have talked about with the aunt and uncle she lived with. She was slotted into a house in nearby Bird Rock with five people with whom she had in common only the fact that they all worked for Seaside.

After a few weeks of initial discomfort, though, everyone fell into a kind of casual routine. Kerry, Josh, and Mace shared the house with Scott Banner and Brandy Pearson, who had come out from Harvard as a couple, and Rebecca Levine. The couple didn't get to share a room since there were only two bedrooms in the small cottage, and nobody was willing to cram four into one room so that two could have the other. But Brandy and Scott still managed plenty of alone time in the house, and they'd both had tonight off. They had said they were going to a movie, and as Mace pulled his massive baby blue Lincoln Continental onto the narrow driveway, Kerry noticed that Scott's RAV4 was still gone.

"Guess the lovebirds are still out on the town," Josh pointed out, echoing Kerry's observation.

"Too bad for them," Mace said, without a hint of sympathy. The driveway ran alongside the house, crowded on one side by the neighboring house's oleander bushes and on the other by the cottage itself. There was room for both cars if the RAV4 got tucked in first, but when Mace's monstrosity had pulled in as far as it could, the RAV4's rear end wouldn't clear the sidewalk. Which meant he had to park on the street. Mace had urged him just to block the sidewalk a little, but Scott was full of Harvard-induced social activism and refused to in case someone came by in a wheelchair. Kerry admired the stand he took, but couldn't have said for sure if she would be as noble if she had to be the one looking for street parking late at night.

The cottage was dark, as if Brandy and Scott had left during the day and had forgotten that no one would be home until after eleven. Rebecca had been working early shifts, and was no doubt already sound asleep—the girl could sleep anywhere, through anything, Kerry had decided.

The nearest streetlight was half a block away, largely obstructed by a big willow tree that overhung most of the miniscule front yard. A low hedge ringed the front of the house, bisected by a flagstone walkway that led from the sidewalk to the front steps. Their landlord paid for landscaping. If it'd been left up to the six of them, Kerry was sure everything would have died by July.

"Somebody could've left a light on," Josh complained, fumbling in his pocket for keys. "I can't even see the front door."

"Like they're gonna think of that," Mace replied quickly. "Probably too heavy into lip-lock mode when they walked out. And Sleeping Beauty was most likely out before the sun went down."

Having no flashlight handy, Kerry, who was not yet out of the Lincoln, hung back to hold the door open in case its dome light could cast a little illumination to help Josh. With considerable and fluent cursing, Josh managed to jam his key into the lock and got the door open. Inside, he flipped switches, and light blasted out from the coach lamp by the door, the windows, and the gaping doorway.

Light that etched, among other things, a pair of legs sticking out of the hedge. Male legs, it looked like, clad in dark pants, feet in what Kerry guessed were expensive leather ankle-high boots. She realized that a far more appropriate response to noticing the legs would have been to scream rather than, well, *noticing* them.

But the scream, practiced so often recently in dreams, wouldn't come. It caught in her throat like a chicken bone. Instead she barely rasped out Mace's name, since his back was still visible in the doorway.

"*Mace . . .*"

He turned, gave her a questioning look.

"Mace," she said again, a little more forcefully.

"What's up, Kerry?"

She pointed toward the hedge. Taking a step closer, she could see that the man, whoever he was, had crashed through the brush and was laying mostly covered by its greenery. "Umm . . . he doesn't belong there."

Finally Mace noticed him. "Oh, Jesus, Kerry. Get inside, I'll call the cops."

"I don't know if he needs cops," Kerry said, inching closer. "An ambulance, maybe."

"He's just some drunk, Kerry," Mace argued. "Fell down there and couldn't wake up."

But Kerry didn't think so. She'd been around enough drunks—held the hair away from friends' faces when they got sick, dodged clumsily groping hands at parties, even tucked her own uncle Marsh into bed a time or two or ten—to know the stink that wafted around them like a foul cloud. The closer she got to this man, though, the more she knew the smell was all wrong. Instead of the miasma of alcohol, there was a familiar metallic tang. The man in the hedge was very still and silent, and she moved closer still, as Mace watched, frozen, from the doorway.

The smell was blood, and it was thick in the air around the man.

Crap, she thought. *He's been stabbed. Or shot.*

She knew there was no way he hurt himself that much falling through the hedge. He'd have been scratched up—*could even have put out an eye on a branch*—but he wouldn't have opened enough veins to kick up a stench like a blood bank on two-for-one day. Kerry had nursemaided her mom for years while cancer had spread throughout her body, finally taking the older woman. Kerry was no trained doctor, but she'd learned a little something about emergency medical care during the ordeal, and she had a feeling that this guy was going to need everything she could offer and then some.

Another smell, underlying the one of blood, nagged at her, and Kerry suddenly realized that it was a faint electrical stink of ozone, as if lightning had struck close by.

"I don't think he needs the police," she repeated, leaning

forward to find the man's wrist in hopes of checking his pulse. By now, she noticed, Josh's lean form had appeared in the doorway, silhouetted behind Mace. "At least not first thing. He needs a paramedic."

The hand she had been groping for clamped around her forearm with surprising strength. "No," the man said, his voice an anxious rasp almost indistinguishable from the rustling sound his motion made in the hedge. "No doctors."

Her heart jumped to her throat, and she tried to yank her arm free. But the man held fast to it, even raising his head a little to look at her. A stray beam from the streetlight shone through the leaves onto his right eye, making it gleam like something from a Poe story. "Promise me, no doctors," he insisted. "Take me in and give me shelter or leave me here, but let me live or die on my own terms."

Mace and Josh had both come down from the doorway and hovered over Kerry and the wounded man like anxious seagulls at the beach, looking for handouts. "Dude, let her go," Mace ordered, snarling. "Or I'll really put a hurtin' on you."

She heard Mace shift as if he really did intend to attack the wounded man, and then she did something that surprised even her. She spread her one free arm—the man on the ground continued to clutch her right arm with a grip so powerful she didn't think she could have shaken it—over the man, as if to protect him from whatever Mace might have in mind. "No!" she shouted. "He's hurt bad enough. Leave him alone or help me bring him inside, but don't be stupid."

"I've got to wonder about your definition of stupid," Mace said, sounding petulant.

"He's right, Kerr," Josh added. "You want to bring some bloody stranger into our house?"

"You guys both missed Sunday school the day they talked about the good Samaritan?" Kerry shot back over her shoulder. "If you don't want to help me, just get out of the way. He's losing blood and he can't stay out here overnight." She pushed her way deeper into the thick hedge, feeling the branches scratch and tear at her skin like a hundred cats' claws, snagging her long, fine black hair and the fabric of the white cotton dress shirt that, with snug black pants, was her restaurant uniform.

She reached around the stranger's head with her left hand, hoping she could ease him up out of the hedge. Holding back the worst of the branches with her own body so he wouldn't suffer any further injury, she found the back of his head and slipped her hand down to support his neck. His hair was long in back, and matted with sticky blood. Never mind the tears, the bloodstains would make her uniform shirt unwearable.

"That's crazy talk," Mace complained behind her. She ignored him and drew the man slowly forward.

Josh unleashed another string of colorful profanities, but he knelt beside Kerry and shoved branches out of the way, helping to bring the wounded man out of the hedge. "I guess we need to get the mug out of our bushes anyway."

"You're both crazy, then," Mace opined. Kerry couldn't see Mace, but from the sound of it, she gathered that he had given up on them both and was on his way back inside. She found herself hoping that it wasn't to get a baseball bat or to call 911.

What do I care? she wondered. The good Samaritan thing had been a flip response to Mace and Josh's moaning, but it wasn't any kind of lifestyle choice she had made. She guessed that, as Josh might say, it meant the reaction she was having in this case was situational. Something about this battered, broken man in their bushes played on her sympathy, and she was unwilling to leave him there or to go against his stated wishes by calling the authorities.

With Josh's assistance she was able to disentangle the man from the hedge. In the light, the blood on his face was shocking—dark and glistening and obviously fresh. He might have been handsome once, but age and the damage caused by whatever had done this to him had taken care of that. She felt, more than ever, an urgency about getting him inside, getting his bleeding stopped, and trying to prevent shock.

"Can you stand up?" she asked him, not sure if he was even still conscious. But he forced his eyes open again, raised his head, and looked at her with something like kindness. His mouth curled into an agonized smile.

"Not a chance," he whispered. Then his head drooped, his eyes closed, his muscles went limp. For the first time, his grip on her forearm eased. She touched his neck, felt the pulse there.

"He's still alive," she declared.

"But he's deadweight," Josh said. Josh was, well . . . "lean" was a polite way to put it. "Scrawny" was more the truth. And the stranger was a big man, probably a little more than six feet tall, weighing a couple hundred pounds. "You think we can carry him?"

Kerry spoke without hesitation, without doubt. "We can carry him. You take his feet."

"Oh, I almost forgot," Josh said. He used the name that the housemates had applied to Kerry ever since they'd become familiar with her stubborn streak, "Bulldog."

Hoisting the stranger's shoulders, she grinned at Josh way down at the other end. "Woof."

Kerry Profitt's diary, August 11–12

Just for fun I looked back to see my first impressions of my housemates. Thinking to compare them, I guess, to current impressions.

Just goes to show how wrong you can be sometimes.

"Can you say insufferable?" I had typed about Josh Quinn. "Gay, Goth, vegan, and obnoxiously adamant about all three. If he keeps it up, I'll be surprised if he survives the summer. Not that he could be 'voted out' or whatever. Not that, to push the metaphor to the breaking point and beyond, this is a reality TV show or anything. *The Real World*, *Big Brother*, *Survivor*—they have nothing on the trials and tribs of six genuine strangers trying to get along in a house without cameras, supercool furniture, and a cash prize on the other end."

There was more, but why cut-and-paste all night when

I can simply scan the folder menu and look it up? Suffice to say, his first impression was the kind that almost makes you hope it'll also be a last impression.

Mace Winston, on the other hand. Then, I wrote: "Hmm . . . he's got a body like Michelangelo's David—not that I've seen under the fig leaf, figuratively speaking. But handsome, buff, and he tooled up in this sky blue Lincoln Continental—except for the left rear, I think he said quarter-panel, which is kind of rust colored and clearly taken from a different car. He said he found the whole thing in a desert canyon somewhere in New Mexico, full of bullet holes and snakes, but he cleaned it up and fixed it up and here he is. He really does wear the boots and one of those straw hats and he has squinty, twinkly eyes like some movie cowboy and somehow it all works for him. I don't know if there's a brain in his head. Ask me later if I care."

But tonight, when the chips, as they say, were down, Mace turned away and Josh came through. Although the heaving and ho-ing would have gone better had it been the other way around, I'm sure.

Okay.

Ms. Harrington, in eleventh-grade speech, used to give us holy hell when we started with "okay" or "umm." She said it was just a verbal time waster, a way of saying that our thoughts obviously weren't well enough organized to begin with because if they were, we'd start out by saying what we really wanted to say.

Boy, was she right.

So . . . okay. Umm . . .

There's a man in our living room, passed out on that butt-sprung lump of fabric and wood that passes for a sofa. We managed to stop most of the bleeding, put bandages on the worst cuts, got a couple of blankets (mine, since no one else would volunteer theirs) over him, elevated his feet higher than his head. Near his head there's a glass of water, in case he wakes up and is thirsty, and he seems to be breathing okay.

He looks like he lost an argument with a wood chipper. I can't even imagine what happened to him. Hit by a truck that hurled him all the way across our lawn? Picked up by a stray tornado and dropped there?

But he said no doctors, and that's exactly how many he's getting. Why? And why did I argue against calling the police? Rebecca woke up just before Scott and Brandy finally came home. I had the same argument with them that I'd had with Mace, although Scott came over to my side pretty quickly and Rebecca, bless her huge hippie heart, lit a candle and dug right in to help with the bandaging. With Josh already allied, that made four against two—Mace and Brandy. Brandy did a lot of huffing noises and is now either sound asleep, or pretending to be, as I laptop this. Is that a verb yet? If not, how soon?

Other good verbs: To delay. To procrastinate. To put off.

Okay.

Of course, what I wanted to do with my summer was to lead a life that might, by some reasonable definition, be normal. As opposed to the life I've led for the past, well, lifetime. Summer job, summer friends, maybe a summer boyfriend, even. Just, y'know, normal stuff.

I don't think this qualifies.

And to be fair, they're entirely correct (and "they" know who they are). We don't know who he is—he could be dangerous, a felon, a crazy person. Or even, you know, someone from Katy Perry's band, although maybe a little senior for that. But, to continue being fair, he's not the one who said "no cops." That was, not to put too fine a point on it, me. He just said "no doctors," and maybe he's a Christian Scientist or whatever. I was the one who said "no cops," and I'm still not sure why I did that. But it was the right thing to do.

I hope.

Journaling is supposed to help one figure out one's own emotions, right? Tap into the unconscious, puzzle out the mysteries therein? Not tonight, Dr. Freud. I don't know why I trust the old road-kill guy snoozing on the couch. But I do.

Go figure. Go to sleep. Go to hell. Just go. See you tomorrow, if we're not all murdered in our sleep. Or lack thereof.

More later, I hope.

K.

2

Scott Banner was one of those guys who did lots of things well. Kerry hadn't known him all that long, but then it didn't take long to figure that out about him. He got good grades in school, hence the Harvard bit. He worked hard, he could cook and clean quickly and efficiently, which were pluses where Kerry was concerned because that meant fewer household chores that she had to do around the summer house. He played soccer, and he looked fit and trim in the polo shirts, khakis, and Topsiders that he favored, and while Kerry thought he was dressing about twenty years ahead of his age, he somehow managed to pull it off.

His girlfriend Brandy, black, athletic, and as graceful as Kerry was not, appreciated those things about him too, confiding to Kerry that he would make someone a great husband one day, hoping that someone would be her. Kerry thought they made a wonderful couple, occasionally wishing she had someone who matched her as well as Scott and Brandy did each other.

One of the most important things to know about Scott was that he made really excellent coffee. And for those occasions when he wasn't available, there was a spot called Java Coast in downtown La Jolla, next to an English as a foreign language school that attracted vast numbers of young, available men—all foreign, of course, but Kerry had picked up a few words of Spanish, French, German, and Russian over the summer. The mornings that she worked early or that Scott was otherwise unavailable for barista duties, she allowed herself to splurge on the pricey brews there. All of which went to the fact that, on this particular morning, having slept almost not at all, Kerry had the distinct feeling that there just wasn't going to be enough coffee in the world to get her through the day. She had developed a serious caffeine habit over the summer. But some days it was more crucial than others.

Today she sniffed the air hopefully, even before she rolled out of the sack. No fragrant aroma of the glorious bean. So Scott was sleeping in, or Brandy had been ticked enough about the way last night's argument had gone that she had kicked him out of the house or dragged him away for an early breakfast (and accompanied by a stern talking-to).

Or, of course, it meant that the stranger in their living room had in fact been an axe murderer, and all of her housemates were dead.

With that image in her mind, she kicked off the sheets and glanced at herself. Green cotton pajama pants and a tank top provided enough coverage. She padded barefoot across the hardwood floor, pulled the door open. A short hallway led to the living room, and she could smell the man before she saw him. He was still there, and he needed a shower more than ever. But if he had, in fact, murdered the rest of the household, she'd have expected him to smell more like fresh blood—as he had last night—and less like stale sweat.

So all in all, an improvement over where things *could* have been.

And there had been no nightmares during the night, she realized, which was a bonus. She'd had recurrent nightmares before, but not since the days when she was young enough to comfort herself by hugging the rag-doll clown she'd named BoBo. He was long since put away, though, stored in a trunk in her uncle Marsh's attic. Approaching the stranger, she found herself wishing for a moment that she had BoBo here with her, giving her courage as he had done when she was a child.

The living room was dimly lit—curtains still drawn, but they were moth-eaten and sunshine leaked through—and nobody was around. Kerry approached the stranger, whose breath was ragged but steady, and looked at his pale, drawn face. He looked different, somehow, than he had the night before. Still gaunt, but his cheeks seemed less sunken, the hollows of his eyes shallower than they had been. It was almost as if, she thought, the night's sleep had not only allowed him to heal but had made him younger at the same time.

Even so, Rolling Stones young, not Radiohead young. Big difference.

A sound from behind her. Kerry turned. Rebecca, her short-cropped orange hair reaching in every direction at once, stood there in blue fuzzy slippers and a cotton nightgown. Rebecca took a bath every day, never a shower, and she spent a minimum of forty minutes—more often an hour—in the bathroom. Lit candles, put in a bath bomb or bubble bath, something floral. Pampered herself. Kerry admired her dedication even if—in a house with six people and only one bathroom and a half—she often resented the time it took. But a cloud of flowery fragrance usually surrounded Rebecca, as it did now, wafting to Kerry's nose across the room, providing relief from the stranger's stench.

Rebecca blinked away sleep. "I stayed up last night," she said in a quiet voice. "Watching him."

Kerry felt an unexpected surge of jealousy, as if the strange man sleeping on their couch was her find, not anyone else's. She knew it made no sense. *Just tired,* she decided. She hadn't stayed up watching him. Thinking about him, though. "Did he do anything?"

A shrug. "Just slept. Maybe dreamed some—he moaned a little, and kind of scrunched his face up, you know."

"How long did you watch him?" Kerry asked, hoping the answer wasn't long enough to be creepy.

"Just awhile," Rebecca said, shrugging some more. Kerry had learned that was one of her signature moves. Maybe a sign of low self-esteem, as if to accompany her statements with a shrug meant that they shouldn't be taken too seriously. "I think he's getting better."

Kerry had to agree, though it was absurd to think that just a few hours of sleep would make much difference to a man as wounded as he'd been. *Well,* she mentally corrected, *a few hours of sleep and some basic first aid.*

But she had thought the same thing when she first glanced at him. Now, as if disturbed by their soft conversation, the man on the couch groaned and rolled away from them. She waited another few moments, thinking that he might wake up. When he didn't, she looked at Rebecca and stifled a yawn against the back of her hand. "Let's make some java, Beck," she said.

Rebecca happily agreed.

A few hours passed. The day, as they had a tendency to do in San Diego in August, heated up. Kerry put on a green V-neck T-shirt with soft, faded jeans and the red-and-white zigzag sneakers that were even more comfortable than being barefoot, and brought a book into the living room. She sat in the big easy chair that had come with the furnished house, silently turning pages while she watched over her patient. The last thing she wanted was for him to wake up alone, in a strange room, not knowing where he was or who had brought him there. She plugged in a freestanding fan over by the doorway, hoping its whir wouldn't be too loud. The breeze wasn't exactly cool but at least it moved the air around.

Occasionally one of her housemates—none of whom, as it happened, had been murdered in their sleep—would wander by. When Mace came in he stood with his hands on his hips and cocked his chin toward the sleeping man. "Dude still alive?"

"Seems to be," Kerry told him. "Disappointed?"

"Surprised, I guess," Mace answered. "Didn't think he'd make it to dawn."

"I guess he's tougher than he looks," Kerry observed.

"Seems like." He shook his head and moseyed on.

When it was time for Kerry to leave for work, she called in sick. It was the first time she had done so all summer, and a pang of guilt caught in her stomach when she hung up the phone. But her boss, Mr. Hofstadter, wouldn't have understood or accepted the real reason.

Through it all, the man slept. And Kerry wondered about him.

What was his story? How had he wound up in their yard? What had injured him? Was anyone looking for him? These questions, and many more, kept her from concentrating on her book, a paperback chick-lit novel she'd borrowed from Brandy. Her own tastes tended more toward suspense and thrillers, and if there were some exotic locations and romance mixed in, so much the better. But she would read anything she got her hands on, and this one was available.

Every time the man shifted in his sleep, she tensed, thinking he was waking up. The rest of the household went to work. She paced, or sipped a soda, or tried to read, and waited.

Eventually she dozed off in the chair. The book slid to the floor, but that didn't wake her.

Neither did having a blanket draped over her.

Later, she did open her eyes, startled that they had been closed at all. More startled to see that the man was sitting up on the couch, watching her. On her lap she clutched the blanket that had once covered him.

"You didn't have to do all this," he said. His voice was soft and smooth, not the ragged husk of the night before. His eyebrows raised as if to encompass the "all this" to which he referred.

He was definitely younger than he had looked, even that morning. Sleep and recuperation had erased wrinkles, filled furrows. Still years older than her, but not decades. His eyes were steel gray and clear, dancing with a light all their own in the poorly lit room.

She patted at the blanket. "It looks kind of like you're the one who's been taking care of me."

"I owed you," he said, as if that explained everything.

Or, really, anything.

"All I did was—"

He cut her off. His smile was, she realized, quite enchanting. "All you did was take me in, against the wishes of most of your friends. Clean and dress my wounds. Allow me to sleep, undisturbed, for as long as I needed. Accept without question my desire not to be taken to a doctor. Refuse to call the police. That, I have to say, was more than I could have asked, even if I'd been capable of asking, and I appreciate it."

Kerry blinked a couple of times. "Weren't you, like, unconscious for most of that?"

"Yes," he said, flashing her that grin again. She felt it down to her toes. She hadn't noticed what a handsome man he was—or, more accurately, how it had been obscured by the apparent years with which his pain and exhaustion had saddled him. "But not unaware. Thank you for everything."

As he spoke he made to rise from the couch, pushing off with his right hand. But he hadn't even reached his full height when his legs buckled, and he flopped back down. He tossed her a sheepish smile that dimpled his cheeks. "I guess I'm not as strong as I thought."

Kerry rushed to his side to help him, dropping the blanket to the floor. "You shouldn't even be awake, much less trying to stand," she insisted. He was already sitting by the time she reached him, so she wasn't sure what to do with herself. She stood there a few moments, feeling embarrassed, then simply sat down beside him as if that had been her plan all along.

Graciously he ignored her awkwardness and extended a hand. "My name is Daniel Blessing," he said.

She took his hand in her own. His was large, engulfing hers, and as warm as if he'd been holding a cup of hot tea. Holding it felt comfortable, like being hugged by an old friend. After a few moments she realized he was waiting for her to let go, to say her own name, or both. She couldn't understand why she was so flustered around this man.

Except maybe because he should be dead, she thought. *Or at the very least, still comatose. And years older.*

There was something very strange going on here. Part of her wanted to know what it was, but a bigger part—the dominant part, she realized—wondered why she wasn't more concerned about why she trusted him, almost instinctively. Why she had brought him into the house and dismissed the concerns of housemates who didn't want to leave her alone with him.

"Kerry," she managed at last. "I'm Kerry Profitt."

"Yes," he said, as if that name meant something to him. Though, obviously, it couldn't have. His voice and his manner were both, Kerry thought, oddly formal. "Yes, of course. It's a pleasure to meet you, Kerry."

"You too . . . Daniel," she replied. She had almost called him "Mr. Blessing," something about his age and that strange formality making her feel like she ought to treat him as she would a friend of her aunt Betty and uncle Marsh. She regarded his handsome face again: high forehead; intense, heavy-lidded gray eyes; a straight nose that she might have considered large on a different face but that here seemed somehow fitting. His lips were thin but quick to smile. When he did smile, his whole face took part, cheeks creasing, eyes crinkling, dimples at the edges of his mouth carving themselves into his skin. His jawline was pronounced but firm, his chin square. Thick brown hair, which could've used an encounter with water and shampoo, swept away from his brow, covering his ears, flowing over the collar of the Deftones T-shirt they'd borrowed from Mace when his own torn and blood-soaked shirt had to be cut from his damaged body. Impossibly he looked even closer to her age than he had when she'd suddenly awoken—within a decade of her, she guessed now.

"You have questions," he said. He tried to stand again, stopped mid-rise to wince and grasp at his ribs where his worst injury had been, an open gash that looked like he'd been attacked with a meat cleaver. His skin blanched, eyes compressing against the evident pain. But he composed himself and pushed through it.

"Well, yeah, Sherlock."

"I wish I could answer them for you, Kerry. Really, I do. But if I did—well, you saw what I looked like when you brought me in, right?"

She had hardly stopped remembering. His body was lean, with the stringy musculature of someone who worked hard rather than worked out, and yardstick-wide shoulders and a deep chest—but after last night, bruised and shredded, as if he'd made a dozen laps in a demolition derby, only without a car. "Yeah, I saw."

He nodded gravely. "If I answered your questions, then

you'd be at risk for the same. And, I suspect, you'd have a harder time surviving it than I did."

"So this is, what, a regular thing for you?" she asked, surprised at his use of the present tense.

He showed that grin again. "Not to this extent, no. And I don't know if I'd use the word 'regular.' But it has happened before and likely will again. I'd rather you didn't get mixed up in it, so that's all I'll say about that." He walked away from the couch, away from her—stiff-legged, clearly sore, but still, considering the shape he had been in, miraculous. "If you don't mind," he called over his shoulder, "I'm starving. Okay if I raid the kitchen?"

Kerry Profitt's diary, August 13

He's gone.

I can't quite sort out how I feel about it. Night before last I risked the wrath of my homies—and maybe our lives—playing Florence Nightingale to a stranger who could have been just what Mace and Brandy were sure he was—a random drunk who'd been bounced off somebody's fender. But once he woke up, once the years fell away from him and he started to speak, it didn't take long to see that he was not that. Still, mega-mystery man.

But we talked and eventually the others came home from work—where, they lied, I had been sorely missed—and Daniel Blessing seemed to draw energy from them. He became enchanting: witty, interesting, the kind of conversationalist to whom you could apply the term "sparkling" without being too off base. Even those who had distrusted him the most had been charmed.

Did he tell us anything about himself other than his name? He did not. And that name is probably as fake as the phone number Rebecca gives out to the tourists who hit on her at work (aside, in case I didn't mention it: While Rebecca considers herself a few pounds overweight, what she is is zaftig. She hides it with the hunching and the baggies, but the powers at Seaside picked her—being the only one of us over twenty-one—to be a cocktail waitress in their oh-so-cleverly named bar, the Schooner. Part of the cocktail waitressing involves wearing a uniform that, while not as desperately provocative as they probably were ten or twenty years ago, is still, let's just say . . . snug. And short-ish. So the aforementioned hitting on? Happens a lot).

So no personal details from (possibly) Mr. Blessing. But he was informed and erudite, able to discuss books and movies and modern music, as well as the state of the world (about which he's not much impressed), environmental and social issues, and even, much to Josh's amazement, film noir of the thirties and forties. By the time people dragged themselves away from the kitchen table to go to bed, he had won them all over. I'm only guessing, but I think Josh may have fallen a little bit in love.

He may not even have been alone in that.

But then, this morning. Not just early-ish, but genuinely early. The kind of early where your eyelids are sort of glued together and the clock's face swims just out of focus. He taps on my door a couple of times, then lets himself in before I can mumble incoherently. He kneels—*kneels!*—beside the bed, takes my hand, kisses it once, says, "Thank you, Kerry Profitt. Thank you so much, for all you've done," and then he stands up and walks out.

I fumbled out of bed, but I heard the front door close before I reached the entrance to my room, and when I hit the street, he was gone. Out of sight. Maybe there was a car waiting for him, though I didn't see or hear one. Maybe one of those big mythological birds picked him up. Or a UFO.

Gone.

I only knew him for a day. And *knew* may be too strong a word, since I know so little about him even now.

So why does it feel like there's a vast emptiness in the house?

Anyone?

3

I'm worried about Kerry," Brandy confided. She and Scott were both at work—she as a front-desk clerk at the resort, and Scott as a groundskeeper. A couple of times a shift, they made a point of crossing paths, usually when she was on a short break from the desk. With the run of the property, his schedule was less restrictive than hers. And as a groundskeeper whose clothing could frequently be grass-stained or otherwise soiled, him visiting her at the desk was frowned upon. Now they wandered the paved pathways that led from the room complexes down to the tennis courts and pool and the wide sandy beach beyond.

"Why?" Scott wondered. He carried a broom and a long-handled dustpan in his left fist; the fingers of his right hand were twined with Brandy's darker ones.

"It's been, what, four days since that guy left. Daniel?"

"Yeah, I guess so," Scott agreed, not quite getting what she was leading to. But that was the thing about Brandy—directness was not her strong point. She would walk all the way around an issue before she'd step right up to it. "What about it?"

"She's been kind of, I don't know, mopey. Ever since."

"Brandy, she hardly knew the guy. She wanted to play nursemaid, she did, he got better. End of story."

Her grasp tightened on his fingers, and he saw the fire flash in her eyes that always told him when he'd said the wrong thing. It was not an unfamiliar event, but it was never a pleasant one either.

"It *should* be," she insisted. "But it's not, and that's the problem. Haven't you seen her? I don't know if she's laughed once since he left. This is Kerry we're talking about. Girl loves to laugh. But instead she's been acting like her dog died."

Scott knew he was treading dangerous ground. Brandy, a psych major, was perfectly content to psychoanalyze anyone who fell onto her radar screen. Scott preferred life a little closer to the surface of things, where motives and rationales were not examined so closely. And he admired Kerry's surface a great deal. She was absolutely gorgeous—he'd thought that the moment he'd met her, and hadn't stopped since. Long, silken hair of purest jet, big emerald eyes, a lean body that was not as athletic as Brandy's or as curvaceous as Rebecca's, but still feminine and attractive. He'd been with Brandy for three years, and loved her completely. But that didn't mean he didn't think once in a while about what it would be like to be with Kerry, who was almost Brandy's exact opposite, physically.

"You're right, I guess," he ventured, shaking off the mental image of Kerry to focus on Brandy "Maybe seeing him on the couch like that, taking care of him, reminded her of her mom. When she had to take care of her for so long."

Brandy nodded. He'd scored one. "There you go, Scotty," she said, her tone congratulatory. She stopped, released his hand and faced him, moving into lecture mode. Behind her, the Pacific surged up onto the beach, then slipped back into itself in an unending, slightly irregular rhythm. "What defined Kerry for years? Being her mom's nurse and caretaker. Then what happened to her? Her mom died anyway, and she had to move in with an aunt and uncle she can barely stand. Now she's got a nice insurance settlement, but she's working anyway, trying to supplement the money with income from a summer job. She's looking to redefine herself in some other role, but when that guy fell into her lap, almost literally, it took her back to the same place she had been, emotionally, with her mom. And when he left too . . . well, that brought back a lot of feelings, most of them the bad kind."

"Do you have a suggestion?" Scott asked. He readily admitted that he was nuts about Brandy. She was smart and beautiful and very caring, so what was not to like? But when she got like this, sometimes he felt antsy, eggshell-walking.

The first time he'd introduced her to his brother Steve—six years older, married with a kid of his own—Steve had taken him aside and said in a conspiratorial tone, "She's great, Scott. Doesn't seem like someone who puts up with idiots."

"She doesn't," Scott had confirmed.

"Then I have one piece of advice, bro. Don't be an idiot."

Brandy's little brother DJ had been less subtle. "You ever hurt my sister," he said with a sinister smile, "I won't have to do jack. That girl'll have you for breakfast and pick her teeth with your bones."

All things considered, eggshells didn't seem so bad.

"She's got to work through it her own way," Brandy prescribed, drawing Scott back to the current situation. "All we can do is be as supportive as we can, let her talk it out if she wants. Show her we care about her, but not that we want to meddle."

If amateur psychiatry wasn't meddling, Scott wasn't sure what was. But he kept that opinion to himself. Anyway, there was a stretch of lawn that needed mowing, and Brandy's break was over, as was his own. He agreed with her, kissed her goodbye, and went back to work.

With so many new faces to look at every day, Kerry found herself looking forward to getting acquainted with the resort's regulars—those who stayed for a week or so and ate in the restaurant several times instead of availing themselves of La Jolla's many other fine dining opportunities. Some she got to know, on the most superficial of levels, as people on vacation who sometimes had a tendency to talk about their lives—family members, pets they left behind, the old neighborhood back in Lincoln or Tempe or Fort Wayne. Others kept their own confidences, and sometimes Kerry entertained herself by making up her own stories about them, giving them colorful, mysterious histories and reasons for visiting southern California.

Some of these fictions she had e-mailed to her best friend Jessica Tait, who had moved to Florida the year before. Lately Jessica had seemed more and more distant, as if her new life and friends were drawing her away from the bond they'd shared. Kerry mourned the change; losing her mother had been bad enough, losing her best friend on top of it was heart-wrenching. The way she'd grown up had left her with precious few friends anyway, and she valued the ones she had.

Tonight one of the diners in her section was a woman she'd seen several times recently—not for days in a row, as was typical with vacationers who came to the resort, but spread out over many weeks. This was unusual, but not unheard of. Sometimes local residents decided they liked the kitchen's offerings. Carolyn Massey, the chef, had, after all, trained at Le Cordon Bleu in France, and then had a stint under Alice Waters in her Berkeley restaurant, Chez Panisse, before taking over the resort's kitchen. Her meals were always delicious and frequently adventurous.

This guest, though, Kerry noticed partly because the woman always dined alone, and partly because, while she was unfailingly pleasant and polite, there was an air about her that made Kerry believe that she was terribly sad. She was a beautiful woman, with skin so soft and smooth it could have been freshly poured from a bottle, and hair that reminded Kerry of a ray of golden afternoon sunlight shining down on fresh straw. Upon closer inspection, the color of her shoulder-blade-length hair spanned a spectrum, from platinum white to a dark auburn, and the overall effect was lovely. Her features could have belonged to fairy tale royalty, or to the Hollywood kind: wide-set, sparkling blue eyes, a refined yet expressive brow, a nose that was petite but was not so small it was an afterthought. Her lips were full and finely sculpted, and the determined set of her jaw implied that she was no pushover.

In Kerry's mind, the woman was a widow whose wealthy husband had died tragically young. She had tried to put his death behind her, to carry on with her life, but everywhere she went, simple things reminded her of the joy they had felt in their few years together. A song on the radio, a particular vintage of wine, even the cries of gulls on the beach, could bring an unexpected tear to her eye. Nonetheless, she made herself go out, eat in restaurants, drink that wine, listen to the radio, walk on the beach at sunset, intent on enjoying her heartbreaking memories as if he were still there beside her.

Sometimes Kerry added an extra twist to the woman's tale. She was a spy, and her husband had been killed in the line of duty. Or she was an international jewel thief, and he wasn't dead at all but simply doing a long stretch in a prison in

Monaco or Majorca. She came to La Jolla because she wasn't wanted for anything in California—yet.

The woman's beauty was ageless, which inspired Kerry to even greater flights of fancy. She could have been in her mid-twenties, her late forties, or any place in between. Her outfit was just as timeless—a loose-fitting white silk top that suggested rather than revealed her figure, a tan jacket, also silk, and matching pants with heels, no doubt some Italian brand that Kerry could pronounce no better than she could afford. There were hints of lines at the edges of her eyes and mouth that would, with the years, deepen and most likely make her even more lovely. She would carry her years and experiences well, Kerry believed.

After dinner the woman lingered over a cup of coffee. She exchanged pleasantries from time to time, but whenever Kerry tried to engage her in conversation, she expertly steered away from any personal topics. *Just adds to her mystery,* Kerry thought with some satisfaction.

When she went into the kitchen to pick up an order for the next table over, a party of five who had come in late after what looked like a scorching day on the beach—lobster-red foreheads, shoulders, and arms that would be painful and peeling before long—the last person she expected to see was Daniel Blessing.

But there he was, hovering near the open back door like an unwanted houseguest who wouldn't quite leave. When he saw Kerry, his lips parted in a sudden smile. This time, she noted, it didn't engage his eyes. She smiled back and arched a quizzical eyebrow his way.

"Daniel?" she said, surprised. "What are you doing here?" The cooks, bus staff, and dishwashers all ignored him, as if by prior arrangement. But Kerry had been out in the dining room for several minutes, and he could have had time to slip each one a twenty for all she knew.

He came toward her, unmistakable urgency in his step, and took her by the arm. His grip was so firm it hurt. She tried to pull away, but he held on. "Kerry," he whispered. "I hoped that you'd be safe, that helping me wouldn't put you in danger. I was wrong. You've got to leave here, right now."

Kerry laughed, but it sounded forced even to her. "In case you hadn't noticed, I'm kind of working here, Daniel."

"You're in terrible danger, Kerry. I'm not joking. Or exaggerating. You have to trust me."

That, in spite of herself, she had always done, even that very first night. And she certainly couldn't imagine any reason he might have had for trying to play a trick on her now. Unless this whole thing was one of those ridiculous TV stunts, set up to ridicule her in front of millions, he seemed absolutely serious.

"What's going on, Daniel? I can't just walk out of here."

"You have to," he insisted. He blew out a frustrated breath. "There's a woman out there, sitting by herself at a table."

"The blond one?"

"That's her."

"She's a regular. She's perfectly harmless."

"You're wrong," he said with finality. "Remember how I was the night you found me?"

How could I forget? she wondered. *Three quarters dead, like an animal by the side of a busy highway.* "Of course."

"She's the one who did that to me. She's still after me. And now she's connected me to you." His voice had gotten louder as he tried to convince her, and Kerry noticed that some of the kitchen staff was now paying attention to them. She had to calm this guy down, fast, or she'd be out of a job.

"Look, Daniel," she whispered, "I don't really know you or anything, you know. I'm glad you're better and all, but I kind of need this job, and—"

He squeezed her arm even harder than he had before. "Kerry," he said. She found her gaze drawn to his eyes, such a strange color of gray, but steady and profoundly persuasive. "There's no time for this. She'll be—"

The kitchen door swung open and the woman was there. Now the staff did react. Carolyn Massey, the head chef, came forward with a knife in her hand. She'd been using it to chop fresh vegetables, and she didn't hold it threateningly, but it was still a big, sharp object. "I'm sorry," Carolyn said, "but this kitchen is off limits to everyone except staff." She glanced meaningfully at Kerry and Daniel. "Everyone."

The blond woman barely spared her a glance, but focused her attention on Daniel and on Kerry, who stood between them. "I thought you were nearby," she said. Her voice was ice.

Then, she spoke another word, or maybe two. Kerry couldn't make them out, couldn't even tell what language they were in. As she spoke, she gestured toward Daniel with her right hand, a kind of swooping curlicue of a motion that seemed to encompass much of the kitchen before settling on him.

Daniel was already in motion when the big gas oven's door flipped open, seemingly of its own accord. He shoved Kerry to the side and spoke some equally strange words of his own, making a different sort of two-handed gesture. Kerry couldn't quite process what happened—it was all too fast, and way, way too weird—but it seemed that, in response to the woman's combined words and movement, the oven door had opened itself and a huge gout of flame jetted out toward Daniel, dragon's-breath-like. She felt the blast of heat suck the air from her lungs. But then it seemed that in response to whatever Daniel had done, the flame stopped in midair, as if striking an invisible shield, and turned back toward the woman.

The questions this raised were, of course, innumerable. But she didn't have a chance to ask so much as "What the hell?" before Daniel tugged her out the back door. He kept a tight grip on her arm as he ran for the parking lot, and she had to sprint to keep from falling down and being dragged along behind.

He was silent as he ran, and she had the impression that he was concentrating, intent on something she couldn't even sense. She guessed the woman was probably following them, but if she'd turned to look she'd have fallen for sure. So she let herself be led to a dark, low-slung sports car parked close to the restaurant. The doors sprung open before they reached it, and Daniel pushed her into the leather passenger seat. He ran around to the driver's side, and she could have sworn—though by this point, the evidence of her own senses was clearly not to be trusted—that the engine turned over before he was even sitting down. Slamming his door, he threw the car into reverse and backed from the parking space, then he shifted gears and the little car darted toward the exit.

Finally risking a glance behind them, Kerry saw that the blond woman had indeed followed. She had just gotten into a car of her own, and before Daniel's vehicle had even cleared the first block, she was racing after them.

4

Daniel hung a sharp left turn on Avenida de la Playa, the car's rear end fishtailing through the intersection as they entered the main drag of the La Jolla Shores neighborhood. From outdoor cafés and restaurants, patrons stared as the screech of skidding tires battled the growl of the engine for supremacy. This time of night, there wasn't much vehicular traffic on the street, so Daniel floored the accelerator and the car burst forward like an animal released from a cage.

At La Jolla Shores Drive, he made a screaming right. This street, which connected with Torrey Pines and the "village" section of the resort town, was busier. Kerry gripped the edges of her bucket seat as Daniel swerved around cars and a city bus, then pulled back into a proper lane and rocketed through the major intersection at Torrey Pines. Kerry barely had time to notice that he had gone through a red light—the blare of horns from cars and trucks was lost behind them.

On the other side of Torrey Pines, the road was narrow and wound up the side of Mount Soledad, the hill that loomed over the town, providing a scenic backdrop and multimillion dollar views from its many estates. As they started the climb, Kerry heard another blurting of horns, which she figured was probably caused by the blond woman pulling the same stunt Daniel had.

Daniel cursed under his breath.

"She's still behind us, isn't she?" Kerry asked. The run had shaken her fine hair free from the ponytail she wore for work, and she tried to regather it, but her hands were shaking as much as her voice.

"Sounds like it. I'd be surprised if she wasn't."

"So when are you going to tell me what this is all about?" Kerry demanded, trying to sound more forceful than she felt. "And what that little display in the kitchen was?"

"Another time," Daniel said. His teeth were clenched in concentration. "Hard enough getting to know this car so I can squeeze every last drop of juice out of her."

Getting to know? Kerry thought. A horrible notion struck her. "Isn't this your car?"

"I don't actually *own* a car," Daniel admitted.

"And this isn't a rental?"

He didn't answer. But then, he didn't need to. It was clear now that he'd stolen the car. *And,* she realized, *effectively kidnapped me.*

"I think you should let me out here," she suggested. "I'll walk back to work."

"You really don't want me to do that."

"I really do."

Daniel risked a glance at her even as he muscled the car around a hairpin turn. The floodlit walls and thickly hedged iron fences that separated La Jolla's wealthy from the rest of the world rushed past in a blur. "Kerry, I'll explain everything, I promise. But right now I'm trying to not get us killed, and I'm trying to leave Season behind. Which is another form, need I add, of not getting us killed. If I dropped you off, not only would she slaughter you, but it would slow me down enough to let her catch me. And I have to tell you, I'm not ready to go through that again."

He sounded convincing, or at least convinc*ed*, and Kerry discovered that once again, she trusted him without knowing why. She stopped arguing and let him drive. A moment later they spotted an electric gate sliding shut behind a Mercedes that had just pulled into a driveway "Hold on," Daniel muttered. He stomped on the brake and cranked the steering wheel at the same time. The little car shuddered and turned in an almost ninety-degree angle, and then he shot through the gate just before it closed. On the other side of the gate, he pulled off the driveway so that a high wall hid the car from the street. As he came to a stop and killed the engine, he said another word in whatever unfamiliar tongue he had used at the restaurant, and waggled his hand.

The air around the car seemed to shimmer, as if enveloped by the most severe heat waves this side of the Sahara. Through the weird haze, Kerry saw a silver-haired man and woman emerge from the Mercedes and stare in their direction. "Keep quiet," Daniel warned her in a whisper. "They can't see us, but they can hear us."

"What do you mean, they can't see us?" Kerry wanted to know, echoing his hushed tones.

"Invisibility spell," Daniel replied, tight-lipped. She could see beads of sweat forming at his brow and dripping down his temples as if from intense effort. Outside, the man and woman looked at each other in confusion, and the man shrugged. They turned away and went up to the door of the house, then disappeared inside. A moment later the exterior lights went dark.

Daniel faced Kerry, a finger across his lips in the universal sign for "keep quiet." She did. There would be plenty to say later. For now, though, she would let him call the shots. He was clearly playing with forces way beyond her understanding or control. That fact stirred her to unexpected anger—she'd been swept into a game to which she didn't know the rules; hadn't known, a half hour ago, even existed. She hadn't asked to be included. And yet here she was. She fumed, but silently.

But when he says I can talk again . . .

From the other side of the wall, they heard the growl of a powerful engine, and headlights swept past, shining through the iron gates. Kerry and Daniel sat in silence until the engine noise faded away, moving higher up the hill. A few moments later Daniel started the stolen car again. With a word and a wave at the gate, it slid open and Daniel drove back out onto the street.

Instead of turning right to continue toward the top of Mount Soledad, he made a left, back down the hill toward where they'd started.

"Are you taking me back to work?" Kerry asked.

"I can't do that," he said. "You're not safe there anymore. She knows she can find you there."

There was so much that Kerry didn't understand. "But she wasn't after me," she insisted. "She was after you."

"She'll consider you an ally of mine now. She's ruthless, Kerry. If I took you back there, the rest of your life would be measured in hours, maybe days at the most. I'm sorry, but you can't go back to work, and you can't go back home—she has probably located the house by now. I'm almost sure of it, in fact. How else could she have traced you to the restaurant? I never visited you there, so she must have followed you from home."

"I told you, she eats there all the time," Kerry said. She was still upset, still ticked that this guy had come along and upended her life, yanked her into his own personal drama.

If it hadn't been for what she had seen the woman do in

the kitchen, she'd think Daniel suffered from paranoid hallu-
cinations. But she *had* seen it. That overruled her rage and
earned him the benefit of the doubt, at least for a while.

Daniel seemed to puzzle over what Kerry had pointed out
for a few moments as he drove to the bottom of the hill and
hung a right on La Jolla Parkway, heading away from town. "I
didn't think that precognition was one of her gifts," he said.
"But I suppose it's possible. Maybe she was staking you out,
knowing that you and I would somehow come into contact."

The talk of precognition and gifts made Kerry's blood run
cold. It sounded like something out of one of those movies
full of pounding death metal, where everyone in the audi-
ence dresses in black and none of them could pass through
an airport scanner without setting off sirens. She shivered and
hugged herself, but at the same time felt a sudden weariness,
as if all her strength had left her at once. Since the woman
had walked into the kitchen, Kerry had been frightened and
furious in more or less equal measures. Then the chase, the
invisibility, the escape . . . she realized that adrenaline had
been charging through her system, and now that the immediate threat had passed, it drained from her. She remained
scared—probably more so than before, a combination of fear
that she was in the company of a crazy man, and worse, what
it might mean if he were not crazy at all—and angry that she
had somehow been punished for what she had believed was
a simple good deed. *See if I ever help a half-dead man in my
bushes again. It's just not worth it.*

"You're going to have to do some explaining, Daniel," she declared. "And it better be good."

"It will be," he assured her with a hint of a smile. That smile, on another occasion, might have won him points, but not now. Now it implied that things were less awful than they were, and Kerry wasn't sure that was possible. "Let's just get someplace safe and comfortable. I'll tell you everything. I owe you that much."

"Got that right." Another horrible thought crossed her mind. "If the house isn't safe, what about the others? My friends?"

"They've got to get out too," Daniel replied. "As quickly as possible. Are they at the house now?"

"Some of them, maybe." Kerry knew Rebecca and Josh were at Seaside. Mace had the day off, though, and Scott and Brandy had worked earlier in the day. She almost reached for her cell phone, but then remembered that her purse was still in her locker at the resort. Cell phone, ID, money, keys . . . everything she needed with her on a daily basis was gone, unless she could somehow get back to work.

And of course, by leaving the way she had, she was pretty sure there would be no job left, even if she could get back. Which meant no further income. She had put aside a little bit over the summer, depositing it via ATM to her account back in Illinois. But her ATM card, naturally, was in her purse.

All in all, this pretty much sucked.

"You've got to warn them," he said. "Get them away from there."

"What am I supposed to tell them? I'm in the dark here, remember?"

"We'll find a safe place," he promised. "When we do, just tell them to meet us there—without telling anyone else where they're going. I know it sounds melodramatic, but their lives really are in danger now."

He took one hand off the steering wheel and squeezed her left shoulder. "Kerry, I truly am sorry you got involved in this. If I could undo it, I would."

Kerry shrugged, and he took his hand away. "Yeah, well, that makes two of us."

5

The apartment Daniel rented—one he found when cruising, stopping after sighting a sign in the window of a building, going inside, paying with enough cash that the landlord was willing to dispense with the paperwork—was on the second floor of a two-story, fake-stucco monstrosity with a red tile roof and an empty pool except for a few inches of scum-filmed rainwater. It had three bedrooms, a long, narrow living room with high ceilings and a skylight, one bathroom, and a kitchen in which two people couldn't pass each other without turning sideways and inhaling. The carpet was microthin, bunched up in spots and separating at the seams in others. Josh, when he saw it, said something about it gloriously representing southern California's "seamy underbelly," but to Kerry it was just a dump.

It was two blocks off Palm Avenue, the main drag of Imperial Beach, a community ten miles south of downtown San Diego, which was about that far south of La Jolla. At the corners on Palm were a fast-food restaurant and a gas station with a minimart, but down the side streets there were only small cottages and low-rent apartment buildings. TVs and music—salsa, hip-hop, classic rock, and Top 40 pop—could be heard from open windows most hours of the day, and night, as it turned out, competing with the constant drone of air conditioners.

It was, Kerry knew, a place she'd be very unlikely to find for herself, which made it perfect for their purposes. The electricity hadn't been turned off yet, and the landlord had agreed to let it stay on under his name for a while in exchange for yet another handful of cash. There was no phone, but Daniel had a cell so she used it to call the summer house, then Seaside. After a couple of tries, she reached everyone and convinced them to leave work or the house and to join her in Imperial Beach. She pleaded, cajoled, and threatened, but they all came. Scott and Brandy brought her laptop and some clothes from the house, in addition to their own things and everyone else's. She gave Rebecca her combination so her friend could get her purse and personal items from work. Within four hours of her escape, as she had come to think of it, from the resort's kitchen, they were all seated together on the floor of the apartment's living room, backs against the walls, legs crossed. Daniel cleared his throat. He was on stage, and, Kerry believed, he knew it. *Looks like you got some 'splainin' to do, Lucy,* she thought, à la Ricky Ricardo.

He started by flashing his friendly grin, but Kerry was having none of that. "I know what I'm about to tell you will sound ridiculous to you," he began. "Unbelievable, even. But I swear to you, it's true. I could make you believe it—that's not a terribly difficult stunt for me—but I won't do that. Instead I want you to believe it on its own merits. Such as they are."

Kerry, having already experienced some of his "stunts," was thrown by his passing remark about being able to make them believe. She interrupted before he could continue. "Daniel, when we first met you," she said, "and I found myself trusting you, for no particular reason . . . was that just because I really trusted you? Or did I have . . . I don't know, *help?*"

"And by 'help,' you mean . . . ?"

"You tell me."

"Was I enchanting you?" he asked. "Even through my pain and semiconsciousness?" He smiled again, looking at the others instead of Kerry. "Yes, I was. I apologize now, but I couldn't take a chance that you'd send me to a hospital, or call the police. I had barely escaped from Season with my life, and she knew that. She'd have been watching for me to show up at a hospital. I needed a place to hide out, to recuperate, and you guys gave me that. I don't know if I thanked you enough for that, for giving me a chance to live."

Rebecca cleared her throat. "Season? Who's that?"

"Is that who we saw at the restaurant?" Kerry asked. "The one who chased us, and—"

"They're still talking about that all over the resort," Rebecca broke in. "You guys are, like, famous. Or infamous, I guess."

Daniel was nodding. "That was her. Season Howe is her name. She's a witch."

Josh made a snorting noise. "Do we get the Ouija board out now?" he asked. "Commune with the spirits of the dead? I think Rebecca has a Stephen King novel we could use for reference."

"It's not as easy as all that," Daniel said matter-of-factly. "It can be done, but according to their rules, not ours."

"Come *on*!" Scott said angrily. His features were long and narrow, their length accentuated by the large lenses on his wire-rimmed glasses and his gaunt cheeks reddened with emotion. "What kind of game are you playing here, Daniel? Why don't you get to the point and tell us what this nonsense is all about?"

"I understand your feelings," Daniel replied, staying calm. "I *am* telling you what it's about. It's about Season Howe. It always has been."

"Maybe you need to give us a little more detail," Brandy suggested. "And the kind we can believe would be good."

"But if he can enchant us," Rebecca tossed out, "how do we know *what* we can believe? We might believe him only to find out that he *made* us believe him!"

"Which, if he could do that," Mace observed quietly,

"would mean that he really is able to do this magic stuff he's claimin' to do."

"If I could go on," Daniel said, "without enchanting you or somehow causing you to believe a word that I say, except perhaps by convincing you—"

"That'd be good," Kerry said. "Because our lives? Pretty much uprooted now, thanks to you. It'd be nice if there's a good reason for it all."

"There is," he assured her. He met her gaze for a moment, solidly, and she felt once again the trust she had before. Of course, now it was tempered by the knowledge that he had helped that trust along a good bit, or at least he claimed he had.

"You have seen, Kerry, things tonight that you would never have believed a few days ago, true?"

She blinked a couple of times. "I . . . I *think* I have."

"Trust yourself, if not me," he suggested. "Trust your own senses."

"Well, then . . . yes. I saw what looked like some kind of . . . mystical battle between you and that woman—"

"Season."

"Yeah, her. Season. In the kitchen. Then we ran, and you stole a car—only without a key, or taking any time to hot-wire it, or whatever. Then later on you turned it . . . invisible. So yeah, I guess it's safe to say I've seen some strange things tonight."

"The merest glimpse into my life," Daniel said, his voice grave. "Our lives. Season's . . . and mine."

"What is she, some kind of psycho ex-girlfriend?" Mace asked.

Daniel chuckled. "Hardly. An enemy. Always an enemy."

"So you've known her for a long time?" Josh wondered.

"Too long," Daniel said. His gaze had gone distant, as if he were searching his memory for something he couldn't find. "You'll find this hard to believe, I'm sure. In *spite* of the evidence you've seen tonight, Kerry. It all happened so long ago."

"How long?" Kerry asked.

Daniel cleared his throat and met her gaze again, as if only by looking into her eyes could he persuade her of the most outlandish things. "During the spring of 1704, in a town called Slocumb, Virginia—you can still find it on the map, a good map, anyway—Season was accused of witchcraft. There was plenty of evidence against her. She was, after all, a very powerful witch, and she remains one today."

Mace let out a snickering sound, and Daniel fixed him with a heated stare. "I said you'd have a hard time believing me," he reminded them. "But let me finish, please, then question me all you like."

Mace shrugged, and Daniel continued. "Season was guilty, there was no doubt of that. The town's fathers weren't hasty about this accusation. Nonetheless, Season objected to it. She objected with fire and wind and destruction. Her powers were greater than anyone in Slocumb suspected, and when her assault was over, so was the town. There was only one survivor."

"You're kidding," Kerry said, as surprised by the unexpected brutality of the story as by its outlandishness.

Daniel shook his head. "Not at all," he said. "Some of this you can find corroborated in history books. Except they don't know, or don't tell, the real reason the town was destroyed."

"Who was the survivor?" Brandy asked.

"I suppose if you look at it another way, there were three survivors," Daniel said quietly. "Since my mother was pregnant at the time with twins."

"Your mother?" Brandy was the one who spoke up, but it was obvious from the general response that they all had a hard time with this sudden twist in the tale.

"That's right," Daniel said. "Everyone called her Mother Blessing. She was also a witch, but she used her abilities to help the people of Slocumb, and she was not only accepted there, but loved. When Season's rage came, though, Mother Blessing was only able to protect herself . . . and her unborn sons—myself and my twin brother, Abraham. We were born seven months later."

"So you're sayin' you're, like, three hundred years old," Mace stated.

"Close to it," Daniel confirmed.

"No offense, bud, but the femme fatale plot is way old hat," Josh said, looking disgruntled. "And no way I buy the old man bit."

Brandy stood up, shaking her head, face clouded with anger. "Okay, now I know you're yanking our chains. I don't know why or what your scam is, but I don't appreciate you trying to play me and my friends!"

Daniel was silent while she remonstrated him, and when she was finished he spread his hands placatingly. "I told you that you'd have a hard time believing me," he reminded her. "I also said that it might be easier for Kerry, who had already seen things tonight that she would never have believed possible."

Brandy turned to Kerry. "Okay, then, Kerry," she said. "Take a look. Do you believe he's a day over a hundred? Or forty, for that matter?"

Kerry swallowed hard. She wasn't sure what she believed anymore. She wouldn't have believed he could make a car invisible, but he seemed to have done just that. And she had seen how old he had looked when they'd first brought him inside—maybe not three hundred, but certainly far older than he had even a day later.

"I . . . don't know," she admitted. "Given what I have seen, though, I'm willing to give Daniel the benefit of the doubt. At least for now."

"Until what?" Brandy pressed. "Until he makes some even more ridiculous claim? How far out there do you want him to go?"

"What will it take to convince you, Brandy?" he asked, remaining utterly calm in the face of her barrage.

"I don't know," she said. "You keep talking about Kerry, what she's seen. What about the rest of us? Why don't you show us something?"

"I don't use my abilities casually," Daniel explained. "They're not for show-and-tell—"

"Lame excuse," Brandy snapped, pointing at him.

"—but if it will help to convince you," Daniel continued, "then I'll try. Nothing fancy—I'm still getting my strength back after Season's sneak attack the other day."

"Is that how you ended up at our place?" Rebecca asked. "A sneak attack?"

"She took me by surprise, yes. I was unprepared, and she very nearly finished me right then." He closed his eyes, as if to end the conversation, and it worked. The room was almost silent. Kerry heard the breathing of her friends, her pulse pounding in her own head, and that was all.

Then Daniel's eyes snapped open and he turned to glare at Brandy, gesturing toward her with both hands and speaking a soft phrase Kerry couldn't make out. Brandy's pose remained the same—arms clenched tightly across her chest, chin jutting defiantly, legs spread a little—but her location changed. Now, instead of a couple of feet of empty space above her head, the space was beneath her feet. Her head brushed the ceiling. When she realized this, fury danced in her eyes. "Put me down!"

Daniel obliged, and a moment later Brandy was standing once again on the floor, and the others gaped at her, open-mouthed. "What the hell was that?" she demanded.

"A demonstration."

"Mass hypnosis, more like," she insisted.

"Touch your hair, Brandy," Kerry urged. Brandy glared at

her for a moment, but then put a hand to her head. It came away dusted with the debris her head had scraped off the popcorn-style ceiling. "That's not hypnosis."

Brandy rolled some of the plaster dust between her fingers, examining it as if the truth lay inside. In a way, Kerry figured, it did. Daniel's demonstration didn't make the rest of his absurd story true, but it at least showed that there was more to him than was readily apparent.

More to the world, for that matter.

Kerry Profitt's diary, August 18

So after that my friends, being who they are, couldn't shut up long enough for Daniel to finish telling his story. Which, I don't know about them, but I'd have liked to have heard more of.

I mean, sure, he told bits of it. His mother dedicated her life to hunting down Season Howe, bringing her to some kind of witchy justice for what she did to their town. And when her sons were grown, she dedicated them to the task too. Season, he explained, has been in hiding ever since. She goes where people are—resort towns in season, like La Jolla, are a favorite because the population temporarily swells and it's easy to stay anonymous. She'll go to one for a few years, then move so people don't get to know her too well. Once everyone she's encountered has moved on or died off, then she can start going there again.

Having figured out her pattern, Daniel said, he has been able to get close a few times. But as powerful as he is, she is more so, and she's always managed to avoid or defeat him—or, like this time, turn the tables so that the hunter is the hunted.

But the others were all over him with questions. Stupid ones too—did he know Humphrey Bogart, Josh wanted to know. Answer, no, in case anybody cares. Not that anybody's reading this except me. No way I'm posting it to Facebook. Brandy got completely corny and wanted to know if he'd ever lived on Elm Street, in reference to nightmares, I guess. Which is my department, after all, although not so much lately, blessed be (as they say, or do they, in witchy circles?). Did he fight in the Revolutionary War (Civil War, World Wars I and II)? I think Mace asked him about every war except the Spanish-American. Answers, no, no, no, and no. His war is private, and all-consuming.

War sucks, and his seems to be no exception. To look at him you wouldn't think he had paid too high a price. I mean, he's an older man—way older, if you believe him (do I? "Ask again later," to quote the Magic 8-ball), but for his age, especially the more advanced one he claims, he looks good, or even fantastic. No visible battle damage anymore.

If you look at the whole story, though . . . his mother lost everyone she knew, everyone she cared about, including her husband, to Season Howe's little temper tantrum. She then spent the next several hundred years trying to get revenge. Or justice. Her sons carried on the same fight for her, giving up anything that might resemble a normal life. Every human Daniel has known, until the very recent past, has aged and died on him.

And his brother, Abraham? Oh, yeah, Season killed him. Late 1880s, I think he said.

So it's no wonder he's just a little pissed, right?

More later.

K.

6

The next couple of days reminded Kerry of an extended *Survivor* episode as her roommates shared whispered conversations with one another, formed and broke alliances, and generally acted as if their world had been turned upside down. She was willing to concede that maybe it had. Daniel spent most of his time away from the apartment, not wanting to attract "undue attention," which Kerry took to be synonymous with "Season Howe."

Maybe because it had become clear that Kerry shared a bond with Daniel that the others didn't, she felt as if she were being excluded from most of the discussions. Every now and then someone would come to her, trying to sway her over to their side, but she hadn't been involved at all in the initial choosing of sides. Still, her opinion seemed to be valued, and she had a hard time being left alone at all. When she wanted an ice-cream sandwich one evening and was about to walk to the corner to buy one, Mace insisted on joining her. She found Brandy far more solicitous than usual, offering her tea, cookies, and a sympathetic ear whenever she wanted one. It was, she thought, as if she was the key to something but she didn't even know where the door was, much less what was behind it.

The basic positions were, it was true, pretty clear. Brandy and her camp thought that Daniel was some kind of charlatan, and that they should call the police on him, at the very least. Rebecca's side believed he was practically a messiah, and that they should all team up with him and do anything he asked. Kerry came down somewhere in the middle—she believed most of what Daniel had told them, but she wanted to maintain a healthy skepticism about him until she had a better idea of what he was after.

Besides Brandy and Rebecca, who had staked out positions early, the sides were vague and shifted as often as the wind. Scott kept his opinions mostly to himself, but sided with Brandy more out of default than reason. Josh flew back and forth, depending on who made the last argument, which was not even necessarily the best. Mace felt a powerful loyalty to Rebecca, with whom, against all odds, he had formed a fast friendship over the summer, but he didn't mind telling her from time to time that she was acting stupid.

Daniel hadn't, as yet, made any particular requests of

the group. He had moved them from the La Jolla house, he explained, because he felt responsible for exposing them to Season's wrath, and he wanted to protect them. He hung around for the same reason, spending his days out in search of the witch, and his nights close to the apartment in case she sought them out.

The rest of the apartment was quiet one night when Daniel and Kerry sat around the second-hand kitchen table he'd scrounged from somewhere. She traced designs in the cheap linoleum tabletop with the tip of her finger while he sipped from a can of Barq's root beer. He'd been talking about some of the changes he'd seen during his long life. "In those days," he was saying, "you could walk from the Atlantic coast to the Mississippi River without ever coming out from under trees. If you were a monkey, you could make the whole trip without ever touching the ground, limb to limb. It wasn't until you reached the Great Plains and the southwestern deserts that the trees gave way to other sorts of landscapes."

"Could anyone have predicted what would happen?" Kerry asked him.

"That the population would swell and all those people would need places to live, and that those forests would be cleared to provide lumber and paper, until the land was a sea of houses instead of trees? No, I don't think so." His mouth was a grim line, and there was a sadness in his eyes that Kerry could barely fathom.

He's seen so much, she thought. She had come to believe

that he was as old as he claimed and that he had abilities far beyond any she had ever conceived of.

"No," he said again. "Some people speculated, of course, that the United States—once we'd given it that name—would grow quickly. But the land, the trees, the animals, the water—we thought those things were abundant enough to last forever." He took another sip from the aluminum can. "Obviously we miscalculated." He smiled. "We should have thought to recycle our aluminum back then, I guess."

She laughed with him, which she was finding easy to do. "Yeah, why were you guys so backward?"

He finished the root beer and set the empty can down on the table. But before he could speak again, one of the bedroom doors opened and the rest of the roommates filed out, grave expressions on their faces.

When Brandy stepped forward as their spokesperson, Kerry was pretty sure she knew what was coming.

"Daniel, we've taken a vote," she began.

"I didn't vote," Kerry interrupted. "Don't I get a say in whatever this is?"

"You can vote, but your vote won't be enough to change the balance," Brandy told her. "If it had been, we'd have included you."

"Thanks for the consideration," Kerry snapped, feeling betrayed by the very people she'd thought were her friends.

"Anyway, Daniel, here's what it comes down to. We've all upset our lives over this mess, some of us have lost our jobs, worried our parents. It's got to end. Summer's almost over anyway, and we'll all be going our separate ways. But for the rest of the summer, for as much of it as we can salvage, we'd like you gone."

There was a moment of silence. Nobody met Kerry's eyes.

"Gone?" he echoed.

"That's right. Don't come around, don't call."

"But Season—"

"None of us has ever seen Season, except Kerry. She's left us alone so far. We'll take our chances."

"You don't know what you're getting into," he warned.

"Whatever it is, you're the one got us into it," Brandy countered. "Now, we're telling you we're done with it."

Daniel glanced at Kerry, but she couldn't bring herself to hold his gaze. She looked away from him, at his pop can sitting on the table, forgotten now. "What . . . what was the vote?" she asked hesitantly.

"Four to one," Brandy answered.

Four to one. That meant . . . Kerry looked at Rebecca. The girl's huge, soft brown eyes brimmed with tears. Brandy and Mace were the only ones who appeared certain. Scott shifted his weight from foot to foot, while Josh looked at his Converse sneakers, his eyes lined with black, the studded stainless steel collar he liked to wear, when not on duty, as tight around his neck as a strangler's hands.

"Four to two," Kerry corrected. But the world tilted sharply up around her in a vertiginous spin—the overhead lights seemed to reverse on themselves, giving out black rays that fought against a pale white background, and blood roared in her ears like an express subway past an abandoned station.

Daniel shoved his chair back on the bunching carpet and stood up. "Thank you, Kerry," he said. "But majority rules, right?"

Does it have to? Kerry wondered. They'd been talking about American history, and she knew there had been times when majority hadn't ruled at all, times when the powerful forced their will upon others. And Kerry had as strong a will as anyone—"stubborn," that's what most people called it, except her mother who had always preferred "determined." Or "Bulldog," as her housemates had named her. She wasn't sure how she could force the others to change their minds, but that didn't mean she couldn't try.

Except she was unable to form a sentence with the floor spinning beneath her feet. "I'll get my things," Daniel said, apparently interpreting her confused silence as acquiescence.

He didn't, as far as she had been able to tell, have many things to get. When they'd found him in their bushes, he had only the clothes on his back. He had been living someplace, though, and he had a knapsack's worth of possessions that he'd gathered from there after installing them all in this apartment. Kerry supposed that it was possible he had a house full of stuff somewhere—obviously, there was still far more that she didn't know about him than that she did. Since the apartment, shabby as it was, actually had more bedrooms than their house had, Brandy and Scott shared one, while Josh and Mace bunked together in another, Rebecca and Kerry in the third. Daniel, when he slept, did so in the living room on a worn, thrift-shop sofa, next to which he stored his leather pack. He crossed the room and picked it up now, moving with graceful economy, surely knowing that all eyes were on him.

Kerry felt her own eyes growing misty. She wasn't sure how much of that was because Rebecca was sniffling, huge round tears rolling down her pudgy cheeks, and how much was because, as briefly as Daniel had been part of her life, she would miss him. She sniffed once, determined not to cry.

"Daniel . . . ," she began, but she wasn't at all sure where she was going with it, and she let it hang there.

He looked at her, as if reading her meaning anyway. "Don't, Kerry," he said. "If you need me, I'll be there."

"But not here," Brandy chimed in.

"Not here."

"And no stalking, dude," Mace added.

"Not a chance," Daniel assured him. He hoisted the back-pack onto his shoulder, took a last look around at everyone, gave a smile and a friendly wave, and walked out the door.

Kerry Profitt's diary, August 20

How many times can you lose a person that you never really got a chance to know?

7

For Mace, the whole crazy thing was just too much to cope with.

He'd lost his job the night Kerry had run out of the restaurant with Daniel. He'd been back at his station in a corner of the kitchen, washing dishes, iPod screaming The Strokes into his ear, completely unaware of what was happening until a burst of light caught his attention. His first thought was that someone was taking flash pictures, though why anyone would want to do such a thing in a busy restaurant kitchen was beyond him. But looking up, he caught a glimpse of Kerry and Daniel diving out the door, pursued by a blonde with a reasonably high hotness quotient.

The whole thing was more than a little freaky. Kerry was

a friend of his, though, so he dropped a stack of plates, which caught the edge of the big sink and shattered onto the floor, and ran past the stunned kitchen staff and into the parking lot. Two cars roared away. His own car was parked in an employee lot a quarter mile away. He ran for it and lit it up, but way too late—the car Kerry had jetted in was history.

When he made his way back to the kitchen, the restaurant manager, Emil Hofstadter—who Mace was pretty sure had been born John Smith, or something like it, and whose name was as phony as his Swiss accent—had been furious, though he denied having seen anything out of the ordinary. But with no Kerry to take out his anger on, he'd directed it at Mace. Knowing it was completely without justification, Mace sucked it up anyway, figuring it might help protect Kerry from any fallout. But then, a couple of hours later, when Rebecca came in and told him that Kerry had texted her and said they all needed to get out of there, now—even though his shift would have been over in twenty-five minutes—Mace had gone along with her, walking out right in front of a raging Emil. He knew then that the job was history. Emil's arms were crossed over his chest and his face was the color of an eggplant, with veins standing out on his forehead like they were about to burst.

So he'd given up the job, and willingly. Not happily, mind you—he didn't have money in the family like Scott and Brandy, or an insurance settlement like Kerry, and had to work for what he got. But friends came first, even when they had only become friends over the course of the summer.

Besides, when Rebecca directed those puppy-dog browns at him, he didn't know how to say no.

But the whole crazy deal with Daniel was just too much to put up with. Even though Brandy had won the battle, and the man had been exiled from the apartment—which he had paid for, which meant, Mace supposed, that he could show up again at any time—Mace still wasn't comfortable hanging around anymore. Occult stuff really gave him the chills. He didn't even like horror movies, unless they were so ridiculously slasherific that there was no way to believe in them. But he thought that messing around with magic was just asking for trouble, the kind that he didn't want to have to cope with.

He didn't *believe* in magic—who would, in their right mind? He figured the stuff Daniel had shown them was nothing but trickery of some kind. And even though Kerry swore some kind of magical battle had gone on in the kitchen that night, there had been no damage left behind and he hadn't seen it, had only observed some bright lights. That didn't mean he was comfortable with it, though.

So the morning after the final confrontation with Daniel, he got up early and packed up Susie, his baby blue Lincoln Continental. He said adios to his summer friends, after coffee and churros from the taco stand on the corner of Palm, with lots of hugs and handshakes. Rebecca cried, as she would, and pulled him close to her, and the curves and valleys of her lush figure beneath her loose clothes made him think twice about what he was doing. But then he saw Kerry, ivory pale, green eyes looking bruised and bloodshot from worrying about Daniel, he guessed, and knew that of all of them, she'd have the hardest time giving up the strange old man—and he her— and if the guy was going to come back into their lives, Mace just didn't want to be there for it.

Susie started right up, as she always did. Rebecca stood on the sidewalk and waved until he was out of sight. He connected his iPod to the cassette deck—damn thing was built before CD players; that and the gas mileage were Susie's main drawbacks—and headed for Interstate 5, which would connect with the I-8, which would merge with the I-10 and take him all the way to Las Cruces. From there the I-70 would lead home to Clovis. In minutes he was on the freeway, and he lowered the window a few inches so the wind would blow on his face as he drove. To Mace, that was one of the joys of a road trip—wind in your face, tunes blaring, blacktop spooling out behind you like film running through a projector.

He'd only gone a few miles, though—hadn't even reached the I-8, which ran east-west across the bottom edge of the southwest—when Susie started to act up. Susie, for whom he cared as if she were a precious thing, started to bump and knock and rattle like she'd been inhabited by a family of poltergeists. There was no reason she should have any problems, given how carefully and meticulously he maintained her, but he couldn't ignore the noises and the shuddering that got worse with each passing mile.

With a curse and an angry slap on the steering wheel, he

gave up and pulled off at the next exit. Downtown San Diego loomed ahead of him, the I-8 a few miles beyond that. But here, off to the side of the freeway, there was only a vacant industrial area—warehouses and a railroad track and then a stretch of sloughs and shipyards close to the shore. Mace pulled Susie over in the shade of one of the warehouses and killed the engine.

He sat behind the wheel listening to her tick for a few minutes, letting the engine cool a little. Inside, he fumed, but he tried to keep that from her. A car was a sentient being, or close to it, he believed, and you didn't want to let one know when you were genuinely mad at it. Talking nice was almost always preferable. He apologized for having struck the steering wheel, and then popped the hood.

He couldn't have said where the woman came from. The neighborhood had been deserted, the only sound the steady rush of the nearby freeway, the only smell the sour, fecund stink of the standing water between here and the ocean. But between the time he opened the hood and glanced inside—to see an engine that looked just as cherry as it ever did—and the time that it took for him to go back into the car to get a rag to wipe his hands on, she had come up behind him. He stood up, rubbing at a spot of oil on his left index finger, and she was just standing there, a dozen feet away, looking at him. Tall, blond, wearing faded jeans and a black tank top and an expression like a stern librarian giving her last warning.

"Where is he?" she demanded. As soon as she spoke, Mace

realized who she had to be. "Season," Daniel had called her. Mace had seen her before, in the kitchen that night, though only from behind. He recognized the honeyed hair, however, her statuesque carriage, her muscular form.

And anyway, who else could it be? This is just too perfect.

"I don't know what you're talking about," he replied.

"Just tell me where to find Daniel," she said, "and you'll be fine."

He started to speak again, to deny that he knew who she meant, but she narrowed her eyes and parted her lips just a little and he knew that it was pointless. He didn't know *how* she knew—didn't want to know, for that matter. But she did.

"I have no idea," he said. "He was hanging around, but we kicked him out last night. I don't know where he went."

She started toward him then, walking slowly, with pretend casualness, but he didn't trust her intentions for a second. "Let's just see about that," she said. Visions of aliens with mind probes leapt into his head, and he knew that the last thing he wanted was this woman, whatever she was, rooting around in his thoughts.

He ran for Susie's open door and hurled himself inside, grabbing and twisting the key that still hung in her ignition. The engine grumbled but caught, and he yanked the door shut as he stomped on the gas. The blonde stood in the roadway before him, coming toward the car as if she intended to stop it with her own body and tug him out. Mace wasn't thinking clearly, wasn't processing. *Get out of here,* that's what went through his mind, over and over. *Get out of here. Get out—*

But she was in the way and she didn't look like she was moving, and anyway she was trouble, anyone could see that . . .

—of here.

. . . and instead of swerving around her, he turned the wheel ever so slightly, and pointed Susie's enormous bulk right *at* her.

The big car ate up the feet between them. He braced himself for the inevitable impact.

Which didn't come.

He reached the spot where she should have been, but she didn't seem to be there anymore. It took him a moment before he realized it wasn't that she had moved, but that *he* had—his direction of travel had changed. Instead of pushing through her toward the open road, he was hurtling *toward* the cement block wall of the nearest warehouse.

Mace pawed at the wheel and started to correct his course, but even as he did, he knew it was too late. He was moving too fast, had come too close. The wall loomed huge in his windshield, and then—

8

"Mace is dead."

Daniel stood in the doorway, his face drawn, looking worse than at any time Kerry had seen him since that first night. This time it wasn't physical pain he felt, she believed, but emotional. He had come to deliver bad news. And he experienced the hurt of that news himself, maybe even some complicity.

"I'm so sorry," he went on, filling the silence when she didn't say anything. "I feel just terrible."

Confirming her theory. "Did you have anything to do with it?" *Cold*, she thought, *but necessary*.

"No. Yes." He looked at the ground, then back at her, eyes wide and solemn. "Just that . . . while he was allied with the rest of you, he was under my protection. Once he made the decision to leave, he slipped from my sphere of influence. She must have been waiting for something like that, for the scent of any of you. She must have caught up to him. It's the only thing that could have happened."

Somehow the explanation, perfunctory as it was, made it all more real to her, and she herself turned numb. "How . . ." she began, but couldn't finish. She swallowed hard and stepped aside, wordlessly inviting him in.

"He had pulled off the freeway in an industrial area, for no reason that I can discern, and drove straight into a warehouse wall. The speed and force must have been incredible. Do you want to know more?"

"I . . . want to know everything," she said. Josh, Brandy, and Scott were at work. Rebecca had lost her job at Seaside when she and Mace bailed from the kitchen, and she had gone down to the nearby branch library for some books. Kerry knew that they'd all have questions, lots of them, and she wanted to be able to answer whatever came up.

"The force of impact drove the engine block through the passenger compartment," Daniel elaborated. "He would have been killed instantly. I'm sure he didn't suffer."

"But . . . if it was her . . . why? Would she have . . . tortured him?"

Daniel shrugged, but his face remained grim as he considered the possibility. "Maybe. I doubt it, though. The way they found him . . . if she had had any time with him,

I don't think he would have been in the car."

Kerry flopped down on the couch, suddenly feeling unsteady on her feet. A darkness seemed to close in around her, but she didn't know if it was actual or spiritual. Or if it really mattered, in the long run. People died—in the thrillers she liked to read, and her own parents had died—but she had never known of a violent death before, and the thought of it staggered her, made her feel sick. "What, is she just evil? Why would she do that?"

Daniel sat beside her and put a hand on her knee. "I'm sure she's still trying to find me, to use my association with you all to track me and finish me off. I've regained most of my strength since our last serious encounter, but if she still expects that I'm weakened, she'll want to press her advantage." He looked away from her, at the plastered ceiling. "Which makes his death my fault," he said, sounding very somber. "One more in a long line."

Kerry felt that she should argue with him, should claim somehow that Mace took his own chances by leaving. But that wasn't right, she realized, since he had no way of knowing what might have been in store for him if he left. None of them had known that they were still under Daniel's protection, so how could they be aware of what might happen if they left it? No, he was right—Mace's death was on him.

On him . . . and Season Howe.

"As to whether she's evil," Daniel continued, "the answer is very definitely yes. I thought I'd made that clear."

"I guess I don't understand what her game is," Kerry said. Daniel's hand still rested on her knee, and it was getting to the point where she'd have to acknowledge it with a squeeze of her own or shift away from it with whatever message that would send, or it would become like the elephant in the room, impossible to pretend wasn't there. But then probably she was only dwelling on it to distract herself from the fact of Mace's death—the real elephant in the room. "What is she after?"

Apparently he caught on to the knee situation too. He gave a final pat and took his hand away, raising it and his other one chest high in a gesture of uncertainty. "Who knows? I like to think that by keeping the pressure on her, keeping her on the run, I've prevented her from putting any grand plans into motion. But bad things happen every day, everywhere on Earth. Might she be responsible for some of those? Of course."

Kerry rubbed her eyes, as if that would help her discern Season's motives. "But you don't have any proof that she's still up to bad things?" she asked. "Nothing you can pin on her recently?"

"Murdering Mace," he reminded her.

"Yeah," Kerry agreed, feeling the numbness overtake her again. There had just been too much going on emotionally this last week or so. She hadn't been sleeping well, hadn't been eating right. It wore on her, and she was afraid that she was simply shutting down, one part at a time. "Yeah, there's that."

* * *

Josh had just parked a Lexus at the north lot and was starting to hoof it back to the valet station when one of his coworkers, Kevin, pulled up to the curb nearby in a gigantic black Escalade. Kevin rolled down the driver's window and leaned his head out. He was big and shaggy, with the sunstreaked blond locks of the surfer he was. He mostly worked nights because he preferred the morning waves. "Dude!" he called. Josh jogged over to him.

"What's up?"

"Hey, you knew that guy Mace, right? Dishwasher?"

"Yeah, he's my—" Kevin's use of the past tense suddenly struck him, and Josh felt his insides turn to hot liquid. "What do you mean?"

"Dude, he got killed," Kevin said casually. "There's some cops askin' for anyone who knew him. Detectives, I guess, in suits. They started with valets because we're right out in front, but it looks like they're gonna work their way around."

"Killed how?" Josh demanded. His legs felt like pipe cleaners, like they were about to buckle under his weight.

"I don't know," Kevin answered. "They were into asking questions, not answerin' 'em."

The specifics of it, Josh knew, weren't really the important thing. The fact was, Mace was dead—unless this whole deal was some colossal misunderstanding, which seemed unlikely. Mace was not the kind of guy to whom Josh would normally be drawn, but over the summer they had become friends anyway, and to think his life had been suddenly snuffed . . .

Then another thought burst into his consciousness, and he believed—no, he *knew*—that this was somehow related to those freaking witches, Season and Daniel. Somehow Mace had been caught in their crossfire and had paid the price for it.

Which meant that any of them could be next.

Scott and Brandy, he thought suddenly. They were working today too, and they had to be found and warned. If the cops could find them, so could the witch.

Without a parting word to Kevin, he broke into a panicked run. Scott could be anywhere, but Brandy would only be one place—the hotel's front desk. It would be the second place the cops would go, after the valet stand. He needed to call her, get her out of there. As he ran, he tore off his red valet's vest, not wanting to be easily recognizable to the police. He hurled it to the ground, followed it with his bow tie. Now he was just a guy in a white shirt and black pants, running full tilt across the resort grounds, digging a cell phone from his pocket as he did.

Kerry Profitt's diary, August 21

Much to my astonishment, Rebecca didn't cry when we told her about Mace.

I'd have put money on it. The girl is such a soft touch she wants to take in every stray dog, cat, or homeless person we see on the streets, of which, especially that last one, there are plenty. But then, San Diego in summer?

Relatively mild, no humidity, not too bad in the bug department (I haven't suffered a mosquito bite since I got here, which is more than I could say for Illinois in the summer). If I was homeless, which so far is only a borderline possibility, there aren't many places I'd rather live.

She said, changing the subject.

Then again, I didn't cry either. Mace Winston, not my favorite person (can you say that about the dead?) was gone, and I felt—and feel—just horrible. I'm sure Rebecca feels the same way. I've never seen her look so sad as when she came in the door, a bunch of library books under her arm, and we told her. But no tears fell. They will tonight, later, I expect. She's still out in the living room as I write this, and I have a feeling that when we're both in here tonight, with the lights out, there are going to be tears on both our pillows.

Mostly what I feel is empty. And angry. As if Mace, who as I pointed out was not my best friend in life, has left a giant hole inside me through his absence. And even though I never expected to see him again anyway after he drove into the sunrise, the idea that he's not out there anymore, the idea that I couldn't call him or see him even if I wanted to, is somehow too horrible to really process.

I'm sure the police notified his parents. Mace had ID on him, they knew who he was. Fortunately not where he was living most recently, because a whole lot of questions

could come up that we have no interest in answering.
I was a little surprised to find that, on that question, at
least, Brandy and I were in agreement.

More later.

K.

Later, Kerry heard a clatter on the outside stairs, which meant
that Scott, Brandy, and Josh were home, earlier than antici-
pated, and the heavy footfalls indicated that they were upset
too. She tossed a wan smile Daniel's way—he was still on the
couch, but she had paced for a while and then settled in a
chair—and waited for the inevitable. Rebecca heard the noise
too, and drifted in from the bedroom she and Kerry shared,
exchanging glances with both Kerry and Daniel.

When the door flew open, Brandy was the first one inside.
She took in the scene quickly. "So you've heard," she said.

"We've heard," Kerry confirmed.

Brandy dropped her purse unceremoniously to the floor;
she seemed to carry the approximate weight of a small city
with her at any given time, Kerry thought. "This is your fault,"
she said, boring in on Daniel with her glare.

"You're right, Brandy," Daniel agreed. "I am so terribly
sorry. It was because of my association with you that Season
Howe killed Mace."

Scott and Josh crowded in behind Brandy, who had
stopped just a couple of feet in front of the door, and had her

arms folded, legs wide. *An aggressive stance*, Kerry thought, *like she's spoiling for a fight.* Sunlight splashed in through a part in the curtain, giving her caramel-colored skin a soft glow.

"Do you know for sure it was her?" Scott asked.

Daniel gave a little shrug. "I didn't witness it, if that's what you mean. But in my heart, yes, I'm certain. Unless you think Mace would have intentionally driven into a wall."

Scott pulled his glasses off and wiped them on the tail of his tan uniform shirt. "That doesn't sound like him."

"Not at all," Josh agreed. He squeezed behind Scott and planted himself on the floor, legs crossed, back against the wall. Kerry wouldn't have believed he could be any paler than his usual paper-white, but he seemed almost gray now. "Mace was, like, the least suicidal guy I've ever known. And a good driver besides. And even if he would kill himself, which he wouldn't, he'd never do anything to hurt that car."

"No," Brandy echoed. "He wouldn't do that."

"It was Season, then," Scott said, replacing his glasses and blinking behind them. He sounded like he was trying to convince himself, and was slowly coming around to that position. "She killed him."

"That's right," Kerry found herself saying. "That's what Daniel's been telling us."

"But if it wasn't for you he'd still be alive," Brandy declared.

Daniel looked at her calmly. "Most likely, yes."

"And we'd all still have our jobs," Josh said.

Kerry had already noticed that they were home early, but

now she realized that Josh wasn't wearing his vest or tie, nor had he carried them in. Brandy still had on the conservative gray skirt and tight short-sleeved top she'd worn that morning, and Scott was in his groundskeeper uniform, but neither of them had work accessories that could as easily be abandoned as Josh's. "You didn't all quit, did you?" she asked.

"Effectively, since we just walked away from them," Brandy said, her dark eyes smoldering. "It was either that or talk to the cops. As it is, I'm sure they'll be calling our families pretty soon, trying to track us down. We're in a serious situation here."

"The police were already there?" Kerry asked, surprised.

"Looking for us, apparently," Brandy replied. "There's an investigation into Mace's death."

"That makes sense," Daniel said. "It just doesn't look like an accident."

"So you saw where it happened?" Scott asked him. He still stood, a half step behind Brandy.

"I did," Daniel answered. "After the fact. I had a sense that something had happened, something involving one of you—"

"Then why weren't you able to stop it?" Brandy demanded.

"It was *after* the fact," Daniel repeated. "As I explained to Kerry and Rebecca, by leaving the rest of you behind, Mace took himself outside my protection."

Brandy shook her head. "There shouldn't even *be* protection," she fumed. "We told you to leave us alone! What part of that don't you get?"

"I couldn't, not completely," Daniel said by way of defense.

"I had involved you in something dangerous. Without my protection, what happened to Mace would have happened to all of you by now. Unless—"

"There's an unless?" Rebecca asked, her voice so high it squeaked.

"Unless you give me up," he finished. "If you tell Season where to find me, then she might let you live."

"But Mace didn't . . . ," Kerry began.

"You had sent me away. Mace had no idea where to find me. Even if he'd wanted to save his own life, he wouldn't have been able to."

Brandy slumped as if she'd been deflated. "So really, I . . ."

Scott grabbed her shoulders from behind, like he was trying to keep her from sinking into the floor. "Brandy, no!"

"But it's true," she said quietly. "If I hadn't insisted we make Daniel leave, Mace would still be alive."

"Possibly," Scott countered.

"No," she snapped, turning on him. "I was the one who pushed and pushed to get Daniel out of here. If I hadn't—"

"Scott's right, Brandy," Daniel said, trying to console her. "There's no way to know what might have happened. Mace might have gone anyway, and then he still would have been outside my protection. He could have given me up, told her to find me here. But that doesn't guarantee that she wouldn't have killed him anyway."

"I guess." She sat down on the floor, with Scott helping her down. He remained beside her, like a bodyguard. "But still . . ."

"You can never know what might have happened, Brandy," Daniel assured her. "Or what's going to happen. The best you can do is try to make the right decisions when they present themselves."

"So what's the best decision now?" Josh asked. "I mean, we're basically screwed, right? The cops are looking for us, we've lost our jobs, and this Season witch is going to try to run us down one by one."

"Unless . . . ," Daniel began.

"Unless what?" Kerry asked.

"Unless," he continued, "we take the fight back to her."

9

Daniel didn't have much in the way of a plan, Kerry learned. *But then, if he had, he might not have spent the last three centuries chasing her from place to place.* He admitted as much over fast-food burgers and milk shakes in the apartment that he had moved back into, taking the now-vacant bed that had been used by Mace.

"Season's survival skills are well-honed," he told them. "She's hard to get the drop on, virtually impossible to ambush. Every now and then I get a lead on where she is, but even then, she's so much more powerful than me that I have to plan my strategy carefully, and that's just to give me a fighting chance. I can't say that I've ever had the advantage."

"Can you beat her?" Scott asked. His neatly trimmed col-

legiate hair, Kerry noticed, was starting to grow a bit long and
unruly. "Or is it just not even worth trying?"

"Am I spinning my wheels?" Daniel rephrased Scott's
question. "I like to think I'm not. But then I suppose the same
is true of anyone on a long, fruitless hunt. Was Ahab wasting
his time chasing the white whale all over creation? A lot of
people would say yes." He took a deep breath and blew it out
slowly. There was, Kerry thought, a sadness in his eyes while
he considered the question. "Certainly there are other things
I could have done with my life. I could have helped more
people, I suppose. Saved more lives in some other capacity.
But I believed—I continue to believe—that Season is a threat,
a real danger, to everyone whose path she crosses. She's not
going away on her own, so someone has to step in and deal
with her."

"That's not exactly what I meant," Scott said, his elbows
on the cheap table as he wrested a fry from its paper bag. "I
meant more, like, can you take her on, or is it pointless to try?
But since you bring it up—not to be too nosy or anything—
but just how long can you guys live?"

Daniel smiled briefly. "Got it," he answered with a chuckle.
"I didn't mean to be evasive. Short answer, this time—yes,
I believe I can take her. Not easily, as I've mentioned, and
probably not one-on-one in a fair fight. But I've long since
given up the idea of fighting her fairly. Question two—I'm
not entirely sure. I knew a witch once who claimed to be well
over a thousand. He said that he'd narrowly escaped death at

the Battle of Hastings, and when I knew him he looked every single one of those thousand and some years. He died shortly after that, of natural causes. Or at least that's what I was told."

"So the fact that Season was an adult when she wrecked your town doesn't necessarily mean that she's likely to die of old age any time soon," Brandy suggested.

"You've seen her, Kerry," Daniel pointed out. "She look like she's on her deathbed to you?"

"I wish," Kerry replied. "But, no. I could only hope to look that good when I'm thirty-five."

Josh had been staring blankly at a corner of the room, and Kerry wasn't sure he had even been tracking the conversation. But now he swiveled his head, neck stiff as if it needed oiling, and fixed his gaze on Daniel. Outside, the sun had gone away, and the glow from the overhead light in the kitchen left the table half dark. "How do we off her, man?" Josh asked. "That's what this is all about, right? How do we freaking kill her?"

Kerry shuddered to hear the question phrased so bluntly. Josh was right, of course. And he had been closest to Mace—well, he and Rebecca. But Rebecca wasn't the kind of person who would think along those lines, under any circumstance. Josh, though—the set of his chin and the hardness of his eyes reminded Kerry of a character from the hard-boiled movies he loved so much. *He could be turned into a killer,* she realized. *Maybe he already has been, and now he just needs the opportunity.*

Daniel shrugged. "First we find her," he said, as if it was

that easy. "Then I kill her. Not you. Not any of you. You wouldn't stand a chance against Season Howe."

"Try me," Josh said.

"I'm serious, Josh," Daniel assured him. "Not a chance. She wouldn't even break a sweat against you. But . . ." He paused before he went on, as if choosing his words carefully. Perhaps debating whether to say them at all. ". . . you can help. You can track her down."

"How?" Rebecca asked. "Wouldn't that, like, make us even bigger targets? Like Mace was?"

"Mace was outside my protection, so he was no longer shielded from her," Daniel explained. "It's not a physical thing, not a matter of distance or anything like that. Mace left the rest of you behind, and by doing so he opted out of my protection spell. But the rest of you—you could walk right up to Season, and she'd never know you were the ones who helped me. As long as you all work together." He looked at Kerry. "Except you, Kerry. She's seen you. She can't sense where you are, but if she sees you again, she'll know you."

"I understand," Kerry said.

"But if we find her, then what?" Scott asked. "Aren't we back to square one? We have to let you know where she is, and then you have to get there and somehow do battle against a superior opponent."

"Sounds so easy when you put it that way." Daniel was smiling when he said it, but his grin didn't look particularly mirthful.

* * *

Under Daniel's direction—and more significantly, he promised, his protection—they split up the next morning to go look for Season Howe. Kerry was impressed by his visual aid: he generated, or rather, projected, an almost-photographic image of Season in the inch of black coffee left at the bottom of Scott's cup, clear enough that even those who had never seen the witch in person would recognize her. Daniel didn't want to let the image last for long for fear, he said, that she would somehow be able to lock onto it. So he told everyone to take a good look, and then he stirred the coffee and the image went away.

Season liked crowds, Daniel had said, and transient populations, where strangers weren't unusual. So to cover the most ground possible, they paired off—Scott and Brandy, of course, Rebecca and Josh, Daniel and Kerry. Rebecca and Josh decided they'd scope out downtown San Diego, look into the coffee shops and boutiques of the Gaslamp Quarter and the stores of Horton Plaza. Scott and Brandy—who, since Mace died, was willing to go along even though he still hadn't come around to believing in Daniel—went to scout the beaches. Daniel and Kerry knew that it was impossible for six people to cover the entire city—plus there was always the chance, though Daniel insisted it was remote, that Season had already moved on—but they also knew they had to make the best possible effort. So Kerry and Daniel went to a place where they knew there would be crowds: the San Diego Zoo.

At Daniel's suggestion, everyone had contacted their parents or other adult caretakers—in Kerry's case, it had been a simple e-mail to Uncle Marsh's work account, which Kerry knew would suffice—to let them know that there had been a change of address and phone number, but that they were okay. Since most of their folks used their cell phones anyway, the change wouldn't be a big deal to them. Kerry had rarely spoken to her aunt and uncle since she'd been in California, but then again, she rarely talked to them even when they lived in the same house. Rebecca was close to her parents and three brothers, as were Scott and Brandy to their families, but Josh almost never mentioned his, and Kerry was pretty sure only his mother was still alive.

The zoo was nearly always busy, but on a warm summer afternoon it was almost overwhelmingly so. The line from the ticket booths extended most of the way to the parking lot. Kerry thought she'd die of sunstroke by the time they got inside, the sun not being a friend to her fair skin. But Daniel told her to wait in the shade while he stood in line, and in a few minutes they had passed through the turnstiles. Inside, the air had a different quality—the exhaust of cars and tour buses was left behind on the other side of the walls, and they moved into a world of exotic scents—scores of plants mixing with the rich, pungent odors of the birds and animals that surrounded them. The scenery was a riot of colors—the Hawaiian shirts and casual clothes of zoo-goers battling for supremacy with the bright plumage of the flamingoes near the front entrance.

Daniel didn't add much to the display in his jeans and dark blue T-shirt, but Kerry had opted for a crimson-and-white striped rugby shirt, with the long sleeves pushed up, and white hip huggers.

"Flamingoes were used as the hieroglyphic symbol for the color red, in ancient Egypt," Daniel told her as they threaded their way through the crowd. "And to represent the reincarnation of Ra, the sun god."

Kerry studied his face, looking for signs of age that weren't there. "You're not *that* old, though," she said.

Daniel laughed. "No, not that old. Just old enough to have picked up lots of totally useless information along the way."

"Not totally useless," Kerry argued. "There's the sheer entertainment value. Not to mention the possibility of scoring big on TV game shows."

He smiled, but he was standing up on the balls of his feet, scanning the crowd for any sign of Season. "Yeah, I guess that's true," he admitted.

"Speaking of cash," she pressed. "How do you survive, anyway? You don't seem to be gainfully employed, not that I can tell."

Daniel looked away from the crowd long enough to meet her gaze for a moment. Just under his right jaw line, where she usually didn't notice it, was a scar like a half-curled worm against his skin. She had meant to ask about it before, but never had. "Turns out if you take the long-term view—and I mean, really long term—the stock market isn't a bad place to keep some money. And even a bank account will do pretty well after a hundred years or so of collecting interest."

"What about government records? Social Security, the IRS, stuff like that?" She'd been too absorbed in the craziness of the hunt to give much thought to such mundane questions before, but now that they'd occurred to her, she couldn't stop the flow.

"Nothing that can't be doctored with a simple spell," Daniel explained.

"And doctors? Doesn't your family doctor wonder if you never age?"

"We tend to take care of our own. Don't have much need of doctors." He touched her arm. "And sometimes an angel of mercy appears from nowhere when you need her most."

She felt herself blushing, and turned away. But then she reached up, almost as if she couldn't stop herself, and touched the curled scar. "What's this one? Seems like that might have needed some medical attention."

His face changed slightly, as if a shadow had passed over it, and he rubbed the spot she had just touched. "I could have removed it," he said. His voice had turned to steel. "But that one I got the day she killed Abraham."

"Your brother," Kerry remembered. Twins, he'd said, born shortly after Season had destroyed their town.

"That's right." They had stopped walking, and the flow of humanity coursed around them like a river around boulders. A woman pushing twins in a stroller shot them a dirty look, as if they had intentionally blocked her path, but then picked a side and moved on. "Season did that, with an enchanted blade she carried in those days. Nearly killed me. Took me out of action long enough for her to finish Abe. He was trying to help me, and she cut him too. Left us both for dead. Unlucky for her. She should have finished me off then."

He touched the spot again and then shook his hand, like he could shake off the memory as easily as a few drops of water. Kerry felt bad for bringing up something so obviously painful, and thought she should change the subject. "Why here?" she asked, starting to walk again. Signs ahead of them pointed toward the children's zoo and the Absolutely Apes exhibit. "Why would she be at the zoo?"

"She would be here, or at the beach or the mall or some other place, because her whole goal is not to stand out. She is probably living in a hotel, although it's possible she found a summer rental. Either way, there would be someone—neighbors, hotel staff, a cleaning service—who would notice if she spent these warm summer days holed up in the room. She wants to look like every other out-of-towner here for the season, so she goes to places like this, even if she has no special interest in them."

"And you can't just magically track her down?"

"No more than she can track me, or you while you're under my protection. I've got counterspells, and so does she. If we see each other, then it's war. But if I can't find her before she leaves town, then I've got to start all over."

They made the turn toward the apes exhibit area, for no particular reason that she could determine. There was a part of Kerry that enjoyed just walking through the zoo with a handsome, interesting man. She wished there didn't have to be some kind of epic death hunt going on to darken the day. But at the same time, she knew it was the death hunt that had brought them together, and it remained the main thing they had in common.

"Do you ever get tired of it?" she asked. "Just want to give it up and let her go?"

Again, he stopped in his tracks. Kerry was starting to feel like the queen of hurtful questions. "You don't have to answer that," she said quickly. "It was over the line. I'm sorry."

"It's okay." He took her upper arms in his hands and held on tightly until she thought he might leave bruise marks. "I don't feel like I have to hide anything from you, Kerry. I don't quite know why that is, yet. But I kind of like it. I hope that doesn't scare you."

The only answer that came to her was the honest one. "Yeah, it does, a little. But I'll try to cope."

"The truth is, I get tired of it every day, and every day there are times when I want to give up. But I never do."

"Why not?" *You just have to push,* she thought, even as the words left her mouth. *You big dope.*

"Honestly?" Daniel looked toward the sun, and blinked a couple of times. "I don't know what I'd do with myself. Daytime TV gets pretty dull after a few decades."

Kerry Profitt's diary, August 23

The zoo was a big strikeout, Season-wise. Brandy and Scott washed out too. As did, need I say, Rebecca and Josh. No Season, no Season, and no Season. Not that, in a city the size of San Diego, with more millions than I can remember, but several of them, it's an easy task to find a single person who doesn't especially want to be found. And as Daniel put it, better twelve eyes looking for her than two—especially since she's no doubt looking for us, too, and whoever spots the other first has the advantage.

Can't argue with the reasoning. Of course, to take it a step or two further, twelve hundred eyes would be better yet. Twelve thousand, and maybe there'd be a chance of finding her. This needle-in-the-haystack routine seems so, I don't know, eighteenth century somehow. Like we ought to be able to Google her instead of just looking.

Which, by the way, I just did. There's a hockey player named Howe who's had several good seasons, and likewise some squash news. No witchy stuff, though. So I guess, as Daniel told me while we walked past the big cats (side note—the snow leopards are spectacular!), she has done a good job of maintaining a low profile.

What is most amazing to me is that this works, he says. The low-tech thing, I mean. He has found her before, several times. Done her some damage, too, he says. Of course, she's done the same to him. Many clinches, no knockouts. Sports page girl today, that's me.

Actually, not, so don't ask why the various jock references. I might recognize Tiger Woods or A-Rod on the street, and not many guys can carry off bicycle shorts like Lance Armstrong, but that is, I confess, about the extent of my sports smarts.

I'm frustrated, of course, by the lack of forward momentum of our day—the first real day of what I presume to be many (at least until school beckons and we have to go our separate ways) of hunting Season Howe. But the truth is, it wasn't a bad day at all. I got to roam the zoo, and then the open spaces of Balboa Park as well as its museums and walkways, with Daniel. Who, as it turns out, is full of stories. Living three hundred years would give one plenty of material, I guess. But I sometimes have a hard time remembering what I did last week, and he's coming up with bits like the time, a hundred years ago, when he sat in a dark nickelodeon in New York and watched *The Great Train Robbery*, one of the first movies ever made.

Well, I guess I might remember something like that too. Having spent my "formative years" not exactly going to a ton of movies, I think I remember all the ones I've seen in theaters. Cried at *The Notebook*, but at the wrong parts. Laughed at *The Hangover*, ditto. Guess I'm just culturally illiterate.

But the point is, walking around with Daniel, being entertained by his stories, even as we kept our eyes open for any sign of the big bad witch of the west, was nice. Balboa Park is as beautiful a spot as one could hope for.

It all helped drive horrible thoughts of Mace from my mind, and I hope that somehow, wherever he is, he's found some peace. Being with Daniel felt easy, comfortable, even though I haven't known him for long and he is as different from me—being essentially immortal, many-powered and all—as it's possible to be.

All the crazy witch stuff? Turns out when you're faced with it, right in front of you, it's not so hard to believe. A month ago—two weeks ago—I would've sworn that it was all bogus. Today I'll swear till I'm blue in the face (and just what does that old cliché mean, anyway?) that it's true, that there are people—witches—among us with abilities far beyond our imagining.

I asked Daniel, while we walked and searched, about Wiccans. I think the way I phrased it was less than charitable, something like, "so those people who sit around in circles and worship trees and stuff—are they just wannabes? Do they even know that witches like you and Season really exist, and is that what they aspire to?"

But Daniel is, apparently, kinder than I. "A few of them are," he told me. "Aware of us, I mean. Very few. To others, we're nothing more than whispers, rumors, maybe legends, if that. They aren't necessarily trying to become like us, or even thinking that's a possibility. It isn't quite as if they're acolytes. But their activities can help to power us, like we're batteries, recharged by the forces they release into the ether. So they do us a major service. And much of what they do is effective, as far as it goes. Spells to find love or employment, or to help friends through difficult situations: These can all work quite well if carried out correctly."

Okay, the colon I put in there? I made it up. Don't know if that's what he intended, or even if I'm quoting verbatim. He could probably quote something Abraham Lincoln told him in 1862 (kidding, he never met Lincoln, he says), but I don't have that particular skill.

Point is, something about Daniel—maybe because of his special abilities—has made him remarkable in other ways too. He has an astonishing memory, and my guess is that he's just developed his mental faculties in ways most people can't even comprehend. So living for centuries just enhances his recall instead of—as I suspect would happen to me—jumbling experiences together.

Hey, I've been to Disneyland and seen the animatronic Lincoln. If I'd been alive in the 1860s, I probably would think I'd seen the real one.

I pummeled him with questions, over the course of the day. Who he had met, what he had seen. Finally, he told me he kept journals, and he'd let me read them if I was interested. I think it was a ploy to shut me up.

Didn't work.

But I'm still going to read them. How cool is that?

More later.

K.

10

The day after that, they rotated partners and continued the hunt. Kerry found herself paired with Rebecca. She felt an unexpected pang of sorrow at not getting another day with Daniel, who teamed up with Scott, while Brandy and Josh went out together. But she understood the reasoning. If the same two people searched together every time, Daniel suggested, they'd fall into patterns of looking, and maybe become complacent. If they were changed up frequently, they'd be more likely to remain alert and aware. Anyway, she liked Rebecca so she had no real problem with it, just a sense of longing to be with Daniel.

They spent a long day mall-crawling, figuring a woman who looked as good and dressed as nicely as Season Howe would probably be a serious shopper. They started south, at Plaza Bonita, and worked their way north, through Horton Plaza, Mission Valley, and its more upscale neighbor, Fashion Valley; east as far as Grossmont and Parkway Plaza; then up to La Jolla's University Town Center. Each mall seemed to have its own personality, its own core group of shoppers, in spite of the fact that most had the same national chain stores. They saw, throughout their day, a lot of attractive blondes.

Rebecca also saw at Mission Valley a pair of turquoise drop earrings she just had to have. She was wearing a blue chambray work shirt open over a white-blue tank, the tails tied across her belly, with a sky blue and green-and-yellow batik skirt. The turquoise looked like it had been plucked from the ground especially for her.

What they didn't see was Season.

Kerry had seen Rebecca sad, but she'd never seen her anything resembling grumpy before. Driving home from UTC in the Honda Civic Daniel had acquired for them was the closest the girl had come, in Kerry's memory. "This sucks more than anything," Rebecca groused, thumping the steering wheel for emphasis. "I've been trying to think of something that sucks worse than this, and I just can't. I mean, how many stores are there in San Diego county? Thousands? A hundred thousand? How are we supposed to find Season in the middle of all that? Why do we live in such a materialistic society, anyway? If this was a simple village of hunter-gatherers, we'd have come across her long before now."

"If we see her, we see her," Kerry countered. "If we don't, we don't. But if we don't see her and she sees us, we're going to regret it."

"Yeah, but . . ." Rebecca didn't finish the thought.

"I know," Kerry sympathized. "I feel the same way, Beck. We just have to keep trying."

"For how long, Kerry? Are we in this for the rest of our lives?"

"I don't think so," Kerry said. She wasn't entirely sure herself, though. She couldn't see the hunt lasting forever, even though it had already gone on for many lifetimes. "From what Daniel says, I think it's just a summer thing. Season will move on after that, and we'll be able to split up, go back to our own lives."

"And she won't keep looking for us?"

Let's hope, Kerry thought. "I figure she's got other things on her mind. She'll keep an eye out for Daniel. But I expect we'll be okay."

"But you can't be sure," Rebecca challenged.

"No, of course not. Not a hundred percent."

They were just about to pass by the off-ramp that led into La Jolla when an idea flashed into Kerry's head. "Rebecca!" she shouted. "Turn off here."

Rebecca cranked the wheel to the right and shot off the exit, cutting off another car that blared its horn at her. The look on her face was one of near-panic. "Why?"

"Just a thought," Kerry said. "I didn't mean to startle you.

I just figured we should swing by the old house, while we're out this way. If Season's looking for us, she might be staking it out."

"So if she is, should we go there?"

"She's never seen you," Kerry reminded her. "I'll keep a low profile. Just one pass."

"Okay. . . ." Rebecca didn't sound convinced, but she drove toward the house they had once shared, in the part of town known as Bird Rock. Kerry wasn't sure what to expect when they got there. The place was full of memories, most happy, some frightening, as when they'd first discovered Daniel. And, of course, memories of poor, lost Mace that weighed on her like a lead blanket.

When they reached their old block, Kerry scrunched down low in the passenger seat, so that only her eyes and the top of her head showed over the window. "Drive slow," she instructed. Rebecca's knuckles were white on the wheel, and there was a bit of a shake to her arms. "We'll be fine." She probably didn't sound all that reassuring, but then, she found that she was more nervous than she had expected to be.

The street, at first glance, looked the same as ever. It was a little after seven thirty, the sun lowering toward the distant horizon, and the trees that lined the street cast long shadows across the blacktop. Houses had lights on in kitchens and living rooms and over front doors, but there was no one visible on the sidewalks, no one out in their yards. On a Saturday morning at least three or four people on the block would be mowing or weeding, trimming hedges, clipping trees. Now, though, the street might as well have been in a ghost town, or a movie set after filming had wrapped for the night.

Rebecca glanced anxiously at Kerry as she slowed the car, bringing them to a crawl as they neared the house. It was dark and didn't look as if anyone new had moved in since they'd left. Kerry tried to scan the cars parked along the sides of the road, in case Season was sitting in one of them watching the place. They all looked empty, and she began to think the detour was yet one more waste of time in a long day full of time wasted. As they passed the house, though, she rose up in her seat a little, staring hard at the building that had, for a brief time, contained her life on this coast. *Funny how a building can be so small, so limited, and yet hold so much inside its walls,* she thought.

And then all other thoughts vanished from her mind. Through a window, she saw something move.

"Stop!" she said, clutching hard at Rebecca's knee.

Rebecca gave a frightened squeal and jammed on the brake, lurching the car. "What?"

"In there," Kerry said, her voice quaking. She pointed toward the house's living-room window. "Look."

The window had four panes. There were curtains over it, the same moth-eaten ones she remembered, still tied back as she'd left them her last day here. In the faint light that filtered in from the street and the setting sun, she could see figures— not just one, as she'd thought initially, but at least two or three—moving about inside. They moved in an odd, graceless fashion that somehow didn't feel right.

"Is it her?" Rebecca asked.

"No. I don't know who it is, but that's definitely not Season."

Rebecca started to lift her foot from the brake, but Kerry stopped her. "Wait a second. I want to get out."

Rebecca's eyes widened in fear. "But, Kerry," she argued, "you don't know who's in there, and you don't know if Season's around."

Kerry agreed, but she didn't want to admit it, even to herself. She had to know what was going on inside that house. Maybe it was something completely innocent—maybe those guys were exterminators or painters, preparing the house to be rented again.

But she didn't think so.

"If Season was hanging around," she pointed out, "she'd have seen us while we sat out here in front of the house."

Rebecca slowly pulled the car to the curb, swiveling her head in every direction to watch for sudden attack. "I'm not too sure about this. . . ."

Neither am I, Kerry thought. She knew better than to give voice to her hesitation, though. She didn't want to freak herself out, much less Rebecca, and she wanted a closer look while she had her courage worked up for it. She couldn't help wishing it were Daniel at the wheel instead of Rebecca, convinced that he'd know what to do. Or at least make her feel safer.

As soon as Rebecca killed the engine, Kerry lunged from

the car. Rebecca had coasted a little past the house, so Kerry darted back toward it, hunching over in hopes that she'd be less noticeable. She knew that if whoever was inside looked out, she'd be spotted. But the way they were moving around, it looked like they were searching for something, and she hoped all their attention was inside.

The light was fading fast. Already shadows covered the lawn, and the bushes in which Kerry had first found Daniel took on a dark, menacing appearance. Through the streaked window, she could barely see the forms she had seen just moments before, when the light was slightly better. Trying to get closer, she shoved her way through the thick bushes and pressed her face to the glass. The evening hadn't cooled off, and a film of perspiration coated her forehead, threatening to blind her, but she blinked it away.

From this spot, one could see the whole living room and into the kitchen. The kitchen had a window over the sink facing onto the tiny backyard, which meant it faced west, toward the sunset. She had loved to look through it when it was her turn to do dishes, watching birds and butterflies, and the occasional stray cat, raccoon, or opossum. Now, though, as Kerry focused on the shadowy interior, a shape crossed in front of the kitchen window, and she felt her stomach lurch.

Its form was distinctly human. It wore what seemed to be a long, dark coat, and some kind of shapeless slouch hat. But its features—unless the bad light and her own nervous system conspired to play really unpleasant tricks on her—were barely human, kind of doughy and indistinct. Her first thought was that maybe she was looking at a man who had been scarred in a horrible fire. As she watched him, though, trying to wrap her mind around what she was seeing, another came into view briefly, and he had a similar aspect. Two fire victims seemed unlikely.

Then a third appeared at the window right in front of her. Kerry screamed and ran for the car. She'd left her door open a crack, but had barely touched the seat with her butt when Rebecca peeled out like a race car driver. "What? What'd you see?" Rebecca demanded.

"It was . . . they saw me," Kerry rejoined. "They were horrible, and they saw us!"

11

Josh enjoyed hanging out with Brandy. She was lovely, for one thing, which made her easy to be around. He liked her cocoa-colored skin and athletic body and her ready smile. She was tight with Scott, of course, but that was okay—kind of relieved him of any pressure to pretend he might be interested in her as a boyfriend, since, being a girl, she definitely was not his type. But that didn't mean he didn't like to look upon beauty of whatever gender.

The day was a scorching one—each day seemed more so than the last, until Josh had to admit that a heat wave was upon them and even he, accustomed to Vegas summers, was uncomfortably warm—and she wore a knit halter top, a denim mini, and strappy sandals. Josh thought the halter was a bit much—or a bit not enough, maybe—but either way, a fashion faux pas as far as he was concerned. He'd have chosen a nice tank top, maybe, with spaghetti straps and a little more substance. The whole knit thing just smacked of eighties to him. In his baggy black jeans, Maltese Falcon movie-poster T-shirt, and spiked collar, he knew he was nobody's idea of a fashion god, but he knew what he liked.

They went into the village section of La Jolla, walking the streets of the shopping district, which centered around Prospect Street and Girard Avenue. The village retained its small resort-town air, with buildings and natural scenery reminiscent of some Mediterranean port of call. The name La Jolla, according to some, meant "the jewel," though others disputed that Chamber of Commerce–sounding translation and claimed that it was really a version of *la joya*, or "the hole," so-called because of an enormous cave that opened to the sea. Small specialty stores lined the streets, intermixed with a few nationwide chains like The Gap and Ralph Lauren. Because restaurants and bars abounded, stores stayed open late, so even though they'd taken time to watch the sun sink into the Pacific from across the grassy expanse of Ellen Browning Scripps Park, most of the shops were still occupied when they went back to browsing.

Season had never seen Brandy or Josh, so they didn't feel too exposed walking in the same general neighborhood where she had last been observed. Kerry had said Season had eaten in the restaurant at Seaside a few times, so chances were good that she was staying in or near La Jolla.

"You think we'll recognize her if we see her?" he asked as they meandered out of what seemed like the fiftieth shoe store they'd visited. "That coffee-cup picture seems to be staying with me pretty well."

"I think he magically implanted it or something," Brandy agreed. "I don't like the idea of him messing with our heads like that."

"There isn't much about him you do like," Josh pointed out. They had agreed not to use names when they talked, because it was possible—remote, but possible—that she or some associate of hers would overhear them. Not that they thought Season had any idea who they were, but caution was the order of the day. "Smoke break," he called.

Brandy scowled at him. "Didn't you just have a smoke break?"

"That was hours ago," he argued, snaking a cigarette from the pack he kept in his hip pocket. "Or at least five shoe stores ago."

"It's like every person in La Jolla needs a new pair of shoes every day." Brandy looked at her own sandals and grimaced. "No wonder they all look so hopeful when we walk in. I really *could* use some."

Josh lit his cigarette and sucked in a lungful of smoke. He knew that Brandy was far too thrifty to buy shoes at one of these trendy shops, though. Her family had some money, according to Scott, but they had climbed to an upper-middle-class lifestyle during Brandy's lifetime, and she still knew what it was like to go without. For his part, Josh would have been happy to try life with money, having never experienced that particular sensation. Since he wouldn't wear leather, his own shoes were canvas and rubber, but the rubber was wearing awfully thin on the bottom. Soon a new semester would start up at UNLV and with it, the cost of textbooks, board, and so on. Even with financial aid, going to college was an expensive proposition.

Of course, if he'd quit smoking, he could save a few hundred bucks a month. But some sacrifices were too terrible to consider.

"I'm serious," he said, trying to draw the conversation back to where he had interrupted it. "You hate him, right? You don't even buy his whole line. So why are you putting yourself through this?"

Brandy squinted at him. "You want to end up like Mace?"

"You really think that's what happened to him?"

"I don't know what else to think. If we'd heard about his death on the news, or if cops had knocked on the door and told us, maybe I'd think it was some freak accident or something. But since Da—since he came and told us about it, I figure it had to be her."

Josh blew a series of smoke rings into the still air. "Or him."

"You think he . . . ?"

"As an entrée back into our good graces? I'm just saying it's possible."

Brandy shook her head. "Anything's possible, Josh. But is it likely? Or have you just watched too many conspiracy movies?"

"He's just one guy, so it's not exactly a conspiracy," Josh observed. "And yeah, maybe I've read a lot of noir crime stories with some pretty convoluted plots. But hey, if those writers could think those stories up, then regular people can come up with some twisted ideas too. And to hear him talk, it sounds like he's loaded with twisted ideas."

"What, now you're saying you don't believe any of this?" Brandy asked.

Josh dropped his cigarette butt to the sidewalk and ground it under his shoe. "I didn't say that," he countered. As much as he liked being with Brandy, sometimes talking to her was exhausting. She had a tendency to question and analyze and interpret even the most casual comments. "At first I thought somebody scared his momma with a Twilight novel when he was in utero, but there's obviously more to him than there is to us. We've all seen that. I'm only saying it doesn't hurt to keep an open mind, you know? Cooperate with him, but keep an eye on him at the same time. Just in case."

Now Brandy nodded her agreement. "You know I've never liked him or trusted him. I'm trying to because if he's right, then our lives might depend on him. Probably they do. But if he's pulling some kind of fast one, I want to be ready to put some major distance between me and him in a heartbeat. And I don't want anybody getting in my way. You know what they say about what you have to do when you're hiking with a friend and a bear charges you?"

Josh spread his arms, indicating his slight frame and his utter lack of a tan. "Not exactly Mr. Outdoors here."

"You don't have to be able to outrun the bear," Brandy elaborated. "As long as you can outrun your friend."

Josh laughed, surprised to hear a sentiment like that coming from Brandy. He guessed he shouldn't have been. *Girl has a pragmatic streak as wide as the Grand Canyon,* he thought. It seemed to put her at odds, sometimes, with her hopelessly idealistic boyfriend Scott, to whom every newspaper or news broadcast held fresh outrage.

"What's the matter with this state?" Scott had exploded at breakfast that morning. "California drinks half the bottled water consumed in the country. But less than thirty percent of the bottles are recycled! Billions of bottles a year go into landfill."

Brandy had calmed him down, as somehow she seemed supremely able to do, but Josh had felt a little sorry for Daniel, having to go out hunting with Scott today. He was sure to return to the water-bottle crisis several times during the search.

"So you're of the 'keep your friends close and your enemies closer' school?" Josh asked.

"Pretty much," Brandy replied. "I'm not saying he's our enemy. So far he hasn't done anything to hurt us, unless he really is responsible for Mace somehow. And this Sea—the other one," she caught herself, "sounds like a real piece of work.

So I'm willing to give him the benefit of the doubt, at least until he proves otherwise."

Josh shrugged. "Works for me," he said. "Let's check out the next shoe store."

The next store, in fact, was a children's clothing store—children's clothing for millionaires, Brandy pointed out when she saw the price tags—and they only stayed a moment, long enough to ascertain that Season was not picking up a new bib or a thousand-dollar velvet toddler's dress. After that came an art gallery specializing, it seemed, in pieces that made no sense at all to Josh's untrained eye, and then an Oriental rug shop. *Then* a shoe store.

But it wasn't until they had reached a woman's boutique with a cutesy name that Josh forgot as soon as they had passed beneath the sign, that they saw her. Josh was eyeing the salesman, who wore bleached-out jeans and a tight, striped shirt, its sleeves rolled back over muscular forearms, when he felt Brandy's fingers dig into the flesh of his upper arm.

He looked at her, and she ticked her eyes toward the other side of the store. An attractive blond woman held up a purple silk shirt in front of herself and examined the look in a mirror.

"Is that her?" Josh whispered. He couldn't be sure he had actually made any sound at all. His heart was suddenly pounding as if a marching-band drummer straddled his back.

But when Brandy said, "It's her," he could hear that. Brandy still hadn't let go of his arm, and it hurt when she forcibly turned him around and marched him from the shop.

"What are you doing?" he asked as soon as they hit the sidewalk. "She's inside."

"Right. You see a back door? I didn't. She's not sneaking out. But we need to get *him* down here—nothing we can do by ourselves."

"Gotcha," Josh agreed. He fumbled his cell phone from his pocket.

"Not here," Brandy hissed. She grabbed him again and tugged him down a couple of storefronts. "We don't want her to see us and know something's up. You heard what he said— she's too strong unless he has surprise on his side. If he can take her when she's walking out of a store, unsuspecting, he might have a chance. If she sees some freaked-out Goth boy screaming into his cell phone, she'll be on her guard."

"He'll have to be close by," Josh pointed out. He gestured with the phone, which was still undialed, to where Season was walking out of the store, empty-handed, a small purse dangling on a long strap from her shoulder. *Leather, too,* he thought. *I hate her.*

"We'll just follow her," Brandy said. "Keep tabs on her."

But even that simple plan wouldn't work quite so easily since, apparently done with her shopping, Season approached a BMW Z4 convertible parked at one of the angled spaces by the curb, underneath a streetlight. "Oh, no," Josh moaned. "She's driving."

Street parking being a precious commodity in La Jolla, especially in summer, their own wheels were in a parking garage beneath an office building, more than a block away. "I'll go for the car," Brandy said urgently. "You call him, and keep her in sight."

She took off running without waiting for an answer. As he watched her disappearing form, Josh had no doubt she was, in fact, faster than the bear. Or at least faster than him.

He punched up Daniel's number and hit send. A moment later, the now-familiar voice came on the line. "Yes."

"Sh-she's here," Josh stammered. "In La Jolla. The village. On Girard. She just came out of a store and got into a car, a silver BMW."

"I'm on my way," Daniel said. "Keep watching her. Let me know where she goes."

"One problem. I'm on foot. Brandy's gone to get the car."

The silver BMW waited for a couple of cars to pass and then began to back carefully from its parking space. Josh started walking quickly toward it, torn between not wanting to attract attention and not wanting to let Season escape his sight.

"Do you know how to hotwire a car?" Daniel asked him. The witch sounded breathless, and Josh figured he was already running to his own wheels.

"Only in theory," Josh said. "I've seen it done in movies. Not in real life."

"Never mind, then. Just keep an eye on her, any way you can."

"I'm trying." Josh broke into a run then, because Season had cleared the parking space and begun driving up Girard, away from Prospect Street and the ocean. There was traffic, though, and she wasn't going very fast. When he reached an intersection, he hurtled into it without looking, and a car trying to cross the wide expanse of Girard squealed its tires, stopping for him. "She's driving," he panted into the phone. "I don't know how long I can keep up."

"Don't lose her!" Daniel ordered. Josh could hear the roar of his engine over the phone. "Can you get the license number?"

Then he heard Scott's voice. "Is Brandy there? Is she all right?"

"Tell him she's fine," Josh replied, huffing. "And I can see B523 . . . can't make out the rest. . . ." Ahead of him the BMW started to accelerate up a long, traffic-free stretch of road. He broke into a sprint, awkwardly trying to hold the phone to his ear as he ran. Every few paces he craned his neck to see if— *please, please!*—Brandy was drawing up behind him.

"Do you still see her?" Daniel demanded urgently.

Josh ran with everything he had, but the BMW reached the intersection. Her brake lights flashed once, and she made a right turn, immediately vanishing behind the building on the corner. "Nooo!" Josh yelled.

"What?" Daniel wanted to know.

Josh kept up his pace, swallowing sidewalk with every step. But the corner was still too far away—more than a city block, on the other side of a supermarket parking lot. He'd never make it. She would be long out of sight before he could reach it.

"She turned a corner," he breathed into the phone. Finally he stopped running. "I lost her."

"Are you sure?" Daniel asked.

Josh did a quick scan. He could cut through the supermarket's lot. If she'd been stuck at the next light, where Fay Street crossed Pearl Street, he might still get a glimpse of her at that intersection. "There's one more thing I can try," he said, though he wasn't sure how he was going to get his legs to take another step.

"Do it!"

Josh was about to obey when a horn honked on the street beside him. Brandy was finally there in Scott's RAV4. She popped open the passenger door and he forced himself to hurry the four steps to the car. "Up to the corner," he managed, folding in on himself from the ache in his chest and lungs, trying to ignore the sweat that ran in rivers down his sides and soaked his back. "Turn right."

Brandy floored it, racing up the street, braking just enough not to lose control as the car screamed around the corner. The car's rear end fishtailed a little, but the tires bit and held on to the road. Josh put his left hand on the dash in front of him and searched Pearl Street.

No BMW in sight. Brandy drove the length of the street, and he watched every parking lot, every side street. In a few moments they were dipping down toward the ocean. "Which way?" she asked.

Josh could only shake his head.

"We're almost there," Daniel's voice said. Josh had forgotten the phone, still clutched in his right fist. "Do you have her?"

"She's gone," Josh admitted. "We can't see her at all."

"Keep cruising," Daniel said. "Maybe you'll pick her up again. Did she know you were onto her?"

Only if she looked in her mirror and saw a maniac running up the sidewalk, Josh thought. He felt defeated, broken. "I don't know."

Brandy took the road down toward the water. It wound between luxury apartments and condominiums, then, on the ocean side, a few sprawling homes and then nothing but cliffs and coast.

"Where are you?" Daniel asked after another few minutes. "We're at Girard and Pearl."

"She went right there," Josh told him. "We went toward the water."

"We'll turn up La Jolla Boulevard, then," Daniel reported. "Maybe she's heading toward Pacific Beach."

"I'm sorry, Daniel. I really did try."

There was a long moment of silence from the other end, and Josh wasn't sure if Daniel had even heard him. But then he answered. "It's okay, Josh. You guys found her. We can do it again."

12

Scott Banner was pretty sure he was going to die.

Daniel had magical powers or whatever, so he could probably survive the collision of the rented (or stolen, he wasn't entirely sure which) Ford Taurus with any of the half-dozen vehicles it had almost smashed into, not to mention lane dividers and walls, as Daniel piloted it at breakneck speeds from Del Mar to La Jolla. But any of those near misses could have spelled instant extinction for Scott, who held onto his seat belt's shoulder strap for dear life on each occasion.

Fortunately Daniel seemed to have an inordinately sure hand with the wheel, and his touch with the brake—though used sparingly—was also confident and precise. Of course, he drove one-handed, with his cell phone glued to his ear by the other, which made the whole experience that much more nerve-racking. They raced down the coast road (ocean to their right, lagoons to their left), then up the hill past Torrey Pines State Reserve, along the cliffs between the Scripps Institute and the University of California at San Diego, of which the campus looked lovely, if a bit blurry, finally speeding down the hill into La Jolla proper. Fortunately they had already been headed in that general direction, having stopped at one of the beaches to see if Season was there. If they'd been far from the car, or going the other way, Scott wouldn't have wanted to see what shortcuts Daniel might have made to save time.

A few minutes after reaching La Jolla, they rendezvoused with Brandy and Josh in the parking lot of a chain drugstore. Josh still looked out of breath, his pale, sunken cheeks rosy with the effort he'd put into the chase. Scott climbed gratefully from the car and enveloped Brandy in a hug, pulling her close and sniffing the vaguely vanilla-like scent of whatever she used on her thick, luxuriant hair.

"Are you okay?" he asked. "Did she see you?"

Brandy disengaged, shaking her head. When she answered him, her usual antagonism toward Daniel had vanished. "She might have seen Josh. I'm sure she didn't see me—if we'd been close enough for that, we'd still be on her tail. Woman can move."

"How did you find her?"

"We just walked into a dress store and there she was, looking just like she did in that coffee cup," Brandy announced.

"Did you . . . like, cement that image in our heads some-how?" Josh inquired of Daniel. "Because when we saw her, both of us were, like, pow, that's her."

"When I conjured it there was a retention spell involved," Daniel admitted. He didn't sound reluctant or embarrassed about it, Scott noted. Just as if it had been something so mundane he'd forgotten to mention it. *A retention spell. When I conjured it. Like I'd say, "I flipped on the light switch."*

Of course, Scott realized, *to me it is basically magic how the electricity gets from the river, or the coal plant, or whatever, to the light socket. So I guess to him it's just another kind of science. Maybe something anyone can do with the right kind of calculator and test tubes. To the liberal-arts undergrad, all science is magic.*

Daniel turned to Josh. "Can you show me where she was standing?"

Josh pointed in the general direction. "Over there," he replied. "On Girard."

"No," Daniel corrected. "I mean, precisely. Can you show me a spot where you know, with absolute certainty, her feet touched the ground?"

"I can," Brandy volunteered. "In the store. Her bag was bumping into a top I thought looked really cute. Unless they've rearranged the display in the last thirty minutes, I can show it to you."

"Let's go," Daniel said.

Parking being the losing proposition that it was, they left the cars in the drugstore lot—risking tickets or towing, Scott noted, because the lot had FOR CUSTOMERS ONLY signs posted in huge red letters—and walked back to the boutique. On the way Daniel called Kerry's phone and told her to meet them back at the drugstore's parking lot.

In the store the salesman looked at them expectantly when they walked in, but Josh waved and said, "We're only looking," and the guy went behind the counter and sat on a stool with a glum sigh.

Brandy pointed out to Daniel exactly where the witch had been standing when they'd seen her. "Right here," she said. Turning to Scott, she fingered a shimmery green blouse and added, "And if you want to pick up an early birthday present, check this out."

But Scott couldn't even get close enough to see the price tag. Daniel squatted down on the ground and touched his fingers to the floor. Scott was reminded of trackers in Western movies, feeling for the oncoming thunder of a buffalo herd. Then Daniel stood and sniffed the air. After a few moments of that, he froze, standing utterly still, eyes closed, lips parted slightly. It was, Scott believed, exceedingly strange behavior. But he presumed that it meant something. Either that or Daniel was a gifted con man, pulling a fast one on them by acting out the oddest routine he could come up with.

While Daniel performed his awkward gyrations, Brandy took Scott's hand and squeezed. "I guess we did okay," she said softly. "I mean, I wish we hadn't lost her. But at least we spotted her once, right?"

"You sound like a convert," he responded. Secretly he was

glad. He'd believed in Daniel almost from the beginning—
or, more precisely, he'd believed in Kerry's judgment, and if
she wanted Daniel around, that was good enough for him.
Brandy had doubted him with such rabid certainty that it had
put Scott in an uncomfortable position. If she was coming
around, that would make his life easier.

"I wouldn't go that far," she hedged. "But maybe I'm mel-
lowing about it. A little. Now that I know Season Howe is
real, I guess."

"Nothing wrong with that," Scott said, hoping he sounded
neutral but encouraging.

Without a word to the rest of them, Daniel stalked outside, nose in the air as if he were following a scent. The sales
clerk watched them go, confusion written all over his face. Josh
tossed him a shrug and a smile, and then trailed after Daniel.

On the sidewalk, Brandy squeezed Scott's hand again
and nodded toward Daniel, who came to a stop underneath
a streetlight. "He's following her path exactly," she reported.
"Walking exactly where she did."

"Weird," Scott uttered. He'd been with Daniel the whole
time, so he knew the man couldn't possibly have seen Season's
moves. Which meant that somehow, even after this long, he
was able to sense where she'd been.

"Uh-huh," Brandy agreed. "Like I said, the realer this gets,
the more I'm into it."

"You never said that," Scott reminded her. "At least, not to me."

"Maybe not. But I meant it."

* * *

Kerry and Rebecca hadn't been far from La Jolla, still working south through Pacific Beach, when Kerry's phone trilled like an agitated bird. She answered it and heard Daniel's voice, sounding strained and urgent. "Are you all right?"

"Fine. What's up?"

He didn't answer the question, but instead gave her instructions to meet the rest of the group at a drugstore's parking lot. Kerry relayed the message to Rebecca, who turned the car around—avoiding the street they'd raced away from, not so long before—and drove back up to La Jolla. When they got there, they found the RAV4 and the Taurus parked side by side, but saw no sign of the gang. Kerry and Rebecca stood by Rebecca's car, waiting, making uncomfortable small talk. Both of them were still freaked by what Kerry had seen in their old house—Kerry by the sight itself, and Rebecca by Kerry's reaction to it. Kerry thought about the conversation they'd had when she'd jumped back into the car.

"You look like you're being chased by ghosts," Rebecca had said to her.

"I don't know what they were," Kerry had admitted, trying to bring her voice under control. "'Ghosts' is probably as good a word as any."

"You're kidding," Rebecca had said. She had stared at Kerry for so long, Kerry worried they'd run off the road.

"Watch where you're going," Kerry had ordered. "I'd like to live long enough to ask Daniel what those guys were."

"You think they were, like, Season's familiars or something?"

"I thought a familiar was like a black cat. Anyway, he hasn't said anything about her having any. But maybe."

Rebecca had offered a couple more suggestions, but Kerry found she wasn't interested in hearing the theories of someone who—while truly wanting to help—could not possibly have any idea what they were up against. Her monosyllabic answers discouraged Rebecca, who eventually stopped trying to talk to Kerry. Then the phone had gone off. And here they were; Kerry still lost in questions she couldn't answer, Rebecca keeping her distance.

As they waited in the parking lot, though, Kerry understood what had happened, and how she'd shut out Rebecca, who was just about the most well-intentioned person she'd ever known. "Hey," she said apologetically, "I didn't mean to be a shrew or anything. I was just, you know, kind of preoccupied."

Rebecca smiled, her whole face seeming to brighten, though in the harsh light it was a little hard to tell. "That's okay," she said. "Perfectly understandable, considering . . . you know. Whatever you saw."

"That's the big question, isn't it?"

Rebecca reached for Kerry as if to give her a hug, but Kerry didn't feel quite that sisterly yet. Rebecca caught the vibe, though, and just rubbed Kerry's shoulder instead. "One thing I do want to say, though, is how impressed I was."

"Impressed?" *Color me confused,* Kerry thought. *Maybe I*

set some sort of Olympic sprinting record when I ran away from the house.

"The way you walked right up to the window, even though you'd seen someone inside," Rebecca explained. "I couldn't have done that. I just about left a puddle in my car seat, waiting for you. I don't think I've ever seen something so brave."

Kerry was complimented to hear her say that, but puzzled by the sentiment. "All I did was check it out," she said. "Nothing special about that."

"You don't think so," Rebecca countered, "because you're a brave person. So it doesn't seem like much."

Kerry felt herself blushing now, heat rising from her chest, engulfing her neck and face. In spite of her pale complexion, she didn't blush often, but once she did, her body committed to it. She turned away from Rebecca, just in time to see Daniel and the others walking from the corner of Girard Avenue and Pearl Street. Daniel led the way, his gait purposeful. Kerry was surprised to feel a small thrill at the sight of him, more or less encompassing the same region as the blush she'd experienced moments before.

When he reached the parking lot, he looked around, and she thought—or hoped—that meant he was seeking her out. His face gave a spark of recognition when he saw her, she believed—a lift of the jaw, a twitch of a smile, a brightening of the eyes. It might have been a trick of the light.

But maybe not. "You're okay?" he asked when he reached her, holding out his hand for hers.

"Why wouldn't I be?" She liked the pressure of his hand grasping hers, engulfing it with warmth and concern.

But after a moment Daniel released her hand and glanced up and down the street. The others caught up to them as he was doing so. "She was here," he said. "You lost her here, on Pearl, right?" This was directed to Josh, who nodded morosely.

"Right."

"She was here?" Kerry asked. "Season?"

"That's right," Brandy said. "Josh and I saw her, but we lost her."

Daniel's gaze darted about again, and Kerry realized he was as alert as a cat in an aviary, ready for Season to return to try something, or just to pass this way again. "I can almost sense her," he explained. "It's like an aftertaste, kind of metallic somehow. It happens when I get close to her."

"Even when you're running from her?" Josh asked. "Like the other night, with Kerry?"

Daniel nodded. "It's how I knew she was in the restaurant."

The admission startled Kerry, though it didn't seem like anyone else realized its import. If he hadn't known Season would be at the restaurant, then he'd have had no reason to go there.

Unless he'd gone to see Kerry.

She couldn't say, at that moment, exactly how she felt about that possibility.

But she thought she liked it.

13

Somehow the seating arrangements for the cars going back to Imperial Beach were shuffled, and Kerry wound up riding with Daniel. Not that she was complaining. In fact, all other considerations aside, she still wanted to ask him about what she had seen in the house. Her initial fear was that he might want to drive by and check it out for himself, but he put that to rest immediately.

"They're simulacra," he said quite matter-of-factly, when she described them.

"They're what?"

"Simulacra. Not really human, but human in structure. They can pass for human, if no one looks too closely."

"Are they . . . do they work for her?" Kerry asked nervously. "For Season?"

Daniel laughed softly as he tooled down the freeway in the dark. "No. No, they work for us."

Shocked, Kerry wasn't sure what to say to that. *Seems like something you should have mentioned,* she thought. But the words wouldn't come out of her mouth.

"Well, for my mother, to be more exact," he went on. "It's a little stunt of hers."

"Your mother?" Kerry realized she sounded stupid parroting what she had just heard, and she had a vague memory of Brandy saying the same words, with very nearly the same surprised tone, many nights before. But the words slipped out of her mouth before she could rein them in.

"Mother Blessing," he confirmed. "That's what everyone calls her. Myself included."

"Seems a little formal," Kerry suggested. "For someone you've known for three hundred years."

"Maybe," Daniel agreed. "But then, she's not much like other mothers. Or at least that's the impression I get, having only had the one."

Kerry felt herself reddening for the second time tonight. "I'm sorry," she said. "I guess I . . . when you told the story about Slocumb, you said your mother had survived. I didn't realize you meant she was still alive."

"Still alive," he confirmed, glancing out the rear window and changing lanes to the right. "Not as well as she used to be,

I'm afraid. Witches do age, just more slowly than most."

"And she's still hunting for Season?" Kerry pressed.

"She does what she can."

Daniel moved farther right, exiting the freeway. A couple of minutes to the apartment, and their brief time alone would be over. She found the prospect sad. But then she mentally chastised herself, knowing she shouldn't even be thinking like that. There was nothing between her and Daniel, and there couldn't ever be. He was not just an older man than her, he was older than her great-grandparents would have been if they were still alive. Which, of course, they weren't, because, hey, *old*. She didn't see that when she looked at him. He looked like a man in his mid-twenties, perhaps, now that he was fully healed.

And in addition to being easy to look at, he was charming and fascinating. From time to time she thought him humorless, but then his dry wit would show through, and she'd realize that it was simply that he was preoccupied and that his quest was more important to him than the ability to crack jokes. She could honestly say that she had never known anyone quite like him.

"These simulacra you saw," Daniel said, after they'd reached the surface street. "Mother Blessing didn't tell me she was sending them, but from your description I'm positive that's what they were. They were doubtlessly searching the house for signs of Season."

"But that was our house, not hers."

"Right," Daniel agreed. "And by now she has surely found it and gone inside looking for similar signs of me. In doing so, she might have left behind an energy signature the simulacra could pick up on."

"But you're just speculating, right?"

"Informed speculation, let's say. If Season had developed the ability to manifest and control simulacra, I think I'd know about it."

"Can she just come up with new powers like that?"

Daniel laughed again. "You can, in fact, teach an old dog new tricks," he said. "Or an old witch, at any rate. But creating simulacra really is one of Mother Blessing's trademarks. So chances are good they were hers. Even so, they can be dangerous, so its good you kept your distance."

"I thought they were on our side," Kerry said.

"They are. But they're not truly human, and their powers of reasoning are essentially nonexistent. They take orders, that's all. If you should see any again, I'd recommend you keep well away from them."

"I'll do my best," Kerry promised. Their apartment building loomed before them in the night. "I'd like to know more about her. Your mother, I mean," Kerry heard herself saying, though the thought had never before crossed her mind.

"I told you I'd let you read some of my notebooks," Daniel reminded her. "Why not start tonight?"

* * *

I knew the weather was changing as soon as I walked outside and felt the north wind on my face, cold and crisp as a winter's day. The trapper's cabin was in a clearing with a creek running behind it, and ponderosa pines as far as I could see in front. Through the trees I could just see a snowcapped mountain peak. I shouldered my rifle and began the day's hunt.

She had been here, this much I knew. Not so long ago. The cabin I had slept in the night before had been inhabited by her within the past week. I could still smell her on the walls, the floors, the scant furnishings. Not long ago she had slept in that place, though not for the last few nights. The night before I had rested with eyes half open and no fire, just in case she returned. But she did not.

Kerry put the dense leather book down on her bed. Daniel had handed her two of them, both wrapped with leather thongs to hold them closed, both heavier than modern books by almost double. The journals were about six by nine inches, she figured, and held a hundred or so leaves of thick paper on which Daniel had written in an ink that had turned the color of rust. His handwriting was meticulous, and even on the yellowed, flaking pages she found it easy to read. "I don't know what years these cover," he said. "I never have bothered to date the outsides. But I'm sure you'll find one just as impenetrable as the next." She took the volumes, surprised by their unexpected weight, and her fingers had brushed his as she did. He smiled and left her alone in the room. Rebecca was out with Brandy and Scott, talking over the day's events, but Kerry had retired early, anxious to start on Daniel's journals.

During the few minutes that I slept soundly during the night, horrifying nightmares had been my reward. This only confirmed my belief that Season Howe had found refuge under this same roof—even the air inside had been twisted and distorted by contact with her, by the evil miasma she leaves behind everywhere she passes. My dreams had been full of death: carcasses missing their heads, blood flowing freely from their necks; disemboweled men with innards yanked out as if by butcher's hooks, streaming from their bellies; worms and vermin crawling about in the midst of all this carnage. These were not, need I say, normal dreams for me, but were surely caused by her proximity.

I knew, therefore, that she was not far away. But the wind from the north meant two things to me. One, by the time the sun set, the day would be far colder than it was now, and two, a stiff wind would scour her tracks, making it even harder to find her. I had come close, but missed her by days. Now I had to follow a trail that was already growing cold, and I had to do so before weather made the task impossible.

At first I had an easy enough go of it. The same

tracks that had led me to the cabin were still visible to me, though most of them would not be to a normal, human tracker. Season had been traveling fast, heedless of such things as broken twigs on the forest floor, or bits of fabric, or long blond hair caught on limbs. And less visible to others were what I have taken to calling her miasmic tracks, the traces of evil that glow in her wake with a foul green tinge. The color of sickness.

I was right where the weather was concerned. By midmorning the air had turned frigid, and the wind bit at my cheeks and hands like a whip. Shortly after noon, a time I marked only by removing a lump of hardtack from my sack and chewing it as I walked, the first snow flurried around me.

My other fear was borne out as well. The ever more powerful winds scattered leaves where her feet might have made impressions, picked up and hurled away those stray hairs and threads, and generally slowed my progress. I began to hope some other trapper's cabin would present itself by dark, or the night would be unpleasant indeed.

To my surprise, though, when I crested a low hill I saw before me a valley containing a small settlement. A mining community; even from the hillside I could see headframes on the opposite slope. A score of buildings, mostly of wood, huddled around one *sad-looking, rutted wagon road. The sun had become a cold, flat disk that looked impossibly distant, and even if Season's tracks had not led me this way I would have sought refuge in the town for the night. As it was, dark had fallen by the time I reached it.*

But when I approached the buildings on the road, I noticed something I had not from above while the sun yet shone. Though it was past dusk, there were no lights in any of them, no flicker of candle or lantern or fireplace glowing through windows. The same wind I had battled all day whistled between the cold, stark buildings. Somewhere a shutter banged; that and the wind were the only sounds besides that of my own feet, trudging on hard-packed earth.

Seeing no one, hearing no other noise, I felt a chill to my core. I should call out, I knew, to see if anyone was about. But what if she was here? Would making my own presence known put me at her mercy? I feared that it might, and decided to investigate at a more cautious pace. I started with the nearest house, and rapped upon the door.

Hearing nothing from within, I opened it. Instantly the reek of death assailed me. Bracing myself I went farther into the house's cold bowels, only to find, in the kitchen, the remains of three people. I could not be certain, but it looked like a man, a woman, and their daughter, a girl of perhaps twelve or thirteen. Fat, lazy flies sated themselves on pools of blood. Gagging, I hurried away from the grisly scene.

But similar sights greeted me in the next house and the next. The town had been massacred—one house, one family, at a time. I was put in mind of Slocumb, although in that instance, of course, the town's death had come all at once in a horrible swirl of destruction, according to the stories Mother Blessing tells. I felt sure that the cause was the same; that the tragedy that had struck this town, whatever it was called, wore the name of Season Howe.

Finally I went into a house and heard, or thought I heard, the scuttling sounds of inhabitants from somewhere in the back. Rats, I told myself, or some other vermin, no doubt feasting on the dead. I readied my rifle and kicked open the door behind which I had heard the noises.

It was no rat, though, or other creature of field and fen. It was a man, wild-eyed and unshaven, staring at me from behind a flintlock pistol of his own, and from behind a mask of madness. His clothes were tattered and covered in blood, but it took me a moment to see the source of the blood. In the corner behind him were the ravaged remains of three other people. My first instinct was that I had caught him in the act of despoiling the remains, possibly even cannibalizing them. But upon regarding him further, his stance appeared defensive, as if he were simply trying to protect them. The antique firearm trained on me enhanced this impression.

"Rest easy, friend," I said. "I am here to help if I can."

When he replied, the madness that flitted across his face came through in his voice as well, high-pitched and anxious. "Nothing to be done. Nothing anyone can do. Go 'way."

"How did this happen?" I asked. "Who did all this?"

He twitched the gun at me. "Go 'way, while you can. Sickness here, sickness spreads."

"I might be able to do something," I said. I knew not what I could truly do to help, but my abilities were beyond those of others, so I prayed that perhaps there was still hope for someone in this forsaken place.

"Too late, way too late," the man said. He giggled when he said it, a sound so girlish it seemed unnatural coming from such a grizzled old man.

"Was there a witch here?" I demanded. "A woman with blond hair and smooth features hiding the evil beneath?"

"She was here, she was here," the man answered. "Too late, though. Everyone's too late. Months too late. Years. Too, too, too."

"She did this?" I was sure I knew the answer. This looked like Season's handiwork to me. "She killed everyone?"

"Too late, too late," the man said again. His face twitched, and I worried that if his finger tightened on the trigger of that weapon, I would be in sorry shape as well.

Sensing that I would get no useful answers from this tragic soul, I shouldered my own weapon again. "I am sorry to have disturbed you, sir," I told him. "I shall find myself someplace in town to sleep tonight, and then tomorrow I will be on my way. If there is anything I can do to help you, just ask."

The man let out a plaintive mewl then, like a kitten begging for milk. He spoke not, though, made no intelligible request of me, which I would gladly have done my best to fulfill. So I took my leave, shaking my head sadly at the wretched state to which he had fallen, which had, indeed, beset this entire town. If he was the sole survivor, as seemed to be the case, then the town was tragic indeed.

I had barely reached the front door of his house when I heard his ancient weapon discharge. I turned and rushed back into the room in which I had left him. He was still there, but there was no life in him. A new hole had appeared in his forehead, and a spray of blood and bone decorated the horrific scene behind *him. The gun was still clutched in his right hand, a thin plume of smoke issuing from its barrel.*

I write this in a room of the town's boarding-house, denoted by a sign beside the door. Downstairs are more dead, but this room I found empty and clean. If there is sickness here, it will affect me not at all. Tomorrow I will perform a cleansing spell to make doubly sure of that and to ease the way for whatever visitor comes here next. But I am not certain that it will do any good. Despite what the man told me— and his madness, I feel sure, makes all of his words suspect—this looks to me like yet another town that has fallen prey to Season's hatred.

I mourn for this nameless town and its people. And I renew my vow to find her, to destroy her, in the name of the people of Slocumb, and now of this place and of any others who have crossed her path.

My candle gutters, my eyes grow heavy. Even in the face of terrible tragedy, sleep makes its demands.

I remain,

Daniel Blessing, Fifteenth of September, 1854.

Kerry closed the book. She hadn't expected to have read this long—Rebecca had come in, wished her good night, and gone to sleep, while Kerry sat turning pages by the light of a bedside lamp. But then, she hadn't expected the story to take on such a horrific aspect. She had thought it would be a record of days, like most she had spent with Daniel—looking for Season, not finding her, getting up and doing it again.

Having read it, though, she felt like she had a more visceral understanding of Daniel's quest, of the urgency of it. *If "urgency" can be applied to an effort that's been ongoing for hundreds of years,* Kerry thought. But who knew what terrors Season had cooked up in that time, if this sort of thing was a habit with her?

Kerry remembered the nightmares she'd been having, in the weeks before Daniel had appeared in their yard—nightmares that had ended at that time, and about which she'd forgotten until reading about the ones that Daniel had in Season's proximity. Could there be some connection to hers? She didn't know how that could be, though. Anyway, they hadn't recurred, even though there was more in her life that might lead to bad dreams now. She felt tired, but she wasn't sure how she'd sleep that night. Determined to try, though, she switched off her light, put her head down on the pillow, and closed her eyes.

14

I'm going to try to pick up Season's trail where we lost it last night," Daniel announced the next morning. Scott and Brandy hadn't shown themselves yet, but the rest of them were up, eating breakfast, and sipping tea or the coffee that Daniel had brewed.

Having read the part of his journal that she had, Kerry understood that the effort wouldn't necessarily be as hopeless as it sounded. "I'll go with."

Daniel shook his head. "It's not safe."

"Safe?" Kerry echoed, incredulous. "With Season out there somewhere, what does safe even mean? Is there such a concept?"

"I wouldn't argue with the Bulldog if I were you," Rebecca warned Daniel. "She's a tough one."

"I know that," Daniel agreed with a hint of a smile. "Believe me, one doesn't have to know Kerry long to figure that out."

"So?" Kerry pressed, oddly pleased to hear Daniel acknowledge a personality trait she wasn't always so fond of. "There's some forward momentum here, and I want to be along in case anything happens."

"When I find her, I don't want you close by," Daniel protested. "Any of you. The next time we meet it's going to be bad, and I don't want to have to worry about you getting hurt."

"Is that why you didn't take her at the restaurant that night?" Josh wondered. "Because you didn't want Kerry or Mace to get hurt?"

"That, and I wasn't fully recovered from our previous encounter," Daniel admitted. "I am now. And there's Mace to hold her accountable for, on top of everything else she's done."

"I didn't know Mace meant that much to you," Brandy put in sleepily. She shuffled in from her room, rubbing her eyes, a bathrobe tied with a sash over her silk pj's. "You sure didn't show it when he was alive."

"Brandy—" Kerry began, but Daniel cut her off.

"You're right, Brandy," he said. "Mace was no fan of mine, and I probably didn't do enough to win him over. I misread him or I would never have let him try to drive off alone. But he was one of you, and I consider myself responsible for the lot of you, in some ways."

"We can take care of ourselves," Josh countered, sounding defiant.

"You could, before I came along. Now, not so much."

"We've been over this before," Kerry said, casting a sharp look Brandy's way. "Rehashing it now doesn't do us any good."

Brandy stifled a yawn. "Yeah, I know. Sorry." She didn't sound much like she meant it, but Kerry figured that was as good as it would get.

"So when do we leave?" she asked Daniel.

He put his cup into the sink with a clatter and ran hot water over it for a moment. "No time like the present," he said. "Let's go."

Back to La Jolla again. Again Daniel parked near the inter-section of Girard and Pearl, which was the last place Josh had definitely seen Season. The morning sun was bright, the skies blue and cloudless, and she could smell the slightest trace of sea air on the gentle breeze, reminding her how much she missed her daily communion with the ocean. Daniel got out of the Taurus and walked to the corner, waited a moment for traf-fic to clear, and then went out into the street. Glancing both ways to make sure it was safe, he squatted down and touched the pavement with his right hand. He shook his head, moved to a spot farther toward the edge of the lane, and repeated the same process. This time Kerry saw a smile curl the edges of his mouth. He jogged back to the safety of the sidewalk as the next wave of cars came toward the corner.

"She was here," he confirmed. "She came this way."

"That's what Josh said, right?"

"And I didn't doubt him," Daniel explained. "But Season can be trickier than most people think. I needed to know for myself."

"Okay," Kerry said. "So now what?"

"Now we follow." He began walking down Pearl, eyeing the street as if he could see her trail. Maybe he could—maybe that green-tinted track Daniel had followed in the journal still existed.

"On foot?" she asked, surprised. Season had been driving a BMW, according to Josh and Brandy. Following on foot seemed pointless.

"It's much harder to track from a moving vehicle," Daniel told her. "But once we have an idea of what direction she's heading, I may ask you to drive ahead, just so the car is never too far from us."

Kerry shrugged and watched him move on, his face turned toward the street, ignoring the curious looks of people in passing vehicles. That image summed him up, she believed, the intrepid seeker, carrying on his quest no matter what the obstacles, or the opinions, of others might be. She couldn't decide if it made him a humorous figure or a tragic one . . . or simply heroic. *Probably a combination of all three. But considering what Season's done, weighted toward heroic.* She hurried to catch up with him, mindful that she might be sent back for the car at any moment.

Kerry Profitt's diary, August 25

This is when the world stopped making sense:

Daniel and I had spent the morning tracking Season, and making good progress. At least according to Daniel. As far as I could tell, he was just following one random street after another, but he insisted that her car had driven on all these streets. Through Bird Rock and into Pacific Beach we went, me running for the car from time to time, and him even getting into it once in a while, when it looked like she was going in a straight line for a long stretch.

But the day wore on and even he gets hungry sometimes, so we stopped for a pizza at a place on Turquoise Street. We're waiting for the food, sipping our drinks, tired and hungry. And his hand is resting on the table. It's just a hand, tan and muscular, I guess, if a hand can be muscular, with long, lean fingers. Well-shaped, I suppose you'd call it, if you called it anything at all. Little scars here and there, and I know from experience that it's a working man's hand, not an indoors hand. Callused and rough sometimes.

So out of nowhere—and I mean that literally, because as surprised as he was, I think I was even more so—I took his hand in mine. Both of mine, actually. Picked it up off the table and held it, kind of caressing it. He closed his fingers around my hand, but there was shock in his eyes, and a kind of hesitant half smile on his lips.

"I know I have a long way to go in the journals," I said. "But are there many women in there? Besides Season, I mean. You've lived so long, and you're so wonderful and handsome, there must have been some in your past. You never talk about them, though."

Daniel sighed and nodded. "There have been some," he said. "Not so many. And fewer who really meant anything."

"Why?" I felt like someone peeking through her fingers at the scariest part of a horror movie, not wanting to see but wanting to at the same time. Was I sure I needed to hear this?

"Ask again later," quoth the Magic 8-ball.

But he answered me anyway. "It's hard. I'm always on the move, always on the hunt. If I did fall in love with someone, would that slow me down? Probably. Would it give Season an edge she could use against me? Certainly. And then there's the other problem. . . ."

"What problem?"

"If she was a mortal woman, she would age at a normal rate," he said. "I would not. She would grow old and die, and I would still look like I look. That would be so hard, for both of us."

About this time it occurred to me that we were still holding hands, and that his thumb was moving softly over mine in a kind of circular pattern. What are you doing? I asked myself. How awkward was this whole thing going to be?

At the same time, though, I liked it . . .

. . . a lot.

"So you've been playing the field for three centuries," I said, trying to make something vaguely resembling a joke out of it all. "Sounds rough."

"Believe me, there have been times when I've wished

it were otherwise," he said. "Times when I wished I could just give up the hunt and settle down with someone. I can't bring myself to do that, though. Not until Season is gone."

The waiter brought the pizza then, and we separated our hands. But even afterward I could feel his hand on mine as if we had never let each other go. I changed the subject, aware that I'd probably been too personal, gone too far.

And anyway, what is my deal? Here I will psycho-analyze myself in hopes of figuring out why I practically threw myself at this guy who is (a) older than me and (b) not quite human.

I haven't, to understate the point, had a lot of experience with boys. Or men, which Daniel clearly is. These last few years—the dating years, according to my friends—have mostly been spent taking care of a sick, and then dying, mother. Friday night, Saturday night? Just as dateless as the rest of the week. Sure, I saw guys at school, during the day. But when school was over I had to rush home, leaving little to nonexistent social time. The occasional party, the occasional groping post-adolescent. Not exactly "seventeen and never been kissed," but close enough.

That being the case, is it surprising that I seem to be hurling myself toward the first male who gives me the time of day? Hormones are hormones, after all, and mine are just as demanding as the next female's. There have, of course, been other males who have looked at me for more than twenty seconds. Mace, I think, I could have had in a heart-beat, if I'd wanted him. But, in spite of the physique, sooo not my type. And Scott has made it clear—not out loud, but through glances and signs and the occasional too-long hug—that he might toss Brandy aside for me, but I couldn't do that to her even if I wanted that. Which I so don't.

But Daniel—unattached, mature, attractive . . . I mean, what's not to like?

Did I mention mature? It keeps coming back to that, doesn't it? And yet my inner Freud says, didn't your father die when you were very young? And didn't that make you feel abandoned as a girl, even before your mother became ill? Is it not possible that you are merely trying to fill the hole left in your heart by a father who was gone from your life all too early?

How do I answer the old Austrian? Or even Brandy, who has her own theories about things psychoanalytic but would surely be in agreement here. Yes, it's possible, Doc. Maybe even likely. But there's something to be said for the way my heart quickens when I'm around him, the way he can make me smile just by being there, the way his touch curls my toes. His scent sends those hormones racing, even when it's only a lingering aroma on the pages of his journal. This is definitely something I'd tell my one-time best bud Jessica about, if I thought she'd be at all interested anymore.

But really, what could I tell her? There's this guy, and he's got magical powers, and he's three hundred years old . . . I guess this is something I just need to work out solo.

On the other hand maybe what I need is to stop thinking about this so much and just feel for a while. Feeling would be nice. . . .

Pacific Beach was loaded with apartment complexes, large and small. In some neighborhoods almost every block had at least one, and in other parts, especially closer to the ocean, apartments greatly outnumbered single-family homes. If Season was living in this area, she had picked a high-density locale with lots of places to hide.

"She's here," Daniel said with what sounded like absolute certainty. It was midafternoon, and though they'd taken a break for lunch, he had essentially been on his feet all day, tracking, tracking.

Kerry looked at the literally dozens of dwellings she could see from this spot. "Which here?"

"I don't know," Daniel answered, and the anger was evident in his voice. "Around here the tracks go every direction. I know this is close to home for her, because she has been over just about every inch of these streets—these, and the ones nearby. Tracks are everywhere. Too many of them—I can't possibly narrow it down any further."

"So you've got, what, six square blocks? What now, door to door?"

"More like a dozen," he said. "Door to door, solo, would take weeks. And I'd be exposed the whole time."

The moment they'd shared while waiting for pizza had

seemingly passed as they'd eaten and then returned to the hunt—*I'll have plenty to write in the old diary tonight, though,* Kerry thought—and they were back to business as usual. Except she couldn't quite shake the feeling that something had changed between them, possibly forever.

"Fortunately for you," she said cheerfully, "you aren't solo. Door to door probably isn't absolutely necessary, but if we've got it narrowed down to a dozen blocks, and five people she has never seen—well, four, anyway, and me, who she's only seen briefly—we can cover the neighborhood pretty well. We'll find her, Daniel. We've got her boxed in."

He thought about it for a moment. "The closer we get to her, the more I worry about you," he said. She was pretty sure that, in that instance, the "you" was specific to her and not referring to the whole group. But that might have been wishful thinking.

"It's what we're here for," she reminded him. "I mean, there's nothing else keeping us in San Diego now, right? No jobs, no other friends. We've been stalling our families, especially Brandy, whose parents got a call about Mace and threatened to fly out here. We're in this deep, Daniel. We are here to do this thing. So let us do it."

Daniel considered a few seconds longer, but Kerry didn't see how he could possibly reach any other conclusion. "Okay," he finally said. "Let's round up the others and set a game plan."

15

The next day the stakeout was in place.

Such as it is, Kerry thought. Three cars, six people, and one of the cars, with herself and Daniel in it, had to stay out of the immediate vicinity because they would be too easily recognized. Of course, Season usually kept to herself, Daniel reasoned, so chances were slim that she'd see them. But then, he usually worked alone too, and now he had recruited help. There was nothing to say that Season couldn't do the same, and if she had, Kerry and Daniel would be the ones they'd be watching for.

So Scott and Brandy took one car and parked it on the route that Season would most likely pass by on her way back to La Jolla, since it seemed she still frequented that community. Josh and Rebecca were roamers, cruising the streets of the dozen blocks Daniel had identified as the ones Season used most often. Daniel and Kerry had moved around outside the perimeter, spending most of the day cramped up in the car. Now that it was night, they had parked in a busy neighborhood, near the beach on Garnet Avenue, where restaurants, nightclubs, and bars kept things hopping all day and most of the night.

Everyone was connected by cell phones, though they were instructed only to use those in emergencies. Everyone knew that "emergency" was defined as a Season sighting.

Daniel parked in front of a store that had already closed for the evening. Most of the people on the sidewalks were young and fashionable, drifting from one trendoid watering hole to another. Men were dressed in jeans and untucked shirts, high-heeled women in short skirts with low-cut tops. The crowd was college age, or just a little older. Kerry felt a momentary pang that she was missing out on the fun, instead sitting here on a life-and-death mission that she barely understood. Sure, she was here with Daniel, not alone. But they had been together all day, studiously ignoring the issue of what had happened between them at lunch the day before, while those people were out laughing, eating and drinking, enjoying the San Diego summer night. She didn't have that luxury and couldn't help being a little sorry she was on this side of the windshield instead of that one. *What must a "normal" life be?* she wondered. She'd never had one, and it didn't look like she would any time soon.

"Tell me why we're here again, Daniel," she said, after the silence between them had grown uncomfortable.

"That's a complicated question," he replied with a chuckle. "Do you mean in the cosmic sense? Or the strategic one?"

"I mean, why we're doing all this. Why you don't just accept that Season is always going to be there—if not her, then someone like her—and move on with your life? Try for some happiness while you can, instead of spending all your days on the hunt?"

In the glow from neon signs and streetlights, his face, when he turned to regard her, was serious, even stern. She thought she'd pushed him too far—between the flirting at lunch the day before, and now this, she was losing her grounding, forgetting to switch on the filter that would keep her from saying and doing stupid things. "That is a tough question," he answered. "You know the facile answers. Because Season is evil. Because she destroyed my town, killed my family."

"Before you were born," Kerry reminded him.

"That's true. Have you read my journals yet?"

"Just started," Kerry said. The night was warmer than was typical for San Diego, as if the heat wave that had started up ruled the dark as well as the light, and the windows were open to let air circulate. From outside she heard a burst of laughter, causing her to look out at a group of men seemingly sharing a joke. "But I haven't had much time."

"When you make more progress you'll see that there are other reasons as well," he assured her. "As for what makes me think that I have to be the instrument of justice? That's more complicated, and I'd have to be a smarter man than I am to figure it out."

"But how do you even define justice in a case like this? Does she have to die for justice to be served? Does she have to die by your hand? Where are the boundaries?"

"My preference," Daniel said, after considering for a few moments, "would be to kill her myself. I know that's going to be difficult—if it was easy, I'd have done it long ago. But that's the ideal."

"Is there a second best?" she asked him. "Something you can settle for?"

"In fact, there is." He shifted in his seat, bumping his knees against the steering wheel. "Next year there's an event we call the Convocation, or the Witches' Convocation, more correctly. It comes around twice every millennium, or every five hundred years."

"Like a Woodstock for witches?" Kerry asked.

"More or less. Maybe more like a trade show. But with elements of Woodstock, for sure. It's a gathering. Virtually all the world's serious witches come together—a few hundred of us, all in one place. We share stories, complain about problems, offer one another help and advice. Witches go to learn new spells, to see friends and family, and so on."

Kerry did the mental math. "But you've never been," she observed. "The last one would have been before you were born."

"That's right. I haven't. We all hear stories, though, and I've heard a lot of them. I can't wait for it."

"It does sound kind of fun," Kerry admitted. "But I don't see what it has to do with Season Howe."

"Because I haven't told you yet," Daniel teased. "One of the things that happens is that tribunals are gathered, crimes between witches dealt with. There's also a lot of politicking that goes on—this is the witch world's main chance to form alliances or partnerships, and to push various agendas."

"Now it sounds like a political convention."

Daniel nodded. Outside, a partyer with a few too many drinks under his belt bumped into the car as he made for the curb. Daniel shot him a sharp glance, then turned back to Kerry. "There is an element of that to it," he agreed. "Where Season comes into it is this: If necessary, we can convene a tribunal, effectively putting her on trial for her crimes."

"That sounds like a good thing."

"It is, to a point," Daniel said. "But there's also the chance that she could be acquitted, just like with any trial in your world. There's also the chance that she could form a powerful enough alliance to block any tribunal. She could even use it as a platform to sway more witches over to her side—the Dark Side, to use *Star Wars* terminology. The side of chaos and destruction. If that happened, and the Convocation ended with that alliance intact, the whole world could be looking at a new Dark Age. The last Dark Age, according to all reports, was bad enough. With new technology, new weapons, and current global stresses, the world might never survive another one."

This was a lot to take in, maybe too much. "So . . . you're saying the Dark Age—as in, *the* Dark Ages, medieval times, whatever—was the result of a bunch of bad witches teaming up to make trouble?"

"That's about the size of it," Daniel said. "Look, it's getting a little raucous around here. What do you say we find another place to wait for a while?"

Kerry agreed, and he started the engine and drove around the neighborhood for a few minutes. The phone had been silent all night, and Kerry was pretty sure Season was either staying inside, or she had managed the not-so-difficult task of evading the other two searching vehicles. After circling a particular block a few times, a parking space opened up, and Daniel nosed the car into it.

"We're a block from the beach," he said. "Take a walk?"

She had hardly had a moment to go to the beach since meeting Daniel, and she realized that she missed it fiercely. "Absolutely," she said quickly. "Do we dare leave the car?"

"We'll keep the phone with us, and stay close by," Daniel promised as he opened his door. "I don't really think she's going out tonight."

"I was just thinking the same thing."

"Great minds . . ." Daniel came around to her side of the car and opened her door. Then, like a perfect gentleman, he reached for her hand and helped her out. She could have easily done it herself, but there was something unexpectedly charming about this, a hint of old-fashioned chivalry absent in the males she had known before.

"Why, thank you, sir," she said, beaming at him.

"It's my pleasure, madam," he replied.

Here on the beach, the noise on Garnet was behind them by a couple of blocks, drowned out by the gentle thunder of the surf rolling forward, collapsing on itself, and pulling back, over and over. Wind off the water carried the scents of aquatic flora and fauna and snapped away the sounds from the couple of bonfire parties spread about the beach. Water and sky were equally black, with white stars glittering overhead and glimmering in the sea of foam and moonlight.

When their feet hit the sand, they still hadn't released each other's hands. Without letting go, Kerry kicked her sandals off and picked them up with her free hand. Daniel held on, helping her maintain her balance.

But that, she knew, was only her physical balance. It was her emotional equilibrium that was dizzy now. The cool sand between her toes felt comfortable, and so did his hand in hers, and she decided that it was time for one more push. Either it would go well . . .

. . . or it wouldn't.

"So, this is all a little confusing," she said after a short while.

"What is?" Daniel asked. "The Convocation? Season?"

She gave a little laugh. "I'm past all that," she said. "No, I mean this." She gave his hand a squeeze. "Us. If there is an us. Just what exactly are we doing here?"

"Ahh," he responded. "I think I see what you're getting at. You mean what makes me think that I, an over-the-hill, overly serious geezer with a mission, would have a chance with a beautiful, lively, spirited young woman such as yourself?"

Laughing again, she kicked sand at his feet. "That wasn't exactly what I meant. But I guess it was close enough."

"Then the answer is . . . I have no idea." He stopped walking and turned to face her, releasing her hand but putting both of his own on the sides of her waist. She dropped her sandals to the ground and pressed her hands loosely against the backs of his arms, not trusting her own emotions at this moment, not confident in her own impulses. "I don't know what we're doing," he elaborated. "But I know what I want, and I hope you want the same thing. I think you do." He stopped, took a deep breath, blew it out. "I've been wrong before, though."

"I don't think you are. Not this time," Kerry assured him. "That is, if you want what I suspect you do."

He pressed his hands more firmly against her waist, then took a step forward, sliding his hands around her back and pulling her toward him. She went willingly, happily, letting him guide her to him, loving the feel of his big hands spreading across her back. At the same time, she moved her own hands up his arms and around him, across his wide shoulders, and pulled him down toward her. As if choreographed, she tilted her head back and rose up on the balls of her feet, and he leaned forward. She felt her chest press against his, broad and muscular beneath his light cotton shirt, and then his lips were on hers and his hands moved hungrily across her back. Kerry returned that hunger, and then some, and they hardly noticed as the sea surged toward them, soaking their legs, then pulled back and left them standing in the wet sand, deeper than they'd been just a moment before.

Kerry Profitt's diary, August 26

Dear Diary,

Oh, never mind.

More later.

K.

16

My first impression of New York City, for this trip, anyway, is that they haven't finished building it yet. But it's definitely changed a lot since the last time I was here, which was, I think, 1899 or maybe spring of 1900.

I flew into LaGuardia and caught a cab into the city. I loaded my gear into the cab, and when I told the driver I was going to the Carlyle, his mouth dropped open. "I've been saving up," I told him.

"No foolin'," he said. Apparently I don't look much like your average Carlyle sort. But it's comfortable and centrally located, right next to Central Park. A good location is important when you're trying to

find a single woman somewhere in America's biggest city, and you don't know where to begin.

Back to the first impression, though—it was just about dusk when I got my first good look at modern Manhattan. Tall buildings, of course, but all over the skyline are these giant cranes. It's like the Empire State Building and the Chrysler Building and those others I don't know the names of aren't enough—every building in the city has to be a skyscraper.

After the cranes, what I notice next are the lights. Millions of them, twinkling everywhere I look. Lighted windows, lighted signs, lighted billboards. The cabbie drives me through Times Square, at my request, and it's just a crazy riot of light and color. There are signs and posters plastered everywhere for Look Homeward, Angel *at the Ethel Barrymore Theatre, which I guess opens this week. Tony Perkins is in it, and it seems to be the talk of the town at the moment. That and, of course, Thanksgiving, which means turkey dinners and the Macy's parade and Christmas lights, adding to the sparkle in the streets. There are people everywhere—on the sidewalks and spilling onto the streets, dressed to the nines, laughing and having a grand time, it seems. It would be nice to join them, I think, but business before pleasure.*

After giving me the nickel tour and running up the fare at the same time, of course, the cabbie drives me to

*the Carlyle, which surprises me by being every bit as
fancy as he had warned me. Thirty-five stories tall, all
beautiful art-deco design, a big fire roaring in the fireplace and formal-dressed staff all over the place—pretty
tony for an old witch. But I can afford it, so why not?*

 *In fact, I'm sitting in one of its deluxe beds right
now and ready to try it out for real. So I'll set this
aside for the night and get back to it when there's
something new to report.*

 I remain,

 Daniel Blessing, November 26, 1957

Kerry put the leather book down and jabbed the power
button on her laptop. Kerry and Daniel had stayed on the
beach, exploring each other with lips and tongues and hands
and eyes, until midnight, when Scott had texted Daniel's cell.
They had all headed home then, recognizing a major flaw in
their plan—that Season could easily slip through their already
loose net while they slept—but also accepting the obvious
truth that people parked overnight in a residential neighborhood might attract the unwanted attention of the police.

 Who still, presumably, wanted to talk to them about
Mace's murder.

Kerry Profitt's diary, August . . . oh, who cares.

I'm writing this in bed while Daniel is in bed in the next room,
probably trying to ignore Josh's snores.

I'm only guessing that Josh snores, but it seems like he would.

But the important fact of my life is not Josh snoring. Rather, it is that he—should that be HE?—is sleeping just twenty feet from where I am sleeping. Or, not sleeping. In my case.

If I were a different person I'd be scribbling the name "Daniel" across the inside cover of my notebook now, a hundred times, in different colored pens. Some with hearts around them, or flowers.

I'm not that girl, though. I'm laptop chick, ever so much more sophisticated.

Besides, I can just cut-and-paste.

Daniel

Daniel

Daniel

Daniel

See? Maybe loses some of the visceral impact. But I'm still all squooshy with visceral, anyway, from earlier, on the beach. I think my toes are permanently pruned, and did I mention that Pacific Ocean water is cold? I mean, at the moment I was sort of disregarding the part of my body called feet in favor of other parts. But when we stopped, I realized that I was, like, frostbitten or something.

Okay, not. But damn cold just the same. Teeth chattering, even.

Which is when Daniel did the coolest thing. Or one of them, anyway.

He got down on one knee, giving me momentary pro-
posal jitters, I must say, and then he took my feet—crusty and
sandy from beach and saltwater, and yuck!—in his hands,
one at a time, and held them. But the thing is, when he held
them, his hands generated some kind of warming field, like
they were mini-toasters and my cold, aching feet were the
bread. After a few seconds in his hands, the cold and the pain
went away, and my feet felt completely rejuvenated.

He's a one-man spa, that Daniel Blessing.

So we got home and talked for a while about the fruit-
lessness of the day's long, long stakeout. But we don't have
enough people to pull different shifts, so we pretty much
have to be out there as many hours as we can, and just
tough it out. Meanwhile, Daniel and I were trying hard not to
make googly eyes at each other, and we managed not to
tell the others what had happened, even though I want
to, but on the way home we agreed that it might make them
feel awkward, and maybe we should hold off telling anyone
for a while.

So then we went to bed. We were able to clasp hands,
just for a moment, as we passed in the hall. That was it.

Fortunately I can still feel his lips on mine, still taste him,
still remember the crush of his hands on me.

Giddy? Me?

Forcing myself not to write in here until after R had gone
to sleep because I was afraid I might just start giggling, or
crying, or both, and she'd want to know what was going on

and I'd have to tell her. So I got out the journals and skipped around for a bit, finally finding what looked like another story instead of just the "woke up, didn't find her, went to bed" reportage of so many days, read that for a while. Until R's breathing was regular. I'm sure she's out now.

So here I am. Instead of being crushing schoolgirl with my friends, I'm being crushing schoolgirl with a box full of wires and . . . well, whatever is inside computers. Chips? Whatever they look like.

It's all magic to me. I touch keys and words appear on the screen. Magic. Daniel touches my feet, and they warm and stop hurting. Magic. Daniel's mouth presses against mine and every worry I ever had flies out of my head. Magic.

Daniel? You're not just playing a game, are you?

silence

silence

silence

Didn't think so.

More later.

K.

New York is a funny town.

So many people. I'm certain that Season is here somewhere, but I roamed the city all day and didn't pick up a trace of her. Just about wore through my shoes, though—I'll likely need a new pair before I leave.

The good thing about New York is that you can buy anything here. No problem finding a new pair of shoes. The only hard part might be deciding: loafers, wing tips, what? I guess it'll depend on my mood when I'm in the store.

After having spent all day wandering around in the cold, though—and I'm talking COLD—I decided to check out the balloon preparation for the big parade tomorrow. I braved wind and weather (and skies that promise rain, I fear, for tomorrow) to hike the Upper West Side, watching colorful stretches of rubber slowly take shape. Mighty Mouse, clowns, Popeye the Sailor, a tremendous dachshund, toy soldiers, and other fanciful forms began to billow and shake as gigantic helium tanks filled them. The streets were crowded with revelers and volunteers, the latter working to control their balloons, the former hindering that effort, as often as not.

One old geezer buttonholed me as I watched, anxious for any target for his stories. "I was at the end of the route in '30," he told me. "Right in front of Macy's. In those days, they let the balloons go at parade's end, you know. Just let 'em float away. Most of 'em popped before they cleared the store—noise was terrible, and the bits of rubber raining down stank something awful too. But some of them got away, and Macy's had a reward out for their safe return—one year, two tugboats each caught an end of one of them wiener dogs, and pulled it in two."

"That's fascinating," I told the codger. But I tried to work my way clear of him because I was getting a strange feeling. One I didn't like a bit. Was it Season? I thought it over for a couple of moments, but no, it wasn't that. I was still trying to figure it when I heard a woman scream, not too far away— around the corner, I thought, and about half a block down.

A couple of us took off running toward the sound, but I was the fastest. When I reached her—forty, perhaps, nicely dressed, in a fur-lined coat, with boots and gloves to protect against the chill—she shouted something about her purse and a guy with a knife. She pointed down the block, and I just kept running.

I don't know what happened behind me, if the other men who ran toward her stopped to comfort her, or to call the cops, or what. All I knew is that a few minutes later I was on a block that seemed hundreds of miles removed from the swank Upper West Side blocks where the parade balloons were. Here the brownstones were run-down, with broken windows covered by boards, and trash in the streets. There seemed to be no one out. I could see the blue glow of television sets *in a couple of windows, and hear radios blaring from others, but there wasn't a soul to be seen.*

Part of me wanted to give up, to turn around. The lady had a fur, she could probably afford the loss of the purse and whatever dough was inside it. And if the guy who hiked her purse lived in this neighborhood, chances were that he'd just gotten away with more than he usually saw in a month. But there was a matter of principle, too. A thief is a thief, whether he steals from rich or poor.

I had touched the lady as I ran past her, though, so it wasn't a terribly difficult thing to track the progress of her purse. Eventually that trail led me to an alley, and in the alley were a half dozen hoodlums, counting out their take. Leonard Bernstein's West Side Story *opened on Broadway this year, and these guys could have been extras from the rumble scene, Sharks or Jets in their leather jackets and pomaded hair.*

And, I was to learn momentarily, switchblades.

One of them looked up and saw me. "You lost or something, Pops?" he asked.

"Pops," I said. "That's funnier than you know."

"I didn't mean it funny," he said back. "You guys think it sounded funny?"

They all agreed that I was the only one who found it funny in the least. Which only made sense, considering I was the only one who knew that I was old enough to be this punk's great-great-grandfather, at the very least.

"Anyhoo," the spokesman said after they had discussed it for a while, "this here is our alley, and unless you have some business with us, I think you oughta scram."

"I do have business with you," I said. "That purse you've got. I've come to take it back to its owner."

They looked at one another then, as if surprised by what I said. I guess they were. They couldn't have known I'd be able to track it this far. They thought they were home safe.

I guess they still did think that. "He's a funny man," the spokesman said. "A truly funny man, is old Pops."

"I'm not being funny," I said. "I'd like the purse, please. And all the money that was in it."

This is when the switchblades came out. Snap, crackle, pop, like the cereal, and suddenly all eight guys had steel in their hands.

I just looked at them, still hoping they'd do it the easy way. "The purse, please," I repeated.

The spokesman grabbed the purse from the one holding it, and waved it toward me. "Whynchoo come get it?" he asked. I'm just putting it down the way it sounded. Whynchoo.

"If that's the way you want it," I said. "I was hoping to spare you some trouble."

They looked at one another again. This time a couple of them looked nervous. I think they were getting the idea that I wasn't someone who was going to back down easily. Since they were used to people who did back down easily, that meant I had some kind of gimmick. Maybe a gun, maybe some friends, they didn't know what. But some secret weapon, because no one would be foolish enough to face down eight switchblade hoods without one.

In fact I did have one. Not any of the ones they might have thought. But a good one, just the same.

There were any number of ways it could have gone. I wanted them to remember it, though. I wanted them to learn something from it. I didn't want them to write it off later as some kind of hallucination, bad liquor or dope, or whatever else they might have imbibed that night. I wanted it to seem as natural as possible. So instead of just knocking them all out, or lifting them off their feet and slamming them magically into the walls of the alley, I decided to go hand-to-hand.

Of course, my hand was a little stronger than their hand. Even with the knives, which would never touch me. But they didn't have to know that. All they'd know was that a seemingly unarmed civilian could stand up to the bunch of them, and win.

I advanced on them at a regular walking pace.

Some of the switchblade-wielding fists shook now, as they realized that this was turning ugly. Maybe they were afraid they'd have to kill me, and while they were hoodlums and punks, I thought they probably weren't killers by nature. Maybe they were just plain afraid.

I started with the spokesman, because he annoyed me the most. Easily dodging his knife, I caught his jaw with a right hook, followed with a jab to the gut and then an uppercut to the chin. He went down hard. Now the others were all stabbing at me, but I took them one by one, letting their blades slip past me. A few punches here, a couple of karate chops there, some judo throws for variety. Finally the last two broke out running, down the alley away from me. But that was okay. I wasn't going to chase. I gathered up all the money the ones left behind had on them, on the theory that even if it hadn't come from the purse, they'd stolen it from someone, and tucked it inside the lady's wallet. Then I left them in the alley. They'd wake up in a few hours, never again quite so confident, I hoped, in their own invulnerability.

I found the lady about where I'd left her, answering questions from a uniformed cop who wrote slowly, and with obvious difficulty, in a little notebook. Gave her the purse. Explained that it had been dropped, several blocks away, and I hoped she wasn't too inconvenienced. Ignored the look the cop shot me, like if I wasn't the snatcher, I was probably in league with him. Back on 90th I caught a cab back to the Carlyle, and here I am. It's starting to rain outside.

Interesting day. Interesting city. No Season.

I remain,

Daniel Blessing, November 27, 1957

17

You get any sleep?"

Scott looked at Kerry like she was some kind of lab specimen. Then again, she felt like some kind of lab specimen, so maybe that was how she did look. When she'd been in the bathroom, she hadn't quite been able to focus on the mirror, which, judging from Scott's greeting, was probably a bonus.

"Not much," she admitted. "I was reading."

"You were?" Rebecca asked. "I didn't even know."

Because you could sleep through nuclear war, Kerry thought. *Or Ozzfest, at least.* She just shrugged and tried to smile, though.

She felt strange this morning. As if she was the same person she had been yesterday, but everything around her had changed. Like she had gone to bed at home, but had woken up in a foreign country. She didn't know the language, the customs, the lay of the land. But she'd made the trip willingly—buying her own ticket, bringing her passport. A strange feeling, that was the only way to describe it.

"Must have been a good book," Scott said. "Keeping you awake and all."

"One of Daniel's journals. It's pretty interesting reading."

"Does it have any advice in it about how to survive a stakeout?" Brandy asked, coming into the kitchen from the bedroom she shared with Scott. "Because all day in a car . . . I thought my legs were permanently frozen in a sitting position."

"You took enough bathroom breaks," Scott teased. "You could have walked around a little more then."

"I'll have to today," Brandy shot back. "I go back into that mini-mart, they're going to start charging me rent."

"Josh suggested using a bottle or a can," Rebecca offered. "I told him if I even saw him bring a bottle or can into the car, I was throwing him out."

Brandy cracked up. "Good for you."

"That's how they do it in real life, I guess," Scott said. "Not that this isn't, you know . . ."

Rebecca flapped her hands at him. "I think that's how it's done in those crime books and movies Josh likes," she replied. "I don't know about real life. I just know I'm not sitting there while Josh whips out a soda bottle."

Daniel wandered in then, hair still mussed from sleeping and a crease from his pillow on his face. Kerry liked it. As she learned more about him, sometimes it was hard to remember that he was human—not quite like her, obviously, but still, at his core. A pillow mark on his face, though—that was as human as it got. He was a long-lived, incredibly powerful man, but he was still a man.

She'd have to remember to kiss that cheek later, where she saw the crease. Maybe some other spots, too.

"I don't blame you a bit, Rebecca," he said as he rummaged in the cabinet for a clean cup. "This is serious business, I'm afraid. But just as I don't want any of you to try to engage Season on your own, I don't want you to injure yourselves, or to be any more put out than is absolutely necessary. We'll stake her out, but we won't kill ourselves doing it, okay?"

"We're already about as put out as we can be," Brandy observed. "Unless you don't count our lives being turned upside down and put in danger."

"Oh, I do," Daniel said. He poured coffee from the pot into his cup, took a sip, grimaced. Kerry had noticed that he nearly always tasted it, even though he invariably put in sugar afterward. *Old habits,* she figured. "Believe me, I know how seriously I've inconvenienced all of you."

"But if we get Season," Kerry put in, "then it's all worth it. Everything. Even . . . even Mace."

She felt Brandy's gaze burning into her. "You sure you want to go there?"

"I feel terrible about Mace, Brandy, you know I do. But Season is responsible for so many deaths, so much sorrow and loss. If we could stop her, think of everyone we'd be helping. All of her future victims."

"We're on board," Scott assured her. "Doesn't mean we have to be thrilled about it. But you don't see any of us turning away, do you?"

"Josh tries to bring a bottle into my car," Rebecca said, trying to sound hard-boiled, "I'll turn him away."

"Yeah, you talk like a tough cookie!" Josh called from behind the closed bathroom door. "We'll just see how tough you really are when the chips are down."

Rebecca laughed and blushed, lifting her breakfast dishes from the table and carrying them to the sink. So far, Kerry decided, she was impressed with all of her friends, for even sticking it out this long, and for being willing to go to all this trouble.

The chips, she was pretty sure, had been down for a long time.

The shopping center was wood-sided, painted brown, reasonably busy. It wasn't much more than a glorified strip mall containing a coffee shop and a bagel shop, a drugstore, office and pet supplies stores, a couple of restaurants, and at one end, a supermarket. But there was enough traffic in and out so no one really noticed that one nondescript Ford Taurus had parked in the slender shade offered by a tree and hadn't moved for a long time.

Anyone looking into the car, though, might notice that the couple in the front seat was locked in passionate embrace, as often as not.

"Should we really be doing this?" Kerry asked when they broke once. It was midafternoon; they'd been on the stake-out since eight that morning. The windows were half open so the occasional breeze could help cool the car's interior. They'd taken one break for ice-cream cones, and a couple of others to replenish their supply of cold bottled water. "The others . . ."

"We don't kiss so loudly that we wouldn't hear the phone," Daniel assured her. "But if you want to stop . . ."

"That's not what I said." At the moment, she could hardly imagine a more pleasant way to pass the time than sitting and talking with Daniel Blessing, interrupted from time to time by a bout of feverish kissing.

"Tonight," Daniel announced, somewhat abruptly, "we'll tell them."

For a moment Kerry was confused. "Tell them . . . oh. *Tell* them. About us."

"There's no reason we should have to keep it a secret," Daniel said. "We're both adults. You're young, yes, but you're as mature a woman as I've ever known."

Kerry felt herself crimsoning. "Thanks. I guess . . . I guess I had to grow up fast, with my mom and dad in the condi-tions they were in."

"You've done an admirable job." He traced a pattern on

her knee with his finger. She wore khaki shorts and a red cotton T-shirt, almost the color she figured her face had turned, because in spite of the August heat, they couldn't run the air-conditioning the whole time they were parked, and his touch was cool, comforting. Somehow Daniel stayed crisp in a white linen shirt with the long sleeves rolled up and faded jeans. "I told you before, I've been with a few women over the years."

She didn't necessarily like to think about that. "Yeah."

"But none of them . . . ever . . . have meant what you have come to mean to me, Kerry. You . . ."

He paused, and she waited for him to finish his sentence. He worked his jaw, she could see the little worm of a scar under it twitch, but nothing came out.

Finally she decided to take him off the hook, finally allowing herself to say what she'd been holding inside, not even certain of her own feelings until just this moment. "I can't say I've been with a lot of guys," she said. "And obviously never with an age difference like we have. But I think I feel the same way. Like there's something about you that I just respond to, that I'm at ease with. It's hard to remember when you weren't in my life, and hard to imagine a future without you in it." She laughed, suddenly even more nervous than she'd expected. Whenever she'd had this kind of conversation in her head, growing up, it had all flowed so easily. "God, isn't this the kind of talk we should be having six months from now, maybe? I'm so bad at this I don't even know what the timing is supposed to be like."

"It's supposed to be whatever feels right," Daniel said, squeezing her leg. "And this does."

"So tonight?" Kerry asked, aware that maybe she was, once again, about to push too hard. "When we tell them? Do you think maybe we can get Rebecca and Josh to share a room?"

Daniel smiled at her, obviously pleased by the suggestion. "It's worth a try," he said.

He leaned toward her, drawing her closer with subtle pressure on her leg, and their lips were almost in contact when his phone chirped at them. He raised an eyebrow in annoyance. "Great timing."

"It's not like we haven't had a chance to kiss today," Kerry reminded him, biting back her own disappointment. "Or like we won't have plenty of time later."

Fishing the phone from his pocket, Daniel pouted. "But I wanted one now."

Kerry stretched toward him and planted one on his cheek, right where the pillow-crease had been. "There you go," she said. "Now answer your phone."

"Pick up, pick up, pick up," Rebecca pleaded, listening to Daniel's phone ring.

"Trying to drive here," Josh said with a growl. He had the wheel of the Civic, and he wore an unpleasant scowl as he tried to maneuver around a Buick that had lurched from an apartment complex's lot into their way. "You want to put the kibosh on the whining?"

Pick up, pick up, pick up, Rebecca thought anxiously. Josh's mood was foul enough that she didn't want to aggravate it any more. But—

"Hello," Daniel's voice spoke in her ear.

"We found her!" Rebecca realized she'd shouted it, but didn't care. She could almost feel Josh's glare.

"Where are you?"

She glanced at their surroundings. "Heading toward the water, so west, I guess, on Emerald."

"She's driving?" Daniel asked.

"Yes. Driving."

"In what?"

"A car." Rebecca said, flustered. She'd known a minute ago, but the tension and excitement of the chase were getting to her.

"Forest green Nissan Maxima," Josh informed her.

She relayed the message, and added, "We were driving down Emerald, and she passed us, going the other way. Josh pulled over, then turned around. She's a couple of blocks ahead of us."

"Okay, good job, Rebecca," Daniel said sharply. "I'm going to alert Brandy and Scott now. I'll check back in a minute."

He ended the call, and Rebecca put the phone in her lap. Two- and three-story apartment buildings flashed past her window; the fronds of tall palms strobed the sunlight that raked across the windshield. Ahead she could see a van and a big black SUV. "Where is she?" she asked Josh. "I don't see her."

"Don't sweat it, I have her," Josh assured her. "I'm hanging back so she doesn't make us." He tossed her a sideways grin. "You act like I don't know what I'm doing."

"You watch a lot of movies, read some books," Rebecca countered. She was fully aware that her anxiety was making her edgier than usual, more argumentative. But she had every right to be edgy. They were chasing a killer—and worse, a killer with unknown magical powers. "I'm not sure that makes you a genuine expert on surveillance techniques."

Josh's grin turned into an unpleasant sneer. She had always liked Josh, even when the rest of their housemates found him a bit obnoxious. But now that he was in his element—or what he believed was his element, even though he had no particular experience with, or real-life knowledge of, the seamier side of life—he got all bent out of shape when she dared to question his abilities. As if to prove her wrong, he mashed down hard on the accelerator and the car lunged ahead. At the same time he twisted the wheel to the left, swerving into the oncoming traffic lane, which was blessedly empty. He stayed on the gas, pulling ahead of the van, then cutting back into the correct lane. The van's horn bleated, the SUV in the other lane ticked to the side as if worried about being hit. But three blocks ahead of them, just making a right turn, she spotted the green Nissan.

Josh glanced at her, wordlessly triumphant.

18

Brandy flipped the phone open as soon as it rang. "Hey," she said.

"She's on the move." Daniel's voice, brittle with anxiety. "On Emerald, headed west. Toward you."

"Okay," Brandy answered, not sure what other response was needed. If any. She and Scott were parked on Mission, near Beryl, on the route one would take from Pacific Beach to La Jolla.

"Dark green Nissan Maxima," Daniel added.

"We'll watch for her," Brandy promised.

"Don't get right behind her," Daniel warned. "Let her get a few car lengths ahead. Josh and Rebecca will be following too, so you should both take turns pulling up and slipping back. Make sure she doesn't see the same car in her rearview the whole time."

"I got it," Brandy said.

"We're on the way over. I'll check back in a few." Daniel signed off, and she folded the phone. Scott looked at her, curiosity on his face.

"What's up?"

"Get ready for action, Scott. She's coming this way." Brandy repeated the details Daniel had given her. "Let's not lose her this time," she said. "I'd sure love to get all this over with."

Scott nodded as he turned the key in the ignition and gunned the engine. The air inside the car was charged now; the urgency of imminent contact, the anticipation of some kind of conclusion to the summer's madness striking them both. "That makes two of us."

A couple of minutes later the phone rang again. "It's Rebecca," their housemate's voice said when Brandy answered. "She's not coming your way after all. She turned south on Mission, not north."

"We're on it," Brandy acknowledged. She hung up and filled Scott in. So Season wasn't heading for La Jolla this time—or to the freeway, at least, not right away. South on Mission would take her through Pacific Beach, and into Mission Beach. But that would become a dead end; eventually she'd have to turn inland, crossing Mission Bay. Then she could go out Point Loma, which would trap her on a long peninsula, or toward downtown and the freeways.

Scott pulled out of the parking place, waited for a break in traffic, and performed an illegal U-turn in the middle of the block. Now he was headed south on Mission, as well. He stomped on the gas and the car shot forward. Traffic was light, but there were cars on the road, and he wove between lanes to get around them. Brandy found herself clutching her seat, trying not to show fear. They'd have to live through the chase if they would ever get a chance to die at Season's hands, she knew.

Of course, there was the other option, too—the one where they defeated Season and ended the summer in triumph. She hadn't been willing to give much consideration to that scenario, unwilling to get her hopes up. Life, she had found, was somewhat less disappointing if she didn't expect too much out of it to begin with. Allowing herself to imagine that she'd be some kind of hero, would help save the world—*okay, not the world,* she thought, *but at least lives, someone's world*—had been too ambitious for her to even consider.

Now, though, she couldn't help it. She had the sense that some kind of conclusion was coming, some ultimate confrontation. Either they'd walk away from it or Season would, but no way would the status quo be unchanged at the end.

So she hung on and let Scott drive, silently watching the road ahead, his hands tight on the wheel. A trickle of sweat ran down the side of his face, dripping from beneath the temple-piece of his glasses. Brandy worried a little about him, about how he'd deal with this whole thing. He was a smart guy, and she loved him, really loved him like no other boyfriend she'd had. But confrontation wasn't his forte. He was smart but not strong, not in the physical sense, although he was no weakling, either—no Mace, but no Josh, either, and soccer had given him great legs—but in the emotional sense. When life battered him around, he didn't bounce back easily. Even something as seemingly minor as a disagreement in traffic— someone cutting him off or flipping him off—unsettled him for at least a day.

She'd been pleasantly surprised, so far, about how well he'd handled all this, with Daniel and Mace and everything. When things turned really bad, he seemed able to rise to meet the challenges. But she couldn't help wondering when he'd reach his breaking point, when it would all just be too much for him. Judging from the expression on his face now—lips clamped together, eyes wide, jaw as tight as a violin string—that time just might be close. She'd have to keep an eye on him.

"There's Josh and Beck," he said a few minutes later. Brandy saw them too, in the rented Civic they drove.

"We should pass them," she said. "So when she looks in her mirror—"

"I know," Scott interrupted. Brandy had already explained the theory, when reporting what Daniel had told her. She guessed the stress was getting to her too.

"I know, sorry."

"Yeah," he said. "Anyway, that's what I'm doing." He

pulled even with the other car, and Brandy waved at Josh and Rebecca. Josh made an ushering gesture with his hand, indicating that they should pull ahead. He had an unlit cigarette clamped between his teeth. Rebecca wouldn't let him smoke while she was in the car, but it looked like he'd been chewing on it. Brandy thought she could see flecks of tobacco on his chin.

Brandy and Scott pulled ahead, though, and all her attention was on the dark green sedan a block or so ahead of them, with only a driver inside.

"That's got to be her," Scott said.

"Yeah," Brandy agreed softly, more nervous than ever now that Season was in view again. This time there would be no losing her, she determined. This time it would all play out to the end. One way or another.

Suddenly every vehicle in San Diego was in Pacific Beach, either stuck in traffic on Garnet or trying to cross it. That was how it seemed to Kerry, anyway. She drove Daniel's car. He had his hands full with his cell, trying to coordinate the movements of three different vehicles, all in pursuit of a fourth, and he'd spread a city map on his lap. He tried to anticipate where Season might be headed, based on where she was. Kerry knew that was a fool's game—Season had proven her unpredictability plenty of times in the past, and could as easily turn around and head right back where she'd come from as continue on any given path. But she didn't bother to share her opinion with Daniel, who, after all, knew his enemy far better than she did.

Ahead, the traffic light turned green, and she started inching forward even before the car in front of her had moved. But three cars in front of that, a pick-up truck with surfboards spiking from the bed was trying to turn left, and sat at the light waiting for a break in the oncoming traffic. By the time the truck had passed through the light, it was turning yellow again, then red. She had moved up all of one space.

"She's not doing this, is she?" Kerry asked, only half-joking.

"What, manipulating the traffic? No, I think that's beyond even her abilities," Daniel replied. "That's the problem with traffic, it can't be controlled. Too much human element. It's barely contained chaos. Almost makes one long for the days of traffic cops, standing in the streets directing the flow."

"Or horses and buggies?" Kerry teased.

"Say what you will," Daniel said. "There were definite advantages. Quieter, safer, less polluting. The world has given up a lot in the name of progress."

"But we don't have to worry about stepping in horse manure when we cross the street," Kerry pointed out.

"That's true. Then, though, you didn't have to worry about global climate change or growing holes in the ozone layer. You didn't have to worry that you were breathing in carcinogens every day. And that's without even bringing nuclear arms or biological weapons into the equation. Life is easier now, in many ways, and safer in some. But in others, the world has gone completely, screamingly insane."

The light changed again, and Daniel fell silent as Kerry silently urged the cars in front of her to just go straight already. And it worked. This time, she made it through the light. Ahead, Garnet had the undisputed right of way for several blocks, so it was relatively clear sailing.

"Do you really think that?" she asked after a while. "That the world is insane?"

Daniel considered the question for a long moment. "In some ways, I said. And the answer is, yes, I do. Certainly, there have been remarkable improvements, amazing technological advances. We've essentially beaten the worst diseases of history—plague, polio, whooping cough, and so on. We can vaccinate against measles and chicken pox. These things used to cripple and kill, and now they're merely inconvenient, if that. But we've also changed the world in ways we don't even understand, so that we have to deal with new cancers, STDs, various pandemics. We've poisoned the air and water. We build nuclear power plants that have the potential to kill tens of thousands if something goes wrong. In many ways, large and small, from the individual to the corporation to government, we keep inventing new ways to kill, new ways to tyrannize, new ways to destroy people's lives." He chuckled dryly. "I'm sorry, Kerry, I don't mean to pontificate."

"That's okay," she said. Listening to him talk helped her cope with the frustrations of the traffic.

"No, it's not. We have other things on our plate right now." He punched some buttons on the cell phone, listened for a second. Then, "Brandy, where are you? Good, good. We'll be there in a few minutes; just trying to get through traffic."

After he hung up, he pointed at a stop light ahead, at Mission Boulevard. "Left on Mission," he told her.

"Okay," she said. She really did find his diatribe intriguing. When most people talked about the differences between older days and the present, she knew they were only basing their opinions on what they'd read or heard. He had actually lived through the whole thing, though—the settling of America, the westward expansion, the rise and fall of global powers. He was history made flesh.

But thinking about his flesh made her mind veer in other directions, and she shook her head, not wanting to let herself get distracted with thoughts of that. Plenty of time later. Right now she had to drive a car. Daniel was on the phone again, with Rebecca this time, when Kerry made the left onto Mission.

Daniel continued to direct her, and she went where he told her to—left, left, right. Through Crown Point and across the bay on a narrow bridge, then they were on wide avenues and moving fast. Past Sea World, and eventually onto I-5, heading south, but then an abrupt turn onto I-8, going east. That way was the desert and the rest of the country, eventually. Kerry found herself wondering how far they'd go today. Was the witch finally leaving San Diego behind? Part of her gloried at that idea—it would be over then, for her.

But Daniel would go too, wouldn't he? Continuing the hunt.

At Daniel's urging, she sped up, and soon she had the other two cars in sight. They slowed a little, letting her pass, acknowledging her and Daniel as they did so.

And then she could see Season, up ahead, cruising along in her dark green car. Daniel put a hand on Kerry's leg and squeezed. "No closer," he said quietly. That made sense—if she could see Season, then Season could see them. She hung back.

In the city of El Cajon, a few miles east of San Diego, the green car exited the freeway. Josh was back in front by this time. He flipped on his turn signal and followed her, and the other two cars did the same. "It's good we have three cars to work her," Daniel said. "She obviously left Pacific Beach the hard way to try to spot, or avoid, pursuit. I don't think she's seen us yet, but she still might. We'll need to be very careful on these roads."

El Cajon was a small city, and traffic there was nowhere near as heavy as it had been back in San Diego. All three vehicles stayed well behind Season's. Daniel was silent now, grimly focused on the Nissan ahead of them. The three chase cars did a dance, each taking the lead for a while, then falling back to let a different one move closer—never sticking to a pattern, but changing things up each time. Now and again one would pull into a parking lot, and then out again, or stop by the side of the road, only to pull back out after the other two had passed. The last thing anyone wanted was for Season to get stuck at a light long enough for them to catch up to her, to risk stopping right next to her or being obvious about holding back.

The streets Season chose became increasingly empty. She led them away from El Cajon's small downtown area, through residential neighborhoods where the streets were lined with small cottages or faded apartment complexes in shades of salmon or aquamarine. Overgrown yards, sometimes with cars parked in them, were not uncommon here. Fences tended to be chain-link, in various states of repair. Behind some of them, dogs stood guard or lazed in the sun. Being inland and therefore farther from the coast, El Cajon was even more brutally hot than San Diego, and there weren't many people on the streets, but Kerry spotted a few, sitting on shaded porches or walking on the sidewalks under sun hats or, in one instance, an umbrella.

"You have any idea where she's going?" she asked Daniel.

She could see his shrug from the corner of her eye. "No clue," he said. "Up to no good, I'm sure."

"Doesn't that go without saying?"

The question was answered in another couple of minutes, though. Daniel's cell rang, and when he answered, Kerry could make out Brandy's voice, which sounded agitated. Daniel listened for a moment, thanked her, and disconnected. "She's stopping," he told Kerry. "Brandy and Scott are driving past, Rebecca and Josh are stopping behind her."

"What do we do?"

The other cars had already turned a corner that Kerry had not yet reached. Daniel pointed to the parking lot of a strip mall, before the corner, on the left-hand side of the street. "Pull in there," he said. "We'll get closer on foot."

She did as she was directed, parking in front of a taco stand, and they both got out. Daniel kept his phone in his hand. He punched a button. "Rebecca," he said. "Where is she?"

He frowned as he listened to her response, then he put away the phone and looked at Kerry. "There's an herbalist around the corner," he explained. "She's gone in there. Picking up supplies for some kind of spell, most likely."

Anxiety gnawed at Kerry's stomach, as if she'd swallowed a mouse. They were close now, as close as they'd been since that night in the kitchen when Daniel was too weak to give his all. A battle might be only moments away. She wanted it, ached for an end to Daniel's long quest. But was he strong enough now? And if he wasn't, what then? She hardly dared to imagine. "What now? Do we just go in there after her?"

"Three reasons why we don't do that," Daniel said. "One, we don't know who's in there. An herbalist may well be a cover for a witch, maybe an ally of hers. Two, we don't know if she spotted us and is trying to lead us into a trap. She may be watching the street right now from inside, waiting for us to make our move. Three, we don't know the territory. We've had no time to plan, to scout out escape routes, to know what cover there might be. Going in there now could be suicide."

Kerry was confused. "Then why have we followed her all this way?"

"Because we found her," he said simply. "We're not losing her again. That just isn't happening."

19

ut they did.

Season stayed in the shop less than five minutes. Kerry and Daniel made their way around the corner and had taken up positions in the recessed doorway of an empty, boarded-up storefront. They could see the Civic up ahead, and Season's Nissan, parked right in front of a shop with a green painted sign that read HERBS 'R' US: REMEDIES AND ROMANCE, and farther ahead, Scott's RAV4. But Season's abrupt reappearance took them by surprise. Daniel and Kerry both had to turn away from the shop, facing into the doorway of the vacant store. They stayed there until they heard engines starting, and then the squeal of tires as Season pulled hurriedly away from the curb.

As soon as she was gone, Daniel grabbed Kerry's hand. "Come on!" he urged. His phone rang, and he answered it as they ran for the car. "I know!" he shouted. "Stay on her!"

By the time they were back in Daniel's Taurus, though, Kerry once again driving, Brandy had called to tell them that Season was gone.

She had made a quick right at the first corner, then a sudden left into an alley. Scott hadn't wanted to be so obvious as to follow her down the alley while she was still in it, so Brandy called Rebecca, intending for that car to go straight instead of making the right. She and Scott would go past the alley and then left, and whichever way Season turned when she reached the alley's end, one of the cars would be nearby.

Except what Season did, apparently, was to go partway down the alley, then back out and go back down the original street, in the opposite direction. Both cars were more than a block away by this time, and Kerry and Daniel, who had started at a disadvantage, weren't close enough yet to catch her.

"Do you think she saw us?" Kerry asked after Daniel explained what had happened.

"Maybe," he said. "Or maybe she's just being careful. She would know that if anyone had been following, her few minutes in the store would have given them time to catch up, maybe even lay a trap."

"I guess it wasn't her trap, though," Kerry observed.

"I called it wrong," he admitted. "Couldn't be sure, though."

"Better safe?"

"Exactly."

"So what now?" she wondered.

"Back to I-8," he said. "As fast as you can. Let's assume she's heading back home, and not away from the city." He began punching buttons on the phone. "I'll text the others."

Ten minutes later, they had her again. She had taken a roundabout way back to the freeway, apparently hoping to shake anyone tailing her. Rebecca and Josh were the farthest back, and when they saw her coming up fast behind them they called the others. Daniel and Kerry pulled off the freeway altogether, so she wouldn't recognize them when she passed. The other two cars stayed on her, and Kerry just re-entered at the same place, so within a very few minutes they were all behind her again. Kerry felt a powerful sense of relief, as if it was all over.

Which, of course, it isn't, she thought. *It hasn't even really begun.*

Forty minutes later, having gone back into Pacific Beach through La Jolla—prompting Daniel to point out that she hadn't taken a direct route anywhere—Season was back on Emerald, with Josh and Rebecca not far behind. She made a right on Everts, and pulled into the driveway of a small clapboard bungalow, at the corner of the alley that ran up the block between Emerald and Felspar—Pacific Beach's east-west streets being named after minerals. This time, Rebecca and Josh drove past, and the other two cars stopped a block away.

"Isn't that more or less where you picked her up in the

first place?" Daniel asked when they called in the report. He listened, nodding, then said, "Okay, sit tight. We're on the way." He made another quick call, telling Brandy and Scott to stay where they were, motor running, just in case. Then he turned to Kerry.

"Okay, drive past the house. Not too fast, not too slow. Just like you're out for a drive with no special destination in mind."

"But won't she see us?" Kerry wondered.

"She might," Daniel said. "If she's looking. Chance we have to take. I need to check out her place."

He sounded a bit too casual about it for her tastes, but Kerry did as she was told. She pulled away from the curb and drove at a slow, steady speed past the bungalow. Its exterior walls were painted white, with brown trim. A front porch seemed to sag under the weight of an old overstuffed chair that had suffered the elements for too long. A screen door was closed, but the heavier door behind that stood open. It looked like the kind of place a college student might live in, Kerry thought, or a young professional still a long way from her potential earning plateau. Not one of the world's most powerful witches. She wasn't sure where the Season of her imagination might live—a gingerbread house or a crumbling castle surrounded by thorn trees, maybe. The yard of this cottage was dried out, mostly dirt with a few hardy weeds, but no thorn trees. The only thing she saw that suggested Season at all was over the door, where a small bundle of greenery had been tacked.

"Is that a charm of some kind?" Kerry asked. "Above the door?"

"Keeps us out," Daniel explained. "It's a ward."

"Really?" Kerry couldn't keep the surprise out of her voice. "That little bunch of leaves can keep you out of a place?"

"It's not just the leaves," he said. They had passed the house now, but he kept looking at it until he couldn't see it anymore. "It's what they represent, how she prepared them, and the way she put them up. Those leaves, properly prepared and blessed, have the power of the trees behind them. Strong enough to stand through the ages, limber enough to survive wind, structured to use rain instead of being worn away by it. With her help, the power of the trees is transferred to the bundle, and then applied to the whole house. I could no more walk in there right now than I could step through a redwood tree."

"Somehow I didn't think a little thing like that would be beyond your abilities," Kerry said, mostly joking.

But Daniel took it seriously. "I didn't say it was," he rejoined. "It just takes some preparation."

Rebecca, Josh, Brandy, and Scott were assigned to keep an eye on the bungalow while that preparation took place. Kerry drove Daniel back to their apartment, way down in Imperial Beach, phone on his lap the whole way in case they called to say she was on the move again. But the phone remained quiet.

Kerry was uneasy about leaving the others behind. The

fact that they didn't call was no consolation—what if Season had somehow caught them unaware and done the same to them that she'd done to Mace? She could have called them, but that could be the same as demonstrating a lack of trust in them. She would have felt much better if Daniel had been able to stay close. But that wasn't an option, he assured her. He had work to do, work that couldn't be done until he knew just what they were up against.

The first thing he did when they got into the apartment was to borrow her laptop and go online. There he went to Google Earth and typed in the location of Season's apartment.

When he had zoomed in as far as he was able to online, he gazed at the image for a while. It lost clarity as it got closer, Kerry noted. And they didn't have a printer, so all he could do, she figured, was to look at it on the screen. But he asked her to find a piece of blank paper, and she rummaged through her belongings until she did, a brief letter from her aunt Betty, written on only one side of the page. Daniel spread the paper out flat on the tabletop and then put his hands on the computer screen. He spoke a couple of words in a language that Kerry didn't know, and then touched the paper.

As if it had run through a color laser printer—*or as if by magic, more accurately,* Kerry thought—the image that had appeared on screen transferred to the paper. But looking at it more closely, she realized that it was much more distinct now, that somehow in transferring it, Daniel sharpened it. Now it could have been a photo taken from a few hundred feet up, if that, showing the bungalow, its yard, and the houses and streets around it in crisp detail.

She was astonished. "If you could patent that, you could give Microsoft a run for its money."

Daniel shook his head. "Witches have gone up against Bill Gates before. He still wins. We're not all-powerful, you know."

He turned back to the image he'd made, and studied it. A couple of times he pointed out features to Kerry—the way the fence at the back of her place was leaning in one spot, suggesting weak support posts there; the fact that a neighbor's house behind hers was unfenced so that there was access to Emerald through that property. He traced his finger across the picture like a general planning a military campaign, which Kerry figured wasn't too far from the truth. For the most part, though, he was silent, working through details in his head without sharing them. Kerry knew that if he wanted to share, he would, and that quiet contemplation was probably more important right now.

When he finished with the picture, he excused himself and went into the room he shared with Josh. "I'll be in here for about twenty minutes," he said. "Don't come in, no matter what you might see or hear. I'll be fine. What I'm going to do isn't dangerous, but it's necessary, and it might sound unpleasant from the outside."

He gave Kerry a last kiss and closed the door. She crossed her arms in front of her chest and stood by the open front window, grateful for whatever breeze slipped through. The apartment was just small enough to be stuffy on these hot days, and though they got a decent cross breeze at night, during the day the air outside wasn't much of a relief. *I always heard San Diego was supposed to have perfect weather,* she thought. She had found out, though, that while it was mostly pleasant, it was far from perfect. She'd learned about June gloom, during which the beaches stayed socked in by overcast skies most of the day, so travelers who had come from far away for the fabled southern California coastline were disappointed by gray, cool days. July had been about as good as it gets, with warm, sunny weather all the time. Even August had started nice, but these last few days had reminded her that San Diego is essentially a desert, albeit one close to the ocean. She hadn't seen a drop of precipitation all summer, which cemented that impression.

Musing on the climate was just one way she tried to ignore the sounds that issued from Daniel's room. The first noises she heard were just strange—deep-sounding bells, like cowbells or heavy wind chimes, with a low moaning sound twining through them. But the sounds quickly became more disturbing—the moan less like wind, more like human voices, then turning to a keening wail, a mourning sound. When Daniel's voice entered the chorus, in evident agony, Kerry started to rush for the door. Remembering his warning, she kept herself from throwing it open, but it took every ounce of willpower. She went back to the window.

When he screamed again, she turned away and crossed to

the bathroom, running water full force in the sink, wetting a washcloth and laying it over her face. She pressed the corners against her ears, trying to keep all noise out, to amplify the blood she could hear in her own head, drowning out everything else.

Finally he emerged. He looked like he'd been through hell. His cheeks were drawn and pale, with red splotches on them. His eyes were glassy and unfocused. It looked like he might have blow-dried his hair in a wind tunnel. Kerry went to him and grabbed his hands, which were clammy. "Are you okay, Daniel? What happened in there?"

"I'm fine," he replied. His voice was a dry rasp that sounded like it reached her from some faraway place.

"But . . . what . . . ?" She didn't even know how to finish the question. It was obvious to her that she needed to know more about this whole business before she would know what to ask. He tugged absently at his hands, and Kerry released them.

"Another time," Daniel said. Already he seemed to be improving: color flooding back into his face, eyes clearing. He ran a hand over his head, smoothing the flyaway hair. Now he looked at her, really seeing her for the first time, she thought, since he'd come out of the room, and he smiled. "I'll tell you all about it later," he said. "It's just . . . preparations that have to be made. A little easier if I could have made them over the span of several days, as they should be. But since we didn't know precisely when battle might be joined, I had to hold off." He leaned forward, kissed her forehead. "You okay?"

"I'm . . . I'm not the one who was screaming in pain."

"Is that what you heard?" he asked. Kerry nodded her head, but Daniel didn't elaborate. "Let's go," he said. "We have a wicked witch to kill."

20

Have you ever been in love, Kerry?" Daniel asked as he drove north on I-5, back toward Pacific Beach and the confrontation they both knew was imminent. "I mean, totally and completely head over heels?" Her heart leapt at the question. *Where is this going?* she wondered. She knew where she hoped he was taking the conversation. She had decided that—lack of personal experience with the emotion aside—she believed she was in love with Daniel. She couldn't stop thinking about him, worrying about him when he was away from her. She wanted to be with him every moment, wanted to feel his hands on her, his lips, the comfortable way they fit together when they walked or stood together, her weight on him and vice versa. There had been a hole in her life, and that hole had been Daniel-sized and Daniel-shaped, and now there was a Daniel in it.

She recognized that she was letting her silence last an awkwardly long time. "No. Never before." She hadn't wanted to come right out and say it, but figured that her reply was ambiguous enough to leave plenty of room for his own interpretation.

"Season was, once," he said simply. Kerry was stunned by the comment, which was so totally opposite from where she had hoped he was leading. "I killed him."

"You did?" was all she could manage.

He sat in silence for a moment, guiding the car up the busy freeway. "That's right. He was a witch—not a terribly powerful or influential one, not in her league or mine, definitely. But probably a nice enough guy, with a few talents of his own. He fell into her sphere of influence somehow, and . . . well, you've seen her. She is a very beautiful woman."

"Yes," Kerry had to agree. "She is that."

Daniel laughed. "Not in your league, of course. But beautiful just the same." Kerry felt her cheeks warming. The thing was, she got the impression he really did feel that way. He wasn't just saying it. When he looked at her and that smile illuminated his features, he seemed to be looking at something glorious, radiant. He could have been admiring one of the world's great pieces of art. But it was Kerry he was looking at. Just Kerry.

"Anyway, he fell in love with her almost at first glance, I guess. I only pieced it all together later, from things I heard.

She came to return the feeling, and after a while—this is about two hundred years ago, I guess, in the early nineteenth century—she was as hopelessly in love with him as he was with her. They were together for a decade or so, completely wrapped up in each other. It was kind of sweet to see, but it made her weak. Distracted. Almost like she forgot we were out there, Abraham and I, looking for her."

There was really nothing Kerry could say to this, so she just tried to pay attention while her thoughts thundered along at a thousand miles an hour. *Is this a brush-off?* she wondered. *Is he telling me that he can't afford a relationship, that it's too dangerous, too distracting?*

"We found her in Philadelphia, in summer. It was hot, like this, but humid, too, I remember. Thunderstorms in the afternoons that sounded like the world was falling apart around us. She and her lover—his name was Caleb—had taken a suite of rooms in a fine hotel. But they went out at night, became part of the social scene, and of course stories spread and people talked about the beautiful stranger, and we heard about it. When we got to Philadelphia we watched the hotel for a few days, saw them coming and going, learned their routine. That was what did them in: the routine they had developed."

The freeway exit loomed, but Daniel was so involved in his story, so lost in the past, that he almost missed it. When he noticed the exit, he ticked down the turn signal and darted across three lanes of roadway, just making it.

"Sorry," he said, sounding sheepish. "What was I saying about distraction? It's a dangerous thing."

"I guess it is," Kerry agreed, a little glum.

"We're almost there so I'll make this short," he continued. "Shorter, at least. Abraham and I came to know when they would be in and when they wouldn't. One night we waited until after they had left and then we went in, enchanted the hotel staff, let ourselves into their suite. We waited. We were ready for battle, but Season . . . Season had been making love, not war, for ten years. We knew we could defeat her.

"When they came back to the room, we were ready and they were utterly surprised. Shocked. I still smile when I think about the look on her face, that beautiful face with the blue eyes so wide, the brows raised, the mouth gaping open, lip quivering. Then rage set in. And Abraham and I attacked, both at once, as we'd planned. Season and Caleb both raised defensive shields, but Caleb's wasn't strong enough. Like Season, he was out of fighting fettle, soft and complacent." Daniel's tone changed, became quieter, with an edge that sounded almost bitter, Kerry thought. "I tore him in half without even thinking about it. Literally. Cut him apart at the waist. When his torso slid off his legs and fell to the floor, I could see Season changing in front of me. She hardened, right there, as if the last decade had never happened. She turned ferocious, throwing everything she had at us. We had believed it'd be a rout, but she turned out to be far more formidable than we'd expected, especially with the fury of a love lost powering her."

"Can't really blame her for that," Kerry opined. "I'd be really ticked if . . ." She let the sentence hang, unfinished.

He didn't seem to notice, though. He let go of one hand and fingered the scar on his jaw. "From someplace she drew an enchanted blade, and she pushed—physically pushed, like someone walking through water—her way past the spells I was casting at her, and she cut me with the knife. That put me out of the fight. I was in agony, losing blood, weak—any mortal would have been dead. I went down, passed out, I guess. Meanwhile she finished up with Abraham.

"When I came to"—His voice was tight now, his eyes narrowed to slits—"Abraham was dead. In pieces, like Caleb, only more of them. It looked like she had done it fast—a few slashing blows, one that cut off his right arm at the elbow, one across the left thigh, one at his throat. I must have appeared dead to her already—not surprising, really, since I was covered in blood, and my neck was cut wide open. I woke up in a hotel suite that was drenched in blood, with the remains of my brother and Caleb scattered around me, a knife on the ground, no Season in sight, and hotel personnel staring at me. One of the men vomited on the spot, and another ran to call the police. I was wanted for decades in Philadelphia after that—probably still am, since there's no statute of limitations on murder, but it's not like anyone is still expecting to find me.

"Things got more personal between us after that," he went on. "Season and me, I mean. I had killed someone she loved;

she had done the same to me, and nearly finished me as well. However inadvertently, she had framed me for the brutal murder of my own brother. I had always hated her, thanks to my mother's stories, but now the depth of my emotion changed. I didn't just want her dead; I wanted to tear her apart with my bare hands, piece by piece, glorying in the expression of sheer agony on her face while I did it. You've heard the cliché about wanting to dance on someone's grave. I want more than that—I want to dance on her body while it's still steaming, still bloody and warm."

Daniel made the turn onto Emerald. Season's house was less than a block away. The conversational thread was worrying Kerry—instead of leading up to Daniel confessing some kind of deep feelings for her, he was, frankly, freaking her out with his talk of bloody revenge. She supposed he was steeling himself for the battle at hand, preparing himself by remembering the reasons for it. But she didn't like it at all.

He braked the car around the corner from Season's bungalow, behind Scott's RAV4, in the shade of a jacaranda tree. "Sorry, I didn't mean this to be so grim," he said as he shut off the engine. "What I really meant to say, Kerry, is that I don't want to see anything happen to you today. I don't want to repeat what happened to Season and Caleb. Now that I've found you . . . I don't want to lose you, Kerry. Ever."

Well, that's better, Kerry thought. *Not quite a declaration of undying love, but close enough for now.* She leaned over and kissed him on the cheek before she opened her door. The doors of the RAV4 opened at the same time, and Scott and Brandy stepped out. Even from the sidewalk, Kerry could feel the heat radiating from the blacktop. She blinked against the sun and scorching air.

"She's still in there," Scott reported. "Unless she's got teleportation technology or something. We've been on this end, and Josh and Rebecca are parked on the other. She hasn't budged."

"Season has a lot of talents," Daniel said seriously "Teleportation is not, to my knowledge, one of them."

"Then she's in there," Scott reiterated. "How do we get her out?"

Daniel shook his head. "*We* don't," he said forcefully. "I take it from here."

Brandy wagged a finger at him. "You got us into this, mister," she declared. "You can't just shut us out of it now."

Daniel's gaze flitted from one to the other, and even down the block where Kerry knew Rebecca and Josh were waiting for the word. "This is where it gets well and truly dangerous," Daniel said. "Deadly. I don't want you guys anywhere near here. You've done your part, and then some. Today Season Howe dies, and you can all go about the rest of your lives knowing that you've done a good thing, you've saved people you'll never meet."

Except we couldn't even save Mace, Kerry thought. "I think we want more than that, Daniel," she told him. "I know I do. After what we've been through, we want to be there for the end.

We want to see Season finished, with our own eyes. We want to help if we can."

Brandy nodded, smiling. "Bulldog's got that right."

Scott didn't look as convinced, but as usual he was willing to go along with Brandy. "It's unanimous," he announced.

"What about Josh and Rebecca?" Daniel asked. "They can still get out of here if they want to."

"You'd have to ask them," Scott replied. He handed his cell phone to Daniel. "But I have a feeling I know what they'll say."

Daniel declined the phone, but used his own and called the other two. They walked down the street and around the corner, joining the rest of the group. Kerry felt pleased that they were all together for this—all except Mace, of course, but he wouldn't have wanted anything to do with it anyway. She thought it was important, though, for reasons she couldn't even really enumerate, that they be absolutely unanimous on this one.

As it turned out, they were.

Once the vote had been made clear, Daniel relented and outlined his plan. As soon as he started describing it, Kerry realized that he had expected them to want to take part from the very beginning—that the finger-tracing he'd done on his self-printed aerial photo had taken all of them into account, not just himself. She should have known he couldn't be in all of those places at once. As he'd said of Season, he had many talents, but some things were beyond even his abilities.

Five minutes later, everyone was on the move.

21

Kerry didn't have as far to go as most of the rest. Daniel had pointed out a big red SUV halfway down the short block, almost directly in front of Season's house but across the street, and instructed her to go sit on the ground behind it—right at the rear wheels, so Season wouldn't see her feet beneath the vehicle. Scott and Brandy hopped back in the RAV4 and drove past Season's place, then around the block. An alley bisected the block, lengthwise. Because Season's place was on the short connecting block between the main streets of Emerald and Felspar, the alley ran beside the fence enclosing her yard. They parked the car and got out, positioning themselves so they could see the whole line of Season's back fence. If she tried to run, they'd see her.

Not that they could stop her, at least not for long. But, as Daniel pointed out, all they had to do was slow her down.

It was, they all knew, potentially the most dangerous thing they'd ever attempted. Kerry found herself swallowing, again and again, as if her terror was something stuck in her throat. But it wouldn't go away. She felt cold and raw, like she'd been through a punishing hailstorm.

When Brandy and Scott were in place, a quick text alerted the others. Daniel started Rebecca and Josh on their way— what Josh called the Long Walk—down the block to take up positions at the front corners of Season's yard. While they walked, Daniel tossed Kerry a grin, blew her a kiss, and went to take his own position on the far side of a gray sedan parked on the street in front of the house next to Season's, on the corner of Emerald and Everts. Like Kerry, he ducked down behind the car, hidden from Season's view by the wheels. The dark sky of gloaming made hiding all the easier.

When they were all in position, Daniel gave Rebecca and Josh the high sign. Standing at the corners of her yard, they began to call her name. "Season," they chanted. "Season Howe."

Hearing the chant begin, Brandy and Scott picked it up at the rear of the house. Within moments, all four were calling in unison. "Season. Season Howe."

"When she hears her name, she'll scan you from inside the house," Daniel had warned them. "She'll know that you don't have any magical abilities, though. I'm counting on her being too curious to resist checking you out further, to see what's going on, how you know who she is. She'll come outside."

Apparently Daniel knew her well. Kerry couldn't see what was going on—she was under strict orders not to make any part of herself visible to Season—but at one point, shortly after the four-part harmony kicked in, she thought Josh's voice caught, and then a moment later Rebecca's did the same. *She's scanning them,* Kerry realized with dismay, *and they can feel it. Feel her digging around inside them.*

Ick.

The chanting continued for another thirty seconds or so. Kerry had been worried that other neighbors would freak out at this undeniably odd behavior and call the police or interfere themselves. Daniel had assured her that it wouldn't be a problem, and she hadn't been anxious for him to elaborate on that.

So when she heard a door open and then close, she was pretty sure that it was Season. Doubly so when she heard the woman's voice.

"Who are you? What do you want?"

She would, Daniel had warned, be on full alert when she came outside. She would obviously know that something was going on, that her cover had been blown, but at first she wouldn't know why and by whom. The key to taking her was to keep her off guard, keep her wondering just what was happening, and not to let her raise the proper defense in time.

Now she was outside, though, and that was Kerry's cue. She could barely get her legs to cooperate, and her hands were shaking like crazy, flopping around like two fish on a line. But finally she got her appendages in order and emerged from behind the SUV. When she spoke, her voice even surprised her with the authority she managed to put into it.

"We're here for you, Season Howe," she said. "We know who you are. We know what you are. And we're here to make sure this is your last day on Earth."

The witch was standing on her front porch. Now, she turned to face Kerry. A storm of emotion washed across Season's beautiful face. A moment of shock when she recognized Kerry, or at least a realization that she had seen her before. That was followed by amusement, when, Kerry believed, she understood that she was being called out by five powerless mortals who hadn't even come bearing traditional weapons much less mystical ones. Kerry was gratified by what looked like a moment of doubt, as if she was second-guessing herself, wondering if these five were as powerless as they looked, because if they were, how would they have dared to confront her?

But her face settled into anger, clouded and red, as she regarded Kerry across the street. "I know you," she said, her voice quaking with rage. "You . . . you were with him. With Daniel Blessing."

"That's right," Kerry answered. This part hadn't been scripted, and she was winging it. But she felt emboldened by Season's anger—the witch wouldn't be so mad if she wasn't concerned, she figured.

And she has every reason to be concerned.

Season stepped down from her porch, beckoning Kerry with one crooked finger. "Come here," she commanded. "I want to talk to you."

Kerry maintained her position next to the SUV, so she could duck behind it for cover at any moment. She didn't have to wait long, though. As soon as Season's shoe clicked on the sidewalk in front of her house, Daniel made his move.

He rose up from behind the gray car like a jack-in-the-box. Spoke one of the words that Kerry still couldn't understand, but which Daniel had told her were in an incredibly ancient tongue, long since forgotten by most humans. Made a hurling motion with both hands toward Season, who only now noticed his presence. Again, her expression changed rapidly, rotating through a variety of emotions—surprise, fear, fury—in the space of a quarter second.

That was all the time she had.

Formed from empty air, picking up apparent mass and force as it went, Daniel's spell had created, manifested, or otherwise brought into being a roiling ball of pure energy At least that's what it looked like to Kerry's admittedly untutored eye. Transparent, it seemed to warp the view behind it, the way heat shimmers the scenery on a summer day. She could only see its outline by watching where the background was clear and where it wavered and shifted.

Season barely had time to register it before the energy ball struck her with a sound like a thunderclap.

The force of the impact drove her to her knees, blasting

her hair like a hurricane wind, shredding her blouse. When it was past she glared up at Daniel with fire in her eyes, a thin trickle of blood running from the corner of her mouth.

And another one hit her, laying her out on her back.

Season swore, scrabbled to turn over, to regain her footing. The next one slammed into her before she could stand steadily, but when she went down this time, it was on her stomach.

Daniel kept up the attack. Kerry watched in dumfounded horror. The destructive potential contained inside Daniel had always been theoretical to her—potential, not actual. Seeing it at work was terrifying. She knew it was for the best possible reasons, knew it had to be done.

But that didn't make it easy to watch.

Daniel changed weapons now. Instead of the roiling energy balls, he spoke different words of the ancient language, and bolts of violet lightning seemed to issue from his fingertips, blasting at Season like the weapons of Zeus. Where they struck her, her clothing tore, her skin smoldered.

Still, she lived.

Still, she fixed Daniel Blessing with a murderous glare.

She hadn't had a chance since he had launched his attack to counterattack. He had never let up, not for a moment. His plan, simple as it was, had worked to the letter.

Season Howe was finished, Kerry thought. Daniel had fulfilled his lifelong goal.

Finally, after what seemed an unbearably long and torturous assault, Season was still.

She lay on the walkway leading up to her front steps. Blood streaked the pale cement. Her body looked, in the pale remnants of daylight, as if it had lost an endurance contest with a threshing machine: cuts and tears everywhere, clothing ribboned.

Kerry started toward her, but Daniel waved her away. She glanced around, saw that Brandy and Scott had come up from the back and joined Rebecca and Josh in the street. Brandy's eyes were wide and glittering with fear—at last, Kerry understood, even she believed what the rest already accepted. Kerry would go stand with them, she decided, and wait for Daniel's all clear.

It never came.

Season was dead, anyone could see that. She'd stopped moving long before, except for involuntary motions, her body buffeted about by the force of Daniel's attack. Even then, he had not let up. Finally she was as limp as BoBo, the rag-doll clown Kerry had slept with from the time she was three until after her mother got sick, when Kerry had decided it was time to grow up, to stop playing with toys, because she was the only functional person left in the house.

Still, Daniel approached her with caution. Stood a dozen feet from her and watched the body, looking for any sign of breath, of life. Satisfied, he moved closer. Stopped, watched again. Closer.

Finally crouched over her. Touched her shoulder, rocking her over, onto her back, and releasing.

Limp. Lifeless.

Kerry knew Daniel by now, knew him well enough to recognize the look of relief that washed across his face. Relief, and something else.

Accomplishment. He had done it. *They* had done it—distracted her, made her forget to look for the real threat.

Daniel locked eyes with Kerry, smiling. Kerry tried to look into those eyes, from this distance, tried to tell him with her own gaze that she loved him. That she always had, somehow, from that first night. That she always would.

So neither one of them noticed that the witch moved her hand—just a simple move, really, a flick of the wrist, almost casual. An observer might have thought it was a postmortem reflex.

But it wasn't. There was purpose behind it. Season's lips moved at the same time, uttering an ancient phrase of her own.

And Season's attack, at such close range—even through her own pain, her own seeming defeat—was devastating.

One second Kerry was looking into Daniel's gray eyes and the next, those eyes were scrunched shut, his face twisted in agony, his knees buckling. *Oh, no,* Kerry thought, but the rest of her thought was wordless, just fear piled upon horror upon the misery of seeing the man she loved brought down by a sudden, treacherous blow.

Season moved again, not much more than a twitch—this time, Kerry watched her, a soundless scream on her lips—and again, Daniel was wracked with pain. He fell to his hands and knees in Season's yard, still facing away from her, toward Kerry. His head hung down toward the lawn but he raised it, his gaze meeting Kerry's once again, holding it, and he was trying to mouth something to her when Season struck a third time.

The last time.

Season managed to push herself to her own knees now, and clearly she wasn't dead, after all—should have been, anyone else would have been, but not her. Her face contorted in rage and she moved both hands this time, mouth speaking words Kerry couldn't even hear over the thunderous roar that accompanied her motion, and Daniel—

Kerry tried to focus on his eyes, those warm, loving eyes, not on the rest of it.

—and Daniel let out a last cry, a wail of loss and longing, as Season's blast crushed him like a squirrel under the wheel of a semitruck. His body collapsed, his spine splintered, his limbs suddenly giving out, blood jetting in every direction, landing with a wet splatter like a lawn sprinkler. His eyes shone for a brief moment and then closed, and with a final shudder he fell onto the grass.

And Season stood, rose up to her full height, fists clenched, face still showing traces of anger but also something else, something that looked like sorrow, and she ignored the others huddled in the street, looking only at Kerry.

Kerry swallowed. Season had defeated Daniel—*killed Daniel,* she corrected herself, she never wanted to let go of that knowledge. She would never forgive Season for that. But at the same time, she didn't exactly want Season to unleash that power against her.

Season didn't. Instead she spoke words Kerry could comprehend, though it took her a few moments to track them, to realize what the witch was saying to her.

"This is done now," Season said without preamble. "This was between me and Daniel Blessing. At long last, it's over. He lost. I won. That's all there is to it. Go now, and don't concern yourselves any longer with issues far beyond your ken. Know that I could easily do to you as I did to him, but I'm not. I won't. Just go."

"But . . . ," Kerry began. "You . . . you killed him."

"As he very nearly did me." Season crossed her arms defiantly across her chest. "Go. Before I lose patience."

"He . . ." Kerry felt hands on her arm. Rebecca's voice whispered to her.

"Kerry, for God's sake let's get out of here. You saw—"

"I saw."

"—what she did to Daniel. We can't fight her. Come on."

"But . . ."

"She's right," Josh said. "This is lose-lose. Cut your losses and let's go."

Now there were other hands on her, tugging on her. In her yard, standing over Daniel's lifeless form, Season nodded her head. She looked almost sympathetic now, as if she understood what Kerry was feeling.

Maybe she did. Kerry remembered the story Daniel had told, just a few minutes ago, really, about Caleb. The one man Season had loved.

Maybe she'd just had her long-delayed revenge for that.

Well, Kerry thought, *revenge can go two ways.* She let the hands tug her away, toward the waiting car.

Away from Daniel, and Season.

Her eyes filled with tears, her heart with sorrow.

Daniel . . .

Kerry Profitt's diary, September 1

I'm writing this at 33,000 feet, scrunched into the window seat of a 737, nonstop from San Diego to Chicago. The guy next to me is snoring, his bulk slopping over the armrest into my space. It's a red-eye, of course—only appropriate, given my bloodshot, puffy peepers. The plan is to meet Aunt Betty and Uncle Marsh in Chicago, then spend a couple of days there together before I go on to Northwestern. I'm hoping that we'll be able to fill the days—Field Museum, shopping on the Miracle Mile, pizza at Gino's East, coffee in Wicker Park, etc.—enough so that B & M won't fight with each other, or me, too much.

I called Aunt Betty and asked her to bring a few things from the house with her, most especially BoBo the clown. I'm feeling the need for some comforting, some retreat, some healing. Hoping he can help with that.

It took us a couple of days to get past what had

happened enough to clear out of the apartment and separate. Josh off to UNLV, Rebecca to UC Santa Cruz, Scott and Brandy beginning the long cross-country drive back to Harvard. And me, on a plane to O'Hare, and a life that suddenly feels like someone else's, not at all like the me I expected a month ago to see sitting on that plane in the dark. !n my suitcase, along with my clothes and a couple of personal things, are Daniel's journals, all of them that I could find, anyway. And the letter.

Oh yeah, the letter.

It was on my pillow when I got home that night. It had not been there when I left the apartment—I was in the bedroom last, and Daniel didn't go in at all after coming out from his "preparations" in his room. So, no letter then.

But letter after. Go figure. Daniel has his ways.

It's not long, and of course I've read it so many times it's committed to memory. But considering the way it came into being, who knows when it might vanish again? So I'll put it down here, and if I have a word or two wrong I'll correct it later.

Dearest Kerry,

I liked the way that looked, and read it several times, right off the bat. Even spoke the words out loud, much to Rebecca's surprise. Plus, I was not looking forward to the rest of it, since I was pretty convinced it wasn't good news.

Dearest Kerry,

If you see this letter, it means I did not beat Season after all, and that she destroyed me. If you had to watch that—and, knowing you, I'm guessing you did; certain I couldn't dissuade you if you had put your mind to it—I am sorrier than you will ever know.

It was, of course, never my intent to involve you in this whole business. My fight, not yours, and all of that. Still, since we were thrown together, by fate or whatever you might choose to name it, I am proud and honored that you chose to throw in your lot with me.

But now it's over for you. I know you'll be angry at Season, and sad to have lost me, but please, please don't get it into your head that you can somehow avenge my death. I think I told you once that Season is quite possibly the most powerful of us. I had a chance, though a slim one, and apparently not a good enough one. You wouldn't. You are a remarkable woman, wise and mature and breathtakingly lovely, but you wouldn't last ten seconds against Season Howe.

So put this summer's experiences into your box of memories. Treasure the brief time we had together. Mourn me for a short while, and then get on with the rest of your life. It will be an incredible adventure, and I only wish I could be there to share it with you.

Death, Kerry, is not the end. It's a passage, a process. In some fashion I will be forever with you, and you will always be a part of me.

In life, though I never said it—I didn't want you to feel any obligation to me, and I knew that our time together might be short and end brutally—I loved you. In death, I love you still.

So, forward! Aspire! Achieve!

I remain,

Daniel Blessing

Yeah . . . so what do you do with that?

Captain just announced that he's beginning our descent. In another few minutes, laptops will have to be put away, tray tables stowed, and all that stuff. Then Aunt Betty and Uncle Marsh will be there, and then college. Endings, beginnings. Passages.

More later.

K.

FALL

Kerry Profitt's diary, October 14

So, okay, college? Not exactly what I figured it'd be.

I mean, the campus is nice, the classes moderately interesting. My favorite is an American history lecture from one Dr. Page Manning, who is not only a terrific and often funny speaker, but can really make the subject come alive.

Not in the way that Daniel Blessing could, of course. But then, Daniel lived a lot more of it. I think it is his influence, though, that inspired me to take the class in the first place, letting me see history in a way that I never had, as something more than just dates and battles and the names of dead white men. I'm thinking about it as a major.

Minoring in depression, I guess.

I miss him SO much. Like I said, college is okay, but it's full of skimpy-outfitted Rihannas and baggy-pantsed, backward-hat boys trying to grow goatees and personalities at the same time, and after what I went through this summer, what WE went through, Scott and Brandy and Rebecca and Josh and poor Mace, and me—and Daniel, who, like Mace, paid the ultimate price—sitting in lecture halls, taking notes, doing homework in the dorm . . . it all just seems so tame. So removed from the rest of the world.

Not that I'd know what the rest of the world was really like, having spent most of my life removed from it by one thing or another. But still, you know.

It's like the summer was in Technicolor and campus life is in sepia tones. Washed out sepia, at that. I keep finding my mind flashing back to San Diego, to the hunt for Season Howe that consumed us all. And to the final battle that Daniel didn't survive.

I don't know where Season is now, obviously. I couldn't fight her if I did. But I feel like if I saw her today, I'd rip her apart with my bare hands, so pumped up with righteous wrath that she couldn't begin to hold me back.

The nightmares haven't come back, so that's one small blessing (a word I have to remember not to capitalize, or to precede with "Daniel" on certain occasions). But my waking thoughts are so dark, so violent, sometimes so hopeless, that it's hard to see the difference.

No, I take that back. I never really knew where the nightmares came from. I know perfectly well where this darkness originates, though. It comes from having watched the man I love get killed. Murdered, right in front of me, by an evil witch named Season Howe.

And some day, somehow, she's going to pay.

More later.
K.

1

K erry?"

Kerry Profitt tore her gaze away from the screen of her laptop. She had lost focus anyway, the words she'd been typing blurred behind a film of tears. "Yeah?"

Sonya, her roommate in Northwestern University's Elder Hall, looked at her from her own desk with motherly concern. Sonya's eyes were big and brown, accentuated all the more by small-lensed but thick glasses and an expression of perpetual curiosity, as if she were a visitor to this world, trying to take in everything at a single glance. Sonya tugged a lock of her short, dark hair away from her cheek and positioned it behind her ear. "You okay?" she asked.

"Yeah, I'm . . . you know. Fine."

"Because you don't look so okay," Sonya went on. "What with the tears kind of splashing on your keyboard, I thought maybe there was something bothering you."

"Well, I guess maybe a little," Kerry admitted. She hadn't given Sonya the What-I-Did-On-My-Summer-Vacation talk, not expecting that her roommate, or, when it came right down to it, anyone else, would believe a word of it. And maybe it'd be worse if they did believe it, because she knew how hard it was to deal with the fact that the world was so much different than she had thought it was. Things she had always believed to be unreal, to be fantasy, had turned out to be absolutely true. It made "real" life seem like a cartoon, like someone else's version of reality. Why force that knowledge onto others?

She had, to cover her sometimes abrupt moments of grieving, told Sonya about the deaths of her parents, and said that they had been topped off by the death of a boyfriend over the summer. She just avoided the minor details, such as precisely how the boyfriend had died, and the fact that he had been a very powerful witch who was almost three hundred years old.

"Daniel?" Sonya asked.

Kerry nodded. "I miss him. A whole lot."

Sonya turned in her chair, and Kerry thought she was about to give her the You've-Got-To-Move-On-With-Your-Life lecture again. But Sonya was wise enough to catch the way that Kerry tensed—a pose that said, *If you start that again I will pummel you*—and she restrained herself. "I'm going out with Dougie and Ben," she said instead, naming the two guys she was juggling, though it seemed that Dougie was winning out. "Maybe get some falafel, have a beer. You want to come?"

Kerry appreciated the invitation, and said so. "But I'll stay in," she added. "I still have a bunch of homework to get done before tomorrow."

Sonya shrugged. "As long as you're really doing homework," she said, "and not sitting here by yourself moping."

"No," Kerry tried to assure her. "I'm okay, really."

The truth was she didn't want to have falafel and beer with Dougie and Ben and Sonya. Their interests were not hers, their lives seemed flat and boring somehow. They would talk about professors and classmates, or the latest band that had captured their fancy, or they'd dis some style they hadn't taken up yet but would soon. She'd been part of such conversations in the past, and probably would be again—she remembered, with some fondness, how all she'd wanted at the beginning of the summer was to have a "normal" life, like everyone else's. Now she had an opportunity to have just that, and it couldn't have held less interest for her.

"You say so." Sonya gave her short hair a little flip, pulled a jacket off a hook by the door, and left.

The room, with Sonya out of it, suddenly felt twice its real size. She was a perfectly nice girl, but her presence in the room seemed to suck the air out of it. Kerry knew it was her own fault, not Sonya's—anyone else would be glad to have Sonya for a roommate. *I'm spoiled,* she thought, *that's what it is. I want Daniel, or nothing at all.*

She wondered if it was stupid to spend her life wishing for things she couldn't have. It probably was, she decided—a huge waste of time and energy. Trouble was, she didn't know quite what she could do about it. She was who she was, and if there was a way to change that she didn't know it.

She went to the window and looked at the campus spread out below her third-floor window. Trees flamed yellow and red in the glow cast by streetlights and spilling from the dorm. The Illinois air was crisp but not yet cold—jackets were required at night, but the days were still warm enough for shirts and the occasional sweater. She had always liked this time of year, before—the cool evenings, the back-to-school excitement, then the Halloween season that led to football games and Thanksgiving and Christmas. Even now she could feel herself wanting to be caught up in it.

But if you have to want it, she thought sadly, *it's not really happening, is it? More wishing, that's all.*

I wish I didn't wish so much.

Rebecca Levine soaked in the big clawfooted bathtub of the house she and her friend Erin had rented near downtown Santa Cruz before summer break started. It wasn't much of a house—a run-down Victorian with faded green paint, floorboards that creaked like something from a horror movie, and wiring she was convinced would someday burn the whole thing to the ground. But they had a cat, and the plumbing worked fine and the water in the tub was steaming hot, and she had placed scented candles around the room before she got in. At some point Erin would yell at her to get out because they only had the one bathroom, but until that happened she'd make the most of it.

She had always loved baths, but during the last month of summer she hadn't had much opportunity to indulge. Too much had been going on—and it had been so sad. Now that it was all over, at least for her, she was trying to make up for August's privation. It had taken her a couple of weeks just to relax enough to do it, not to jump every time there was an unexpected noise or a shadow fell across her path. She still wasn't back to what she considered routine, and didn't know if she ever would be. But she was determined not to let that prevent her from indulging herself whenever she could.

Sleep? That was hard to come by, at least sleep uninterrupted by horrible visions and memories of Mace and Daniel and Season Howe. But in here, wet and steamy and alone, she could relax, let her mind float to happy places. Private sandy beaches, mountains thrusting up from canopied jungles, sidewalk cafés on wide Parisian boulevards . . . these were comforting images for Rebecca, and comfort was what she needed most. Holding Reynolds, their mutt of an alley cat, and feeling the motor of his purr while she read helped too. She'd gained almost ten pounds in the last couple of weeks, thanks to the comfort foods she had allowed herself. While she had never been skinny or cared that she wasn't, she recognized that eating her way to sanity was never going to work. So, the baths, the pampering, the self-indulgence.

Her classes this semester were pretty cool, though she was having a hard time getting into them. She was taking a poli sci class focusing on twentieth-century American political history, an introductory psych class, and an entomology class, figuring that the only way to get over a lifelong fear of bugs was to learn more about them. No luck on that, so far. Actually, knowing what insects could do to people only beefed up that particular phobia. At the same time, though, being afraid of creepy-crawlies at least took some of the edge off being afraid that Season Howe might come around at any time.

Rebecca breathed deeply, inhaling the aroma of the lilac-scented bath water and the vanilla candle nearest the tub. She luxuriated in the tactile sensation of the hot water against her skin and tried to push aside all other thoughts and cares.

If only she didn't ever have to come out . . .

"Pop-Tart?"

"Eeew," Brandy said, just as Scott had known she would. "How can you put that stuff in your body?"

He took a bite and spoke with his mouth full, letting crumbs spill out over his lips. "Kind of like this," he said, facing her and enjoying the way her pretty face twisted in revulsion. This one was strawberry, and fresh from the toaster so the filling was especially soft and gooey. She waved him away from her with an urgent motion.

"Yuck! Go away!"

Instead, he lowered his head toward hers, crumbs dropping onto the chemistry text spread in front of her on their dining room table. "Kiss me, baby," he demanded around the mouthful. "Gimme some sugar."

Now Brandy physically pushed him away, her hand against his shoulder. "All the sugar you're getting is already in your mouth," she told him.

Scott decided the joke had gone far enough and he turned away, finishing the bite in a more mannerly fashion. He loved to gross her out because she was such an easy target, but he knew that her tolerance for it was very limited, and on those occasions when he'd pushed too much her reaction had changed from good-humored to genuinely furious without notice. And a furious Brandy Pearson was a sight that Scott Banner didn't want to see too many times in his life.

"Sorry, babe," he said after he'd swallowed and chased the mouthful with a drink of water.

"Sure you are." Her words were clipped, her tone honestly angry. If he hadn't gone over the edge he'd come close to it, that was for sure.

"I'm just teasing, you know that."

"That kind of teasing I can do without."

Brandy had changed, Scott thought, since the summer. Her sense of humor—never her strongest suit to begin with—had diminished somehow, as if life just wasn't as funny as it had once been. He liked it when she laughed, loved the contrast between her even white teeth and her dark face, but these days it happened less and less. Although she had thrown herself into her studies at Harvard, she didn't seem any more removed from him—they held hands as they walked across campus just as they'd done before, they made love from time to time, they kissed when they parted and when they reunited. But the not-laughing thing bothered him, more than he wanted to admit even to himself.

He touched her shoulder gently. "I know. I'm sorry," he said again. He hoped he sounded sincere. The other thing about Brandy—*okay,* he realized, *this has always been true, but more so since the summer*—was that he really hated to be on her bad side. Not just because he loved her and wanted to make her happy, but because she was a little scary when she was angry. He'd seen the power of rage now—Season Howe had demonstrated that—and Brandy was nowhere near that kind of level. But still, Scott guessed, he was a little gun-shy.

"Just . . . try to be an adult," she admonished him. "Pretend, anyway."

The rest of their apartment was dark, the only lights burning the ones in the dining area, where they did most of their studying. The table was almost lost under mounds of books and papers, with precious little space left for actual dining. A living room opened onto the dining area, with a computer, TV, and stereo system, and past that their cramped bedroom waited. Scott knew that he needed to put some space between them right now—space and time. If he turned on the TV or music, though, she'd complain that it was interfering with her studying. Instead, he grabbed a short-story anthology off one of the stacks on the table. "I'm going to read for a while," he said, and headed toward the bedroom, where he could find solitude and solace until she decided to join him.

Space. And time.

UNLV would have usurped all of Josh Quinn's time if he'd let it, but the casinos beckoned, and he couldn't bring himself to ignore their call. Every time he saw them, neon shining so bright that the stars dimmed, he felt like Ulysses tied to the mast, trying to resist the sirens.

But there was no one to bind Josh down, and Ulysses hadn't fared all that well either, come to think of it. So whenever he didn't need to be in class—and sometimes when he did—Josh found himself haunting the Strip or the older casinos downtown. *Ocean's 11* country—the original, not the lame remake. On this night, that's where he was, downtown at the Golden Nugget, enveloped in a soundtrack of bells and buzzers and clanging coins. He was too young to gamble by a few years but he had a fake ID that no one ever checked. He didn't have much money to risk at the best of times, and this was not the best of times, so he resigned himself to video poker. It was hard to win big at that, but it was possible to play for a long time on a ten-dollar roll of quarters.

He'd been sitting at the machine for almost forty minutes, puffing on a succession of smokes, feeding the coins in one or two at a time, playing his hands with as much care as he could, considering the machine was also the dealer. He punched the deal button and was dealt two fives—hearts and clubs—the jack of spades, ten of hearts, and seven of diamonds. A nothing hand, pretty much, and he'd blown two quarters on it. Two hearts . . . he could shoot for a flush but that was almost a guaranteed loser. He had a pair, but that wouldn't net him much. Keep the jack and dump the rest?

Finally he kept the two fives, pathetic as they were, and drew three new cards. Nine of spades and two eights. Now with two pair, the machine paid off. Still small change, but it would keep him going for a while.

If he ran out of money then he'd have to start the long walk back home. And if he did that, walking through the shadowed streets away from the lights and the action, then he'd think about her. About Season, and how she'd ripped the life from Daniel Blessing.

He didn't want to think about that. Instead, he fed two more quarters into the slot.

2

Home again, after far too long. The journey was an arduous one, as I had been in San Francisco when I received Mother Blessing's urgent summons. Urgent or no, one can only cross this great nation at a certain speed, even by railroad. Arriving at Norfolk, I hired a carriage and drove to the old Slocumb site, where she keeps a skiff for precisely such visits.

Great Dismal Swamp greeted me as it always does, and this was my first real indication that I had indeed come home. The smells of the brackish water and the white cedar, the screams and cries of blackbirds, warblers, and robins, the mechanical knocking of woodpeckers, the incessant drone of mosquitoes: All these things brought a rush of memory to my mind, memories of my youth growing up among these marshes and bogs, learning the craft at Mother Blessing's side. No matter where I travel—to the jagged peaks of the Rocky Mountains, the softly sculpted dunes of Arabia, the villages of Europe—Great Dismal's walls of trees and thick cover of ferns, mosses, camellia, and dwarf trillium remain the standard of natural beauty in my heart.

As I poled the skiff through the swamp, I watched for the long-missed but always-remembered landmarks—the lightning-split oak, the stand of bald cypress shaped like the corner of a log fort, the trio of stumps rumored to have been cut by George Washington himself, rising up from the water like swimmers seeking air—that would presently lead me to Mother Blessing's cabin.

Soon enough, I was here, and that is when I learned the reason for her call. Mother Blessing lay atop her bed, flushed and fevered, writhing and thrashing in evident pain. I quickly performed a healing spell, glad that even through her delirium, she had been able to reach out to me in time. My spell calmed her and broke her fever, and before long she was sleeping soundly.

While waiting for her to recover, I cleaned the cabin, which had been clearly suffering from neglect *due to her illness. By evening she was awake and alert enough to drink some broth I had prepared for her, and to take a cup of tea. After she had her strength back a bit, she told me that a witch down in South Carolina had cursed her after they'd had a disagreement over some small matter.*

I write this now by candlelight, with Mother Blessing asleep again in her room, snoring softly. My spells have helped her, and she is of course powerful enough to help herself now that she's on her guard. But tomorrow I must leave for South Carolina, to find the witch and make her remove the curse.

Or else I shall have to kill her. Either way will work.

I remain,

Daniel Blessing, April 7, 1881

Kerry had just shut the journal and replaced the leather thong that held it closed when Sonya and Dougie entered, arm in arm, laughing at some joke Kerry wasn't privy to. "Hey, Kerry," Dougie said by way of greeting. "That doesn't look like any textbook I've ever seen. What is it?"

"It's an old journal," Kerry replied, not wanting to reveal any more than that. Dougie annoyed her—she considered him a typical frat boy but without the frat, all about using his college years to drink and party and have a good time, knowing that at the end of it his degree and his father's connections would guarantee him a good job even if he never set foot in a classroom. She didn't quite know what Sonya saw in him, but then she didn't know Sonya well enough to speculate.

He disentangled himself from Sonya and reached for it. "Lemme see."

Kerry jerked it away from his grasping hands. "It's very old," she insisted, "and fragile."

Dougie screwed his blunt, good-old-boy features into a mask of hurt. "Jeez, I wasn't gonna damage it," he declared. "I just wanted to look at it."

"Kerry's pretty protective of her stuff," Sonya told him. Kerry noted her tone, as if she were talking about someone who wasn't in the room.

"Just the stuff that needs protecting," she countered. "This journal is more than a hundred years old, and the paper is brittle. I can't let anything happen to it."

"It's okay, Kerry—chill," Sonya chided. "No one's going to mess with it. Dougie's just having fun."

"More than you are, it looks like," Dougie added. "Looks like you need a boyfriend, Kerry. You shouldn't be sitting around here on a Saturday night with some moldy old book."

"You don't have to worry about me," Kerry answered, wishing he'd just go away. She sat on her bed and picked up BoBo, her old childhood rag-doll clown. "I'm fine."

"Tell you the truth, Kerry," Sonya said, dropping her voice to a conspiratorial level, "we were kind of hoping you had gone out for a while, if you know what I mean."

Sonya's meaning couldn't have been more clear. *But do I want to do her that favor?* Kerry asked herself. *Do I want to clear out of my own room so she and her horndog boyfriend can have their fun . . . and maybe paw through my stuff—even Daniel's journals—when they're done?*

Resigned, she gathered up the things she'd need to spend an hour in the common area. For about the millionth time since the semester had started, she wished she had a private room.

By the time she had settled on one of the couches in the third-floor lounge, Kerry was fuming. Two girls she knew vaguely shared another couch and spoke in hushed tones about a project they were working on together, but blessedly the TV was off and the faint smell of microwave popcorn that hung in the air when she entered dissipated quickly. She made it clear that she was there to study, not socialize, and she buried herself in the American history text that she should have been reading instead of Daniel's journal. The words seemed dry and lifeless to her, though, especially compared to the journals, or even more, to Daniel's voice, telling her things about her nation's past that had never made it into the history books.

Kerry was trying, really and truly, to immerse herself in school, to put Daniel and Season and the rest of it behind her. And Kerry was someone who did what she put her mind to—they hadn't called her Bulldog over the summer for nothing. So why couldn't she just focus on the work? Why did images of Daniel pop up, unbidden, every time her mind wandered? Why did she keep seeing Season in every blond woman on campus?

The whole situation was just incredibly frustrating. She turned back to the history text and tried to read about the landing at Plymouth Rock, but the words turned to fuzz before her eyes.

Daniel was there, in her dream, looking just as he had in life. His long-sleeved white shirt was clean and crisp, tucked into faded jeans, the sleeves rolled back a couple of times over muscular forearms. His hair was long and windblown, and he was laughing, head thrown back, mouth open, teeth even and white, gray eyes crinkled at the corners and dimples etched into his cheeks. He stood on a hill, at a slight distance from Kerry; she couldn't reach him or even hear his laughter, which should have been booming.

She moved closer to him, or tried to. But for every step forward she took, the hilltop on which he stood seemed to move back. She tried calling out to him, shouting his name, but even her own voice vanished before it reached her ears.

Then a fog rolled in, as if from offshore—thick and wet, blotting out the view, blocking Daniel, then the entire hillside. Within seconds Kerry was alone, an island in a sea of white mist. Then even she was gone, the mist breaking her body into ever smaller chunks until it had disappeared completely.

Kerry Profitt's diary, October 21

And again with the nightmares, now. All I need, right? Having gotten rid of them once—thanks, I am now convinced, to the appearance of Daniel in my life—they are back, and, it seems, with a vengeance. This one wasn't even all that scary in itself—I mean, the imagery wasn't—but the overall feel of it creeped me out big time. Especially the way that Daniel was there, and then he wasn't, and . . .

Oh, never mind. It's different from the dreams I used to have, which I forgot as soon as they ended. And a year from now I won't remember what the dream was, and this entry will make no sense.

Which distinguishes it from the rest of my life how, exactly?

Now Sonya is sleeping hard and I am wide awake, pretty much giving up on the idea of sleeping tonight. And since it's fresh in my mind, I can't stop thinking about the dream.

Its meaning? Obvious, I think. I miss Daniel. He was taken from me. Duh. Bonehead psych, no-brainer.

The part where I disappear? A little tougher, that. Losing my identity? Maybe.

And maybe I should e-mail Brandy for a more comprehensive analysis. She's the doc, after all. I have her addy—we all have each other's, and have sent a few around since splitting up back in SD after the summer.

But not as much as I thought we might, almost as if everyone wants to forget what happened, wants to leave Season and Daniel and the summer of our discontent well behind.

And really, who can blame 'em for that? It pretty much sucked. Find a great guy, and he dies. Find out witchcraft is real and scarier than you ever imagined, and the baddest witch around has it in for your new BF. Find out he's been chasing her for almost 300 years, so you help him catch her, only to watch her kill him.

Yeah, summer means fun.

Okay, here's the thing. School is just not happening for me. Sonya . . . ditto. Aunt Betty and Uncle Marsh check in from time to time, but I could be gone from here for a month before they knew it. So really, what's keeping me here? Lack of someplace better to go?

Only, see, I have an idea about that, too.

I've been reading Daniel's journals. That's just about the only thing that's held my interest, in fact. And Daniel is lost to me.

But that doesn't mean that part of my life has to be lost. Mother Blessing is out there, in the Great Dismal Swamp. Season Howe is out there too, still at large, and now owing for yet another crime.

One that I take just a little bit personally.

So here's my theory. I find Mother Blessing, convince

her to teach me witchcraft, and then I hunt down Season
Howe and give her what she deserves.

Nothing to it, right?

But did I mention people call me Bulldog?

More later.

K.

3

McKinley's policies, particularly his unwavering support of the gold standard, helped build confidence among business-people and limited the effects of the depression," Professor Crain declared. "Which, incidentally, cemented Republican domination until the 1930s, at which time they lost it, largely due to the much greater Depression, which had been the ultimate result. Short term, the economy seemed to be doing well. But the truth was, that period was called the Gilded Age for a reason. The rich got richer and the poor became ever more destitute, and the gulf between them had never been greater. Long term, that helped lead to a financial collapse that was the most catastrophic in our nation's history."

Rebecca tried to take careful notes when Professor Crain spoke. She had already learned that he mingled historical fact with personal opinion in his lectures, and while he welcomed analysis that differed from his, one had better be prepared to back up one's differences. In any case, she found herself agreeing with him more often that not. Word was, on almost any other college campus he'd have a reputation as a bit of an ideologue, but this was UC Santa Cruz, where nonconformity was the norm and strong opinions were highly valued.

Anyway, his lectures were always stimulating, and the difficulty of his essay tests, while legendary, helped keep her interested. Lately, she'd been having a harder and harder time even getting out of bed in the morning. Reynolds, their cat, had taken to sleeping on the bed with her in the mornings, and as the year progressed and the weather cooled, the cozy comfort of her quilt with a purring cat pressed against her became more and more difficult to leave. Knowing that to miss even one of Professor Crain's lectures would lead to certain disaster come midterms helped spur her up and out of the house. Three afternoons a week, after class, she worked at a local coffee shop called the Human Bean, and that was the other motivating element—if she couldn't make it to school, she likely wouldn't make work either, and she'd be fired long before she flunked out.

After class she stepped from the lecture hall, blinking in the bright sunshine. Hector Gonzales, a classmate she'd become friendly with, followed her outside. "Party tonight," he said as he sidled up beside her. "You got anything going on?"

She didn't. "I don't know if I'm up for a party," she said vaguely.

"It'll be fun. Two kegs, limited guest list—it's at a private house, some friends of mine. Not a frat kind of thing."

She knew that her hesitation stemmed from the same root as her disinterest in leaving the safety of her own bed. One never knew what might happen, around which corner doom might lurk. She'd never been brave, but she also hadn't thought of herself as a fearful person. She was well on her way to becoming one, though. She didn't want to turn into one of those people who were afraid to leave their own homes, but she felt that she was heading down that road. If she never left the safety of her room, she would be okay. It was other people, other places that were dangerous. She didn't want to become antisocial, but if that was the only way to stay safe . . .

She shook her head violently, and when she looked back at Hector he was staring at her with evident concern. "I'm fine, sorry," she assured him. "Just a little fried today."

"I was worried for a second," he said. "You aren't getting that cold that's going around, are you?"

"I don't think so," she said.

"So, what about later then?"

"Give me the address," she replied. "I'll try to make it if I can."

As it turned out, by nightfall she had talked herself into it. She hadn't been to many parties in the early part of this year, and they were, after all, an important part of the college experience. She found the address Hector had given her—a small, Spanish-style bungalow a few blocks from campus—and knew immediately it was the right place. Students spilled out the door into the yard, loud music chasing them the whole way. Strangers greeted her like old friends as she passed them and worked her way through the crowded doorway, looking for Hector. The air inside was thick with beer, hormones, and dance music.

When she found Hector, he was already beyond buzzed, and into the sloppy and obnoxious category. He sat on a couch with an empty bottle in his fist, staring right past her like he didn't even know her. Rebecca felt a twinge of regret—not that she thought she and Hector might turn into anything other than friends, but part of the reason she had come tonight was that she enjoyed talking to him before and after class and wanted to get better acquainted. Clearly, that wasn't happening.

Disappointed, she almost turned and walked out of the house without even having a drink. But the clot of people between her and the door had become almost impenetrable, and the music hammered her skull, so she spun on her heel and headed the other way, looking for a back way out. She was sorry she had come now, just wanted to get home where she belonged.

She pushed her way through a door that she thought led to the kitchen, but there was a girl coming out of it at the same time—a girl a year or two older than she was, Rebecca thought, tall and thin, with a curly mop of dark hair and bright, friendly eyes. "Hey," the girl said, regarding Rebecca carefully. "You're just what we need."

"We?" Rebecca echoed. "What we?"

The girl put a hand on Rebecca's shoulder and leaned close to her ear, as if sharing state secrets. "In the bedroom," she said, causing all sorts of images to flit into Rebecca's mind. "We're holding a séance."

"A séance?" Rebecca repeated. She could barely hear herself speak. "Don't you need, like, quiet and privacy for that?" The fact was, she didn't care what conditions might be required for a séance. She knew, better than these kids, certainly, what the supernatural was all about, and she wanted no part of it.

But the girl hadn't let go of her shoulder. "We'll have all the privacy we need," she assured Rebecca. "Everybody saw the freaky people go into the back bedroom; they won't dare come in. Anyway, there's a lock on the door. We already have four other people besides me, but we want an even number."

"Does that matter?" Rebecca found herself asking.

"I have no idea," the girl said. "It's Shiai's thing. She just sent me to get a sixth person—and a girl, 'cause it's boy-girl, boy-girl, you know."

Rebecca was torn. Mostly, she wanted to get out of here and go home. But she recognized that for what it was—*something*, she thought, *between fear and outright cowardice*. It was silly to be freaked out. These were just kids at a party, wanting to have a good time scaring themselves. The same impulse sent people to horror movies and Stephen King novels. Rebecca decided it wouldn't hurt to hang for a little while, see what these people were like. She could use some new friends, she knew, and maybe she'd find them here. The girl who had stopped her was certainly amiable.

"Okay," Rebecca said quickly, before she could change her mind again. "Lead on."

"I'm Amy," the girl announced, grabbing Rebecca's hand and tugging her down the hall.

"Rebecca."

"Good to meet you, Rebecca." Amy knocked twice on a door, then opened it. "We have success!" she called into a darkened room.

Cheers greeted her entry, and Rebecca started to feel glad that she'd decided to stick around. The room was lit by six candles, marking the six points of a star drawn on the hard-wood floor with chalk. It looked more like a Star of David, Rebecca thought—an image she had grown up with—than any kind of magical pentangle or anything she could remember having seen. But then, Daniel Blessing hadn't really seemed to go in for that kind of thing, and he was her only contact with actual magic. So maybe it was authentic.

A person sat behind each candle. As Amy had described, they were seated boy-girl. Amy pointed and named at the same time, and Rebecca struggled to remember to whom she was being introduced. "Brad, Shiai, Donnie, Mark," she said. "And I'm Amy, like I said. And this is Rebecca."

"Hi, guys," Rebecca said, feeling shy now that she was center stage. At least the room was too dark for anyone to see her blush.

"Welcome, Rebecca," Shiai greeted her. Even though she was sitting down, Rebecca could see that she was short and squat, with chin-length blond hair streaked with green. Her sweater was black and snug, her jeans frayed at the hems. "Come on in. Have you ever been part of a séance?"

"Not really," Rebecca answered. No séances, and the occult activity she had been part of she wouldn't talk about here.

"Then you'll fit right in," Mark tossed out. "Neither have we!"

"But I read a book about it," Shiai added. "So I know basically what we're supposed to do."

Rebecca sat on the floor at the one empty star point, crossing her legs like the others had. She remembered having seen Brad on campus; he was tall, probably six and a half feet, with hair past his shoulders, and so was easy to spot and hard to forget. The others she wasn't sure she'd ever seen. Donnie was handsome, dark-haired and olive-skinned, and Mark was a little on the goofy side, with a short brush of red hair, freckles, and a crooked smile that was friendly and funny at the same time.

The company was comfortable for her, but she still had mixed feelings about the idea of a séance. Though she couldn't tell them why, she knew that messing around with the supernatural was not the safe, casual game they seemed to think. Her only consolation was that she didn't really expect them to be able to accomplish their goal—if indeed they had a goal beyond sitting in candlelight together and telling what would amount to ghost stories.

There were a few more moments of laughing and joking, but then Shiai took the lead, putting a finger to her lips. "We need to be quiet and concentrate," she instructed. "We should all join hands."

Rebecca reached out to Mark on her right and Donnie on her left. Their hands were warm, and she noticed that Mark's trembled a little. Nervous about the séance, or about holding hands with a strange girl, she couldn't tell. *It's not like I've been holding hands with a lot of boys lately,* she thought. *Or doing anything else with them, for that matter.* But she kind of liked the sensation.

Shiai moved a seventh candle to the center of the star. "Focus on the flame," she said in a hushed voice. "Try to clear your minds of any stray thoughts."

She stopped speaking then. Music from the front room rattled the door, but Rebecca, in the spirit of the moment, tried to block it out, to concentrate her entire being on the flickering candle before her. After many minutes, the breathing of everyone around her had settled into a steady rhythm. She felt her own body's breath, her heartbeat, the heat of the hands on hers, and then even those things slipped away She might as well have been floating on a cloud in a night-dark sky, staring into the glow of a faraway star. Sound lost distinction, filling the space around her like soft cotton but without meaning. She became cognizant at some point that Shiai was speaking again.

". . . part the veils between this world and the next, and give us a sign of your presence," she was saying. "Slip the ties that bind you to that world and appear before us . . ."

Rebecca stopped paying attention to the words and let them join the music as just a sound that filled the dark room. Gravity had lost its hold, space and time folded in on themselves, and still Shiai droned on . . .

And then the candle's flame leapt from its quarter-inch height to become more than a foot tall, its bright light blasting her darkness-adjusted eyes like a camera's flash. Amy shrieked and Mark let out a loud curse. Rebecca tightened her grip on him and Donnie, her heart suddenly thundering. *This isn't supposed to happen,* she thought, *or it's a trick of some kind, a fake candle.*

But when Shiai continued, her voice was different, tremulous, and Rebecca knew that it was no fake she was part of. "Now tell us who you are," she commanded. "We know that you are here with us—identify yourself."

The candle had only blossomed for a second, and then its flame had returned to normal. Rebecca stared at it again, its light seemingly diminished even more in contrast to the sudden brightness. As Shiai continued, her voice caught, and Rebecca glanced away from the candle at her.

And she saw—where Shiai should have been—a blond woman, older than Shiai, leaner, taller, with a distinct sense of poise and elegance.

Season Howe.

Rebecca screamed.

She felt hands on her—Mark and Donnie and Amy, crowding around, trying to comfort her. She dared another look, and Shiai sat cross-legged across from her, anxious and frightened. "What is it?" she asked. "What's wrong, Rebecca?"

"Yeah, you scared the holy crap outta me," Mark added.

Rebecca swallowed, trying to regain some composure. It was only Shiai, after all.

But for that moment, it had seemed so real.

"Nothing . . . I'm sorry," Rebecca said haltingly. "I should . . . I should go."

"But we're not fin . . ." Brad began. He let the sentence die. The séance, as far as Rebecca was concerned, was finished. The others could stay here as long as they wanted. Rebecca rose unsteadily to her feet, supporting herself on Mark.

"I'm really sorry," she said again. The others tried to soothe her, to reassure her that her outburst had not been a problem.

But it was a problem for her. She hurried from the party as fast as she could, out into the cool night air for the walk home.

It was not really Season, she thought, trying to convince herself. It had only been her imagination running wild, that and the retinal burn from the candle's flare, making her see Shiai in a different way.

Because if it had been Season, that would mean that the witch was somehow looking for her, tracking them on the astral plane or something like that.

And that would just be too scary for words.

* * *

After dozing for a few hours, Kerry got to work.

She skipped her morning class, staying in bed until after Sonya left. Outside, a leaden sky glowered angrily, so Kerry was just as happy to remain in the warm comfort of her own space. She tugged on a Northwestern hoodie and cotton drawstring pants, tied her long black hair back with an elastic, and began.

Her first task was to pull all four of Daniel's journals from the bookshelf and scan them for any references to the Great Dismal Swamp, or to Mother Blessing's cabin. There turned out to be very few of either, but whenever she found one with useful details, she made notes. She had always thought it an interesting coincidence that Daniel, like her, kept a journal, and concluded that it wasn't just coincidence, it was one of the factors that drew them together, one of the points of similarity that made them appreciate each other. Daniel's journals—*just like a man,* she thought—were long on incident and short on emotion, while her own diaries were almost all about her feelings and reactions instead of recounting what exactly happened in her life.

Gradually, though, piece by piece, she drew together a mental picture of the Swamp and the route one would take to find Mother Blessing's cabin deep inside it. Of course, whether that mental picture would prove to be at all helpful was yet to be seen. Interestingly, according to his vague descriptions, the Swamp didn't change much over the years, but Mother Blessing

seemed to keep her cabin updated, enlarging it and moderniz-
ing it from time to time. It had started as a one-room trapper's
shack, but in the most recent entries Kerry could find, from
the mid-1970s, it was a four-room cabin that sounded almost
luxurious.

Noon had come and gone by the time she finished her
paging through, and she hadn't even had breakfast. Putting the
journals away, she made a trip to the floor's vending machines
and bought a prepackaged sandwich, some chips, and an
orange soda. She said hello to the few people she passed in
the hall, but avoided conversation. Her body was in Evanston,
Illinois, but her mind was far away, and she wanted desperately to stay in that place.

Back in the safety of her room, Kerry went online and
searched the Net for information about Great Dismal. It
turned out to be a national wildlife refuge, which she hadn't
known, straddling the border between Virginia and North
Carolina. Beyond some descriptions of its history and a few
long, scientifically precise accounts of its wide array of flora
and fauna, though, there wasn't much to be found that would
help her. It was interesting that George Washington had organized a company that drained and logged portions of the
Swamp—that backed up Daniel's claim that George had personally cut down some of the trees—but it wasn't information
she could use. She couldn't find any really detailed naviga-
tional charts, for instance, and nothing so helpful as a map
to Mother Blessing's cabin. Not that she'd expected any such

thing, of course, and a quick Google search showed no online references whatsoever to Mother Blessing. That was almost surprising, until she realized that Mother Blessing would probably have the power to maintain her privacy to whatever degree she wanted. Season Howe didn't turn up on Internet searches, and neither had Daniel, for that matter.

Again, though, she made notes. At one point she pushed herself away from her computer screen to rest her eyes, and realized that two more hours had passed. *If I put this kind of effort into my schoolwork, the year would be off to a much more promising start,* she thought. But then there was nothing about her schoolwork that struck her with the same kind of urgency.

Around four, the door opened and Sonya returned, wearing a fluffy yellow turtleneck and dark pants. She dumped some notebooks on her desk, looked at Kerry, and blinked a couple of times behind her big glasses. "Have you even left the room?"

"Once," Kerry replied.

"Obviously didn't bother to put on any makeup when you did," Sonya pointed out. "Are you sick?"

"I'm fine," Kerry said. "Just involved in something."

"What is it? You mean a project for one of your classes?"

"Not exactly." Kerry suddenly felt defensive. Not only would Sonya not understand—she would steadfastly refuse to understand—but Kerry didn't want to share this information anyway. If she was going to leave the campus, go to Virginia and find Mother Blessing, she didn't want anyone to know where she'd gone, or why. Possibly she'd tell her summer friends, Rebecca, Scott and Brandy, and Josh, all of whom would be more likely to get it than Sonya. But no one else—certainly no one who might tell Uncle Marsh and Aunt Betty when they came around looking. "It's more personal," she added.

Sonya shrugged. She had, Kerry thought, become good at that—just about everything Kerry did or said merited a shrug as far as Sonya was concerned. That was okay. She'd started off the year hoping they'd become friends, but it hadn't taken long to realize that that wasn't going to happen. Now she wanted simply to get along well enough to not have her plans actively interfered with.

"Yeah, whatever," Sonya said at length, crossing to her closet. "I just came to get a coat—Dougie and I are going to the game tonight. You want to come?"

It was Friday, a fact that had completely escaped Kerry's notice. That meant one of two possibilities: for the next couple of days, Sonya would either be away with Dougie a lot, which would be great, or she'd be cooped up in the room with Kerry, studying, which would stink.

There was, unfortunately, no way to know which it would be until Sonya volunteered the information. Kerry didn't want to call attention to her curiosity by asking directly. But she tried one vague query, just in case.

"No, thanks. I'm going to stay in and keep working, probably through the weekend. You got any big plans?"

"I'm going to play it by ear," Sonya answered. No help at all. With another shrug and a wave, Sonya donned her jacket and left again. Kerry turned back to the computer.

If Sonya was going to be in the way, that made getting out of here in a hurry that much more important.

Sonya and Dougie went out for an afternoon movie on Saturday, which gave Kerry the opportunity she needed. She had already identified what she'd need to take, so she crammed it all into a duffel: some changes of clothes, especially heavy sweaters and jeans, essentials like underwear and makeup, her laptop, Daniel's journals. Anything else she needed, she could buy. Her bank had Saturday hours, so she'd stopped there earlier in the day and withdrawn what she thought she'd need. Money wasn't a particular problem—if she wasn't going to be in college, then the insurance settlement that she had set aside for that purpose was up for grabs. And she believed that Mother Blessing's would be an education in itself.

Assuming, of course, she doesn't just throw you out, she thought. *And you can find her in the first place.*

Friday's gloomy skies had turned into a driving rain that snatched brown leaves from trees and glued them to the sidewalks and gutters, blown by an icy wind off Lake Michigan. Kerry made a last pass at the room, making sure she was leaving only clothing and schoolbooks she could stand to lose, but nothing of a deeply personal nature. Then she called a cab. Under a yellow umbrella with green frogs emblazoned on it, she waited, half a block from Elder Hall's front door, until it came, its headlights slicing through the downpour. She hopped in as soon as it stopped, tossing her duffel onto the seat next to her, folding her umbrella, and resting it on its point in the empty footwell.

"O'Hare Airport," she told the driver. He was a thin man wearing a bow tie and a cardigan sweater, and when he smiled at her in his rearview mirror his teeth were full of gold.

"What airline, miss?" he asked politely

She told him and he pulled away from the curb, his movements smooth and precise. "Have you there in a jiffy," he said. "Do you mind the radio?"

"Not at all." This seemed like an auspicious beginning to her trip—a cabbie who was considerate and also knew his way around town. He turned the power on and heavy metal music blared from speakers in both the front and back seats.

He smiled again, flashing gold. "Too loud?"

"Maybe a little." Kerry dug at her ears with her fingers, trying to see if her eardrums had in fact ruptured.

"Sorry." He turned the music down until it was a dull roar. She'd been expecting a violin concerto, maybe even opera. But it was nice to know that people could still surprise her. She settled back into the seat, guitars clashing and drums banging, and enjoyed the short ride to the airport.

Once at O'Hare, Kerry paid the driver and carried her duffel inside. She made sure people noticed her, buying a copy of *Sports Illustrated* along with her gum, because a young woman picking that magazine would be more memorable than one who chose, say, *People* or *Vogue*, at one of the WH Smith shops. She got dinner at a snack counter, and she greeted maintenance and security workers with big smiles and cheery hellos. After spending a couple of hours there she went back outside to the ground transportation area and caught a CTA bus to downtown Chicago's Greyhound station.

On the bus, surrounded by working people heading to or from jobs, and now and then by students, Kerry felt a sudden rush of sorrow for what she was giving up. Any life resembling these people's, she had decided, was destined never to be hers. But she had spent years looking forward to college, to the things she'd learn there, the friends she'd make, the professors and books that would swell her intellect and experience. Instead, she was leaving all that behind for an uncertain future, and the loss of her once-imagined life tugged at her heart, like a slender shadow of the pain she still felt at the loss of Daniel Blessing.

At the Greyhound station, she was considerably less friendly, keeping her gaze downcast and her face blank. She posted a letter she'd written to Aunt Betty earlier in the day—a brief note, really, saying essentially, "Don't look for me, I'll be fine but out of touch for a while"—and caught a 3:15 bus to Madison, Wisconsin.

She had a seat by herself on the bus, but the two men sitting behind her, nattering on about seemingly every tiny thought that flitted across their minds, made her wish she'd brought an iPod with her. Instead she turned to Daniel's journals and lost herself in his exploits for the four-hour bus journey. Panic attacks threatened to set in every time she thought about what she was doing, but Daniel's voice, as she heard it through his words, managed to calm her every time.

Madison was freezing. The bus station there was on a narrow strip of land between two lakes, and the evening air, dark already at seven thirty, felt arctic to her. She pulled the sweatshirt hood over her head and walked up South Bedford until she spotted a cheap motel, the Flamingo Inn—the kind of place where, she believed, no one would pay much attention to anyone else's business. The desk clerk sat behind a thick, scratched Plexiglas window, and Kerry passed cash through a slot to him. He coughed, grinned at her with yellowed teeth and rheumy eyes, and gave her a room key. After a quick look at the room—bed, dresser, TV, minimalist bathroom—she went back into the cold, searching for a drugstore to find what she needed. Again she paid with cash, and she carried her bag back to her underwhelming temporary abode. The desk clerk eyed her as she returned, leering at her as if she were some kind of runaway. In a sense, she guessed she was, but she didn't think of herself that way. As she climbed the dank, musty staircase to her equally unsavory room, she decided that the difference was that she wasn't focused on running *away* from anything. She was running *toward* something—toward a definite goal, a new future, a destination that she would recognize once she found it.

Inside the room again, she locked and bolted the door, took a long, hot shower, and then toweled off and found *Saturday Night Live* on the battered hotel TV. She wasn't really in the mood for comedy, but she wanted to drown out any noise that might issue from the Flamingo Inn's other guests or staff and get ready for bed. The day had been long and wearying, the emotional impact of leaving her old life behind was hitting her hard in these last few minutes, and she found herself suddenly near exhaustion, tears welling in her eyes for no reason.

And tomorrow, she knew, would be longer still.

4

Morning came all too soon, and with it harsh light spilling through curtains barely worthy of the name. Kerry groaned and forced herself out of bed, rubbing her eyes and biting back yawns. She had too much to do to allow herself to sleep in, even though the idea of opening her eyes to her wretched hotel room filled her with dread.

The night before she had shampooed her hair carefully—long, dark, lustrous hair she had grown out and tended for years. She almost had to choke back tears as she regarded her reflection in the mirror, knowing what had to happen next. From the drugstore bag she removed a pair of new scissors. *I can't believe I'm doing this,* she thought as she took six inches of her tresses into her hand. *But what has to be done . . .*

Before she cut, though, she drew her hand down three more inches. *No use getting carried away,* she decided. A *little* change was better than none at all. Anyway, there would be more to it than the cut. Once she'd snipped away the extra inches—and the split ends that had resulted from a couple of months of virtually ignoring any maintenance beyond simple shampooing in the shower—she took the blue temporary dye she'd purchased at the drugstore and worked it into her raven locks. She knew she couldn't do much about the color without bleaching first, which she wasn't willing to do. But she figured even this little bit would create blue highlights, which people would remember—and which people who knew Kerry Profitt would never associate with her. This was the theory she had developed of disappearing: be as completely unlike yourself as possible, and they'll never find you.

Of course, she didn't expect that a huge effort would be thrown into tracking her down in the first place. Aunt Betty and Uncle Marsh would make some kind of attempt, but when it came to putting money into hiring a private detective or anything like that, Uncle Marsh would draw the line. She was nearly eighteen, and she'd written a letter saying she was going away intentionally and was fine—that would be enough for him. Really, her disappearance would make his life easier. No more trying to keep track of and care for a teenager he'd never asked for in the first place. No more having his wife's loyalties divided when they fought, which they had done with some regularity during the months she'd lived in their house. Uncle Marsh was a drinker, and when he drank he got obnoxious—loud and demanding and unreasonable. Aunt Betty—Kerry couldn't figure out if she admired this, or despised it—had learned to put up with it, to ignore him or cajole him or otherwise accept his behavior. Kerry never could, never even cared to try, and that attitude had caused plenty of tension around the place.

So okay, she thought, *maybe I am running away a little bit. Running from a life I didn't choose, one that was handed to me without any input from me. But it's what I'm heading toward that keeps me going.*

When her blued hair was dried, she put on a nondescript red sweater and jeans. Much as she loved her trademark red checkered tennies, she chose to leave those in her duffel in favor of plain leather hiking boots—better in Madison's weather, and not as memorable. She packed up the rest of her belongings and checked out of the hotel; the desk clerk was a woman this time, not the same guy as last night, which was what she'd counted on. She dropped the key into the tray under the Plexiglas window, and since she'd already paid cash there was no further transaction necessary Then she took her duffel and waited at a bus stop until a city bus came along. After paying the fare, she sat on the bus for almost an hour, riding through one neighborhood after another until she spotted what she was looking for.

Happy Jack's Wheel World was one of those used car lots

that was not associated with a new car dealership but was simply a wide parking lot crammed with various models of vehicles, from a faded pink Jeep to a plum-colored Toyota minivan that looked as if it had never been on the road. Prices were painted on cardboard signs and leaned up against the windshields of the cars. Kerry had never owned a car and didn't really know what used ones should cost, but these prices seemed reasonable to her. After she looked for about fifteen seconds, a man who could only be Happy Jack—his huge bulk resplendent in a sport coat the color of spilled mustard and plaid pants that could have blinded a pro golfer—came out of a small office, smiling as if to prove his identity.

He shook her hand with all the energy of a spastic squirrel. "Looking for some wheels, miss?" he asked, his voice higher than she'd have expected for someone so large. "I'm sure I can put you into something that's just right for you."

Kerry didn't want a long conversation with this guy. She wanted to get in a car and get out of Dodge, or at least Madison. Her inclination was toward something small and economical, not a gas guzzler—although the Jeep would have been okay too, except for the pink part. Too showy. The last thing she wanted was to call attention to herself.

Finally, she pointed at the minivan—absolutely the last thing she could picture Kerry Profitt driving. "I'll take that one," she declared.

Happy Jack chuckled wetly. "You want me to wrap it up, or are you going to eat it here?"

Fifteen minutes later she drove it off the lot. Even paying cash, she'd had to do paperwork, and since she didn't have a fake ID, her name and former address were down on paper. She decided it didn't matter, though. She was still a long way from her destination, and from this point she would become untraceable, just a girl with bluish hair inscribing an arc across a corner of America.

Kerry Profitt's diary, October 23

On the theory that big cities are more anonymous than small towns, I picked St. Louis to stop in tonight. I've been here before, of course—from Cairo, it's the nearest "big city," so it's where I'd go with Mom and Dad for special shopping trips, cultural events, museums, and of course the zoo. That was a long time ago, though—a lifetime. In THIS lifetime, on this journey, I picked one of the dozens of roadside motels outside the city, more or less at random—they all look pretty much the same, and while free HBO and in-room coffee are nice, I'm not inclined to use a pool, spa, or weight room, so one is basically as good as the next.

Outside my window trucks grind through their gears as they climb the ramp back onto the interstate. My route from Madison, in case posterity cares, was Interstate 90 to Highway 20 to Interstate 39 to 55, with a lunch stop in Bloomington and bathroom breaks whenever the urge struck. I don't have a schedule and no one's waiting for me, so I've decided to move as fast as I can without killing myself too much. I'll drive, I'll stop, I'll drive some more. I think I did as much driving today as in the rest of my life combined, but it was all highway and I got pretty comfortable with it. Tomorrow it's Interstate 64 east, which will take me all the way to Norfolk.

Then things get tricky. Daniel had said that the former site of Slocumb can still be found on some maps, but not on most standard road maps or online. Daniel's journals are a little vague on how exactly to get to his mother's hideaway—and anyway, even when he uses specific directions, it's usually not much more helpful than "turn right at the big tree." Which, by now, might be surrounded by bigger trees, or chopped down, or whatever. I guess the important thing is finding the Great Dismal Swamp, which is easy, since it's a national wildlife refuge and all, and it's on every map. Then somehow, once I'm there, finding my way to Mother Blessing. Which I'm sure won't be easy. But I'm equally sure that I'll do it. It's meant to be.

Yawn, stretch. Sitting behind a wheel for hours on end is hard—I don't know how those truckers outside do it all day and sometimes all night. I feel like I need to walk a couple of miles just to unkink, but I'm too tired to try. After this I'm going to send an e-mail to the La Jolla gang, my fellow veterans of the Season hunt, and then take a hot bath.

Then bed. At least this room is cleaner and more comfortable than the one at the Flamingo Inn. Thank the goddess for anonymously institutional chain motels, I guess.

And hey, free HBO. Maybe I can watch while I sleep.

More later.

K., the vanished one.

Brandy went into the bedroom and shook Scott's shoulder. He moaned and turned over, looking up at her, his pale, narrow face puffy with sleep, eyes blinking blindly. "Put on your glasses," she instructed. "E-mail from Kerry. You've got to see."

"You can't read it to me?"

"You've got to get up anyway," she reminded him. Mornings had never been his favorite time. "You have a ten o'clock lecture. It's almost nine."

He stifled a yawn, grabbed his glasses, pushed back the covers, and swung his legs off the bed. His chest was bare, with striped cotton pajama pants covering his legs. Scott was not a particularly impressive physical specimen, but Brandy liked him and the sight warmed her heart a little. Once he was upright she took his hand and led him into the living room, where the computer monitor glowed patiently. Rubbing his eyes, he sat down on the chair in front of the desk, and she read it again over his shoulder.

"Guys," it began, "I'm dropping off the radar for a while. I'll be fine. Please PLEASE don't worry about me. And don't try to find me (not that you would). I'll be in touch when I can. Where I'm going, what I'm doing, is very important—I think to all of us. I'll tell you about it (broken record here) when I can. Summing up: DON'T WORRY. WHEN I CAN. And I love you guys. K."

Scott read the e-mail slowly, or maybe twice, before turning back to Brandy. "What do you think she's up to?"

"Like I'd know? You have the same information I do."

He rose from the chair, folding his arms defensively over his chest. "I wasn't looking for certainty, just speculation, Brandy. You don't have any guesses?"

Brandy shrugged. "It's Kerry. Who knows how that girl thinks? If I understood her, I wouldn't have been so shocked to find out she and Daniel were, you know, a thing." It continued to annoy Brandy that she hadn't guessed that, since she liked to think of herself as a good judge of character and an astute amateur—for now—psychologist. She had known there was a strong connection between them, but she hadn't realized that it had blossomed into anything physical or romantic. By the time Kerry let on, Daniel was already dead.

She suspected that it hadn't been just romance driving Kerry's feelings. Kerry had lost her father, years before, and then nursed her mother through a long and difficult illness. When they'd found Daniel Blessing in their front yard, he had been injured, near death, and Kerry had once again been drawn to nursemaid duty. Brandy thought that some of what she'd felt for Daniel had been projection, layering her feelings about her parents, who were beyond her help, onto him.

"It's something to do with Season," Scott suggested, worry tightening his voice. Rebecca had called on Saturday afternoon, telling them about the Season sighting she had had—which she had later thoroughly discounted—at a party the night before. She had convinced herself that the whole thing was a figment of her imagination, but she'd been a little freaked by it anyway. She said she'd tried to call Kerry but there had been no answer at her dorm room. Now, apparently, they knew why. "She wouldn't do something like this unless it was. She's got a lead on Season."

"You're probably right," Brandy agreed. "I don't see her getting so worked up over anything else."

Scott's lips were pressed together in a tight line, and he looked at Brandy as if she should have some kind of answer. "We've got to help her."

"Did you read the girl's e-mail?" Brandy countered impatiently. "I'm talking about the part where she specifically tells us not to."

"Yeah, but—"

"But nothing, Scott. She says not to worry about her, and not to try to find her. So your response is, let's worry and then go looking?"

"Of course she'd say those things, Brandy," Scott argued. "Kerry isn't the kind of girl to say, 'Please worry about me.'"

"But you don't think she's the kind of girl who'd ask for help if she needed it?"

"I guess she would. Maybe."

"That's right, Scott," Brandy assured him. "Kerry's not stupid. She knows she can't take Season on by herself—hell, she knows all of us together couldn't take Season. She's not going to do anything rash."

"I suppose."

The good thing about Scott was that Brandy knew all the buttons, all the levers. He could be brought around to her point of view on just about any matter Brandy cared to make the effort on. There was, she thought, a certain amount of satisfaction and comfort in that—in knowing that when it counted, she could have her way.

Manipulative? Maybe. But with a purpose.

And as far as I'm concerned, getting what I want is a good purpose.

5

In addition to Roanoke Island, there was another small town on the eastern seaboard that suffered a mysterious fate, albeit more than a hundred years later.

Slocumb, Virginia, less than a dozen miles from the North Carolina state line, was founded in or around 1641 by John Slocumb, one of the earliest settlers to exhibit any interest in the forbidding region that came to be known as the Great Dismal Swamp. Slocumb, a trapper and explorer, led a group of settlers forty-some strong from the Jamestown colony to this new settlement on the edge of the Swamp, where it was believed oysters; beaver, mink, and deer hides; and alligator skins could provide a steady income for those willing to work hard and brave the Swamp's uncharted depths.

In 1665 the tiny village of Slocumb experienced a bit of a population explosion when William Drummond, then governor of North Carolina, discovered the lake which still bears his name, and commercial activity, mostly trapping, really began to take off.

But from a high point of seventy-some residents, in the spring of 1704, Slocumb's population suddenly—apparently in the space of a few days—dropped to zero. No one seems to know quite what happened, and there are no records to explain the mystery. What is known is that there was a great fire, which not only burned down the township but also ignited the eastern edge of the Swamp. No surviving Slocumbites, if there were any, were ever reported after the fire. Volunteers from the nearby towns fruitlessly battled the blaze off and on for a month's time before giving up on it completely, and they claimed that the fire had overrun the town, burning every structure to the ground.

Mysterious, unpleasant rumors began to spread about what may have happened to Slocumb's populace, including stories of massacre by Indians or runaway slaves, the infernal workings of witches and devils, and the awful idea that everyone in town had been caught by surprise when the fire broke out at night and thus burned to death in their homes.

Whatever the cause, no attempt was ever made to resettle the town's site.

—Edginton's History of the Coastlands, 1937

Kerry spent her third night on the road in Portsmouth, Virginia, where there was a library in which she was able to find a reproduction of a map of Virginia from three centuries before. Of course, the roads that existed now weren't shown on it. But she got a sense of where Slocumb had been, and by comparing that to current maps and skimming through some histories of the Great Dismal Swamp area, she pinpointed where she thought its site must be.

Not sure what to expect there, she bought an inflatable boat, plenty of insect repellent and sunscreen in a handy combination form, a couple of flashlights and batteries, and some portable food and water. It crossed her mind that a gun might not be a bad idea, given that there were wild animals in there. But she hated guns, and she decided she wouldn't sacrifice her principles for a measure of comfort that might be illusory. Anyway, if the place really was a wildlife refuge, shooting at the critters was no doubt frowned upon. Better to just watch her step and not take stupid chances.

Except, the whole thing's a big fat stupid chance.

Fully outfitted, she drove the minivan down Highway 17, past the tiny town of Deep Creek. The main occupations here seemed to be fishing and selling cold beer. Kerry figured that in hotter weather, the cold beer would be a popular item. Even now, it was quite a bit warmer than it had been in Chicago or Madison; there seemed to be some sort of Indian summer thing going on. The people she saw from her van were mostly men wearing T-shirts or short-sleeved shirts, many open over chests burned brick red from years of exposure to the hot sun.

Not far to the east of here was the Intracoastal Waterway, a series of inland channels upon which one could navigate all the way from Key West to Boston, if one had a boat and the inclination. Kerry had the boat—well, *a* boat, though she doubted that her little rubber dinghy would survive such an ambitious journey. And, she had to admit, she also had a little curiosity about the idea of traversing the country north to south on water without ever sailing open ocean. But that adventure would have to wait its turn. She had another one in mind for now, and who knew how consuming it would turn out to be? Maybe if she and her boat survived it, they'd try the Intracoastal next.

After Season Howe had been dealt with.

This region was notable, too, because it was the part of the country she'd been studying in her history class before she made the decision to leave Northwestern. Roanoke Island, the colony that claimed the first child of Europeans born in North America—and from which the entire settlements population had mysteriously disappeared without trace—was on North Carolina's Outer Banks, just a short distance across the state line. She'd always been fascinated by that story, and by the cryptic word *Croatan* that was found left behind in their wake. That had all happened before Daniel was born, she realized, but maybe not before his mother was. Yet another reason to find Mother Blessing.

Finally, she found the spot on the roadway that she was searching for, a turnoff unlabeled except by a mile marker a dozen or so feet before it. She took a narrow lane that led off the highway to the right. Tall reeds towered over the van on both sides of the road, creating the impression that she was driving into a tunnel of some kind. Ahead, all she could see past the tops of the reeds was a wall of trees that looked impenetrable from here. Already, just moments after leaving the main road, Kerry felt as if she'd left civilization far behind her and ventured into some primeval world.

The road wound to the right and then left again, but always leading basically west, away from the sea and toward the heart of the Great Dismal Swamp. Kerry didn't know the names of any of the trees or plants she saw, but their effect on her was overwhelming—everything was green and incredibly lush. *This must be the most fertile spot on Earth,* she thought, *or one of them, anyway.* She'd never been very successful at grow-ing houseplants, but from the looks of things around here if she'd had some of the local climate, soil, and water, she'd be queen of the green thumbs.

She drove with her window rolled halfway down, the warm air brushing her left arm and cheek thick with the rich, fecund aromas of the Swamp. The edge of the road was pebbled, and beyond the stones, the reeds stood in murky, stagnant water. The whole experience was like nothing she'd ever seen—or smelled.

After another ten minutes or so, the road came to an abrupt end. For a moment Kerry's heart fell; she thought she'd figured the way incorrectly or made a wrong turn. But then she spotted an old, unpaved track, made impassable to cars by the trees that had fallen across it, but still clearly something that had been considered a road at one time. Now it was little more than a space between trees, choked with weeds and brush, leading into the darkness of what looked like impenetrable jungle.

This was a development she hadn't counted on. But then this whole trip had been made without a real plan, just flying by the seat of her pants. No reason this part of it should suddenly be easy or predictable. Bringing the van to a halt at the edge of the roadway, right tires on the graveled shoulder, she was sure it wouldn't be.

The heat surprised her. When she'd been driving through it, her movement had made it feel comfortable. But now that she stood in it, listening only to the ticking of the Toyota's engine and the cries of unseen birds, it settled around her in a great, damp blanket of humidity. Clouds of gnats swarmed around her like manifestations of the temperature. She flapped her hands at them, then remembered the combination sunscreen/insect repellent in the van and went to retrieve it. A few moments later, suitably slathered, she braved the elements again. Gnats still crowded her, but kept a slightly greater distance; the sun, filtered as it was through the overhanging trees, still hammered mercilessly upon her.

The stretch of old roadway through the trees was relatively short, and after less than fifteen minutes it stopped, opening onto a wide clearing at the other side of which, Kerry supposed, the Great Dismal started up in earnest. On the far side of the clearing, the woods looked dark, benighted in spite of the early hour and the pounding sun.

But it was the clearing itself that struck her the most. This, she surmised, was the lost town of Slocumb. Not a building stood, but the blackened remains of charred timbers still rested where they had fallen back in 1704. Outlines were visible where once houses had been, and among them the paths of the lanes that connected them. The whole thing looked like a carefully preserved archaeological site.

What was most remarkable about it, though—the part that made her body shiver, in spite of the heat—was the fact that there was not a blade of grass, not a single weed—much less the mass of trees and roots and reeds and ferns that covered the rest of the landscape—anywhere within the confines of the Slocumb site.

It was as if a manic gardener had picked the site clean. The pathways between buildings were sandy and rock-strewn, and there was evidence of broken, crumbled oyster shells everywhere. The burned, skeletal remains of the buildings were as free of vegetation as the lunar surface. Even the air smelled different, lacking the musky, dank aroma of the surrounding swampland. Instead, it had a kind of sour stench that made Kerry think of the meat that had spoiled in her mom's freezer when a power outage had kept the electricity off for three days. Kerry hesitated to enter the space, but after a moment's consideration decided that she had to. All of Daniel's directions into the swamp had been from the other side, where the town site bordered the Great Dismal.

She shook off the sense of unease, as well as she could, at any rate, and ventured into the clearing. The air felt thinner here, rarefied, and maybe five or ten degrees cooler than the humid air outside the space. *This,* Kerry suddenly knew, *is the work of Season Howe. She did more than destroy the town; she put some kind of curse on the land so it would never recover.* It was no wonder the history books tended to ignore Slocumb— how could anyone explain this lifeless anomaly in the midst of one of the country's greatest swamps using only the limited vocabulary of science and accepted belief?

When she reached the first dwelling, its boards long since petrified as fire-blackened cinders, Kerry realized something else about this place. There was no noise here, not even the bird cries that had been omnipresent since stopping the van; no frogs croaking or crickets chirping could be heard from this place. And the cloud of gnats that had followed her every step of the way, even after she'd slathered on the insect repellent, had stopped at the edge of the clearing, refusing to enter. Only

Kerry was foolish enough to tread this ground, it seemed. The silence was unnerving; the complete absence of life nearly terrifying. The tiny hairs on her neck and arms stood on end, as if Kerry had been subject to a jolt of electricity. She tried to swallow her fear and walk on, but her steps, instead of being courageous and determined, were small, hesitant, and she tried to keep a clear path at her back in case sudden retreat was called for.

Perhaps an archaeologist foolish enough to brave the place might have found something of worth in the ruined buildings, but all Kerry could see were ashes and scorched logs. The ground was solid beneath her feet, less spongy than the trail she had taken here from the van, but even so the people who built this village hadn't used stone foundations. A few piles of rocks that might once have been chimneys lay here and there, but rocks big enough for building seemed impossible to find—probably if they existed at all they had long ago sunk beneath the waters of the swamp. So for the most part, the construction had been wood, which had all burned.

After what seemed like hours, but was probably not more than ten or fifteen minutes even at her cautious pace, Kerry reached the other side of the clearing. Here the forest rose up thick and menacing, with patches of thorny blackberries filling in the space between tree trunks. She saw no way to walk through that morass without a machete, which she didn't have, and even with one the going would be slow.

But between the clearing and the trees was a narrow ditch

filled with water that looked like soup, a dark, reddish brown color. Leaves floated on it, and it rippled in spots where there may have been submerged objects. It was maybe a dozen feet across at its widest point, and only half that right where she stood. She couldn't get a sense of how deep it was, even when she tossed in a handful of pebbles from the clearing. They simply plopped against its tranquil surface and disappeared. After rimming the clearing, though, the ditch turned to the west and disappeared into the trees, which meant, Kerry believed, that this was the waterway that Daniel had taken to his mother's house in the Swamp so many years before.

Which also meant, she knew, that it was the path she had to take.

She'd left her supplies in the van while scouting the lay of the land. Now she regretted that decision, for it meant crossing the clearing twice more. But there was no other way to reach the ditch, at least none that she could see—the forest was impenetrable on every other side of the town's site. Biting back terror, she steeled herself and turned back, back onto the most forbidding piece of real estate she had ever imagined, back through the silence and the utter absence of life.

6

Kerry Profitt's diary, October 25

There's this theory that the weight of any object is inversely proportionate to how useless it turns out to be—the less one needs it, the more it ends up weighing, and vice versa. So the flashlight I brought with me weighed about an ounce, or maybe a negative ounce, since the inside of the Great Dismal Swamp at night is so ridiculously dark, but the can of beans I brought, because beans on a camp-out just seemed right, weighed about forty pounds. Had I brought a can opener, it might have dropped to just five or ten pounds—even less if I liked beans to begin with.

Okay, the theory is one I just made up. I don't think that invalidates its scientific truth, though.

Here's the thing. I maybe should have bought the Jeep instead of the van, because maybe I could have driven a bit closer to the barren stretch of land that used to be Slocumb. But I didn't, which meant I had to leave the van where it was and carry all my gear, including the inflatable boat, which—the exception that proves the rule—weighed about a thousand pounds more than it had in the store. Eventually I had to put some of the stuff down and make multiple trips to the ditch at the edge of town (or rather, former town), which I had decided was going to be my pathway into the depths of the Dismal.

Eventually, though—and ask me if I mind saying that walking back and forth across that bizarre, haunted piece of land was freaking me out in a gigantamous way, because it was—I had everything where I needed it. The boat, wonder of wonders, inflated when I pulled on the goobie, just like it was supposed to. And it didn't even sink when I loaded all the junk in it, like the forty-pound beans. If I'd had a bottle of champagne I'd have christened it, except for the part about how shards of glass from a broken bottle would probably shred an inflatable boat, and the other part about how I don't drink, but at this point in my admittedly bizarre journey I might have considered taking it up.

So without christening I just launched. No motor or anything, sadly—it was all driven by Kerry-power. Me and my little toy oar, which was really too small to be useful, but fit in the box with the boat. At first it didn't seem too bad, but after a while it started to get old. And then when the over-hanging brambles and branches and logs (and other names for spiky wooden things) started hanging down so low over the ditch that I pretty much had to lay down in the boat to keep from having my scalp ripped off, rowing became that much harder.

Plus, did I mention the dark? Scrolling back. Yep, mentioned. But hey, if ever there was something that merited repetition, it's that. Seemed like it would have been kind of late evening, in the real world, but inside the Swamp where the sun just doesn't reach, it was full dark way before I was expecting it. When I realized the light was going I looked around for someplace relatively dry and flat to stop, not wanting to spend the night on the boat. And after a while I found it—found this, in fact, the lean-to under which I am sitting and running down my laptop battery.

And what else is interesting is the way insects are drawn to laptops, which, who knew? I wonder if Mac has a way to clean blood and guts off the screen, because they keep committing suicide by slamming themselves into it.

Before the juice runs out, then, a summary of my position. Somewhere in the middle of the Swamp, except I don't know precisely where. I didn't exactly watch for the landmarks I read about in Daniel's journals because I was too busy watching for someplace to spend the night, which means that even if they still exist, I might have missed some of them, which means that I might be hopelessly lost. And

I don't exactly know where I'm supposed to be going anyway. In spite of the insect repellent, I am being eaten alive by bugs. The Swamp makes strange noises—rustlings and hissings and moanings in addition to the more recognizable croaking and chirping, and I think it's really things in the Swamp, not the Swamp itself, which is actually a lot worse.

And all this gab is just a way of not admitting that I am freakin' SCARED TO DEATH out here . . . which, you know, who likes to admit that? But then again, it's the truth, so why not?

The books say people used to get lost and die in the swamp on a fairly regular basis. If I don't find Mother Blessing, will I die out here? If I do find Mother Blessing, will she turn me away, which could still mean dying out here? Or will she take me in like I hope she does? What is she like, anyway? I could write about that for hours, but the battery will never last.

More later.

K.

Mother Blessing was a surprise.

Kerry had begun to think she'd never find Daniel Blessing's mother. The Great Dismal was just too big, too dense, too full of dangers. She saw a black bear her first morning out; fortunately, the bear saw her, too, and turned back the way he had come, vanishing down a trail that seemed too narrow for a human, much less a huge furry beast. She had barely reined in her galloping heart when the creek before her, wider now and flowing faster than when it had merely been a ditch, parted to reveal an alligator drifting to the surface a few feet ahead of her. Kerry had a quick mental picture of it tearing into her inflatable boat with its razor-sharp teeth and sinking her, then finishing her off at its leisure. *This was a bad idea,* she thought, *a stupendously bad idea in a lifetime chock full of bad ideas.*

"I taste bad!" she shouted at the beast. "Really bad! That's what everyone tells me, anyway. Kerry, you taste bad. And you smell funny too."

Apparently she was convincing enough, because the gator drifted past her without biting her boat. For a couple of hours after that, she started to get used to the Swamp, even to enjoy it. Tall trees arced over her head, creating an effect like a green cathedral. The fragrant forest floor was festooned with wide-leafed ferns. Butterflies and birds flitted and flew; squirrels scampered up the sides of trees; great multihued spiders spun webs like fishnets between tree trunks. There was a quiet charm to the place that she appreciated in a way she would never have expected the night before, when she had been so afraid she had barely managed to sleep at all.

As the day wore on, her nearly sleepless night began to catch up with her, and the beauty of the Swamp combined with the gentle motion of the boat to lull her into a kind of stupor. So when she first noticed the men watching her from the banks, she didn't think anything of it. After a couple of minutes, though, she realized that there was something wrong about it. Men shouldn't watch her here—she was a unique enough sight in a place like this that any other human would hail her, not simply observe from the cover of thick underbrush. She tried to focus on the spot where she thought she'd seen one of them, but he was gone. Maybe a leaf shuddered slightly with his passing, or maybe it was a wisp of a breeze that moved it.

But Kerry was on the alert now, wide awake, senses sharpened. If she saw anything else she'd be ready.

Or so she thought.

The creek forked, and Kerry chose to go to the right. But though she paddled that way, the current had another idea, and it pushed her toward the left. She thought she remembered something in the journals about the right fork, and she tried to fight the pull. She lost the struggle, though, and gave it up after a few minutes, concentrating instead on keeping the boat steady against the sudden surge. It was more important not to capsize than to worry about which fork she should take when, for all practical purposes, she had no idea where she was or where she should be.

Just when she had the little boat settled on the water, Kerry caught another glimpse of movement through the thick trees. For a moment she thought it was a deer, or maybe—her heart pounded in fear—another bear. *What are you supposed to do in the event of a bear attack?* She tried to remember. *Make noise?*

Play dead? Run like hell? Making noise seemed like the easiest, especially since trying to run might involve drowning, or a close-up encounter with an alligator or a water moccasin. For a moment she thought maybe she'd be okay if she stayed in the boat and the bear was on land, but then she remembered pictures of bears standing in rushing rivers, fishing for lunch. *So much for that idea.*

She brought the little paddle up out of the water and laid it across the boat's bow, trying to sit very still to minimize any sound. Maybe it hadn't noticed her at all. Through the trees, another flash of motion—something big and dark—caught her eye. This time she heard a noise, too, a rustling of leaves.

So it's not just shifting shadows.

As quietly as she could, she slipped the paddle back into the water and rowed for the opposite bank. The banks on both sides were sheer, with trees right to the edge, roots erupting from the cutaways. She wasn't sure where she'd be able to climb out of the boat, but she wanted to at least have a chance if some creature came at her.

The foliage across the water shifted again, as if something with serious weight were coming through it in her direction. That was all it took to spur Kerry. With two more powerful sweeps of the oar she made the far bank. There was a rope tied to a ring at the boat's bow, and she quickly looped it around the root of a tree. Then, setting her feet widely for best balance, she stood, clutching at a narrow tree trunk for more support. Putting one foot up on the bank, she hoisted herself from the boat and slid between two trees just as the dark figure on the far shore loomed into view.

It was not a bear, but a man.

Everything she'd read about the Great Dismal rushed back into her consciousness: a haven for people dodging the law, runaway slaves before the Civil War and Emancipation, and for criminals in every age, as well as a prime spot for hunters and fishers. If the man across the way had innocent intent he'd have said something by now, surely, not approached her with stealth and silence.

The ground under her feet was soft and spongy, the trees close together, with ferns and trailing vines covering the lower reaches and tangles of thickets tearing at her legs. Placing her feet was difficult, but she didn't intend to just stand there and let someone sneak up on her. As fast as she could manage, she pushed her way through the underbrush and around the trees, putting distance between herself and the creek. Once she had a rhythm going, she was able to get up a reasonable speed.

She was going so quickly, in fact, that she didn't, at first, notice the man who stood in front of her. When she did, it was too late—he swung something heavy at her and she tried to dodge, but a tree trunk blocked her way. A flash of light accompanied the impact, and then everything went dark.

I have to be dreaming, Kerry thought. *This can't be real.*

She seemed to be in an actual bed, with crisp, clean sheets pulled up around her. A dull ache throbbed at her right temple, but it wasn't any worse than an average headache, and there was none of the nausea she might have expected given the fact that she had apparently been clubbed into unconsciousness. The odors around her—she hadn't yet opened her eyes—were clean, almost antiseptic, not the pungent aroma of the swamp. And there were two exceedingly strange sounds: one a kind of electrical hum, and one a labored, artificial-breathing noise, as if Darth Vader were standing beside the bed holding a small appliance.

Or a light saber.

Having gathered as much—seemingly contradictory—information as possible, Kerry opened her eyes.

The first thing she saw was a woman smiling at her from a motorized scooter-style wheelchair. She was an enormous woman in her fifties or sixties, big in every way, from her teased, bleached beehive of a hairdo to her vast bosom and belly, barely confined in a plaid smock the size of a pup tent, to the thighs straining royal blue polyester stretch pants. A clear plastic mask across her nose and mouth was attached by tubes to oxygen tanks mounted on the scooter's rear. The scooter had wide rubber tires and a shallow basket mounted on the handlebars.

"Welcome back, darlin'," the woman said, her Southern accent thick as the trees in the Great Dismal. "I've been wonderin' when you'd be joinin' me. I'm so sorry for the way my boys brought you here."

"Here?" Kerry asked weakly.

"My house, of course," the woman replied. "Y'all were lookin' for me, weren't you?"

Kerry tried to raise herself up on one elbow. "You . . . you're . . ."

The woman breathed loudly into her mask, and then favored Kerry with another broad, slightly grotesque smile. "Folks call me Mother Blessing."

7

"Scott," Brandy said, her tone arch. "What are you doing?"

He turned away from the computer screen. "Checking e-mail."

"Didn't you check it, like, an hour ago? And an hour before that? Since when have you become compulsive?"

Her arms were crossed over her chest and her lips were pressed together so tightly they practically disappeared. Her stance, the tilt of her head, and the tone of her voice put him instantly on edge. "Well, it's just . . . you know. I'm hoping we hear something from Kerry."

Brandy made a *tch* noise and shook her head ever so slightly.

"She said she'd be in touch when she could, right? I'm sure she's fine."

"Yeah, but we don't know that. And if we don't check, how are we going to know if she's trying to get in touch?"

"I swear, sometimes it seems like you think about that girl more than you think about me," Brandy said, turning away from him.

Scott came out of the chair and went to her. "You know that's not true, Brandy," he said. He wrapped his arms around her, but there was nothing yielding about her flesh; she didn't lean into him. Her velour top was soft, but that was just surface. It was like trying to hug a velvet bag of saw blades.

The thing was, maybe she wasn't wrong. "You know I love you, babe."

"You keep telling me so," Brandy admitted. But what she left unsaid was whether his words were convincing to her.

"I do," he assured her. He was about to say more, but the computer chimed softly, indicating an incoming e-mail. He felt Brandy's muscles tense even more. He rubbed a shoulder that seemed to resist his touch, and then returned to his seat. "It's from Josh," he said, unable to keep the disappointment from his voice.

When Brandy spoke again, she sounded distinctly uninterested. "What does he have to say?"

Scott scanned the message. It was short; their friend hadn't heard from Kerry either. "I'll read it," he said. "'Hey guys. Just checking in. School is, you know, school. Grades are fine, so no worries there. The rest of life keeps plugging along. No significant other, although there are a couple of guys here who might be potentials. You have any news from Kerry since she went AWOL? I haven't heard a thing, and I'm a little on the nervous side. Love you, Josh.'"

"See, I'm not the only one who's worried about her."

"I guess it's a man thing," Brandy said. "We women know we can take care of ourselves."

"Somehow I doubt that Josh's interest would be the same as mine," Scott pointed out. Realizing how that might be interpreted, though, he quickly tried to cover himself. "Not that I have any interest of that kind. Just, if I did, you know, Josh wouldn't. Kerry being a female and all."

"I understood you the first time," Brandy said. Her tone had gone from arch to glacial. Scott wondered if it was possible to make more wrong moves in one relationship than he did in this one and have any hope of keeping it together. Before he could add anything, though, Brandy walked toward the bedroom. Her body was tight and confined and there was no invitation in the way she walked; instead he got a vibe from her that was somewhere between a shrug and a flipping of the middle finger.

Just as well, he thought. *Anything else I said would only have dug me in deeper.*

Mother Blessing's house, Kerry discovered, was as surprising as the woman herself. It looked like any average ranch house— hardwood floors, plaster walls painted eggshell white, oak cabinets and avocado-green appliances in the modern kitchen. But outside the windows, the gloom of the Swamp pressed up against it, and through the screens Kerry could hear the buzzing of insects and smell the Swamp's fetid aroma clashing with an indoor odor that reminded her of pine-scented cleaning solutions.

After giving Kerry a moment of privacy to pull on a voluminous pink cotton bathrobe, Mother Blessing led her on a tour of the place, seemingly as proud of her house as a new mother might be of her child. With her motorized scooter making agile turns and pirouettes, the woman took Kerry from the guest room, in which Kerry had awakened, down the hall to the bathroom, pointing out her own master bedroom across the way, then further through the single-story house to a kitchen and dining room, and then past the entryway into a living room that opened onto a screened-in porch. Once Kerry had the lay of the land, Mother Blessing led her back into the kitchen, where she took a pitcher of iced tea from the refrigerator.

"Sweet's okay, isn't it?" the woman asked cheerfully. "I hope so, because it's hard to take the sweet out once it's in there, isn't it?"

Kerry thought she was still in shock from the attack, because this whole scene seemed more than a little surreal to her. "Yes, I . . . I suppose it is. Probably."

"Not that it can't be done," Mother Blessing went on, pouring tea into two plastic tumblers with bright, primary-colored polka dots on the sides. "Just about anything can be done, if one's got the determination and know-how, right?"

Kerry simply nodded. She wasn't quite sure how to broach the more urgent topics that were on her mind, such as Daniel's death at the hands of Season Howe or the attack, seemingly at the hands of Mother Blessing's accomplices, that had brought her to this place. *Not that this isn't where I was trying to get to anyway,* she thought, *but I'd rather have done it without the lump on the head.*

Mother Blessing rolled over to the dining table with the two glasses and a bag of Oreos in the basket mounted on her handlebars and parked herself on the one side that didn't have a steel-framed chair. "Have yourself a sit-down," she urged Kerry, sliding one of the drinks across the table for her. "I know y'all have had a rough few days, and my boys didn't help matters none, I'm sorry to say."

Kerry shrugged and took one of the chairs. She knew that both of Mother Blessing's sons were dead. "By your 'boys,' you mean . . ."

"Simulacra," Mother Blessing said matter-of-factly. "Y'all know what that is?"

"Daniel told me." Simulacra, he had explained once, were humanlike figures magically molded from whatever substance was near where they were needed—in this case, Kerry guessed, maybe from swamp muck, leaves, and branches. He had also said that they were kind of a specialty of Mother Blessing's. Now that his name had come up, she felt she had to tell

Mother Blessing what had become of her son. "You know, about Daniel? That—"

"That he's moved on to the next plane?" Mother Blessing interrupted. The wide, toothy smile half-hidden behind her breathing mask didn't falter. "Yes, I knew right away. As soon as Season did it."

"So you know it was Season, too," Kerry commented. "I was there."

"You meant a lot to him," Mother Blessing said. "Soon as I saw y'all, I knew you were Kerry. That porcelain skin, the big green eyes, the dark hair—course, Daniel didn't say anythin' about it being blue, but I figure that could be new." Kerry was shocked; she hadn't known that he had been in touch with his mother at all during the time they were together. The impression she had had was that mother and son were not particularly close. But then it was clear there was still a lot about the Blessing family she didn't know. She swallowed, fighting back sudden tears.

"It is," she managed. "The blue. And the feeling is . . . mutual . . . about Daniel. You don't seem . . ."

Mother Blessing blinked at her, breathing heavily. Her oxygen tanks hissed softly. "I'm not as angry as you expected? People die—even *our* people. Even witches. It's a passage, that's all."

"Daniel said something like that too. But he still took it seriously. He never forgave Season for killing Abraham."

"Nor have I, child. Season has much to answer for. I mean to see that she does."

Kerry sipped her tea and watched Mother Blessing pull her oxygen mask aside so she could do the same. The older woman followed it with an Oreo. They might as well have been swapping recipes or hair-care tips, Kerry thought. "That's why I . . . why I came looking for you," she said. "I want revenge. On Season. For Daniel, and for our friend Mace, and for . . . well, everything. I want to see justice done." Kerry steeled herself, knowing her request was probably premature. "I didn't know myself why I wanted so badly to find you, but now I do. What I want is for you to help me . . . to teach me. To make me powerful enough to fight her."

Mother Blessing laughed suddenly, little bits of Oreo spraying the varnished wood tabletop. Her laughter shook her enormous frame and turned to coughing, then choking. Kerry was afraid the woman would die right here in front of her, but she didn't know what to do about it. Through her paroxysms, Mother Blessing snatched up her oxygen mask and held it over her nose and mouth until gradually she was able to control her breathing again. When she looked at Kerry again, mascara-streaked tears ran down both cheeks.

"Child," she said finally. "Y'all are a spirited one, aren't you?"

Now that she had declared her purpose, Kerry saw no reason to back down. "I'm sorry," she said, "but I am completely serious. Daniel said the craft could be learned, that one didn't have to be born a witch."

"Daniel was right," Mother Blessing agreed. "It's not easy,

and it's not something that can be taken lightly. It can be done, of course. I'm not sure I'm the right teacher, though. My days of power are somewhat behind me, I'm afraid."

Kerry touched the side of her head where it was still tender. "Powerful enough to have me brought here unconscious by your simulacra," she pointed out. "And, I'd guess, powerful enough to have patched me up, since this doesn't hurt nearly as much as it seems like it ought to."

Mother Blessing made a dismissive motion with her hand. "Nothing," she declared. "A couple of herbs, an ointment. And I am sorry about the simulacra, child. They didn't rightly know who you were, did they? I knew you were tryin' to find me, of course—soon as you entered the Dismal, I knew that. But not the who or the why. If I'd have known it was you, my invitation would've been much more neighborly, wouldn't it?"

You tell me, Kerry thought. She didn't give voice to it, though. She was asking this woman, this utter stranger, for a huge favor. She didn't want to start on an accusatory note. Even if the woman had bashed her head in, however remotely. "I guess that's true," she said, accepting the semi-apology that Mother Blessing had offered.

"Of course I know a little about y'all," Mother Blessing went on. "Through Daniel. But even so, I don't know you myself. How do I know if I can trust y'all with the kind of power you're talkin' about, the kind that could make y'all a challenge to Season? How do I even know you haven't joined up with her?"

Kerry felt her face flush with anger. "I wouldn't!" she

raged. "I couldn't team up with that . . . that . . ." She had been about to say "witch," but realized that in this company that wasn't necessarily a powerful epithet. So she just let the sentence trail off, knowing that her meaning was clear. "She killed the man I love."

Mother Blessing regarded her for a moment, silent. Then she nodded slowly. "So she did."

"You can't possibly believe I'd be . . . in . . . in *cahoots* with her or something."

"I'm just sayin' I don't know what to believe, child. I have years—centuries—of hate built up for Season. Y'all have, what, a couple of months? If I'm supposed to teach you what it takes to defeat her, I have to know you're goin' to stick it out. I have to know y'all are as committed as you say, don't I?"

"Well, I'm here," Kerry pointed out. "I left college, and everyone I know, to come here. I tracked you down—as well as I could, anyway, and if your 'boys' hadn't attacked me I'd still be out there in the Swamp looking for you. I have—oh, crap!" She suddenly remembered her gear, which she'd left in the boat when she ran from the simulacra. "My boat—I have some of Daniel's journals in it, and my laptop!"

"That's all in the closet in the guest room," Mother Blessing assured her with a patting motion of her hand. "Don't you worry about that."

Relieved, Kerry blew out a sigh. "I've been reading his journals, studying them," she said. "Trying to learn as much as I can about Season, her habits, her weaknesses."

"I've got more of those journals here," Mother Blessing told her. "On that bookcase in the living room."

Kerry had known there must be more somewhere, since there were chronological gaps from book to book. "I'd love to read them."

Mother Blessing examined her again. Kerry felt like she was under a microscope, or an X-ray device—as if the woman were somehow looking beneath skin and muscle and bone to what lay deep inside, in the innermost reaches of her heart. "Maybe you will," Mother Blessing said. "Maybe you just will. You know, what you're askin', that's a lot of responsibility. I'm not as young as I once was, and I'm not sure I can keep up with a spirited little chickadee like y'all. Might could be a strain on my heart."

Kerry was heartened by this development. "Does that mean I can stay?" she asked, unable to keep the hope from her voice.

Mother Blessing didn't answer right away. Kerry understood that this was one of her conversational traits: taking a long time to answer, letting the other person feel off guard. Asking questions was another one, even though they weren't meant to be answered. This time, she did both.

"I guess y'all can stay on for a spell. We can get better acquainted before we make any big decisions, can't we?"

8

Josh Quinn's mother was downstairs in her home office, which was where she seemed to live these days. Except, her office, Josh knew, was also the location of her wet bar, and if what she did in there had anything to do with work, then she had given up her real estate license in favor of rehearsing for a role in a remake of *Leaving Las Vegas*. He'd tried to talk to her about it, but nothing doing. He'd even, for what it was worth, left brochures for substance-abuse clinics and a copy of AA's *Little Red Book* where she'd be sure to find them.

But she could ignore a hint just as easily as he could drop it. Maybe easier. All she had to do was pretend not to notice what she was dumping in the trash, whereas Josh had to actually go out and acquire the stuff he brought home for her. Most of it he found on campus without much trouble, but even picking it up and glancing at it meant acknowledging that perhaps he had an addiction problem of his own brewing, and—*like mother, like son*—that wasn't something he wanted to dwell on.

He shut down his computer and headed downstairs. He thought about calling Henry, a friend from school who he had believed might become more than a friend if the circumstances were right. Last time he'd called Henry for a date, though, the conversation had been awkward, and he had ended up not following through. Henry was attractive and articulate, and Josh liked him a lot. But on the phone the other night, there had been a sudden moment when Josh had realized that his friend's experience of the world was so limited that they were like residents of two different planets. They both shared an affinity for noir books and films, for instance. But Henry's entire understanding of violence came from pop culture, and when Josh objected to his hyperbolic comment that he'd like to kill one of his professors, he hadn't understood that Josh viewed killing and violent death through a more realistic lens than he once had. Josh had been unable to overcome that mental hurdle for a few minutes, and Henry had noticed his hesitation. Things had gone downhill from there, and Josh hung up a short while later, thoroughly embarrassed. Rather than put himself through that again, he decided to just go out by himself.

For a moment he considered putting on a light trench-coat, but decided against it. He had on a long-sleeved black T, tight black artificial leather pants, and high boots with silvery buckles running up the insides, and he was pretty sure he'd be warm enough this evening. Stopping outside his mom's office door just long enough to call "I'm going out!"—and hearing no reply—he went out.

Downtown was a couple of miles from home, the Strip even farther. Tonight, though, he didn't want the slightly seedy, no-frills atmosphere of downtown. He wanted to immerse himself in spectacle, in themed entertainment as carefully thought out as Disneyland, albeit with a slightly different focus. The choices were many: Casinos were disguised as fantasy versions of New York, Rio, Paris, Venice, ancient Rome, medieval Europe, the high seas. He could mingle with acrobats and clowns at the circus or pharaohs in ancient Egypt. This time choosing none of the above, he hiked until he could flag a cab, then asked the driver to take him to the Mandalay Bay. He'd never quite figured out what its theme was—some sort of generic Balinese paradise that didn't quite have the courage to commit to its *Gilligan's Island* roots—and that ambiguity suited his mood tonight. Plus, he enjoyed the fact that sections of it had sunk sixteen inches into the ground after it was built, requiring hundreds of steel pipes bored into its foundation to stabilize it. Somehow that seemed to sum up the Vegas experience for him—just do it, and worry about the consequences later.

If Mother Blessing was a surprise, what Kerry saw when she left the house was even more of a shock.

The day had been exhausting, what with the not having

slept much and the various excitements of traveling through the Swamp, including but not limited to being chased and clobbered by simulacra. So, despite her nap and the sweet tea's caffeine, after talking with Mother Blessing for a while, Kerry was ready to sleep again. Mother Blessing took her back to the guest room, showed her where her things had been stowed, and left her to get some rest.

Kerry tugged on a tank top and some pajama pants she'd brought, and climbed into bed, clutching BoBo, the clown doll that had made the journey with her. In spite of her exhaustion, though, the day's events echoed in her mind and sleep was hard to achieve. The double bed was comfortable and roomy, and she had two good pillows—a big improvement over the night before, when her bed was the ground in some hunter's ancient lean-to with the Swamp's wildlife investigating her—but still she tossed and turned for more than an hour before finally drifting off.

Once she finally succumbed, her sleep was deep and without dreams.

She woke early the following morning, when the Swamp was quiet and still and the day's first light was sending yellow streamers across a rosy sky. Curious, Kerry moved through the silent house, still clad only in her nightwear, and slipped out the front door. The Great Dismal seemed a different world from this angle, beyond Mother Blessing's slatted wooden walkway—magical and mysterious, though in a cheerful way, not threatening at all.

But when Kerry turned back toward the house she felt a
sense of dislocation that almost made her lose her balance.
She faced not a suburban-style ranch house, but a tiny swamp
shack, something a trapper might have lived in during the few
days it took to set a line of traps. The boards were old and
warped, with spaces between some big enough for rats to pass
through, the windows covered with what looked like nailed-
down tar paper. The waters of the Swamp seeped under the
walkway right up to the walls, with trees pressing in against
the cabin from three sides.

That's not what I came out of, Kerry thought anxiously.
Worried that the whole house might have been a fevered
dream, a result of the knock she'd taken to the head—or that
it might have been real, but was gone now—she hurried back
to the shack's front door, which was at least in the same place
as the door through which she had exited. She threw it open
quickly, and the scene inside the entryway was just as she
remembered: nicely floored with hardwood, walls of eggshell
white, a sideboard holding a series of potted herbs, and some
framed still lifes hanging on the wall above it.

Confused, Kerry stood in the doorway. Inside was Mother
Blessing's house as she remembered it, complete with the artificial pine scent of whatever she cleaned with. But when she
stuck her head out of the door and looked at the outside, she
saw the ramshackle cabin. The disjunction made her head
hurt, so she gave up trying to figure it out. As she walked back
to the guest room, Mother Blessing's bedroom door opened.

Kerry waited for her to emerge, then described what had happened. She wondered if there was an explanation.

"What do y'all expect, child?" Mother Blessing asked her. "It's magic."

"But . . . which one is real?" Kerry pressed.

"That depends, doesn't it?"

"On what?"

"On if y'all are inside or out, silly," Mother Blessing said. She made it sound like it made sense, and Kerry decided to leave it at that. But she knew that she couldn't take anything about this place at face value.

Kerry Profitt's diary, October 26

After showering in the hall bathroom and dressing in "my" room, I came back out to find that Mother Blessing was up to something in the kitchen that she didn't want me witnessing. Apparently the kitchen is not just where she dishes up the sweet tea, Oreos, and Scooter Pies that seem to be her primary foodstuffs; and by the way, how has she lived to this advanced age (though not necessarily in good health, given the ever-present oxygen mask, etc.) on such a diet? The kitchen is also where she practices her magic, or whips up her potions, or whatever she's doing in there.

Right now, I could go for a Scooter Pie. Or a steak. Yesterday I was too bushed to really care much about food, but today my hunger is catching up to me, and with the kitchen off-limits I only have the stuff I brought in my duffel to sustain me. I've had some trail mix, but the idea that there's a whole kitchen just out of reach is starting to consume me. I'm imagining a pantry stocked with everything I could ever want to chow down on, though in fact it's probably just loaded with more types of cookies, with maybe a few five-gallon jars of mayonnaise and some cases of Velveeta.

Maybe I'm being unfair, or stereotyping the poor woman needlessly. So far, though, I'm getting a really strange vibe from Mother Blessing. She doesn't trust me, that's clear—hence the no-admittance-to-the-kitchen-while-she's-working rule. But it seems like there's more than just that going on—she's trying to be a gracious hostess, I think, because she knows Daniel loved me and maybe because that's what Southern women do. I'd never have pegged her for a witch, though—look at me, Ms. Expert all of a sudden! For one thing, I would expect a witch to maintain herself in a healthier state. Daniel made it clear that he was something of an anomaly, that not all witches spend their whole lives either preparing for battle, battling, or recovering from battle, like he did. But it seems like she would have to be at least a little concerned about Season coming after her, even if she has no other enemies. And except for the simulacra in the Swamp, which seemed to have been dispatched specifically to find me, I haven't seen any defenses at all. Maybe the house's disguise helps with that, though I'm not sure how. If anything, it seems to create the impression of a defenseless place—something a good, stiff wind could knock over.

So the sense of Mother Blessing that I get, obnoxiously prejudiced as it is, is that she's a woman I'd expect to see wheeling her little cart through Piggly Wiggly, stocking up on Ding Dongs and Twinkies, rather than a witch of enormous power and influence.

But Daniel indicated that she was the latter—that when the Witches' Convocation comes around next year, she'll be a participant of considerable importance, though also one that Season might try to railroad in witchy court.

For Daniel's sake, I've got to see if there's anything I can do to help prevent that. But also, and more importantly, from my perspective, I've decided that what I really want is for Mother Blessing to prepare me to take Season on in battle. Daniel asked me not to seek revenge, and I'd love to honor that request. But the truth is, I'm not spiritually advanced enough for that. I guess I'm not as decent a person as he believed I was. Because as small and petty as revenge is supposed to be, it's what I want. The idea of it is one of the only ways I've made it through these last months, since Daniel's death, with any sanity at all.

And of course the other aspect of it is that if Season is allowed to live, she'll keep doing the things she does. I don't have any illusions that now that she's killed Daniel, she'll suddenly reform. On the contrary—without him tracking her constantly, she might feel more free to wreak havoc wherever she goes.

She's got to be stopped. I don't know if Mother Blessing is the right person to help me stop her, but I don't have a whole lot of options at this point. So until she throws me out bodily, this is where I'll stay.

I haven't asked her yet, but my cell can't get a signal and I have my doubts about the place's wireless capabilities. There's not a phone or a computer in sight, so I don't know if I can call or e-mail my buds. I'll just have to hope they're doing okay and not worrying about me.

More later.

K.

Just when Kerry thought she'd either faint from hunger or be reduced to finishing off her camping supplies—which she had hoped to preserve in case she wound up back in the Swamp— Mother Blessing called her into the kitchen. The smells that greeted her were heavenly, and she saw that Mother Blessing had prepared two plates with pork chops, dirty rice, greens, and mashed potatoes.

"I thought y'all might be hungry," Mother Blessing said with a welcoming smile. The oxygen mask hung from its strap around her neck. She delivered a couple of plastic tumblers of iced tea to the table. "Ready for supper?"

"More than ready," Kerry answered happily. "Starving, in fact."

"Well, sit yourself down, child," the older woman invited.

"I didn't mean to leave y'all settin' out there by yourself for so long."

Kerry tried to set aside the anger she'd felt earlier. "I know you didn't plan to have a houseguest," she said. "I can't expect you to rearrange your whole life for me."

Mother Blessing parked her scooter at the table. "It's just a real busy time for me, honey. Just a few more days to All Hallows' Eve, you know."

Kerry didn't follow at first. "You get a lot of trick-or-treaters way back here in the Swamp?"

Mother Blessing laughed so hard that Kerry feared another choking incident. "Goodness no, child," she said when she was able. "It's the most holy day in our calendar."

"Oh." Kerry felt embarrassed by her lapse. "Of course."

"If y'all are serious about learnin' our craft, you've got to know these things."

Kerry could barely contain her excitement. "Do you mean it? You'll teach me?"

Mother Blessing chuckled, but this time without near-asphyxiation. "Did I say that, child? I didn't hear myself say that. But I haven't ruled it out, either, have I? I'll give it some thought these next few days, and y'all think about whether it's what you really want. Once you start down that path it ain't so easy to turn around, is it? You don't want to get into something that you don't really want to see the finish of."

"I do, though," Kerry insisted. "My friends, during the summer? The ones who helped Daniel find Season? They called me Bulldog, because once I put my mind to something, I don't let it go. And there's never been anything I've been more dedicated to than this. I can guarantee that."

Mother Blessing nodded her huge head, that billow of platinum hair twitching around it as if it had a mind of its own. "I won't be surprised to learn the truth of that," she said. "Not at all, child. Not at all."

9

Mother Blessing has told me the story since I was old enough to pull myself to my feet with my tiny hands on her knees, but I realize now that I've never put it down on paper. Since she's not the type who ever would, I suppose, it falls upon me to do so, in case something should happen to me and it should never be told. Here it is, then, as she has told it—and of all the billions of people on Earth, she is the only one who would know.

Well, she and one other. But that person's version of the story, if she tells it at all, is surely not to be trusted. So the best I can do is to commit to history the facts as I know them.

At the dawn of the eighteenth century, Slocumb
was a village of industry and high moral standing.
The village claimed seventy-six residents at that
time, most taking their living from the Swamp, or
farming the fertile land at its edges. John Slocumb
had died but his family had stayed on, with two of his
sons working his fields and a third hunting and trap-
ping, living the life of a swamp hermit deep inside
the Great Dismal. There were other families Mother
Blessing knew well too: the Mortons, the Tanners,
the Wallmers, and more.

Kerry sat back in Mother Blessing's leather recliner
chair—which also, its owner had pointed out, tipped back
almost flat, rocked, and had hidden rollers inside which
would massage Kerry while she read, if she chose—and held
the journal against her chest. Reading it, she heard Daniel's
voice in her head, almost as if he were there with her again.
Missing him was a physical sensation, an ache in her gut that
faded from time to time, but never abandoned her completely.
She wondered if everyone's first love was the same way,
or if this was something unique to them. She had tried to
broach the subject with Mother Blessing, but the woman had
seemed uninterested in or uncomfortable discussing her son's
relationship with a girl who was his junior by almost three
centuries.

This wasn't the only topic Mother Blessing chose to avoid.

While she had hinted that she'd be willing to teach Kerry witch-craft, she hadn't yet committed to a plan of action, or even allowed their brief conversations to drift back in that direction. Now she was back in her kitchen with the door closed.

Kerry had staked out her spot in the living room, anxious to read more of Daniel's journals and to learn whatever she could about his life and craft—especially here, in his boy-hood home, where she almost thought she could sense his presence. There was a tall bookcase in the living room with a few random best-sellers from years past, as well as a stack of the heavy leather volumes that were obviously Daniel's journals. An ancient TV stood in one corner with a lace doily on top and a potted plastic flower centered on that. Kerry didn't understand why anyone would have a fake plant in the middle of one of the most fertile spots in the country, but the list of things about Mother Blessing that she didn't understand was a long one. *The more I learn, the longer it gets,* she thought. *I didn't necessarily have an idea of what she'd be like before I got here, but whatever I thought, she isn't it.*

Besides the recliner there was a wrought iron couch that looked particularly uninviting, and, in the corner opposite the television, a straight-backed wooden chair that looked like something one might see in a Shaker household. The chair looked about as comfortable as sitting on a rock, but it appeared to Kerry to be very old, maybe dating back to the early days of Slocumb itself.

Which reminded her about the journal. She listened for

Mother Blessing for a moment, but all she heard from the kitchen was a tuneless humming. She opened the book again.

The people of Slocumb didn't have a lot of time for fun and games. The Swamp provided for them, but not easily. They had to wrench their living from it, making use of its wood and water, its creatures, its abundant plant life.

But while these were honest and hardworking citizens, God-fearing and sober, near the end of the century a darkness seemed to settle over the village. Crops failed, children died young, and even the Swamp seemed to turn against the townsfolk. A rogue bear came into town on several occasions, attacking, mauling, and killing. Alligators left the Swamp and hid in the creek that ran along the edge of town, preying on swine, young cattle, and even people who strayed too near. Each incident seemed accidental, random, but they added up quickly; within the space of six months a full quarter of the town's residents were either dead or crippled in some way.

Once the extent of the devastation became known, rumors began to spread as to the cause. These were religious people, of course, but also superstitious and ignorant ones. So the explanations didn't revolve around bad luck or unhealthful environmental conditions, but swung to curses and witchcraft.

Living in Slocumb were two suspects: Mother Blessing herself, and Season Howe. Mother Blessing was known as a woman of extraordinary empathy and unusual talents. Season was less beloved, and little trusted by the townspeople. She kept to herself, living in a small house where, it was said, inhuman creatures came to visit her in the dark of night, including the Devil himself on some occasions. Suspicions were voiced in whispers, but no accusations were made, no action taken.

Then, one freakishly cold October morning, as a rare snow dusted the Swamp, a widow woman named Flinders woke to a silent household.

October, Kerry thought. *So this month is an anniversary, of sorts.* Mother Blessing hadn't said anything about that, and Daniel had never pinpointed a date when he told her the story, only mentioning the year. The thought of poor, as yet unborn Daniel and the horrible things that were about to happen to his hometown made her feel sad for him. But she kept reading, wanting to know more.

She had three children under the age of seven, born before her husband was killed in the Swamp by a bear who hadn't been as badly wounded as Mr. Flinders had thought. Most mornings the children were noisy, playing or squabbling in their room, but on this morn-

ing not a sound escaped their door, and when Mrs. Flinders went to look inside, a scene of unimaginable carnage greeted her horrified eyes.

Her three young ones were all dead in their beds, throats savagely torn as if by animal claws, blood soaking the bedding and pooling on the wooden floor. The window was wide open and a chill wind blew flurries of snow into the room. A scream caught in Mrs. Flinders's throat, and it wasn't until she crossed to the window and looked outside to see the tracks in the snow—animal tracks such as a wolf might make, she believed—that it finally broke free, shattering the early morning stillness.

Neighbors came running, and then the town's constable and two of its three clergymen. A hunting party was quickly gathered and the tracks followed through the snow that had fallen during the night. But at the Swamp's boundary the tracks suddenly disappeared, as if, the constable said, the beast had suddenly sprouted wings and taken flight.

The clergymen agreed that there could be only one explanation.

Witchcraft.

The names of Season Howe and Mother Blessing sprang to everyone's lips. The tracking party split into two, one branch heading for each of the suspected witches' homes. Mother Blessing was sound asleep beside her husband—*my father, Winthrop Blessing*—*when a determined rapping on the front door roused them. Both grumbled as they opened the door to find Parson Coopersmith—a dour-faced man whose black clothes and ghastly pallor would have made him as suited for undertaker's work as for the pulpit—standing at the front of a pack of a half-dozen men armed with muskets, axes, and, in one case, a pitchfork.*

Mother Blessing knew at a single glance that this could not be good news. The men's faces were grim, their eyes hard, and of course there were the weapons they bore. "What brings you here?" Mother Blessing asked without preamble. Winthrop Blessing, never a strong man, according to his wife's stories, stood mute beside her.

"There has been an incident," Parson Coopersmith declared. "The widow Flinders's children have been murdered in their beds. Every indication is that witchcraft is behind it."

"Witchcraft?" Mother Blessing asked him. When she tells the story she says that she was acting like a natural performer, since she had never publicly admitted to witchcraft, though many in town knew her ways and came to her for help from time to time. "Then why come to me?"

"There are tales," Parson Coopersmith said diplo-

matically. "You and I have never had any troubles, Mother Blessing. But this . . . this has gone on too long, and we can no longer turn our backs on this activity."

"You believe my wife to be a witch?" Winthrop asked angrily, finally rousing himself. "And a murderer?"

"I believe her to be a possible witch," the parson said, "and therefore suspect in this matter."

Mother Blessing felt her confidence shake at this point. She well knew that it was not their responsibility to prove that she was a witch; rather, the accusation having been made, it was now her job to prove that she was not—an impossible task.

A couple of contradictory ideas came to her. She could run, though that would certainly mean giving up her home in Slocumb forever. She could fight— and win—but that would demonstrate her witchcraft beyond question, and even though these men would never talk, she wouldn't be able to keep their deaths a secret. Or she could go along with them and accept the task of proving her own innocence, which could not be done, since anything she said or did would now be suspect. There were, she knew, no good options. Time and circumstance had gone against her, and all the good she had ever done for the townsfolk couldn't save her now.

"Leave this house at once, Parson," Winthrop demanded, perhaps recognizing himself the impossible choice that confronted his wife.

But she ignored my father's outburst. "Allow me to dress properly," Mother Blessing insisted. "I won't meet my fate in my nightclothes, and you men should be ashamed for facing me in them."

There were murmurs of dissent from the group, but Parson Coopersmith quickly and loudly overruled the others. "As you would, Mother Blessing. Make haste, though."

Mother Blessing closed the door on them. She could hear them arguing, some afraid that she would grow wings and fly out a window so they wouldn't be able to stop her. If she could do that, of course, she could have done so at the door just as easily. But they were frightened and superstitious, and she supposed that she was lucky no one with a musket had fired upon her as soon as she showed herself. She dressed as rapidly as she could, doing her best to ignore their fearful comments, while reassuring her anxious husband that she would be fine.

Of course, she knew that if witchcraft had indeed figured into the murders, like as not Season Howe was behind it. But one witch didn't talk about another, even in such a dire circumstance.

As it turned out, she didn't need to bring up

Season's name. Another group of men had gone to Season's home, and her response had not been as calm and reasoned as Mother Blessing's had been. Instead, she had answered their accusation with the proof they sought, a powerful demonstration of witchcraft that killed them all where they stood.

Her assault was witnessed, however, and even before Parson Coopersmith and his group returned to the town center with Mother Blessing, an alarm had been sounded. From every corner of Slocumb men ran toward Season's home, only to find themselves beaten back by her magical blasts. Parson Coopersmith and his men heard the commotion and charged forward, dragging Mother Blessing along with them. Winthrop armed himself with a musket and joined the group.

Mother Blessing tells me that as they neared Season's the very quality of the air changed. There was so much magic in the air the color of the sky was affected, purpling over Slocumb even though it was early morning, and a smell like burning skunks filled the town. Her guess was that Season had lost control of herself—that in her rage or terror she had unleashed so much magic that it was feeding her own extreme emotions, which then spurred her on to greater efforts in an ever escalating cycle of destruction. Those who had first approached her were all dead now, as were any others who had been nearby.

And still it continued. Parson Coopersmith raised a cross toward Season and advanced on her, shouting out a prayer with every step. But Season uttered words in the ancient tongue and gestured toward him, and a moment later his head was ripped from his body and sent flying, rolling to a stop near Mother Blessing's shoes. The body stood a moment longer, and then dropped the cross to the dirt and collapsed.

Panic spread through Slocumb at that point, and those who had given thought to attacking Season changed their minds. Instead of going after the witch, they ran for cover. Season didn't care, though. Mother Blessing saw her standing in front of her home, her pretty face twisted in unreasoning fury, unleashing wave after wave of incredibly powerful magics. Dust swirled away from Season, choking the streets, and a ferocious hurricane-force wind picked up, bending trees and tearing shingles from houses.

Mother Blessing tried then to stop her. Except for Winthrop Blessing, who proved to have some backbone after all, the men surrounding her had all run away, leaving her exposed in the road. She had left the house empty-handed, though, not anticipating a challenge like this. She tried a few spells, but they were blown back from Season by the furious power of the other witch's magic.

Mother Blessing realized at that moment that even she was powerless to rein in Season's wrath. Season Howe had lost all sanity, all the rationality that normally kept her in check. There was no stopping her now, not unless she could somehow calm herself down. And that didn't seem to be happening. Finally, even Winthrop was caught in her attack: he picked up a fallen musket and fired a ball at her, but Season simply reversed its course, driving it through his skull with enough force to shatter it, blowing bits of brain almost all the way into the Swamp.

Lashed by wind, stung by flying dust, pummeled by chunks of wood and debris, and agonizing over the death of her husband, Mother Blessing had no choice but to retreat. She escaped into the depths of the Swamp, from which she could still hear the screams and cries of dying villagers, could smell the smoke as one building after another caught fire in an inferno that burned in the Swamp for more than a month.

By the time Season's preternatural tantrum quieted, two days and nights had passed. Mother Blessing dared to venture from her safe haven only to find the town leveled, the swamp ablaze, and every last soul in Slocumb dead. Except her, and the two unborn in her belly: my brother Abraham and myself. Season, who had caused the destruction, whose rage had destroyed a town, was gone.

And Mother Blessing dedicated her life, and those of her sons, to hunting her down. That task continues.

I remain,

Daniel Blessing, March 23, 1797

10

Rebecca Levine walked away from campus toward her shared Victorian, her loose, flowing batik skirt fluttering against her legs in the gentle breeze, her soft peasant top open at the neck. She caught glimpses from time to time of the Pacific shimmering in the distance. She had always loved the ocean, loved the natural beauty that surrounded Santa Cruz. But the ocean now reminded her of La Jolla, and that reminded her of Season Howe and Daniel Blessing. Rebecca had never seen anyone killed before—didn't even like violent movies and TV shows—and the sight had been utterly horrifying. She wanted to surround herself with grace and beauty, to forget the vision that would not be forgotten.

She found herself thinking about it at odd moments.

When she was sitting in class, listening to even the most stirring lecturer, she would suddenly realize that her mind had drifted, that she was back on that street in San Diego, watching Season cut Daniel Blessing down with her mystical attacks. Or else she would remember the séance at which Shiai had turned, momentarily, into Season—though she had persuaded herself that she had been carried away by the moment, that it had just been an awful hallucination. Sweat would pour down Rebecca's sides, her fingernails digging into her palms, her heart pounding. She knew her grades were suffering because of the stress, knew that she needed to pay better attention in class, but she couldn't force her mind to comply.

When things had been tough during her childhood, Rebecca's mother had had an odd habit of reminding her that her great-grandparents had survived the concentration camp at Buchenwald. "If you think your life is really so hard, think about theirs for a while," she would say. "Then maybe you'll understand that your problems aren't as big as you think."

It had worked, most of the time, when she was a kid. But then she'd been part of a big family—mother, father, and three brothers—and there was always noise and activity going on that she could use to bring herself out of her occasional funks. Now she didn't have that, her problems seemed far worse than they had ever been, and even thinking of the great-grandparents she had never met didn't quite do the trick.

When she reached the house, she was covered with a thin sheen of perspiration; Indian summer had brought a heat wave to northern California and the walk home had been hot and dry. The house was dark, it was cool inside, and she was almost to the refrigerator for an Odwalla when the phone rang. There was an extension mounted on the wall in the kitchen, so Rebecca reached it almost immediately.

"Hello?"

"Rebecca?" The voice sounded familiar, but strange.

"Kerry, is that you?"

"Yeah," Kerry responded. "It's me."

"Where are you?" Rebecca asked anxiously. She hadn't heard from Kerry since that cryptic e-mail—hadn't even had a chance to tell her about the séance. Now that they were actually speaking, though, it seemed unimportant. "You sound so weird."

"It's a little hard to explain," Kerry said. "And I don't know how much time I have. I'm calling via my built-in microphone, since there's no phone here. Or cell service, wi-fi cable, satellite, or anything else."

Rebecca didn't understand. "So then what are you on? Cable? Satellite?"

"I don't really know myself," Kerry said. "But if I had to guess, I'd say magic."

Rebecca felt herself blanch. "Kerry, you're not . . ."

"I'm fine, Beck. Really. Don't worry about me. You know I can take care of myself."

"But why are you messing around with magic?" Rebecca asked.

"Someone's got to stop Season," Kerry said flatly.

"But . . . you?"

"I don't know if I can," Kerry admitted. "But I know that if I don't prepare myself and try to do it, I'll never succeed."

"I guess that's true," Rebecca said. She felt like there had to be something she could say to her friend to change her course, to make her realize what she was doing. Kerry was brave and capable, and she'd seen for herself what Season could do—had felt it more than the rest of them, Rebecca was sure, because she and Daniel had been in love. Even so, she thought, maybe Kerry underestimated what she might be getting herself into.

"Listen, Beck, I'm being way careful. I'm learning witchcraft—Daniel's mother is starting to teach me. I'm not going to do anything rash. I just wanted to let you know how you could get ahold of me—assuming this connection keeps working. Like I said, I'm not really sure how it's working now."

She told Rebecca she couldn't be telephoned. Or if she could, she wasn't sure how, but that she could check e-mail again at her existing e-mail address, and probably could call if necessary. When Kerry disconnected, Rebecca was confused all over again. How could she get e-mail without being connected to the Internet? But they had spoken, somehow, so clearly the physical laws that she had once believed in didn't apply here.

Having promised that she'd let the others know how they

could reach Kerry, Rebecca booted up her own computer and sat down to write one of the oddest e-mails she could remember.

Mother Blessing had emerged from the kitchen while Kerry sat in the living room trying to fathom what it must have been like to be the last living person in Slocumb, with the homes smoldering pits of ash and coal, the bodies of her husband and friends and neighbors strewn everywhere, acrid smoke painting the air, and a layer of ash overlaying everything. "Are y'all ready?" Mother Blessing asked before Kerry even knew she was in the room.

Kerry started, closing the journal she still had open on her lap. *Is it time for dinner?* she wondered. She knew time had passed while she'd been reading, but she had no idea how much. "Ready for what?"

"Your first lesson," Mother Blessing said.

"Really? Do you mean it?" Kerry asked excitedly. This was why she'd come, what she'd been waiting for. But instead of teaching her a spell or mixing a potion, Mother Blessing sent her into the Great Dismal Swamp to look for a particular type of plant.

Slogging across the wet, uneven ground, Kerry felt more like a lackey than a student. Mother Blessing had shown her a picture of the plant she was looking for—a white, five-petaled flower with broad green leaves—given her a bag, and instructed her to bring back a sack full of its roots.

"The craft is as much about knowin' the natural world around us as anything else," she informed Kerry. "Our Swamp here is a bounty of blessings, but y'all have to know what to ask of it, and how, and it'll help you when it can. Ain't a better place on Earth for a witch to find what she needs, or if there is I'd like to know about it. And there ain't a better way to get to know it than on your hands and knees."

The task took Kerry the rest of the afternoon, and by the time she returned to the house—still ramshackle ruin from the outside, suburban spotless on the inside—she was soaked, cold, scratched, bug-eaten, and miserable. But she had her bag of roots. And that's when Mother Blessing surprised her with the laptop setup, which she promised would be able to communicate with the Internet, even though she wouldn't explain just how. Kerry tried it out for a few minutes, retrieving e-mails sent to her account over the past many days, then using her built-in microphone to try calling her friends. The first one she was able to reach was Rebecca. She knew Rebecca would contact the others and talk to them, and she felt more comfortable spreading the word that way than sending out e-mails she wasn't sure would get through, or that might be magically intercepted somehow. Kerry didn't know if Season Howe kept track of Mother Blessing, but just in case, she didn't want to do anything that might bring Season's wrath down upon them.

At least, not until she was ready.

* * *

After a hot shower and a filling meal, Kerry followed Mother Blessing into the kitchen. Mother Blessing set two cutting boards out on the table with two sharp knives and the bag of roots. When Kerry sat down across from her, Mother Blessing took up one of the knives and one of the roots and, with skillful, precise movements, skinned the outer surface of the root, revealing a moist, white interior, which she tossed into a ceramic bowl. "This is the part we need," she said. "The outside's nothin', might as well be bark. The power's in here, where the root takes in nutrients from the soil, takes in water, and transmits it all up into the body of the plant. A plant's just like a person, has to eat and drink in order to live and grow, doesn't it?"

Kerry almost laughed, thinking of the fried foods and soft drinks and sweetened tea that Mother Blessing seemed to live on, wondering how long a plant would survive on a diet like hers. She was the last person Kerry would expect to give lessons on nutrition—even plant nutrition. But Kerry knew better than to give voice to such a comment. Mother Blessing seemed to be beginning her lessons, and Kerry didn't want to interrupt her, especially with something that might be considered insulting.

"What's the connection?" she asked, picking up her own knife and a section of root. "Between witchcraft and things like plant roots. I just don't quite get it."

"Our power doesn't come from us, child," Mother Blessing explained. "Or from the Devil, as some would have you believe.

It comes from the Earth, through the Earth. It comes from the plants and animals and the rocks and the sky and the water. Some call the source the Goddess, or Mother Nature, or other names. But it's all the same in the end—we don't possess the power, we just channel the power that's around us all the time. That's why I wanted y'all to start getting used to nature—really muckin' around in it, y'know, instead of just moving blindly through it like y'all have been doin' your whole life."

"I haven't been . . ." Kerry started to object. But then she gave it a moment's thought and realized that she probably had been. She had always been drawn to the beauty of nature, the rivers near her home in Cairo, the ocean, the trees and skies and mountains she had seen. But seeing beauty wasn't the same as knowing nature, as being on a first-name basis with it. Kerry thought that that was what Mother Blessing was getting at, and why she had spent the afternoon in the Swamp, digging through mud with her bare hands, uprooting plants. "I guess you're right," she said after reflecting.

"Y'all are gonna find out I often am," Mother Blessing said with a chuckle.

Kerry held her piece of root toward the pot, its outer surface scraped away, its inside liberated. "Can I taste it?" she asked. "Is it poisonous or anything?"

Mother Blessing shrugged. "Find out."

Kerry raised an eyebrow. That seemed like the hard way to learn a lesson. *But hard lessons stick, right?* She brought the root to her lips, opened her mouth, touched it to her tongue.

It was bitter, and a little on the hot side. Not especially pleasant, but she didn't think it would kill her. With the knife she cut off a tiny sliver; she put it on her tongue, feeling its heat, then swallowed it. "I hope that wasn't a bad idea."

"Well, we'll just see if you live or die, child," Mother Blessing said casually. "I expect it'll be live."

"Let's hope."

"Unless, of course, you harbor evil thoughts, right?"

Kerry raised both eyebrows at that. "What if I do?"

"Then it could be bad," Mother Blessing said. She was very matter-of-fact about the whole thing, still carving up her roots.

"But . . . doesn't everyone?"

Mother Blessing laughed out loud. "That's right, child," she declared. "Lesson number two. And three. Life, and magic, are about balance, including the balance of good and evil that exists in all of us."

"That's two?" Kerry queried. "So then what's number three?"

"Don't ever let 'em get you down. Even if they're your teachers. Or your enemies. Psychological warfare, Kerry. It's as important to us as spells and magics. If I'd have let y'all think you'd eaten poison it could've actually made y'all sick to your stomach."

"Like people who believe they're cursed, so they exhibit the symptoms of the curse?"

"That's right." Mother Blessing tossed another root into

the bowl. "Sometimes they just believe it. Then again, sometimes they don't believe in curses, but they get the symptoms anyway. Because sometimes the curses are real, aren't they?"

"I . . . I suppose sometimes they are."

"Better believe it," Mother Blessing said, her tone suddenly serious. "Sometimes they're as real as can be."

11

Kerry Profitt's diary, October 31

So it's Samhain, which Mother Blessing pronounces SOW-waaain, stretching the final syllable out in her Southern way. I've always just called it Halloween, and thought it was all about trick-or-treating and gorging on candy, but apparently there's a lot more to it than that in the Blessing world. This is one of the most important nights of the year in her calendar, up there with the solstices.

She says I get to celebrate with her tonight, but first I had to have another lesson in the Swamp. She gave me a chart and my little skiff and sent me to Lake Drummond, the biggest body of water within the boundaries of Great

Dismal Swamp. There was a jug in the boat that I was supposed to fill with water from the lake. The best tasting water on Earth, she said, because of the cypress trees that constantly freshen it.

"Magic is all in how y'all use the energies that surround us, child," she said when she was giving me my instructions. "Energy is everywhere—how else would trees grow, and the grass, not to mention people? It's how rocks form, how wind blows, how water runs. The world is full of energy, and most people walk around in it without even knowing it's there, much less how to use it. That's where our kind are different." She stopped then, and laughed like she does, a high-pitched kind of titter that seems strange coming from someone her size and age. "Well, like I'm different, anyway, and it won't be too long for y'all now, will it?"

"I don't know," I told her. So far we had been talking only about theory—she hadn't yet SHOWN me anything, or told me how to do anything except chop up roots. In a way it was a complete reversal—Daniel had shown me plenty, but told me precious little. He hadn't, of course, shown me much by way of demonstration; it was mostly just him doing what he had to do to keep me safe. "Will it?"

"Let's us get through tonight, Kerry Profitt," she said— the first time she ever used my full name, I believe. "Then we can see what we see."

Which I took to mean that after Samhain is over, she'll

start teaching me the good stuff. So I went out into the Swamp—it had cooled considerably over the past few days, and was starting to feel like fall outside—and followed her directions. This time I was less scared than I had been before, and more attuned to the world of the Swamp. It's a green world, every shade imaginable and then some. From the thickets at foot level to the tops of the tall trees blocking out the sun, green is the predominant color. I know that if I study with Mother Blessing long enough I'll learn the names of all these trees, and more than that, I'll know their properties: what they can do, what they can provide. I saw, moving about in the trees, a stunning array of birds—black, gray, brown, white, blue, yet more green. Also squirrels, a flash of fur that might have been a fox, and several alligators floating through the still water like sentient logs.

Instead of traveling through the Swamp worried or frightened, this time I passed through it in a state of wonder, breathing in the rich, fertile aromas, listening to the burble of the creeks, the calls and whistles and shrieks of the birds, the buzz and whisper of insects, really SEEING everything for the first time. Mother Blessing's directions were as clear as if the boat itself knew where we were going—which, hey, maybe so, considering who we're talking about—and Lake Drummond was amazing. I dipped my head down to it and drank some of the water straight from the lake, and she was right—I've never tasted anything so fresh and sweet. Rimmed by trees, like castle walls around a big, calm pool, the area was quiet as death, which is a creepy kind of simile—or at least that's what I would have thought before talking to Mother Blessing so much. She is a little strange about death. She misses her sons, but she says that death is just another part of life, just a passage, which Daniel also told me. She says death returns a person's energy to the world, so ultimately it's a good thing. Hard for me to see it that way, but maybe in time I will.

Going back to Mother Blessing's was almost, in a strange way, disappointing—like having to go back inside was punishment because it meant I couldn't stay outside. The sun was lowering, though, and I didn't want to be out in the swamp alone at night, and I especially didn't want to miss the Samhain celebration. She's in her room now, getting ready, and I've washed the swamp muck off me and am just waiting, and waiting . . .

More later.
K.

Las Vegas on Halloween night was a zoo. *Worse than a zoo,* Josh thought, *because in a zoo the animals are contained. In Vegas, they're everywhere.* The Strip was clogged with traffic, and Josh had to shoulder his way through the homeless people, tourists, and partyers filling the wide sidewalks that served no function except to connect the huge casinos. The lights were always glaringly bright here, the cars in the streets always loud, the people always determinedly cheerful, but with an edge of desperation, as if they knew they were expected to have a good time here and thought if they didn't that it was because of some personal failing on their part.

But on Halloween, it was all magnified a hundred times. Walking into the Mandalay Bay, where he had found a slot machine he particularly enjoyed because it seemed to like him, he saw people in costume—women mostly, though a few men as well—drinking and gaming and carrying on all around him. There were an inordinate number of cops around, but tonight they were all female, and their uniforms consisted mostly of hot pants and low-cut, figure-hugging tops, with high heels and maybe a nightstick or a pair of handcuffs hanging from their belts. But it wasn't all police officers: There were similarly sexed-up firefighters, nurses, and maids, and among the men pirates and pimps seemed to be the themes of the moment. For a change, laughter and loud voices clashed with the familiar electronic chiming, dinging, and clanging of the casino machines.

Recognizing that his usual Goth look—augmented tonight by a belted black trench coat that Humphrey Bogart would have worn proudly—could be construed by some as a costume, Josh hugged the casino wall until he reached the bank of slots where the machine he liked was located. It was called the Whirlwind, and whenever two like objects showed up on the pay line, whichever wheel didn't match went into action again, spinning around like mad to give the player one more chance at three matches across. One could play up to three coins at a time, with jackpots commensurately larger the more a player put into the machine. Josh hadn't had any huge payouts, but he'd left the other night with sixty dollars more in his wallet than he'd started with. Tonight he had twenty bucks in his pocket, no early classes the next day, and the intention of making his money last for a while.

His first five credits were no go—he might as well have tossed them down a storm drain. On his next spin, he won two credits. He anted up another credit and played all three. Zero. Ditto the next four credits. This was turning out to be not nearly as enjoyable nor as lucrative as the other night. Of course, there was still an advantage to not being at home, either listening to his mother get wasted or fighting with her about taking better care of herself. That was a pretty big plus.

By the time he had reached his last credit from his first ten dollars, he was lighting one smoke after another with his Zippo, waving away the cocktail waitresses in their skimpy outfits, and trying to ignore an obnoxiously loud couple— she in skintight black leather, he in a Laughlin T-shirt, baggy shorts, and a Utah Jazz ball cap—who were either flirting or fighting but apparently hadn't decided which they wanted to go with. Barely twenty minutes had passed—at this rate, he'd be through all the money he'd brought with him in no time, and therefore reduced to either going home or finding some-place where he could hang out for free. And most of the free options didn't pass his annoyance threshold test.

He started to dig into the pocket of his black jeans for the second ten but stopped himself as soon as his finger touched it. Obviously, the machine was cold. The Whirlwind had worn itself out for now. It needed a breather, and so did he. He left the machine, giving it some time to get its mojo back.

Instead of going right to another game, he wandered into the big lounge in the center of the playing floor. The live band had taken a break, which was good since he couldn't stand their watered-down version of rock music. He didn't order a drink, but instead drifted at the edge of the drinkers, listening to snatches of conversation and looking at the wild Halloween outfits. Throughout most of the casino the circulation system whisked virtually all odor from the air, but here a cloud of smoke hung thick and heavy.

"Video discs," he heard one man say to his companion, a bitter edge in his voice.

"What about 'em?" the other man asked. This man was in his sixties, gray hair long and curled at his shoulders, wearing a Western-style jacket and a bolo tie. The first man looked to Josh like a businessman on casual Friday—he wore a neat polo shirt, khaki pants, and deck shoes and had both a cell phone and pager clipped to his belt.

"I was all set," he said. "Perfectly positioned. Big, beautiful store. Good credit ratings with all my suppliers. Well trained staff. Plowed all my profits back into the business, growing it, ready to be there when every home had a video-disc player."

"And what happened?"

"DVDs." The man practically spat the word. "Freaky little things. Who'd have thought you could even fit a whole movie on such a little tiny thing? And what makes it better than a full-on laser disc? At least you can see the cover art on a laser disc."

"What'd you do?"

"I adapted. Got heavy into DVDs, built seven stores across the region."

"Sounds great. What happened?"

"As soon as I opened the seventh, movie downloads hit. Killed me all over again."

"What are you selling now?"

"Women's shoes. I hate my life."

"Sorry that—" the second man began. He stopped short and was quiet for a long moment. Josh had paused to listen but didn't want to be caught staring, so he was about to move on when the man finally spoke. "Sorry, it's just . . . I was here, I guess, forty years ago. Forty-two, I think it was. Not at this hotel, it didn't exist then, but downtown at the Lucky Strike. I met a woman at the blackjack tables, and we got on well, and next thing you know I was buying her dinner and, you know. We went out a few times, had a kind of a fling while I was in town. I haven't really thought much about her in the last decade or three, I guess. Just one of those things that happens when you're younger, and it's a pleasant memory but a vague one at best."

"What about her?" the first man asked, sounding confused. Josh was equally befuddled, and if the guy didn't get to

the point, he was going to give up and go back to the Whirlwind.

"I could swear she just walked by," the man said. He
seemed a little confused himself.

"Maybe she did. Maybe she never left Las Vegas."

"Yeah, maybe, but . . . well, if it's her, she hasn't aged a
day since then. I mean, it was a long time ago, but she was
a looker, you know, not the kind of girl you forget. I'd say
maybe it's her daughter but there's no way a daughter would
be an identical duplicate of her mother, is there? No, more
likely it was someone who just sort of looks like her, and just
being back in Vegas made me think it was her."

"That sounds right," the bitter man said. "Memory plays
tricks. It's not a perfect storage device like a handy laser disc or
anything, right?"

"Yeah," the guy said again. "Yeah, I guess so. But it's just
weird, you know. Kind of creepy."

Josh was shaking his head, ready to get back to his last ten
bucks and block out the world's strangeness with the rush of
the win and the noise of the machines, when he had a sudden
insight that sent a chill down his spine. *A woman who didn't age
in forty years? That could describe Season Howe.* Daniel Blessing
hadn't aged in hundreds of years, and from everything he'd said
about Season, the same went for her. The chances that it was
Season were slim, he knew. More likely the man was as nuts
as he sounded, or his memory was as bad as he said. Or the
woman under discussion was some kind of female Dorian Gray

with a really heinous-looking portrait out in her garage.

But on the other hand, he knew from what Daniel had told them that Vegas would be just the kind of place Season might go to hide out. Full of transients, all the anonymity she could want. In Vegas people didn't ask too many questions; they didn't want to know a lot about anyone because they didn't want anyone to know a lot about them. If nothing else, Las Vegas was a good place to keep secrets.

Either way, he had to know. He hadn't seen the woman the old guy had been talking about, but he'd never forget what Season Howe looked like. The idea of trying to track her down by himself—even with thousands of people around—seemed absurdly dangerous. But no more so than letting her roam around his stomping grounds without knowing where she was. And Rebecca thought she had seen her once. Maybe Season was regretting having let them live, back in San Diego. *Besides,* he thought, his mind racing now as he tried to avoid surging panic, *if I find her, I can call the others, and maybe someone will have a good idea.*

He wasn't sure where to look, though. Since he hadn't been watching the man, but simply eavesdropping on what had seemed a fairly mundane conversation, he didn't know in which direction the man had been looking when she passed by. And the casino was not only crowded but, like all the big casinos, laid out in an intentionally chaotic fashion so that one couldn't walk a straight line but had to pass the maximum number of slots and gaming tables to get from one place to another.

The best Josh could do was pick a direction and strike out. If that didn't pay off, he'd work his way around and hope that he saw Season before she saw him. The worst thing would be if he couldn't find her, because then there was always the chance that she would find him. She had spared him once—spared all of them except Daniel, that day outside her San Diego hideout—but if she spotted him here and thought he was looking for her, he doubted that he'd get the same consideration again.

Josh had come to think of the casinos as a kind of refuge, where he could go to get sucked into the thrill of the game and forget his problems. He had forsaken most of his friends for them, with few regrets. But if Season was indeed loose here, his sanctuary was violated, his comfort zone suddenly a potential death trap.

Nearly frantic, he chose to go to the left, and he dashed off in that direction, scanning the way ahead, dodging gamblers even as he cranked his head in every direction to eye those sitting at the machines he passed. He kept going that way until he reached one of the far walls, then peered through the windows as best he could into the restaurant there. Plenty of blondes, some very attractive, but no Season. He turned and went to his right, staying near the wall for a while, passing another restaurant, then struck out to his right again, cutting through another swath of casino.

He was afraid that he was calling attention to himself, darting this way and that, looking hard at every blond head he saw. He half expected security to snatch him up at any moment.

Still no sign of her. He tried to carve the casino into a regular pattern in his mind so he could make sure he covered all of it—notwithstanding the probability that she was not sitting still someplace, but was moving around just as much as he was, so he could miss her anyway—but its walkways were so irregular that that was hard to do.

Finally, Josh gave up. There was a plain-clothes security agent giving him a hard eye—he recognized the guy from other trips here, and the man was always loitering, never playing, which marked him as an undercover man. Josh hadn't seen Season anywhere. Probably his first impression was the right one: Either the old guy had been wrong altogether, or he had seen someone who looked like his old flame, but that someone was not Season Howe.

As he headed for the nearest exit, Josh felt his heart rate start to calm, his breathing become more regular. He had been, he realized now, dangerously close to a full-fledged panic attack. It had all been a false alarm, though. He wouldn't be returning to this particular casino for a while, but at least he didn't have to worry about Season Howe.

He was almost out the door when he saw her.

12

Scott didn't pace. It might almost have been better if he did. Instead, he sat down at the couch, turned on the TV, ran through the channels using the remote. Finding nothing of interest, he turned it off again, drummed his fingers on the couch, then rose and went to the kitchen, where he rummaged through the pantry. Again finding nothing, he went back to the couch, drummed for a while longer, then clicked the TV back on.

Brandy, sitting at the dining room table and trying to cram for a midterm, thought she would scream. Or kill him. Or kill him and then scream. Earlier, occasional trick-or-treaters had interrupted his agonized fidgeting, but their numbers had trickled and then they'd stopped coming altogether.

"Can you *please* try to control yourself?" she asked, impatience evident in her voice. She had given up trying to hide it.

"What? Am I bothering you?" *Clueless.*

"Brilliant deduction, Sherlock." She couldn't put a finger on precisely *when* she had stopped loving Scott. But this was the moment at which she became aware that she had, and it struck her hard, like a physical blow, and made her queasy, almost nauseous. She had, for a long time, loved the guy sitting there on the couch looking at her from behind his glasses like some lost little boy. But she didn't now. He had drifted away from her somehow. They had much in common, still—mutual friends, mutual interests—but that was a friendship, not a love affair or a lifetime commitment.

"It's just that I'm worried about her."

"About Kerry."

Scott nodded affirmation.

And there it is, Brandy thought. *The wedge that's come between us.*

"You think about her more than you do about me," she said simply. "About us."

He looked as surprised as if she'd slapped him. His thin cheeks crimsoned. "That's not true. It's just . . ."

"It *is* true," Brandy said. "You can't get her off your mind. Since we came back from San Diego, you've talked about Kerry more than anything else. Your grades are slipping because you worry so much about her. You check e-mail, what, twenty times a day, just in case she's sent one? Thirty?"

"She's important. To us," Scott argued. He came off the couch now, walking toward her, and Brandy felt threatened by his approach. No, not threatened, that was wrong. Disturbed, though—she wanted distance. If he put his arms around her, held her close, if she breathed in the familiar scent of him, it would weaken her resolve. Somehow, this seemed important to her right now. Earlier, they'd taken turns answering the door to their apartment as trick-or-treaters came in search of candy, but since that had petered off they'd been alone with only the sounds of the TV and his finger-drumming disturbing the silence, grating on her nerves, pushing her toward a decision she had never wanted to make.

"She's important to you," Brandy shot back. "Okay, to both of us. But only one of us is obsessed with her. One of us thinks she can take care of herself."

"Not against Season," Scott rejoined.

"We don't know that she's fighting Season," Brandy said. "In fact, we have every reason to believe that she's not, and that she's perfectly safe with Mother Blessing, like she told Rebecca."

"I wish she'd called here—" Scott began.

"Is that it? You're ticked that she talked to Rebecca instead of you? She said she tried here, didn't get an answer."

"We have voice mail," Scott pointed out defensively.

"Yeah, we do. And Rebecca said she was calling via her laptop, with some sort of magical force connecting it to the Net. So maybe whatever magic made that work doesn't play well with voice mail. Maybe it wasn't even Kerry, maybe it was her audio doppelgänger."

"It's just . . . I worry about her. I think she's up to something dangerous. I think she's the key to Season, somehow, and . . . I don't know." Instead of approaching Brandy, he flopped back down on the couch, as if he sensed the coldness with which she would have greeted his advance. It was almost as if she'd put up an invisible force field around herself, which was, in fact, what she had been trying to project. "Okay, yeah, you're right, I worry about her. She's our friend, is that a bad thing?"

"It is when it's to the exclusion of the rest of your life," Brandy offered. "Do you remember the last time you kissed me? I don't mean kissing back if I kiss you, but the last time you took the initiative? The last time you made love to me? The last time you even took my hand as we walked across campus? You've been so distracted, so—I have to say obsessed, again—with Kerry that you haven't been paying attention to anything or anyone else, including me. I've looked through your notebooks, Scott. Your notes are terrible. I don't think you're going to pass any of your classes. You can't live like this—or, I don't know, maybe you can, but I can't."

She paused, and Scott's gaze bored into her as if he were looking for the Brandy he'd once known behind this new, cruel mask. Finally, he spoke again. "What . . . what are you saying? It's . . . we're over? Is that it, Brandy? Because if it is, if you'd let what we have, what we've meant to each other, end because of . . . because of something like this, of me worrying about a mutual friend who's in trouble—she left her school, she went to some swamp—you know, that really sucks."

"Maybe it does." Brandy had to try hard not to shrug, but that would look too callous, even for her. "But it's her *Deliverance* fantasy; she's where she wants to be. You know, I'm sorry, Scott. This is not what I wanted at all. I wanted us to be together forever. But, see, by definition that requires both of us participating, and you haven't been. I don't see that changing. I think you love Kerry—or if not, your concern for Kerry outweighs every other aspect of your emotional life, which might as well be the same thing."

Finally, Scott seemed to understand what was happening, and anger clouded his face. She saw him looking at her, narrowed eyes twitching as if he were searching her face to see if she meant what she was saying. She was pretty sure that she did. At any rate, she'd said it—it was out there in the room now, like a tiger let out of a cage, and it couldn't be put back in.

She only hoped it didn't draw blood.

"Brandy, I . . ." Scott let the sentence hang, unfinished. He swallowed, and she thought she saw a tear forming at the corner of his eye. *At least that would be something,* she thought, *an emotional response that really was directed at me and not at Kerry.* But he sniffed once and rubbed his eyes with his knuckles, and when he blinked and looked her way again it was gone, if it had ever been there.

He looked like he was about to say something else when

the phone rang. *This is a test,* she thought. *If he lunges for the phone, hoping it's Kerry or news of Kerry, then I'm right about this. If he understands that we're fighting for our own survival, as a couple, and lets it ring—*

He lunged. "Hello?"

He was quiet for a minute, his face growing ever more somber. "Okay," he said after a while. "Yeah, thanks. We'll be there."

He hung up the phone, left his place on the couch and came back into the kitchen. She didn't like the look on his face. "That was Josh," he said, and Brandy thought she detected a tremor in his voice. He opened the refrigerator and leaned inside, hunting for something, raising his voice so she could hear him. "He's found Season. We have to go to Las Vegas."

"What, right now?" Brandy asked, surprised. "We're kind of in the middle of something here. And Las Vegas is, like, two thousand miles away."

Scott swung around toward her, a Coke in his hand. "Brandy, you may not like it, but you're in this. You're part of this. Remember when Rebecca thought she saw her? If Season's in Las Vegas she might be hunting Josh—hunting all of us. Or she might just be trying to hide out. Either way, something's got to be done."

"What can we do?" she asked. She felt a sudden panic—she had hoped their Season-fighting days were far behind them, for the rest of their lives. "We can't hurt her. Even Daniel couldn't beat her."

"We can't just leave her alone," Scott insisted. "Josh could be in trouble. And if she's after him, she'll come for us, too. We have to try to do something. Rebecca's going to try to reach Kerry. Maybe with the help of Daniel's mother, she can . . ."

"Kerry's going to save the day?" Brandy asked archly. "You just keep thinking that."

Scott threw his hands into the air. "Okay, whatever," he said. "I'm going to the airport to get the first flight to Vegas. You can come or not. Suit yourself. And anyway, *Deliverance* is hillbillies, not swamp rats." He headed into the bedroom, and a moment later Brandy heard the sounds of drawers being flung open, his closet ransacked, as he packed for the impromptu trip.

She only thought it over for a few minutes, listening to him prepare. She hadn't consciously changed her mind about loving him—almost as if a switch had been thrown, it was just over. He had demonstrated that his concerns were elsewhere, and that was all it took. The process, she was sure, had started a while ago; his obsession with Kerry had simply been the crucial card that brought all the others down.

But notwithstanding that, he was right. She was in this witch-hunt as much as he was, or as much as any of them with the possible exception of Kerry. And even if she was no longer in love with Scott, she didn't want him to be injured. Maybe Kerry could take care of herself, but Scott couldn't. Someone had to be there to keep an eye on him.

She went into the bedroom to gather the things she'd need. *I hope this is a short trip,* she thought anxiously. *I'm going to have to make up that midterm.*

"Samhain is a very special night," Mother Blessing explained. She was wearing a green, velvety robe, and while Kerry bathed in a specially scented tub, she had placed a similar robe on Kerry's bed. After Kerry donned the robe, marveling at its soft, luxurious fabric, they met in what had been the kitchen, except that, through some mystical process Kerry couldn't yet fathom, it had become a courtyard, open to the moon and the stars and an aromatic breeze off the Swamp.

The floor, once vinyl tiles, was now earthen. Candles flickered everywhere—short, fat ones on the bare ground; tall, narrow tapers in multitiered candelabra; tea lights in glass dishes or simply arranged in lines upon the stone altar that stood at one end of the impossible arena. When Mother Blessing had pushed the door open and motored into this place, Kerry hadn't believed her eyes. She tried surreptitiously to feel the ground with her hands, rolling dirt between her fingers to convince herself that it was real.

During her childhood, Halloween had been a very special event for Kerry—the one night she could really lose herself in imagination, in fantasy, giving herself permission to be someone else for the evening. She loved the costumes, the witches and jack-o'-lanterns and black cats, parties with bobbing for apples and other games, knocking on the doors of strangers and being rewarded for it with candy. She had never imagined a night like this one, though . . . had never believed that the witches were real.

"We celebrate the Old Ones on this night," Mother Blessing continued. "We thank them for the gifts they've given us this past year, and we ask them to bless the crops which are to be harvested." She allowed herself a chuckle. "Course, I don't do a lot of harvestin' myself, so that part's just kind of traditional. But still, someone's doin' it, and I use the crops plenty. Just don't pick 'em."

The Old Ones, Kerry knew from Mother Blessing's lectures, were the God and the Goddess. Mother Blessing had stressed that they were two facets of deity, and that other religions and cultures might see them differently—as a single deity, or as an entire pantheon full of gods and demigods. But in Mother Blessing's world, they were two: male and female, opposite sides of the coin. The God represented war, power, rationality, and the seed; the Goddess emotion, beauty, art, and the womb. "Sexist, ain't it?" she had said with a laugh. "But not really, because they're both all of those things. Or they contain all those things within them. Or their aspects can be seen in those things. It's a fluid system, child, that's the important part. However you want to think of it is the way it will work for you. It's only crucial that you do think of it, that you commune with them, because they *are* the power. You channel the power, nature provides the power, but they are part and parcel of the power."

"I think I understand," Kerry assured her. She was afraid of sounding simplistic, but it was a lot to take in and she was still processing. "I haven't done a lot of harvesting myself, but I'm sure happy there are fresh fruits and vegetables and grains."

"That's right," Mother Blessing said. She placed several objects on the altar: a cup, a bell, a knife. "Tonight is also a night of great power," she went on, her voice taking on a warning tone. "So our ritual must be cautious. We want to honor those who have passed, and to prepare for their eventual return. But we don't want to call them—on Samhain, that is far too easy to do and far too dangerous to contemplate."

"The dead can come back?" Kerry asked, hope sparking within her for a moment. Maybe there was a way to see Daniel again, to be with him . . .

"The dead always come back," Mother Blessing replied. "But not as those we remember. And not in frogs or rocks or, I expect, lawyers. Just as new people, with some trace fragments of who they were before buried deep inside them. But if they're summoned on Samhain and they're not ready to return . . . well, you don't want to know, do you?"

Actually, Kerry thought, *I kind of do.* But she decided she wouldn't let on about that. This whole thing was so exciting—finally being allowed to take part in a ritual, and such an important one at that. She felt that Mother Blessing was gradually learning to trust her. If she performed well here—which she figured meant keeping out of the way, not accidentally breaking anything, and doing whatever Mother Blessing asked of her—then surely Mother Blessing would ramp up her training, start in with the real goods. She knew it would be a long time before she could do the kinds of things that Daniel had, but baby steps were better than not walking at all.

Mother Blessing turned her cart around and was about to wheel away from the altar when a look of surprise washed over her face. She stopped cold and stared at the ground, as if listening intently to a voice Kerry couldn't hear. When she looked up again it was directly at Kerry. "Someone's trying to reach you."

Kerry said the first thing that popped into her mind. "The dead?"

"The living," Mother Blessing answered. "I hate to see our Samhain rites interrupted, but you had better see what they want. It's urgent."

"How . . . ?"

"Check your computer," Mother Blessing said. "You'll be able to get through. Tonight, magic is easy. The veils between worlds are thin. Go, child, go."

Kerry took a last look around at the unlikely courtyard, the candles, the objects arrayed on the altar, and herself and Mother Blessing in matching green robes. *I'll never learn this,* she thought angrily, *if I can't have some uninterrupted time to do it in.*

But she knew that Mother Blessing wouldn't send her

away if there weren't a good reason. She went out through the door—into the rest of the house, just as if she'd been in the normal kitchen all along—and dashed down to her room. The laptop was in the cabinet next to her bed. As she booted up, she wondered what could possibly be so important.

13

Josh had figured he'd live his whole life without ever once saying—at least in any kind of serious way—the words "Follow that cab." But when he finally spotted Season at the Mandalay Bay, she was walking out the front door, and by the time Josh reached the door, a doorman was closing a taxi door behind her. Josh had jumped into the next cab in line and uttered those eternal words, and as the taxi pulled out into the street, he was glad he hadn't gambled away his second ten. And hoped the ride would be a short one.

Both cabs rolled out onto Las Vegas Boulevard—the Strip—and were immediately stuck in gridlock. The Strip was thick with vehicles: huge stretch limos, SUVs, hotel shuttles, and cabs mixing with normal passenger cars and the occasional city bus in a ballet of steel, glass, and rubber performed to a soundtrack of honking horns, screeching brakes, and squealing tires. Josh was half afraid that his cab would accidentally catch up to or pass the one Season rode in, and that either she'd see him or his driver would misunderstand the nature of the request and, thinking he was trying to join her, would flag the other driver down or radio him.

As it turned out, though, that didn't happen. Season's cab stayed ahead of theirs, turning off the Strip at Flamingo and cutting down to the Maryland Parkway, which ran parallel to Las Vegas Boulevard but without as much traffic. Josh watched the dollars mount up on the taxi's meter as the car swallowed up the miles toward downtown. He knew he should call the rest of the summer gang, but he didn't want the cabbie to hear what he had to say; bad enough that by not having a destination, but asking the driver to follow another car, he was creating a memory that would stick with the guy.

Finally, the other cab stopped at a motel near downtown, the Come-On Inn. It was nothing special—not the kind of place Josh would have expected Season to stay. But then again, he thought, if privacy was her primary consideration, the big casinos probably weren't ideal. They had cameras everywhere, they had staff who tried to remember the guests, especially regulars. At this place one could probably get a room without even showing identification, and the staff most likely made a point of not prying into a guest's affairs.

Josh glanced at the meter again. Thirteen bucks, and still

climbing. He had just the ten, a few singles, and some loose change on him. "Stop here," he said. He reached into his pocket, pulled out the ten, a couple singles, and some change. When the driver reached around to collect, Josh hurled it all into the front seat. "Sorry!" Josh shouted. He grabbed the door handle, opened it and darted from the cab while the driver fumbled with the money.

The guy shouted at him, but Josh ran into the shadows behind a vacant commercial building. He stayed there for a few minutes, breathing hard, his heart pounding, while the cab circled the block. Josh felt terrible—he hated to rip off an honest cab driver just trying to make a living—but this was an emergency situation. As it was, he'd been left with just a couple of quarters and two singles. *Damn Whirlwind,* he thought.

When the coast was clear, Josh emerged from the shadows, just in time to see an upstairs door close behind Season. He moved a little closer until he could see the number on it: 17. Behind heavy drapes, a light turned on. It looked as if she was alone in the room, and, he hoped, in there for the night.

Now he dug out his cell phone, scrolled through his saved numbers, and dialed Rebecca. "Happy Halloween," she answered cheerfully.

"Beck? It's Josh."

"Hi, Josh, how are you?"

"Listen, Rebecca, this isn't a social call. It's Season. I found her."

There was a long silence from the other end. When Rebecca spoke again, there was a tremor in her voice, and Josh felt sorry for having to put her through this. "If this is a Halloween prank, Josh, it's not a very funny one.

"It's not a joke, Beck. She's here, in Vegas. I just tailed her to her hotel. We have to do something."

"What can we do, Josh? You're better off getting out of there before she sees you."

"But . . . Rebecca, she's not going to stop being a threat. To us and to others. Don't you think we should try to fight her while we have the advantage?"

"What advantage is that? She has all the power."

"We have surprise," Josh countered, hoping he didn't sound as foolishly desperate as he felt.

"We had that before, too. And we also had Daniel. Look at where it got him."

"Yeah, but she was ready for Daniel. She knew he was around, knew she'd be facing him sometime. She doesn't know that we know where she is."

"Because she's not worried about us, because we can't do a thing to her," Rebecca pointed out. "We're powerless against her, Josh. Get out of there while you can."

"Maybe we're not so powerless after all, Beck," he argued. "Didn't you say that Kerry was learning magic from Mother Blessing? Maybe there's something she can do."

Another pause from Rebecca. Her hesitation surprised him. Sure, it was stupid to think they had any chance against

Season. But it was suicidal to just leave her roaming freely around his town. "Maybe," she said at last. "Are you sure she hasn't seen you?"

"I'm sure." Josh realized that another advantage of this crummy motel was that in any of the big hotels, security would have thrown him off the premises before too long. Here, though, he should be able to keep an eye on her door at all times. "Can you try to get through to Kerry? I'll call Scott and Brandy. I'm sure if we all get together we can think of something. But it's got to be fast—I don't want to lose her again."

Rebecca sighed loudly enough that he wasn't sure he needed the phone to hear it. "Okay," she said. "I'll reach Kerry, somehow, and then I'll catch the first plane out there. I'll call you when I get there, and you can tell me where you are."

"That's great, Rebecca. Thanks. I really think this is important."

After he disconnected the call he tried to figure out why he thought that. She was right, of course. They had no way to mount a successful offense against Season Howe. Unless, that is, Kerry had learned some really impressive magic in the weeks she'd been gone. Even so, the chance that in such a brief period of training she had picked up any skills that Daniel hadn't acquired after hundreds of years was worse than slim.

But really, he thought, *that doesn't matter. Daniel died. Mace died. Others will die. Now that we have a lead on her, we have to play it out, no matter what. To turn our backs on her would be the only unforgivable thing.*

He scrolled down to Scott and Brandy's number and pushed talk.

With every passing day in the Great Dismal, Kerry felt more comfortable there—so much so that when she had to leave, she was surprised by a pang of regret, as if she were leaving a home she'd known for years. She bade Mother Blessing good-bye before first light, having missed the whole Samhain observance, which the older woman had said had had to go on as scheduled before midnight changed the date. After the ritual was over, Mother Blessing had called her back into the kitchen, which was, once again, just a kitchen, and they had sat down together at the table with glasses of milk and a plate of cookies between them.

"Y'all have to go," Mother Blessing had said.

Kerry had come to the same conclusion, but she had expected to have to convince Mother Blessing. That the witch herself suggested it came as a surprise. "I know," she agreed. "I'm just not sure what I can do."

"You'll do whatever you can. The woman is just evil. You know why she was at a casino instead of celebrating Samhain like she should've been? She thinks she's nontraditional, but it's the tradition that is so important to the craft. She just likes to do things her own way, no matter what." Kerry could tell from Mother Blessing's tone, and the sneer on her lips, that this was an enormous sin in her eyes. "I want y'all to understand why it's so important that Season Howe be stopped," Mother Blessing continued. "And sooner better than later."

"Well, to start with, she's a killer, right?" Kerry offered.

"She is that, true," Mother Blessing said. "More urgently, though, did Daniel ever tell y'all about the Witches' Convocation?"

"Yes, he mentioned it." Every five hundred years all the world's witches gathered for a festival, a sharing of information, and a combination social and business gathering. Kerry remembered, with a pain in her chest like a spike to the heart, that he had been looking forward to his first one.

"Well," Mother Blessing went on, "this one's the first since Season destroyed Slocumb. I'm fixing to bring charges against her for it. But word is she's got a counterattack planned—that she's thinkin' she'll demand sanctions against us for chasin' after her for so long, and she'll use that as a forum to deflect blame for Slocumb onto someone else. Maybe even me."

Kerry was astonished to hear this. "Could she get away with that?"

Mother Blessing tucked a cookie neatly into her mouth and chewed while nodding. "It's all political," she said when she had swallowed it. "If she could sway enough votes to her side, she could pull it off."

"What would the sanctions be?" Kerry wanted to know.

Now Mother Blessing shrugged. "Could be just about anything. I might have to give up magic until the next Convocation.

I might have to pay a fine of some kind. Could be I'd even have to pay with my life."

Kerry had been about to sip some milk, but now she put the glass down hard. "You're kidding."

"I wouldn't joke about something like that, would I, child?"

"I guess not. It just seems sort of extreme."

Another shrug. "If her accusations were true, it might be a fair judgment. Since they're not, though, I have to keep her from bringin' 'em if I can. Be better to stop her before she ever makes it to the Convocation so I don't have to worry about tryin' to outmaneuver her once we're there."

After sorting through the logistics of how to get to Vegas from the Swamp, Kerry had turned in for a few hours of restless sleep. As soon as the morning light filtered through the trees into the Swamp, she was in Mother Blessing's skiff, rowing for the old Slocumb site, where her van still waited. By the time she reached it her arms and shoulders were sore from the workout, and she was covered with a film of sweat in spite of the cool of the morning. She hiked across the wasted, barren land with a deeper appreciation for what had occurred there than she'd had before reading Daniel's account of that catastrophic day. When she reached her minivan she thought for a moment that she saw shadows slipping away from it into the reeds. She wasn't entirely sure, but it wouldn't have surprised her to know that Mother Blessing had sent simulacra to guard it until her return.

The van started right up. Sitting behind the wheel felt oddly foreign to her, as if hiking through the Swamp had already become her everyday life, and the world of cars and roads and cities a kind of half-remembered dream. But she hadn't forgotten how to drive, so she put the vehicle into gear, turned it around and headed back toward the highway, back toward Norfolk and an airport from which she could fly to Las Vegas.

Season was there. She wasn't sure what she'd do to Season—Mother Blessing had armed her with some potent spells, though she'd had no time to practice them—but that would come. The important thing was finding her again. Confronting her.

Making sure she paid for what she did to Daniel. And making sure she would never make it to the Witches' Convocation, where she might compound her crimes by blaming them on Mother Blessing.

Kerry's resolve was tempered steel. The Bulldog was back.

14

Josh spent the night huddled in the doorway of the vacant building, drawing his coat around him for whatever warmth it could offer, smoking for the same reason, wishing he had a car he could sit in or a credit card so he could take a room at the Come-On Inn for himself. Las Vegas was a desert city, which meant that on summer days the sun could be merciless, but on October-melting-into-November nights, the same lack of cloud cover that let the sun beat down during the day allowed the city's heat to be quickly dissipated. The result was nights that felt positively arctic, at least by Josh's standards. He figured frostbite was not a genuine concern, but he'd spent more comfortable nights, and he couldn't think of many worse.

Finally, though, the sun did reappear above the eastern horizon, and with its glow the city began to awaken. Parts of it, of course, never slept—the casinos were open 24/7—but most of the city, away from the bright lights and high rollers, operated on a more traditional schedule. As the sun warmed the air, birds began to chirp their morning songs, cars and buses emerged onto the streets, and Josh felt his bones start to thaw.

He also realized another downside to his plan. His stomach woke up too, and it began churning hungrily. He'd hardly slept, he'd had nothing to eat or drink, and he'd been smoking like a chimney. He needed to eat something now, and have some water, or he'd be sick. But there was nothing he could see within immediate range, no handy market or diner, and if he went looking for something he could buy or steal he'd run the risk of missing Season, should she emerge from her hidey-hole. He wondered what Philip Marlowe would do in this situation, or Mike Hammer. Fictional private eyes didn't need to eat as regularly as real people, he decided, so they'd probably just buck it up, maybe knock back a shot of whiskey, and continue the surveillance. Sooner or later someone would knock them out, and then they'd have the opportunity to grab a few winks and maybe a sandwich.

The sound of his cell phone's electronic tune startled him. He fished it from his pocket with a shaking hand. "Yeah?"

"Hi, Josh." Rebecca Levine. She sounded close, but that was meaningless.

"Beck, hey. Where are you?"

"At the airport," she said.

"McCarran?"

"Here in Las Vegas."

He moved the phone from his ear long enough to check the time. Seven-fifteen. "Listen," he said, regretting the words even before he spoke them. "I think our bird's gonna stay in her cage a while longer. Why don't you rent a car, but then stay at the airport a while? Brandy and Scott are supposed to get here at 10:12. You might as well wait and bring them when you come."

"I talked to Kerry last night," Rebecca reported. "She'll be here this morning too."

"That's great," Josh said. "I'm glad you were able to reach her."

"Is everything okay?"

"I could use some grub," Josh admitted. "And I'm sure I need a shower. But I'm fine, I guess. No movement from Season after she went into her room last night."

"It's so amazing that you found her," Rebecca said. Josh thought he caught a hint of disbelief in her voice, as if Rebecca questioned whether it was, in fact, simply coincidence that put Josh and Season in the same building at the same time. Josh didn't know how to answer that, because he'd had the same concern himself.

If it's not coincidence, then we could be playing right into her hands.

That idea chilled him to his core. But in fact, he remembered, Rebecca had seen her first—or had thought she had. Which didn't mean this wasn't a trap of some kind. In fact, the more he dwelled on it, the more it seemed to confirm that idea. "Yeah," he said simply. "I don't know what we're going to do now, but at least we've got her pinned down."

"I think Kerry will have some ideas," Rebecca offered.

"She'd better. I sure don't."

"She will." Rebecca sounded more like someone trying to project confidence than someone who actually felt it, but Josh was willing to take what he could get. "You've got my number, so if anything comes up, give me a call, okay?"

"Absolutely," Josh assured her. The fact was, as much as he liked Rebecca, he could think of no one less useful for surveillance or combat, if it came to that. Her manner of dress tended toward flowing skirts and tie-dye, which would make her stand out in a crowd or in a casino—not that Josh didn't, in his Goth blacks and jet hair. But at least during the night his chosen wardrobe had helped him blend into the shadows. Then there was the fact that Rebecca was just about the most peaceful soul he'd ever known. He was vegan, but even so, he was willing to swat a hungry mosquito. Rebecca would argue for the creature's life, then extend her arm to it. She had needed to be informed of Season's reappearance because she was part of the original group that had faced the witch during the summer, but keeping her at the airport, taking care of logistical things like renting a car, was the best use for her.

Still, he thought as he squirmed in the doorway, *I could have had her pick up some granola or something.*

Two more hours had passed when the door to Room 17 opened. Josh looked around anxiously, hoping to spot a cab. If she was going somewhere by car, or had a ride coming, he was out of luck. This was what he had hoped wouldn't happen until Rebecca showed up with the others in her rental. He watched Season step outside onto the walkway that ran past all the second-floor doors, her honey-blond hair catching the morning sun. She wore what looked like a brown leather suit, snug pants and a jeans-style jacket with a white shirt underneath it. Josh pressed himself back against the door, as deep in shadow as he could get, while she slowly surveyed the neighborhood.

Instead of getting into a car, though, Season descended the staircase and walked across the street to a bus stop. Almost no one used public transportation in Vegas, Josh knew, except those so economically disadvantaged that they just couldn't afford a car. Which was probably precisely why Season was using it—if she were hiding out she'd want to vary her routine, not be predictable. Cab last night, bus this morning. Made perfect sense.

But that didn't solve his predicament. He had an idea that might, though. So far, no bus was in sight. Bus stops weren't too terribly spread out around this neighborhood. He had an opportunity, then, if he hurried, to reach the next bus stop down the line, and to get on the bus before Season did. Of course, that came with a couple of pitfalls, too. If he missed the bus he'd lose Season. If she changed her mind and didn't take the bus, or crossed the street and hopped one going in another direction, he was screwed. And if she recognized him once she got on, she'd . . . well, it didn't help to dwell on such things. It was a gamble, but Josh was a gambler. He ran.

He went around behind the building next to which he'd spent the night, knowing as he did that letting Season out of his sight only decreased the odds in his favor. But if she saw him running, her guard would certainly be raised. This way she'd only have a brief glimpse of him, if at all, when he ran across the distant intersection more than a block away from the one where she waited at the bus stop. Josh put aside his exhaustion, his hunger, and his fear, and sprinted full-out. Two blocks beyond Season's location, he cut back over to the street she was on.

From here, he looked in both directions, spotting a bus stop one more block away. He started for it at the same time that a city bus swung around the corner, coming toward him. He had been running with everything he had—he was not, he'd readily admit, exactly track-star material—but now he reached deep down inside, knowing he had to find a little more speed, a little more endurance, if he hoped to beat the smoke-belching vehicle. Feet pounding pavement, head jarring with every step, aching lungs sucking air, he ran, finally reaching the bus stop just as the bus lurched to the curb.

The driver looked curiously at him as he boarded, but it was all Josh could do to drop his fare into the slot and request a transfer. Trying to catch his breath, he moved toward the back of the bus. He spotted an open window seat next to a wrinkled Latino man with a steel lunchbox on his lap, and ignored several empty seats to take that one, to eliminate the chance that Season might sit next to him. The man frowned, but relented and allowed Josh to squeeze past him.

When the bus rumbled up to the next stop, Josh scrunched down in the seat as far as he could, just looking over the seat back in front of him from the tops of his eyes. For a terrible moment he feared that Season had changed her mind, that she wasn't getting on after all, and that he would be taking a bus ride to nowhere while she slipped away. But then her familiar features showed up in the doorway, another ray of light striking her—as if illuminated by an admiring sun—just before she came into the bus's shadow. She didn't even glance his way, but took an available seat near the front.

The horrible thought struck him, once again, that this was not in fact Season Howe, but simply some innocent young woman who happened to resemble her. *Wouldn't Season sense me sitting here?* he wondered. *Wouldn't she just know?*

But when he saw her run her fingers through her hair or glance toward the back of the bus, he knew again that it was indeed Season. At those moments he quickly looked away, lest the old "I know someone is watching me" radar kick in and alert her to his presence.

Josh's next challenge came when she got off the bus, just outside the New York-New York casino. Should he stay on until the next stop and risk losing her in the crowd? Or get off here and risk being seen? He decided that being seen was the lesser of the two worries, since there were so many people in the casino and so many places she might go. He stayed in his seat until she was off the bus, then he rose, pushed past lunchbox guy, and darted for the back door. By the time he made it off, she was already headed toward the casino's entrance.

He tore his cell from his pocket, breathlessly punched Rebecca's number. When she answered, he said, "Beck, she's at New York. Where are you?"

"Kerry's just shown up," Rebecca answered. "We'll be there in a few minutes."

"Okay," he said. "Take Tropicana to the Strip and turn right."

"I've been memorizing the map," she assured him. "We'll be right there. Don't do anything stupid."

Sprinting for the door, he broke the connection. By any reasonable definition, this whole thing was stupid. The fact that Season Howe was entering a small-scale reproduction of New York City—complete with Statue of Liberty, Times Square, and fireboats in the harbor—was absurd.

But that was Vegas.

Inside, she had already blended in with the rest of the crowd: tourists, gamblers, employees, and sightseers gawking at the replica Big Apple that filled the huge building. Josh tried to slow his pace, not wanting to appear frantic or to chance missing her if she'd simply stepped behind something or someone. She was inside now—it'd be a while before she made it back out. He'd find her.

By the time he did, though, panic had almost overtaken him. He felt like the casino was as crowded as the real New York, like there were nine million people in the place and he was only looking for one. He eventually spotted her, though, sitting at a hundred-dollar-minimum blackjack table, looking as at home as if she owned the place. This, he realized, was probably a great way for a witch to generate cash flow: A few magically altered cards at the right moment could keep her in the green for a long time, and the pit bosses would never be able to figure out how she was cheating. Josh felt a moment's envy—this was the kind of action he craved but could never afford. Maybe if he'd been in league with Season instead of with the good guys, he'd be sitting next to her instead of wearing the same stinking clothes he'd had on all night, ragged and hungry and beyond exhausted.

He had made his choices, though. He hung back and watched her play, the pile of chips before her growing steadily After a little while, he realized he wasn't the only one watching her. From a bank of slots nearby, two men glared at her with eerie yellow eyes. There was something not right about them, he noticed. When they started to move it became even more apparent. They weren't men at all; he could see bits of casino

debris stuck to them—no, stuck *in* them, as if it were part
of them—cigarette butts and change cups, plastic and paper
coin rolls. These were manufactured men—Josh searched his
memory for the term Daniel Blessing had used. *Simulacra.* It
came to him just as they headed for her. She hadn't seen them
yet, and he knew that if she did, it would spook her—no way
would she still be around when Kerry and the others showed
up. He was sure the simulacra couldn't defeat her alone; if
they'd been able to, Daniel's quest would have ended ages
before.

He was also pretty sure that Kerry and the gang wouldn't
be able to beat her either. But if she was hunting them down,
then they had to at least try. And he didn't know what tricks
Mother Blessing might have outfitted Kerry with. No matter
what, he had to keep the simulacra from scaring off Season
before Kerry arrived.

He did the only thing he could think of. He moved in
front of them, putting his hands out to stop them. "Wait," he
said urgently, trying to keep his voice low so as not to attract
casino security. "I know what you are. You work for Mother
Blessing, right?"

The two barely spared him a glance. He could see that
he was right, though; there was nothing natural about these
creatures. *Men* was the wrong word for them. They ignored
his entreaties, as if deaf to him. One of them swept an arm
sideways, catching Josh in the chest and hurling him into
the slot machines. Pain shot through his back and flashes of

light filled his vision. But he forced himself to his feet again, and dashed toward the creatures, knowing even as he did so that it was too late now to prevent a scene. His gambler's instincts, though, told him that if the simulacra got to Season first, he'd never get another shot at her, and he wasn't willing to let that happen. "Stop!" he called. "You'll blow everything."

This time one of the simulacra turned toward him. Its face was featureless but its body language spoke volumes, and Josh got the sense that it would not interrupt its mission for anything. The thing snatched up a stool from in front of a video poker machine, tearing it loose from its moorings, and drove its jagged base into Josh's chest. Fire lanced into him, obscuring the comparatively minor pain he'd felt before. This was like nothing he'd ever experienced: The whole world was turning dark, except for the white-hot bolt of agony at his chest.

Josh felt himself slumping backward, falling to the floor. The world moved before him in slow motion. The simulacra, having forgotten him, advanced on Season. She came up from her seat, her pretty face set with a determined scowl, sparing only a glance for Josh before she faced the two not-men. All around, people went into slo-mo action, like something from a Peckinpah battle sequence: civilians ducking for cover, security forces converging on the scene. Josh heard screams, but distantly, as if through some kind of filter.

One of the simulacra overturned a craps table as it rushed

toward her. Chips spun everywhere, arcing through the air like rainbows. Again, voices were raised, but they sounded to Josh like deep bellows, like foghorns on faraway shores, and when the table hit the ground, the crash came to him slowly, as if he were underwater.

But then Season went into action, and it was a beautiful thing to behold: practiced, efficient, without a wasted motion. She spoke words Josh couldn't hear, inscribed gestures in the air that his eyes couldn't track. Bursts of glowing energy pulsed from her upraised hands. The simulacra halted in their tracks, caught in beams of light that pummeled them like hurricane winds. They tried to push forward against her magical field, but it tore at them, tattering their makeshift clothing, keeping them at bay Now they both howled their anguish, and this Josh could hear even over the dull rush that filled his ears: long, drawn-out screams as they began to disassemble. Pieces of trash, a mannequin's arm, a hunk of partially shredded black tire, strips of wire—Josh saw them all come into focus as they tore away from the simulacra's bodies under Season's steady assault. The image was fascinating and terrible at the same time—nonliving beings dismantling bit by bit—and Josh couldn't help being impressed by Season's bold stance as she stood there, unshaken by their attack, unmoved by the commotion around her, until her task was done.

Finally it was.

The simulacra gone, Season shook off the meaty hands of the security officers who tried to grab her and headed straight for Josh. She swam in and out of focus as she neared. Josh was cold, so cold, but at least his chest had stopped hurting, and that was something. He started to think that maybe he'd survive this after all, until he saw Season bearing down on him. His eyes fluttered closed; he fought them open again, and she was nearer.

The expression on her face as she knelt before him was the scariest thing he'd seen yet. It was concerned, almost tender—her clear blue eyes wide, moist lips parted—but at the same time utterly without hope. Her words confirmed this impression. "It's too late for me to help you," she said softly. "But thank you for what you did. Maybe this will help."

She touched his cheek, fingers as gentle as a whisper, and spoke a single word. Instantly, all the pain faded away. The cold vanished. Josh felt as comfortable as he ever had in his life. He was dying. He had known that, but where moments before he had been in utter agony, now he felt at peace with it. That was Season's gift to him, and it was not one he could take lightly.

He touched his chest, feeling the tacky blood that flowed there, soaking his clothing and skin. In the dim distance he saw Season running, twirling like a quarterback to elude the security forces trying to tackle her. He couldn't help thinking that they had all misjudged her, and he knew they were coming, Kerry and the rest, and had to be told. He just had to hang on long enough to let them know. Or he had to send them a message some other way.

He tried to free his cell phone from his pocket but it slipped from his wet hands and clattered away. He didn't have the strength to lift it anyway, he was sure. Dipping his finger in his own blood, Josh Quinn began to write on the side of a slot machine.

15

When Kerry came down the escalator into the central baggage-claim area of Las Vegas's McCarran Airport, Rebecca, Scott, and Brandy were waiting for her, Rebecca holding a big, hastily lettered sign that said "Bulldog Profitt." Kerry began to laugh immediately, the first good, long belly laugh she'd had in a long time. The others surrounded her and enmeshed her into a textbook-quality group hug that lasted until the laughter faded and the import of the trip began to settle among them again.

As Rebecca directed them to the parking structure where the rental car waited, Scott inclined his head toward a young woman dressed in a skimpy showgirl's outfit, complete with feathered headgear, holding a sign welcoming visitors to the resort she represented. Then he pointed at the double rank of slot machines filling the center of the baggage-claim area. "No wonder Season likes this place," he said lightly. "It's like a surrealist's bad dream. No one would even notice her here."

Rebecca, resplendent in a long broomstick skirt and an embroidered denim top, nodded her head. "I read someplace that more fugitives from justice pick Las Vegas to hide out in than any other city."

"I believe that," Brandy chimed in. She looked stylish as ever in a peach-colored, long-sleeve thermal top with low-rise twill pants and black Paul Frank sneakers, and she tossed Kerry a smile like they were long-lost sisters. "After all, Josh lives here."

"He likes crime stories," Scott countered. "I don't think he's so big on actual crime."

"I'm just saying," Brandy shot back. "The spoon doesn't fall far from the kettle, or something like that."

Rebecca cracked up again. "That doesn't even make any sense," she said, her face turning red.

"It's Josh we're talking about," Brandy reminded her. "Who said making sense entered into it?"

The banter continued until they were in the car and Rebecca, after giving them a brief update on her last text from Josh, focused on driving. Scott and Brandy sat in back, hushed, while Kerry watched out the windows.

Emergency vehicles overtook them on the short trip from the airport—police cars, fire trucks, ambulances, lights flashing, sirens blaring. Traffic already jammed Las Vegas Boulevard, but somehow the cars on the street managed to pull to the sides, and the official vehicles wove through. Kerry wrinkled her forehead. "I've got a bad feeling about this," she said. "Hurry up, Beck."

Rebecca nodded grimly and pulled out, beating most of the other cars back into the lane after the emergency vehicles had passed through. "I'm on it," she said, flooring the accelerator. The rented Maxima lunged forward. Kerry was impressed by the way Rebecca handled the car. Ignoring the complaining horns, she muscled it from one lane to the next, pushing her way through before traffic had a chance to jam up again.

Within minutes, New York's skyline, or an approximation of it wrapped by a roller coaster, loomed on the left. Rebecca turned into the self-parking structure and the four of them ran from the car into the casino, Rebecca trying furiously to reach Josh on his cell phone. It rang and rang, she reported, but he did not answer. Kerry swallowed hard, expecting the worst.

Inside, the worst was what they found. Uniformed police officers were shooing away gamblers and onlookers, trying to spread yellow crime-scene tape across a wide swath of the casino floor. People stood around with stunned looks on their faces, some in tears, some strangely excited, as if they'd just seen a show put on by the establishment and felt they'd gotten their money's worth. Kerry shoved her way through the clot of people, craning her head to see around the cops, EMTs, and firefighters. The first thing she noticed was a strange assortment of trash strewn around the floor—the wheel of a shopping cart, a paper cup from an overpriced coffee shop, some general casino litter. Anyone else looking at the random junk would have wondered why it was all there, but to Kerry there was only one possible answer: simulacra had been here. She'd told Mother Blessing she was going to Las Vegas to investigate a Season sighting; the old witch must have sent her own scouts ahead.

But then her eyes rested on another sight, one that chilled her to the core, as if she'd just taken a cold shower inside a deep freeze.

Josh—or rather, a crumpled shape that had once been Josh, had once contained the essence of him—was splayed against a bank of slot machines. In the center of his chest a hole gaped, red and meaty, and blood from it had poured down his torn shirt, pooling on the ground between his legs.

Next to him, on the side of one of the slots, were four letters, scrawled in blood by a shaky hand.

SEAS

As if there were any doubt, Kerry thought. "Leave it to Josh," she said quietly to Scott, who had come up beside her. She pointed to the writing. "He fingered his own killer."

"Just like something out of one of those hard-boiled movies he loves," Scott answered. His voice broke when he said it, and Kerry knew he was close to tears. That was okay.

So was she.

Kerry Profitt's diary, November 1

We couldn't stay at NY-NY—couldn't bring ourselves to—so we're across the street at the MGM Grand. It's my first time here, and I'd like to think there's something grand about it, but the fact is that we are all just staying the night because we're too drained to actually make any moves toward going home.

Three down:

Mace Winston.

Daniel Blessing.

Josh Quinn.

Pausing to look at my friends . . .

Scott Banner sits in a chair, staring out the window. Brandy Pearson's reading a textbook she brought with her, sitting on the bed with her legs folded beneath her, making herself as small as possible. Something's wrong there—trouble between those two, though neither one has said a word about it. Neither has said much of anything, come to think of it, since we saw Josh. They asked me a couple of questions about Mother Blessing and the Swamp, I asked them a few about school and their lives. I don't think any of us heard the answers. But I don't think Scott and Brandy have touched each other once since I got here, if you don't count that group hug. Rebecca Levine, beautiful flower child, has barely stopped weeping since we saw Josh's body. Now she stares vacantly at the TV, watching a moronic reality show with the sound turned so low I can barely hear it. Which is fine with me.

Rebecca also told me something apparently everyone else has known for some time now—that she thought she saw Season at some bogus séance. Which maybe wasn't as bogus as she thought. Maybe Season has been hunting us down, one by one.

So I can't help wondering: Which one is next? Season has taken three friends from me so far. Not just from me, from the world. Three flames snuffed, three lights extinguished. Three people who could have changed the world. Would Mace have discovered a cure for cancer? Not likely, I guess. But he might have coached a baseball team and befriended a sad, fatherless boy, and isn't that just as valuable an accomplishment? Josh might never have composed a stirring symphony but he might have skipped through a park on a sunny spring day, bringing smiles to the faces of everyone who saw him. Daniel . . .

Daniel saved lives, dedicated himself to bringing Season Howe to justice, and still found time to love me. To change my life, to pull me out of my own self-obsessed rut and give me some kind of direction, a goal, a desire to affect something larger than just myself.

We can never measure the impact we have on others, never know when a friendly word to a cashier at the market or a smile bestowed on a stranger or a few bucks to a charity might strike at just the right time to make someone's day, or give someone hope, or lend the tools someone needs to rebuild something that's broken. And so we can never know which life, cut short, might be one that the world needed. Since it's unlikely that Josh, Mace, or Daniel would have eventually become super-villains or anything, the loss of these lives, the tragedy of their early endings, is that their gifts, whatever they were to be, will never be realized. Okay, I guess it's hard to apply that to three-hundred-year-old Daniel, but still, he seemed young to me, and he had an important task that was left unfinished.

Not that their lives were wasted. They gave to me, to the others in this room, to their families, and to strangers. Rebecca wanted us to go see Josh's mother, but the rest of us talked her out of that—considering what we've found ourselves mixed up in, we've all agreed to keep parents, family, and friends out of the loop. Safer for them, safer for us. I'm sure Josh never told his mom anything about us, and if we had shown up with our crazy stories, it would have just made a hard day even worse.

We don't know if Season is still in Vegas. Rebecca was the last one to talk to Josh, but he never told her where he staked Season out last night, so we don't even know where she was staying. Chances are, though, given that she battled simulacra, she knows her cover here is blown and she's already on the move. By plane, car, train, bus? Don't know.

I leave in the morning, back to Virginia, back to the

Great Dismal. So do the others, Brandy and Scott for Harvard, Rebecca for UC Santa Cruz. My college pals, and me, witchy apprentice girl.

I don't know what they're all learning. But I know what my major is, what my course of study has to be. Intense, comprehensive, accelerated.

How to kill Season Howe.

More later.

K.

16

The sky over the Great Dismal Swamp was heavy and gray, lowering overhead like a leaden shroud, which suited Kerry's mood just fine. She had parked the minivan in its usual spot and rowed back through the ever-more-familiar Swamp to Mother Blessing's ramshackle cabin/ comfortable suburban home (depending on whether one was outside or in). Kerry thought she felt eyes tracking her the whole way, but whether it was simulacra or snakes, birds, and other swamp wildlife, she couldn't have said.

Mother Blessing met her with a bottle of Coke and a tray of ham sandwiches on Wonder bread, and they sat together in the kitchen while Kerry filled her in on what had happened. The older woman was sympathetic, listening attentively until

Kerry declared that she was exhausted and needed to get some sleep. Mother Blessing patted Kerry's arm. "Y'all get a good night's sleep, child. Tomorrow'll be a busy day."

"Busy with what?" Kerry asked, stifling a yawn. She had hardly slept at all the night before; images of Josh and Daniel filled her head. Though she'd dozed a little on the flight home, she really was weary to the bone.

"Well, it's time you learned some serious magic, isn't it?" Mother Blessing said. "Someone's got to stand up to Season, and I guess it might just as well be you."

"Are you sure I can do that?" Kerry asked excitedly. She wanted it more than anything, but she'd thought she'd have to persuade Mother Blessing. Now she was almost afraid that the witch had made the promise in hopes that Kerry would realize she was asking too much and back off. She almost wished Mother Blessing had waited until the morning to make this announcement—now, tired as she was, she feared she'd have a hard time sleeping. Everything she'd been shown so far was basic stuff, beginner's tricks and a bunch of theory. But she'd seen Daniel and Season at work, knew there was far more to be learned.

Mother Blessing nodded gravely. "I reckon we'll find out, Kerry," she said. "Tomorrow. Y'all get to bed now."

Kerry did as she was told, and to her surprise, as soon as she put her head on the pillow, she felt consciousness fading away. Tragedy and possibility whirled around in her mind, each feeding on the other, but soon enough they both emptied into nothingness and she slept.

* * *

"Most magical systems won't let one practitioner do harm to another," Mother Blessing explained the next day. They were back in the kitchen, which seemed to be where the woman spent most of her time, day and night. Kerry sat at the table in a heavy cable-knit sweater and soft, forest-green fleece pants, her long dark hair tugged into a tight ponytail. Dressed in her usual stretch polyesters under a shapeless housecoat, Mother Blessing rode her scooter, rolling it this way and that like a lecturer pacing while she spoke. "Violence is limited, in those systems, to the evil, the outlaws or renegades. Black magicians who call up destructive demons, for instance, are hated by white magicians. If Wiccans knew half of what they could do by simply taking their studies a few steps further, applying their powers in different ways, their little flowered headpieces would most likely melt off them." She had a small smile on her face when she said that, and a twinkle in her eye, but Kerry knew that didn't mean she didn't believe what she was saying.

"The difference here is that we use violent magic only in self-defense, or in the defense of others. Y'all know Season well enough now to understand that there's no stoppin' her, short of killin' her. Now, there's plenty of witches out there who'd think we were evil to contemplate such a thing, but when it comes to evil, I have to think that letting Season continue her reign of terror is just about the worst thing a person could do."

"From what I've seen," Kerry said, "I'd have to agree."

"Of course." Mother Blessing spoke as if no other opinion was even worth considering. "Y'all have been touched by her foul deeds. She's impacted your life. Those others, the ones who'd defend her, they don't know her like we do. They haven't lost two sons and a husband to her, or a lover, or a whole town full of neighbors and friends."

"That's probably true."

"Bet your sweet patootie it is," Mother Blessing said with a chuckle. "So the question is, what do we do about her? What steps are y'all willin' to take to make sure she can't keep doin' what she's been doin'?"

Kerry had thought long and hard about just that question. "Whatever it takes," she said decisively. "I'd do anything."

"I'm delighted to hear it, child." She wheeled in close to Kerry, leaning forward, her bulk almost spilling out of her scooter. "What's really required to go the extra step is depth of commitment. If you're willin' to go where the magic takes you, it'll carry the weight."

"I'm willing," Kerry affirmed. If she had any doubts along the way she could simply call up the pictures of Daniel and Josh emblazoned into her memory.

"That's fine, just fine." Mother Blessing wrapped her big, fleshy hands around Kerry's. They felt warmer than human hands could rightfully be, as if they burned with the inner fire of her dark magics. Kerry would embrace that darkness, if it would lead to revenge. This was why she'd come here.

Then Mother Blessing released her hands and backed away from her, rolling toward a kitchen cupboard. She opened the door and withdrew a book—a slim volume, but covered in soft leather like Daniel's journals. It looked incredibly old, the leather creased and cracked, the pages yellow with age. Mother Blessing put it in her scooter's basket and drove close enough for Kerry to reach it. "Take the book, child," she said. "First thing you've got to do is learn the Old Tongue."

"What's that?" Kerry asked.

"The words of power. They come from a language forgotten by humans, a language that predates the written word. There was a time when magic was commonplace, swirling through the air like smog does today. People understood it better'n we do electricity today—course, there wasn't as many people about, and not all of 'em knew how to use magic. But they all knew someone who did, and they respected their shamans, instead of burnin' 'em at the stake or forcin' 'em into hiding."

Kerry figured that there was some personal bias tinting Mother Blessing's commentary—if living a hermit's life in a disguised home deep in the Swamp wasn't being forced into hiding, she didn't know what was. Daniel, too, had been good at disguising his nature. And Season was nothing if not expert at running and hiding. If these three—the most powerful witches Kerry had ever imagined—were all forced into seclusion by the world's distrust of magic, then it was not surprising that Mother Blessing had strong feelings about the matter.

Taking the book from the basket, Kerry flipped through its brittle pages. At first glance, it was completely illegible. There were no words in it, not in any kind of writing she could decipher—just scribbles, seemingly random markings that might have been the scratchings of an animal's claws. She looked up, confused. "How am I supposed to . . . ?"

"Give it some time," Mother Blessing assured her. "Look it over at night, before you go to sleep."

Kerry closed the book and put it on the table, still confused but willing to give her the benefit of the doubt.

"When y'all speak the Old Tongue," Mother Blessing continued, "it draws the power of the Old Ones into you. Since y'all will be taught how to use that power, the right combination of words and gestures focuses the power and directs it where you want it. Gesture is as important as words, Kerry, and don't forget that. It's the combination that makes y'all's magic effective."

She pointed across the kitchen to where a copper-bottomed pot hung on the wall. "As a for instance," she said, "see that pot?"

"I see it."

"Okay, now watch me." Mother Blessing raised her hands and curled her fingers. She took her right hand and, with the thumb sticking up, tucked the two lower fingers flat against her palm, and crooked the middle two as if holding onto a pole. She splayed the fingers of her left hand as far apart as she could while bringing the thumb down crosswise across her palm. "Looks awkward, but it ain't bad," she explained. "You'll get used to it."

Pointing both hands toward the pot, she said a single word that sounded to Kerry like "bibblehead." As soon as the word had escaped her lips, the pot vibrated against the wall, shaking free of the hook that held it there, and floated across the room, as if carried by spectral hands, to land safely in the basket of Mother Blessing's scooter.

"What was that word?" Kerry asked her. Before she spoke it she made sure her own hands were neatly crossed on her lap, just in case. "'Bibblehead'?"

"B-I-B-E-L-H-E-T, I think," Mother Blessing spelled out. "Actual spellin' ain't all that important—it's the speakin' of it that counts. I couldn't define it, either, just know that it'll do what I want it to do. That's what y'all have got to achieve—the knowledge that the words and gestures'll be there when you need 'em, without having to think about 'em too much. Thinkin' things through'll get you killed. It's got to be automatic."

"But . . . that could take years!" Kerry complained. "You've been at it for what, centuries."

'That's right, child," Mother Blessing agreed. "But once y'all start in to learning, you'll be surprised how fast it goes. Power feeds power, Kerry. It's like it's all floatin' out there lookin' for a home, like liquid searchin' for the lowest point, and when it finds one, it flows in fast and strong."

She took the pot from the basket and put it on the table in front of Kerry. "Put it back," she instructed.

Kerry started to rise, lifting the pot from the table. "No," Mother Blessing said sharply. "Not that way."

Kerry understood what she meant, but not how to accomplish the task. "But . . ."

"Do like this," Mother Blessing said. She folded the fingers of both hands toward her palms, making hooks of them, then raised the thumbs and pointed them toward the wall where the pot had been. She held her right hand about a hand's breadth higher than the left. Kerry duplicated the pose as best she could, until Mother Blessing nodded her satisfaction. "That's good," she said. "Now hold the pose."

Kerry did so, and Mother Blessing unfolded her own hands, lowering them to her handlebars. "Now, say the word '*beshitoon.*'"

"Beshi . . . ?"

"*Beshitoon,*" Mother Blessing repeated.

Kerry held the position with her hands and attempted the word. "Bes—*beshitoon,*" she said hesitantly.

Nothing happened.

"Say it like you mean it, child," Mother Blessing chided her.

Kerry hesitated a moment, her hands starting to quake from the effort of holding them still. She visualized the pot floating back across the room and hanging itself up on the hook again. *I can do this,* she thought. *Mother Blessing wouldn't be pushing me if she didn't know I could.*

"*Beshitoon.*"

The pot rattled on the tabletop, as if trying to make up its mind, then ascended into the air. Slowly, taking its time, but moving in almost precisely the line Kerry had visualized, it drifted across the room. Reaching the far wall, it lowered itself until the hook had slipped inside the hole in its handle. Then it was still, and the room silent.

"There you go," Mother Blessing said softly. "Nothin' to it, is there?"

I wouldn't say that, Kerry thought. But excitement coursed through her. She had *done* that! She had taken power from the air around her and directed it toward a specific goal, and that goal, however minor, had been achieved!

"I did magic," Kerry said finally. "I really did."

"You really did, child," Mother Blessing confirmed. "Congratulations."

Kerry Profitt's diary, November 4

I did magic.

Yeah, I know, big whoop. I moved a pot. Could have used some scrubbing—the copper bottom was a bit on the tarnished side—but I didn't take it that far. One step at a time, right? Today I move, tomorrow I may scrub.

Or not.

The thing is, this is why I came to the Swamp. This is why I sought out Mother Blessing. She trained Daniel, right? So she can train me, too. Can, and more importantly, is willing to. Even anxious. She knows that Season is out of control. And the closer it gets to next year's Witches'

Convocation, the more important it is to take Season out of commission. Which means that I don't have much time to perfect my skills. I don't have centuries, or even years. I have weeks, months.

I was going to write in here last night, after my day's training, but instead I did as Mother Blessing suggested, and I looked through the book she gave me, the one with the Old Tongue in it. Look at it before you go to sleep, she had said, in that delightful accent of hers that makes everything sound like music. So I did. Still looked like chicken scratches to me.

But then I went to sleep, and in my dreams the writing became clear. It was so realistic that when I woke up, I grabbed the book and looked again. And guess what?

I could read it!

Well, not READ it, precisely. The words still don't make any sense, words like bibblehead and beshitoon. But it was as if they were all written down using our alphabet. No more scribbles and scratches. Don't ask me how—magic, I guess—but now at least I can sound out the words, know how I'm supposed to say them. I still need Mother Blessing to tell me which ones should be used for what, and what gestures to combine with them—seems like I'm particularly dangerous right now, because if I accidentally spoke one of them while unconsciously making some gesture or other, I could blow something up or hurt someone.

But yesterday I knew squat about this stuff, and today

I've not only done magic, but I'm able to read the words in the book. Power flows to power, she says. The more I achieve, the more will come to me.

I wouldn't want to be Season Howe a couple of months from now. Because I intend to flow a lot of power this way, in a hurry.

Impatient, me? Perish the thought.

More later.

K.

17

Erin pounded on her door.

"You're going to miss class again, Beck!" she shouted. Rebecca tunneled deeper into her blankets, wedged a pillow over her head.

She didn't want to go to class. She didn't want to get out of bed. She hadn't wanted to since Halloween, since . . . since Josh had died at the hands of Season Howe.

She couldn't stop dwelling on the sight of Josh, murdered, body cooling up against a bank of slot machines. Every time she closed her eyes, it seemed, he was there—either that or the image of Season herself. She had become convinced now that she'd been right after all, at that séance—that Season was looking for them, hunting them down. If that was true, there was hardly any purpose in getting out of bed. When Season came for her, it wouldn't matter where she was.

Kerry, at least, was trying to learn how to defend herself against the witch. Rebecca didn't have that option. She was defenseless, and every day that she listened to Erin—every day that she got out of bed—she was only one day closer to the inevitable confrontation.

She knew that she was slipping into clinical depression. Erin had said as much, had even offered to take her down to the student health center and help her sign up for counseling. But Rebecca knew that no counseling could help her with her problem.

Every now and then she talked with Scott or Brandy—Kerry was out of reach again, and their little summer group was getting smaller and smaller—and that helped a little, mostly because she could speak freely with them, didn't have to hide what was really on her mind. But they were far away, and she was here in Santa Cruz, alone.

Erin knocked again and Rebecca shoved her pillow aside. "Okay!" she called. "I'm getting up, okay?"

"Fine," she heard Erin answer.

This would, she had decided, be the last year she and Erin shared a place. She didn't know what would happen next year.

But then, she didn't know if she'd be alive by next year. Certainly not if Season Howe had anything to say about it.

* * *

There was, it turned out, a lot more to the whole witch-craft thing than simply reciting strange-sounding words and making funny hand motions. Mother Blessing made Kerry spend hours in the Swamp becoming intimately familiar with dwarf trillium, silky camellia, fiddlehead, and log fern, discerning Tupelo bald cypress from Atlantic white cedar from maple-blackgum, tasting the bark of red maple, crushing pine needles in her hands and inhaling the bitter scent, picking bunches of paw paw, blackgum, devil's walking stick, and wild grapes for the table. Not all magic could simply be scooped from the ether, she explained. Some had to be distilled from plants and trees, teased from animals, dug from the very earth.

Kerry learned how to tell apart the tracks and scat of the swamp's big mammals: the paw of the bobcat and the black bear, the hoof of the white-tailed deer, the smaller track of gray fox and red, of raccoon and mink and gray squirrel. She came to recognize the calls of different warblers, the Swainson's and the Wayne's and the Myrtle, the chirps of the ovenbird and the hermit thrush, the sounds of the robins and blackbirds that swarmed in as the month progressed as if drawn by the fiery leaves on autumn trees. She took pleasure in the staccato rapping of the pileated woodpecker; she went to sleep at night wondering what the barred owl was talking about, or cringing at the plaintive cry of the bobcat; she woke to the *yakkety-yak* of the wood duck. With great care, Mother Blessing taught her to extract venom from the cottonmouth, the canebrake rattler, and the copperhead, and how to tell them apart from the dozen or so nonpoisonous varieties of snake that lived nearby.

Every night, Kerry went to bed with aching muscles and a head swimming with new information and vivid images, her tongue tripping over the foreign words and phrases she had learned that day. And each day she woke early and leapt from her bed, ready to repeat the process, to absorb more knowledge, to glean more wisdom from the Swamp and its inhabitants—and, of course, from Mother Blessing herself. The days grew ever shorter—darkness came early now—but Kerry packed them full. Makeup was a thing of the past—a quick shower, a brush through her hair and a band to hold it back, some jeans and a sweater or maybe sweat pants and a long-sleeved T-shirt, and she was ready for the day. She barely took time to notice that her physical efforts were making her ever stronger, her arms and shoulders firm and supple, her waist tight, her thighs and calves bunched with strength.

When she was inside, she worked with Mother Blessing on learning the correct pronunciation of the Old Tongue, on practicing magical gestures until her hands screamed with aching. And she read, still working her way through Daniel's journals, front to back, beginning to end. She couldn't remember a time in her life that had been so filled with activity, days so long and with never a moment to be bored—hardly even any time, but for the few seconds between undressing and falling asleep, to reflect on anything.

During one of the rare moments of downtime, she had turned on the TV for the first time, and had not been at all surprised to find that it received more than a hundred channels, none of which seemed worth watching. This house was like that, though—she could take long, steaming showers without worrying that the hot water tank (if there was one; she had never seen it) would run out. The lights and the heat always worked, though there seemed to be no electrical or gas lines to the place. Mother Blessing could, she figured, solve the world's energy problems in seconds if she wanted to. But then the energy companies wouldn't be able to make any money, and they'd probably prove a far more nefarious adversary than even Season Howe.

Kerry knew that this was a time of preparation, a schooling time, but it didn't feel like a step on the way to somewhere; it felt like a destination achieved. As if she had already made it to where she was going.

It was, she decided one night in the moments before sound sleep overtook her, a happy time. In spite of everything that had led her to this point. She had rarely been quite so content.

She found that strange.

> Now that I am older and have seen more of the wide world, I realize that there were great advantages to growing up where I did, to reaching maturity—and spending many months after that—in the Great Dismal. It was, and probably remains, a magical place to be a child, full of mystery and, yes, some danger. The sheer variety of plants and animals made every day an

adventure: How many children my age went to school with alligators and came home with black bears? How many knew that every time they left the house there was the distinct possibility that, before suppertime, they could become hopelessly lost, never again to see their mother and brother? How many could see millions upon millions of blackbirds erupt from the Swamp, filling the sky in a steady stream that blacked out the sun for most of a day before they had all flown away?

Precious few, I'd wager. And though, in the way of small children everywhere, I didn't always appreciate it while it was happening, I certainly do now. I'm glad Mother Blessing didn't let Season drive her away from the Swamp, but only deep into it, that horrible day when she ruined Slocumb, house by house, burning each one with her magical fires until the screams of those inside faded away, keeping the flames hot until every trace of habitation was gone. Mother Blessing did the right thing by hiding out, by refusing to return to Slocumb until a safe period had passed, for in her fury Season Howe was certainly more than herself, channeling evil unknown and unknowable, not to be stopped by any earthly intercession.

But the Swamp: I was writing of the Swamp. Each day a new lesson, a new joy, sometimes a new fear, but always with Mother Blessing, and usually Abraham, to help me through it all. And so many surprises, for anyone willing to open his eyes and look for them. I met George Washington there, in 1763. I didn't know yet, of course, what a courageous leader of soldiers he would turn out to be, but he was already known as an intelligent man, and a decent one, with a sharp eye for business.

And one day in November of 1894 when I was back visiting Mother Blessing—depressed at my inability to find Season, who had been successfully avoiding me for months, and feeling like a complete disaster, a worthless fool who would never amount to anything—I met a sad-eyed young man roaming the Swamp on foot, looking, he said, for the best way to kill himself.

"Best," I asked, "in the sense of most assured? Or most dramatic?"

"I should like it to make a statement," he said after considering my question. "I believe I should like people to talk about it."

"Is there, perhaps, some certain individual who you would especially desire to hear the news?" I inquired, believing I was beginning to understand the nature of his predicament. He sat down on the log of a fallen gum tree and looked at me as if deciding whether or not I was trustworthy enough to reveal his story to.

"I was late in Canton, Massachusetts," said he at length, "where I surprised my lady love by arriving unannounced at her door bearing a most special gift. I thought that this lady would welcome me. Certainly

I hoped so, having ridden all night by train."

"What was the gift?" I asked the young man.

"Two books of poetry, written especially with her in mind," he said. "One for her and the other for me. There existed only the one copy of each book. But upon being given hers, she simply held it at arm's length, as though I had given her a toad or a snake, and closed the door on me.

"In my grief, I wandered back to the railroad yard and tore my own volume to shreds. On the journey home, I determined that without Miss White, I had no reason to live. So I am here, in the most aptly named Great Dismal, where I should like to find an appropriately dramatic way to close the door on my existence."

I scratched my chin again and considered his predicament. "Hmmm," I said. "A number of options present themselves. Have you considered trying to make the acquaintance of a brown bear, or an alligator, or perhaps a poisonous snake? Although any of those might leave you merely crippled or ill, not dead. Perhaps you could find a tree in the process of being felled and stand on the wrong side of it; the woodcutters, though, might see you and insist you move away."

"You seem quite well versed in the ways the Swamp can put finish to a fellow."

"Swamp born and bred, sir, though I have traveled more than a little in my day."

He regarded me for a long time, nodding his head. Finally he said, "I suppose the most certain way would be to walk into the Swamp with no provisions. One way or another I should not survive the journey."

"That seems to work, yes," I agreed.

"But if my body was never found, then the news of my passing might never reach Miss White."

"It is true," I said, "that she would likely never know with certainty."

The young man raised his arms in evident frustration. "What is the point of it?" he thundered. "To come all this way, to the most dismal spot in Creation, and still not find a suitable end?"

"Very little point that I can see," I agreed again.

The young man spared me a smile then, the first that I had seen, and it was like a flicker of sunshine breaking through storm clouds. "Then perhaps it is my plan that is faulty, and the better course would be to go on living after all."

I pointed my index finger at him. "And to live such a life that Miss White would learn to regret having spurned you," I added.

He smiled again, this time as if the sun had warmed the sky and burned the clouds away. "Yes," he said happily. "I think that might be the better course of action after all."

"I am happy to hear it," I told the man.

He took my hand then, and shook it with great effusiveness. "I thank you, sir. Be well, and remember the name of Robert Frost, in the event that some day it should come to mean something to anyone. Especially to Miss Elinor White."

I gave him my own name, and he smiled again and walked away. I felt better about myself immediately: Having saved a life, I felt the depression that had gripped me lift at once, and I knew that I would, in fact, find Season again and destroy her.

And that young man? He did become something special after all.

I remember the story today because I heard on the radio that Robert Frost died yesterday. While I don't believe he was a witch or prolonged his life through any special magical powers, there was certainly magic within that man. He won four Pulitzer prizes for his magnificent poetry, and just over two years ago he became the first poet to read a poem at the inauguration of an American president.

I, for one, salute his passing—much delayed, and we are all the better for that. And his moving on serves to remind me of the special joys and pleasures of life in the Great Dismal, so thank you, Mr. Frost, for all your gifts.

I remain,

Daniel Blessing, January 30, 1963

18

Just when Kerry was starting to think that her life was destined to be devoted to studying and nothing else, Mother Blessing surprised her.

"How long's it been since you got yourself a new outfit, honey?" she asked one morning, startling Kerry from her reading. She was constantly amazed by the things Daniel had seen and done, by the sweep of history he had lived. But the idea that he had effectively saved the life of Robert Frost, whose poetry she had loved in high school, had blown her away. She had been reflecting on that when Mother Blessing mentioned her wardrobe, and the disconnect seemed almost surreal. "I swear, the clothes you're wearin' look like they're fixin' to come apart at the seams."

Honestly, Kerry hadn't even been thinking about clothes, or hair or makeup or anything else. There didn't seem to be time in the day for such things, and there was no one to get dressed up for except Mother Blessing. Since the older woman's idea of dolling herself up usually involved wearing stretch pants with slightly fewer stains than usual, Kerry felt that the bar of presentability had been lowered, and that was fine with her. Now that Mother Blessing mentioned it, though, Kerry remembered that there was a certain therapeutic value to shopping that she appreciated.

"I guess it's been a while," she answered. She didn't want to sound too anxious, though, in case this was some kind of test. "If you think we have time . . ."

Mother Blessing's smile looked genuine, though. She was not an attractive woman, but when she really smiled, a sense of true joy showed through. "Child, we don't answer to nobody but ourselves. We want to make the time, then that's just what we'll do."

A simulacrum rowed Kerry and Mother Blessing out of the Swamp in the old witch's boat, to where the creek went right up, behind Edgar Brandvold's property in Wallaceton, Virginia. Edgar was a man who looked as old as Mother Blessing was, though he couldn't have been more than eighty or so, whereas Mother Blessing, while she looked like someone in her fifties, was obviously several hundred years old. When they arrived, the simulacrum lifted Mother Blessing's scooter up onto old Edgar's driveway, then lifted her up onto it. She cruised up to the front door of Edgar's sagging frame house, which looked as much like a shack as the magical facade of Mother Blessing's place, and rapped on his door. A few minutes later a stoop-shouldered mass of wrinkles with thick glasses and a knob-headed cane came out, waved, smiled at Kerry and the simulacrum as if he'd known them both for decades, and unlocked his garage, a former carriage house that looked to be in even worse shape than the main house.

"Howdy, Mother Blessin'!" he called loudly. His voice was deep and sonorous, unexpected in such an apparently ancient fellow. He wore baggy brown pants and a plaid shirt under a ratty blue cardigan sweater, like some kind of Mr. Rogers gone to seed. "Lovely day. You gon' take a ride?"

"That's right, Edgar," Mother Blessing answered brightly. "Miss Kerry here's got some shoppin' she needs to get done."

Edgar opened the carriage house doors widely and Kerry saw her van in its shadowed interior. "What's that doing here?" she asked. Last time she had seen it, it was still parked in its spot near the old Slocumb site, on the other side of the Great Dismal.

"I had it brought around," Mother Blessing explained. "Thought it'd be best if Edgar kept an eye on it."

The simulacrum stepped toward Edgar, who seemed well accustomed to such temporary creatures, and took the key from the old man's hand. "Y'all drive safe now, hear?" Edgar said.

"Always do," Mother Blessing answered for the voiceless being, which opened the driver's door and climbed up behind the wheel.

"I could drive," Kerry offered, a little fearful about the reactions other motorists might have to the plainly nonhuman thing.

"Wouldn't hear of it," Mother Blessing replied, shaking her hands at the very idea. "Ain't nothing like havin' a chauffeur take you where you need to go."

"But he's . . . not exactly convincing," Kerry argued.

"Folks see what they expect to see," Mother Blessing insisted. "Or if I'm around, what I want 'em to see."

The simulacrum at least seemed to know what it was doing. It backed the van smoothly out of the long, narrow garage, then stopped and climbed out, leaving the engine idling. Opening the big side door, it easily lifted Mother Blessing off her scooter, as if she were weightless, and deposited her in the front passenger seat. Then it put the scooter up into the cargo area of the van. There was a single back seat with a seat belt, and at Mother Blessing's suggestion Kerry got into that. The van had a distinctly earthy aroma to it, but she didn't know if that was from sitting cooped up in a small garage by a creek, or from the presence of the simulacrum, who was composed of leaves, vines, mud, and other swamp debris, in the enclosed space. The simulacrum got back behind the wheel and put the van in gear. With a cheery farewell to old Edgar, they headed up the road toward Norfolk.

"One thing I've been wondering about," Kerry began, after they'd been driving a few minutes. Seeing Edgar Brandvold looking so much older than Mother Blessing had reminded her of her curiosity. "If it's not too personal to ask."

"Well, y'all just ask it, and if it's too personal I won't be shy about sayin' so," Mother Blessing replied.

"It's just . . . Daniel looked like he was in his mid-twenties. Season looks like mid-thirties at the oldest. You look like someone in her fifties, maybe. But I know you're all much older than that—so how exactly does the aging process work for witches? Now that I'm learning, will I stop aging and always look like this?"

Mother Blessing regarded her for a few moments, as if she were weighing the relative merits of appearing to be a teenager for hundreds of years. "It's mostly a function of peak power," she said then. "It takes different witches different lengths of time to achieve their strongest capabilities. At that time, the aging process more or less freezes up. I guess I was a slow learner, and it wasn't until I was in my fifties that I reached my peak. My overall health was better—that's gone downhill in recent years, I'm afraid, though I'm still not aging much."

Kerry nodded. "That makes sense, I guess."

"Don't much matter if it does or not," Mother Blessing answered. "It's how it is."

Twenty minutes later, they turned into the parking lot of a bland-looking discount clothing store. "They'll have everything y'all might need here," Mother Blessing announced.

Kerry couldn't prevent the crestfallen expression from washing over her face. She still had plenty of money left over from her college account; since reaching the Swamp, the only thing she'd had to spend it on was the brief trip to Las Vegas. "Isn't there a mall someplace?"

Mother Blessing eyed her with surprise for a moment, then smiled. "Turn around," she told the driver, who obeyed instantly—had, in fact, been starting to obey before the witch gave the verbal command. "Course there's a mall. Teenage girl needs more than a place like this, don't she? Let's us find you somewhere with real shops."

Kerry Profitt's diary, November 17

In the dream, I'm driving in a car. This one I can remember, so I don't think it's the same dream I used to have in the weeks before I met Daniel. Nothing special about the car—it's not the van I bought or any particular car at all that I can tell. But I'm stuck in traffic.

And as I'm sitting there, looking at all the other cars around me, wishing I could just floor it and move already, water starts to bubble up through the floorboards. (Were they ever actual boards, at one time? Just a digression. They sure aren't now.)

Rapidly, the water rises. I try to open a door or a window to let it out, but nothing doing. I can't get anything open. Now I'm in water up to my waist—it's not cold, I notice, but pleasantly body temperature, and I'm not nearly as panicked as I probably should be. Still, it rises.

And rises. And then it's over my head, and I'm still there, seatbelted in, unable to go anywhere or do anything about it. Noises sound funny, like, you know, when you're underwater. Finally, I notice, traffic eases up a little and I can move again. I press the accelerator down and start to edge forward, unable to breathe now, my lungs constricting, really and truly beginning to drown.

But as I do, I'm looking out the car windows at the other cars around and I see that the drivers of those are all underwater inside their cars too. Only the thing is, they don't seem to mind. They're breathing normally—well, normally if humans could breathe underwater. Bubbles float up from their mouths and noses, but they look just like people do in traffic, some smiling, some talking, some angry or impatient. Just people in cars. And we're all underwater.

But I'm the only one who's drowning.

Once again, I need Doc Brandy to tell me just what this all means, and she's not around. Brandy ain't handy.

My guess? Maybe it's telling me that I'm becoming different from all the normal people out there, the people who are not witches—or even halfway to becoming one. Alienation from my peers. Evidence of my journey and how it diverts from that of everyone else I've ever known.

Or not. Who knows?

More later.
K.

"Strike!"

Kerry heard Mother Blessing's voice in her head, even though the woman was miles away, back in her cabin. She had drilled Kerry on this so many times, though, it seemed as if she were right here with her. Kerry did as she'd been taught: She hurled herself to the peat, tucking her head, rolling on one shoulder, and coming up on her feet, hands splayed out in the proper ritualistic position. *"Hastamel!"* she shouted as she rose, and a burst of energy shot from her hands, tearing a chunk of vegetation off the simulacrum with which she sparred. The thing grunted with pain—part of Mother Blessing's commitment to realism, Kerry figured—and dropped to its knees. Kerry knew she'd missed any vital organs, so she repositioned her hands and spoke a defensive spell. If the thing had been a witch, it could have gotten off a blast.

Since it wasn't, she only defended herself against an imaginary spell, and then she shot an impulse wave at it. The creature's head separated from its shoulders and it went down hard in the dirt. Kerry allowed herself a congratulatory moment, but she cut it short when a noise behind her alerted her to the fact that this one hadn't been alone.

She spun around, throwing up a blocking spell and then following that with another sharp, directed burst that punched a hole the size of a soccer ball through this one's chest. These sparring matches were wearying, and she became frustrated when there was one opponent after another after another, even sometimes half a dozen all at once. But they were also necessary, she knew. Daniel had found himself in all kinds of dangerous situations over the course of his long life, and—until that last battle—had survived them all. If Kerry was going to survive, she needed to train until she dropped, and then pick herself up and train some more.

She may have resented Mother Blessing while she was putting her through the mental and physical agony of the exercise, but when it saved her life some day, she'd thank her mentor. She tried to keep sight of that knowledge, to let it help her through these difficult days.

The second simulacrum fell, and Kerry found that there were only two, for now. She was allowed a moment's respite, a chance to catch her breath and let her racing heart calm a bit. After a few minutes the Swamp's normal sounds resumed: birds cried, insects buzzed, a faraway frog croaked its basso profundo solo.

Kerry stood for a few moments, just enjoying the day. It was cold enough in the Swamp that she had the hood of her new lime-green fleece snugged around her head, and fake fur-lined boots with a fake suede finish—bought out of consideration for Josh's feelings about wearing real leather—on her feet, but the sky was crisp and cloudless. Between the flame-red tops of two maples she watched a great blue heron skate across the sky and out of sight. Her appreciation for the natural world was far greater than it had ever been now that she had a better sense of how inextricably humanity was tied to it.

I wish Rebecca were here, she thought, *and Brandy and Scott, too. I wish they could all go through what I have, learn what I have.* She'd had other friends, of course. But with the loss of her parents, and then her ordeal over the summer, most of those people had drifted away from her. She didn't miss anyone from Northwestern, not really. She barely thought of them at all, except a couple of times when she found herself imagining how much Dr. Manning, her history professor, would love to talk to Mother Blessing and hear some early American history from someone who'd been there. But Rebecca, Scott, and Brandy—they held important positions in her heart, and she couldn't help believing each would find valuable lessons here in the Swamp, even if they didn't care to learn magic.

It's not magic to understand that what happens to nature affects all of us, she thought. *To know that the wholesale extinction of species can only be bad for everyone, that humans won't be the last species to become extinct, or that no species except humans has ever been single-handedly responsible for the extinction of any other. And it doesn't take magic to comprehend that power flows from nature through us, or that we have to give back to nature some of what we take from it, if we want the interrelationship to continue.*

Kerry laughed. *Listen to me,* she thought, even though she hadn't spoken a word out loud, not wanting to disturb the Swamp's natural choir with a human voice. *I sound like some kind of green. And I thought Rebecca was our resident hippie.* But she wasn't thinking along political lines, or about social policy, just about what Mother Blessing had taught her of the need to respect nature and worship it as a manifestation of the Old Ones from whom all witchy power sprang. Along with that respect, which also applied to her tools—her cauldron, her athame, her wand, and the rest of the things Mother Blessing had helped her make or find—came a new appreciation. No tree, rock, implement, or person lasted forever. While it was in one's life, then, it had to be cared for and held precious.

The faintest rustle of a footfall on dry leaves alerted her, and Kerry spun, dropping to a crouch and raising her hands in a warding gesture. *"Shellitush!"* she shouted, generating a protective field around her. But this wasn't a simulacrum, she saw. Instead, emerging from the cover of a nearby cypress stump, an enormous black bear regarded her, one paw up on the stump, one hanging free, back feet firmly on the ground. Its head bobbed a little, as if listening to some silent tune, but its nose wrinkled slightly and she suspected it was sniffing her, catching the odor that sailed on a barely perceptible breeze. Its eyes were obsidian; its mouth open, tongue lolling over big teeth in an accidental impression of a smile. The big animal looked happy, even friendly. But she knew that it was not. Not that it would intentionally hurt her. If it felt threatened or trapped, it would certainly try. Otherwise, it bore her no ill will, just as surely as it didn't want to be her friend.

Kerry tried to project her thoughts toward the bear. She wasn't a meal, she wasn't a danger. She was simply a mildly interesting side note in the day's activities. After a few moments, as if it understood, the bear dropped down from the trunk, turned around, and loped away into the brush.

Kerry glanced toward the simulacra, both of which had decomposed back into the swamp stuff from which they were made, and then disappeared. She had a long walk back to the cabin, and the day was getting no warmer. Looking for the position of the sun to catch her bearings, Kerry headed for home.

19

I died once," Scott said. "You didn't know that, huh?"

Brandy looked across the table at him. Mugs of hot chocolate steamed between them, and outside bundled-up students rushed to and fro, slipping on icy sidewalks. It would get colder, but already the weather had turned sour. Thanksgiving was tomorrow, and Scott wanted an invitation to her place for the day—an invitation that would not be offered.

She and Scott had agreed to get together twice a week for lunch, coffee, or sometimes dinner or a movie. Not dating—she wouldn't go that far, and at her insistence it was strictly hands off. When they'd returned from Las Vegas, she had declared that it was over between them. He had packed up his things and moved out, leaving her in an apartment that she had to struggle to pay for. She had considered getting a roommate, but there was only one bedroom, and she valued her privacy. So far, her parents were helping out, but she knew she would have to move after the first of the year.

"No," she answered. She took a sip of the hot chocolate. It had been topped with whipped cream and just a hint of cinnamon. "No, I don't think I did. You never told me, did you?"

"No, it's . . . it's weird," he said. "I don't talk about it, really. I thought about it, after . . . you know, after Mace died. And then in Vegas, with Josh and everything. But it didn't seem appropriate, somehow. Because I came back, and they didn't."

"You came back? I mean, obviously, you're here. But what happened?" It seemed like the kind of thing a guy would tell someone he was in love with, living with. But hearing it this way just helped cement her conclusion that Scott wasn't ready for a real commitment.

He looked away from her when he told the story. These meetings were hard on him, Brandy knew, but still he insisted he wanted them. She was convinced that he thought she would reconsider, take him back.

He was wrong.

"I was eight," he said. "My dad was driving, mom in the front seat, me in back. I was wearing my seat belt, of course, but I was kind of laying down in the seat, you know, flopping around like kids do. We were going through an intersection when some maniac in a big pickup truck ran a red light and slammed right into us. Dad says the car spun around a dozen times, but he's always been kind of prone to exaggeration. Anyway, we bounced off a couple of other cars, slammed into a light pole. The car was almost cut in half, and I was banged up pretty bad. The paramedics on the scene thought I was gone—they actually wrote me off and went to work on my mom, who was the one with the most minor injuries. There happened to be a doctor there, and he didn't have any trauma equipment or anything, but he checked my pulse, my breathing. He declared me dead.

"I don't remember any of this—I only remember being told about it later on, when I was older. But after they had all turned their backs on me, I revived somehow. I started to scream, and they were really freaked out that I was even alive."

"I can see how that might be surprising," Brandy admitted.

"Yeah. I was out for a couple minutes, I guess. My mom said if it had been any longer they would have worried about long-term brain damage. She said she'd never been so glad to hear me holler bloody murder."

"I bet." Scott's mom was a little stiff, a little too old–New England for her tastes, but still a nice enough lady.

Scott drank some cocoa, went quiet for a minute. Finally, he put his mug down, ran a finger across his lips to wipe away any chocolate remnants. "So anyway," he said, "I guess the moral of the story is that you don't always know for sure if something is really dead. Sometimes it'll surprise you."

And there it is, Brandy thought. *He doesn't give up easily. You almost have to admire that.*

Almost.

She wasn't about to get sucked into it, though. She made up an excuse and left him in the coffee shop. Ten minutes later she was sliding down the sidewalks herself. It *was* over. It was because she said it was, and one person didn't make a couple all by himself, no matter how much he wanted it.

Anyway, she thought, *he only wants it because Kerry's not here.*

They hadn't heard from her since leaving Vegas. She had gone back to the Swamp, back to finish her training, she had said. After Josh's death, none of them had had much to say to one another. Kerry, Rebecca, and Scott had all retreated into their own minds, into their own worlds. She had done the same, Brandy knew. They had promised to stay in touch, and Rebecca had called a couple of times since then, and of course she still saw Scott.

But everything had changed. Brandy had realized it was changing even before Josh's death, but that had hurried it along, made it all somehow more definitive.

Life might be short. *Too short to waste in a relationship in which you're only a stand-in for someone else,* she decided. She didn't know if Season was really hunting them, although it certainly seemed as if that might be the case.

If she was, then Brandy had a lot of living to squeeze into a finite amount of time. Being with Scott wasn't really how she wanted to spend it.

So she had moved on. She just hoped he would be able to do the same.

* * *

Thanksgiving brought a perfect fall day, with a clear sky, a snap to the air, and leaves like brittle flame. Kerry rowed herself to the Slocumb site and tugged the skiff up onto the bank at the edge of that blasted, forsaken landscape. She had listened to some of Mother Blessing's stories about that fateful day, and had read various accounts of it in Daniel's journals. It had made such an impression on his mother, and through her on his own life, that he came back to it again and again.

Kerry found herself drawn to the place too, trying to picture what it had been like on that day so long ago. She walked across the scorched earth, noting the location of each building. Season had burned each one individually to the ground. The places where the roads had been laid out were still clearly distinguishable, now that she knew what to look for, and where structures had been, fire-blackened earth made precise geometric shapes. Wind had blown across this land, softening the edges, but as she'd noticed before, not a blade of grass had grown here since that time, not a dandelion or one of the ferns that were everywhere just a few feet away.

She had never quite understood how Mother Blessing had such precise knowledge of Season's actions on that day, since by her own account she had taken refuge in the Swamp as soon as it became clear that Season's rage had made her too powerful to fight. Kerry had asked, a time or two, but Mother Blessing had glossed over the issue as skillfully as a math teacher dodging the question of just when in life someone might have a need for advanced trigonometry. Probably, she had just relived the incident so many times in her own mind that she thought she remembered things she couldn't possibly have seen. At any rate, the damage had been done, that long-ago day. The Swamp had grown back, even after the fire that burned for months afterward—everyplace but here, of course. Mother Blessing had lived, had borne her sons and raised them. The world kept turning.

But for the people of Slocumb, the people Mother Blessing had known, had lived among, the world had ended that day. Kerry didn't know if Season's murderous ways had begun that day—if, having snapped, she'd never fully regained her sanity—or if she'd already embraced evil, and in fact had been responsible for the initial killings that had led up to the day's events.

Really, Kerry thought, *it doesn't matter. Season can't keep killing people I care about. Or strangers, for that matter. She's got to be stopped.*

She still had a lot to learn, a lot of drilling, a lot of practice before magic became as second nature to her as it would need to be to take on Season. But she was already more powerful than she had been three weeks ago when Josh had been killed, and a far more imposing person than she was a few months ago when she was trying to be a student at Northwestern, wanting nothing more than an "ordinary" life.

There is, she decided, *very little value to being ordinary.*

But there were times she wished for life to be a bit more like what she had grown up expecting, and this was one of them. The days and weeks had flown by; Thanksgiving was upon them. As a little girl, she had always loved that day, enjoying the televised parades, the football games, the way the house smelled, the warmth of her mother's kitchen, and the good spirits of the friends and relatives who came over. Mother Blessing's house couldn't be the same, but being there, so close to the region where the first European settlers made their homes, Kerry felt that some celebration was warranted. The older witch had agreed, so Kerry had gone out to shop for the requisite groceries: a turkey that Mother Blessing would fry, Southern style, in a deep pot she owned, and stuffing, cranberry sauce, fresh potatoes, green beans, and whatever else crossed her mind when she got to the market.

After spending a few minutes at the Slocumb site, soaking in the atmosphere and seeing it differently now that she had heard more stories about it, she rowed all the way over to Edgar Brandvold's place. He came out and unlocked the carriage house for her, wishing her a very happy Thanksgiving and revealing that he planned to spend the afternoon watching football. Kerry got in the minivan and drove to Deep Creek, where the nearest grocery store was. She loaded up with the things she needed and a few incidentals—Nehi and Coca-Cola for Mother Blessing, some herbal teas and a couple of bags of chocolate for herself—and took it all back to the van.

She appreciated Edgar Brandvold's willingness to garage the van for her. She had always been worried that someone would happen across it when she left it out in the open near

Slocumb, and though it hadn't happened yet, hunting season had started and the Swamp was full of strangers. Now that she had met Edgar and knew he was an ally of Mother Blessing's, she felt comfortable asking him to help out.

When she pulled into his long drive, though, she knew at once that something was wrong. Edgar was nowhere to be seen, even when she honked her horn, and the door to his ramshackle house hung open. She remembered that when he'd come out before, it had been closed, and that he had closed it behind him with the unstudied efficiency of long habit. He didn't seem like the kind of man who'd forget and leave it open.

She killed her engine and climbed out of the van. The house and yard were quiet; only the ticking of her van and the cry of some faraway bird broke the silence. Dust that she had kicked up driving in hung on the still air.

Edgar's house was old, and the boards that composed it looked as if they'd never been painted, though surely they had been once. A gallery edged the front and one side, and the roof bowed low over the door. Missing shingles gave it a gap-toothed look. The house's windows were black, empty. Through the open front door Kerry could see nothing at all.

Steeling herself, fear welling up inside her, she walked across the yard and put her right foot on the first of three steps up to the gallery. The wood beneath her was worn thin, with nails sticking up from it. Old Edgar wasn't big on mainte-nance, that much was clear. Kerry had already announced her presence by honking, so she climbed the stairs and rapped her knuckles against the open door.

"Mr. Brandvold!" she called. Now she could see an entryway with a small side table for keys or mail and a worn staircase beyond. Her words echoed in the small space but were not answered.

She went in. "Mr. Brandvold, are you here?" The loud creak of a floorboard underfoot startled her, cranking up her anxiety another notch. In spite of the cool day she felt sweat beading on her lip. She went through a doorway into a parlor jammed with enough furniture for a whole house: chairs, sofas, a TV, a table holding a radio and several magazines, other tables in front of the chairs and sofas and lining the walls behind them, and lamps, all turned off, scattered here and there through it all.

Edgar Brandvold sat in one of the chairs, hands at his sides, eyes open. He looked relaxed, like a man peacefully watching television. But his blue cardigan sweater was purpled and moist, and fat, lazy flies were walking around on it.

His knob-headed cane had been driven through his heart.

Kerry caught the coppery smell of blood—and something else at the same time. The second smell was familiar, but it took her a moment to place it. A smell that reminded her of electricity.

Then it came to her.

The stink of ozone. The smell of destructive magic, of murder.

She turned and ran from the house, dashed across the yard, threw herself into the van and slammed her fist down on the door lock. She hadn't taken the key out of the ignition, so she cranked it, and as the engine roared to life she stomped down on the accelerator, cutting a wide arc across the yard as she sped away.

It wasn't until she was back on the road toward Deep Creek that she realized her mistake. This had been no ordinary killing. This could only be the work of Season Howe. She must have tortured Edgar to learn the whereabouts of Mother Blessing—which meant that Kerry needed to get into the Swamp, back to Mother Blessing, as fast as she could. Instead of driving away, she should have thrown the skiff into the creek and rowed for her life. Convincing herself to go back to Edgar's place, though, was almost beyond her capability, even though the only other place she knew her way well enough from was the Slocumb site . . . and if there was one place she didn't want to go while Season was around, that was it.

Choices . . .

The highway was empty, so when she jammed her foot down on the brake there was no one behind her to smash into her van's rear. She performed a shaky three-point turn and headed back the way she had come, back toward Wallaceton.

Back toward Season's last known location.

Chances were, though, that Season had already moved on. Obviously, she had determined that Edgar was connected in some way with Mother Blessing. So if he knew enough to tell her, before his horrible end, how to find Mother Blessing, then Season was already in the Swamp, and there was precious little time for Kerry to warn her mentor. If he did not, though, then Season would be looking for some other clue, and chances were, Slocumb would be on her list of destinations.

Kerry raced back into Edgar's yard, pulled as close to the creek as she dared, and dragged her skiff out of the van. She spared a moment's thought for the groceries and then abandoned them. There would be no Thanksgiving anyway, if Season got to Mother Blessing before she did. Climbing into the boat, she sat down and dipped her paddle in the water, glad that the autumn's activities had built her muscles. She would need to row as she never had before.

20

By the time Kerry reached Mother Blessing's home— *my home,* she thought defiantly, *as much as anyplace else is*—the once-blue sky had turned dark gray and begun to weep. She grounded the skiff at the edge of the small property and ran inside.

"Mother Blessing!" she called anxiously. "Are you—"

The door to Mother Blessing's bedroom banged open and the old witch rolled out into the hallway on her familiar scooter. Her brow was furrowed, her lips tightly compressed. "I know, child," she said. "Season is in the Swamp."

"Edgar . . ." Kerry began, barely able to formulate a sentence. "She killed him!"

"I thought as much," Mother Blessing acknowledged. "I

have eyes in the Swamp, Kerry. I know she's lookin' for us. Lookin' for me. It's not too late for y'all to get yourself gone, though. Things are like to turn ugly round here."

Kerry hadn't considered running for a moment, couldn't quite believe Mother Blessing was making the offer. "It's my fight too."

Mother Blessing spared her a smile at that. "I was hopin' you'd feel that way. Let's get to work."

"How do you get ready for something like this?" Kerry asked anxiously. She could hear the first heavy drops of a hard rain hammering against the roof. "When Daniel was preparing to battle Season, he locked himself in a room and I heard the strangest noises—bells, wind, screams."

Mother Blessing rolled toward the kitchen as she answered. "He took himself out of the world for a few minutes, sounds like," she said. "Purifyin' is important before a fight, if there's time. If he was pressed for time, then he'd have done it by goin' someplace where time has a different meaning, where a short spell for you was a day or more for him."

"You mean . . . when I was standing outside the room waiting for him, he wasn't even in there?"

The old witch opened the refrigerator and rummaged around inside. "Yes and no," she said. "There's no easy answer to a question like that, and no right one either."

Kerry was almost afraid to ask the next one. "Are we . . . going someplace like that?"

"We don't even have that much time," Mother Blessing

answered quickly. "We just got to be as pure as we are."

Kerry thought about making a crack to the effect that the only man she'd spoken with in a month was in his eighties and dead, but it didn't seem funny, even to her. She let it go and watched Mother Blessing's preparations. As a sudden fierce wind began howling outside, her mentor took out potions made long ago and stored in glass bottles in the icebox, then wheeled around and retrieved various implements from her cupboards. These were, for the most part, things Kerry hadn't seen before: a long sword she was sure she'd need both hands to lift, an old thorned stick that could be used as a wand, and, most frighteningly, a rifle or shotgun, Kerry wasn't sure which.

"What's that for?" Kerry asked, surprised. "Daniel didn't use anything like that."

"And he lost, didn't he?" Mother Blessing answered, her words clipped, her voice glacial. "I don't intend to."

Kerry couldn't argue with that, so she held her tongue. Mother Blessing moved rapidly, mixing the contents of some of the bottles, lighting candles, chanting softly to herself in words that Kerry recognized as the Old Tongue, even though she couldn't make out the meaning. Once Mother Blessing had combined some of the various fluids, she rubbed the mixture on the blade of the sword. She poured another concoction into a bowl, where it steamed like something from a mad-scientist movie, and into that she emptied a box of bullets. Her efficiency was wondrous to behold, even as her actions filled Kerry's heart with terror.

Mother Blessing pointed at the bowl of ammunition and tossed Kerry a dishtowel. "Dry those," she instructed. Kerry held her hand over the rim of the bowl and poured the liquid out into the sink, cringing inwardly as the cold steel of the bullets bumped against her flesh. She spread the towel on the counter and scooped them out onto it, then folded it over them and rubbed them dry. She had always hated guns; the thought that she might be asked to use one repulsed her. After a moment she checked the bullets.

"They're dry."

"Load it," Mother Blessing said.

Kerry looked at the forbidding weapon. "I . . . I don't know how."

Mother Blessing huffed at her and took the gun in her own hands, drawing the towel toward herself over the counter. Kerry felt like she ought to apologize, but then thought better of it. The woman had no reason to assume that Kerry would know how to use a rifle; she shouldn't get upset when it turned out she didn't.

Still, it was true that while Mother Blessing did almost all of the preparatory work, Season—if the weather outside was any indicator, and Kerry couldn't help feeling like it must be—was drawing ever closer. The rain beat at the roof and walls like fists, causing her to wonder if it had turned to hail. The wind buffeted the walls, seeping in through whatever cracks it could. In fifteen minutes the temperature had dropped at least thirty degrees.

Before Kerry could even process the drastic meteorological

changes, though, there was a noise like a clap of thunder right outside. The whole house shook as if a sixteen-wheeler had run into it. Mother Blessing looked up at Kerry with a wry grin. "She's here."

"Do we have any simulacra?" Kerry asked.

"If she's outside, she's already gone through them."

"But . . . are we ready?" Kerry asked.

The witch was already in motion, wheeling her scooter around and heading out of the kitchen, toward the front door. "As we're gonna be. Got no time to be readier." Over her shoulder, she added, "Bring that stuff, willya?"

Kerry gathered up the sword, the stick, and the loaded gun and followed her. She caught up to Mother Blessing just inside the front door, where, to her astonishment, the older woman was climbing off the scooter. She had never seen Mother Blessing stand or walk, and had just assumed that both were impossible for her. But she was doing both now, and though her bulk made it difficult, she was able to maneuver herself to some degree. She tugged open the door, which blew inward with a great gust of wind, and stepped out into the lashing rain.

"This is still the South," Mother Blessing declared loudly. Kerry couldn't see who the witch was talking to, but she knew just the same. "We're hospitable folks here—y'all don't need to raise such a ruckus just to visit."

As Mother Blessing took a couple more steps away from the door, Kerry came closer to it and was able to see Season Howe standing on the firm ground outside the house. She couldn't spot any indication of how Season had arrived—there was no boat visible, nor any other form of transportation. But then again, Kerry couldn't see much; the curtain of rain reduced visibility to just a few yards.

Season looked like she had the last time Kerry had seen her: stern, severe, but undeniably beautiful. Her honey-blond hair was plastered to her head by the rain; wet black leathers, like a motorcyclist's, hugged her slim figure. Arms folded over her chest, she stared up at Mother Blessing on the wooden walkway outside the house, spared a casual glance for Kerry, whose arms were still laden with Mother Blessing's weapons, then looked back at the real threat.

"I decided I'm tired of you sending intermediaries after me," Season said, her voice calm and even. "Especially after I saw in Las Vegas that you are using these children again." Here her gaze ticked toward Kerry for a moment. "And not even children versed in the craft, but simply cannon fodder. You should be ashamed."

"Not that y'all will believe me," Mother Blessing argued, "but those 'children' weren't workin' on my behalf. They got their own issues with you."

"Is that right? I thought *you* were the one who wanted my hide—you and the sons you sacrificed."

Kerry was close enough to Mother Blessing to feel her go tense at that—*surprising,* she thought, *because I've been tense for a couple of hours now*—the woman's spine straightening, her fists clenching. "You leave them out of this."

"If you had left them out of it, they'd still be alive," Season observed. There was no cruelty in her tone, though there obviously was in the words she spoke. Mother Blessing took another step toward her.

"This house is under protection," she warned.

"And how far does that extend?" Season asked, almost cheerfully. "Since you're outside the house."

"Far enough."

The two witches faced each other, neither speaking for a moment. Kerry couldn't see Mother Blessing's eyes, but she was sure they were locked on Season's. The very air between them seemed charged somehow, as if to step into their path would be inviting electrocution.

"This has gone on too long," Season said after a few moments. Her voice sounded tighter now, as if she were starting to feel the tension. "Let's end it."

"Sounds good to me," Mother Blessing agreed. She raised her hands in a gesture with which Kerry had grown very familiar. *Lahatsi,* she thought, even before her mentor spoke the word.

"*Lahatsi!*" Mother Blessing shouted. She raised her hands as high as her bulk would allow and Kerry saw the energy ball that formed between them. Then Mother Blessing drew back and hurled it at Season.

Season didn't even speak, just flicked her wrist, almost casually, and the energy ball was diverted from its course. It hit a stand of cypress trees nearby and burst into flames, which sizzled and were extinguished in moments by the powerful rain. Watching the ease with which Season turned away what Kerry had believed to be a devastating attack, she realized with a shiver of fear that Season was the more skilled, the more potent, of the two combatants.

Which is bad, because Season has to die.

Not to mention that Kerry didn't want to be on the losing side of another fight to the death.

Season brought her hands together in a gesture that Kerry didn't know and then spread them quickly. A wave of power rippled the air, coming right toward them. Mother Blessing raised her hands in a warding gesture, and Kerry reflexively did the same. It worked; the energy wave dissipated harmlessly around them.

Mother Blessing turned partially, glancing behind her to make sure Kerry was there. She took the stick and the gun from Kerry's hands, leaving her only the sword. "We'll need weapons," she said simply. "Use that, Kerry. Kill her."

"Me?" Kerry felt her stomach clench, her insides turn to liquid. She had never fought with a sword in her life. *But then,* she told herself, *there are a lot of things you've never done before. Doesn't mean you can't do them.* Half convinced by her own pep talk, she gripped the sword by its handle, holding it in both of her fists. To her astonishment, flames licked up and down the blade, as if gasoline had been spread on the steel and then ignited. Raindrops hissed on its fire as they struck it, evaporating instantly.

With the fire came new confidence—confidence she thought might have been magically instilled, but was good enough just the same. She pressed past Mother Blessing and went down the steps toward Season, fiery blade held out in front of her.

Season took a step back as Kerry approached, her eyes widening slightly, which added to Kerry's sensation of well-being. *This can work,* she realized. *She's genuinely worried that I can beat her.*

As she moved toward Season, she felt more sure of what to do, how to wield the flaming sword, as if the weapon itself were teaching her its technique. She advanced, blade flicking this way and that, weaving a web of light and flame. Season raised her right hand and manifested a similar weapon, a sword made from pure magical energy. She waved it around for a moment, as if gauging its heft, and it made a whistling noise as it cut through the air. Then she lunged suddenly toward Kerry, right leg thrown forward, left hand back, like a fencer. Kerry didn't even have to think—the fiery sword drew her hand across her body to parry the lunge, and Season's mystical blade slid harmlessly to Kerry's side.

Kerry moved easily from the parry to an attack, her own sword thrusting itself forward at Season, drawing her body into a straight line as it did. Season, her face all intense concentration now, blocked the thrust with a grunt of effort. The move threw her off balance, her feet slipping on the wet ground, and Kerry pressed her attack, twisting her blade around Season's and driving forward again. This time, the tip of it touched Season's leathers before the witch managed to bat it aside.

Season retreated two quick steps and raised her sword again. "This can only end badly for you," she warned through clenched teeth. "You don't know what you're in the middle of."

"The plan is for it to end badly for *you*," Kerry corrected. She stood her ground, feet planted, legs spread for stability. Every muscle that she had built up over the fall was functioning at peak performance. Mother Blessing had been right— she may not have been ready, but she was as ready as she'd ever be, and far more prepared than she had expected.

"Plans don't always work out the way they're supposed to," Season pointed out. "I would have thought you'd have learned that by now."

"You killed Daniel," Kerry reminded her, fury tightening her voice. "That's all I need to know."

"Like I said, you have no idea what you're mixed up in, girl. If you back off now I'll try not to hurt you."

There was something in the witch's blue eyes that looked plaintive, even sympathetic. But Kerry was in no mood for it. She feinted to Season's left and then drove her sword, hard, toward Season's right. The witch parried, then drew her energy blade back and brought it forward again, slamming it into Kerry's with enough force to rip the flaming sword from her grasp. It spun twice in the air and splashed into swamp water, its flames dousing as it did.

All trace of sympathy gone from her face now, as if Kerry's

resolve had steeled her own, Season charged in for the kill.

She lunged, the tip of her mystic blade slicing the air toward Kerry. Before it reached her, though, Kerry heard a sharp report from behind her, then another, and a third. Season's advance halted and she staggered back, blue eyes widening, mouth dropping open. Kerry whirled to see Mother Blessing sighting down the barrel of the rifle, which had a trail of smoke rising up from its opening. The woman fired again, the muzzle flash impossibly bright against the dark sky. Four spots appeared on Season's black leathers, dark against dark, wet on wet.

Then Season bent forward at the waist, hands going up to her mouth. Kerry felt an unexpected sadness. She couldn't decide if it was because she hadn't been the one to finish Season off, or if it was something more than that, a kind of sorrow that the whole affair was ended. But ended it seemed to be.

Season had another surprise in store, though. She moved her hands a few inches away from her lips and spat four bullets into them, each one slick with her own blood. Holding them out before her, she smiled and dropped them to the ground. "You've got to do better than that," she said with a chuckle.

Mother Blessing hurled the weapon away, and raised the stick. "Not the gun and not the sword," she said, "but the rod will vanquish you."

Now Season's dry chuckle turned into a full-throated

laugh. "That thing?" she asked. "Do you forget who gave you that, daughter?"

"Y'all are on my ground," Mother Blessing said sharply. "And Kerry is strong, stronger than she has any right to be. There'll be no walkin' away, not from this fight. Not this time." But Kerry noticed that in spite of the certainty of the words, the hand holding the old stick was shaking a little, and there was a quiver in the voice. She couldn't have imagined Mother Blessing being scared by anything, but there it was.

"I didn't come here to walk away," Season reminded her. "I came to make sure you don't. To make sure you aren't going to continue to haunt me for the rest of my days."

"I don't need to haunt what's dead," Mother Blessing said, her voice cracking even more. She held out the stick like it was a weapon and said, *"Manistera!"*

The stick crackled with energy, traces of blue lightning running up and down its length. After a moment, the energy lanced toward Season. But the witch deflected it with a quiet word and hastily upraised hands. Her magical sword was gone now, back to whatever place she had conjured it from.

Season clapped her hands together hard, creating a sound like a sonic boom. Kerry threw her hands over her ears too late. The boom echoed in them, and she had a feeling they'd ring for hours, if not days. But the blast of power that began at Season's clap and rippled out toward Mother Blessing like a stone in a pond was sliced by the older woman's rod. Where it passed, leaves and bark were torn from trees, mud upturned, water churned in the creek. Mother Blessing, Kerry, and the house seemed unaffected.

Season didn't release her hands, though. She kept them clasped together, and as long as she did, the wave continued. Kerry felt it pressing against her like a surging tide. Mother Blessing felt it too, she saw, and though she tried hard to hold onto her stick—*her rod,* Kerry mentally corrected—the force of Season's attack whittled away at it, bit by bit, until all that was left was the tiniest twig. As that happened, tears came to Mother Blessing's eyes—tears of rage or tears of sorrow, Kerry wasn't sure—and the older woman, who she had come to think of as all but invulnerable, was driven to her knees. The sight filled Kerry with terror more than anything else that had happened so far.

Finally, Mother Blessing threw the twig aside and brought her hands up in a *"Lashifoth!"* defense. Kerry joined in, shouting the word simultaneously with her and making the appropriate motions.

A golden glow engulfed them—the punishing rain actually bounced off its blurred edges—and Season's attack ceased. Still, Season didn't look particularly frightened or upset. "You didn't really think that stick would stop me, did you, daughter?" she asked. "A gift from me to you? Your first rod."

"I remember," Mother Blessing said, almost spitting the words. She crooked her finger at Kerry. "Help me up," she commanded.

Kerry wasn't sure she'd be able to budge the woman, but

she hurried to comply. She didn't want Season to try anything more while Mother Blessing was on her knees.

"You're right," Season admitted then. "I am demonstrably more powerful than you, but on your home ground, and with your little helper, neither of us can get the upper hand. I had hoped to bring this little conflict to a close today, but apparently that's not to be."

Mother Blessing looked at Kerry, her eyes narrow, her mouth twisted into a scowl of utter hatred. "Don't let her go!"

Kerry already had her hands on Mother Blessing's arms, trying to hoist the enormous woman to her feet. "What can I—?" she began.

Season interrupted her question. "Nothing. There's nothing you can do, child. Except perhaps ask the woman you call Mother Blessing to explain what happened here today. Make her tell you the *whole* story. The real story."

Kerry looked from one to the other—Mother Blessing, struggling to regain her footing, her face a mask of fury, and Season Howe, beautiful and calm even though her leather jacket still showed four bullet holes. As she watched, Season grew less distinct. Kerry thought at first that she was walking backward, getting lost in the still-pounding rain. But her legs weren't moving, and she wasn't getting smaller. She was just . . . *vanishing* was the only word that came to mind. Becoming less substantial. Kerry could see the trees behind her, through her, and the rain and the Swamp, and then she was gone altogether.

Mother Blessing got a grip on Kerry's shoulders and forced herself to her feet. She looked at where Season had been a moment before, spat in that general direction, and stormed inside, slamming the door behind her. Kerry opened it again and walked in, wanting to talk to the woman, but Mother Blessing was already back on her scooter, wheeling toward her bedroom. When she reached it, she slammed that door, too.

And Kerry was alone with a million questions.

Kerry Profitt's diary, November 24

There's something very wrong here. I can't ask Mother Blessing about it because (a) she hasn't come out of her room since the battle to end all battles that wasn't, and (b) because if what I think is true IS true, then she's been lying to me all along.

To me, and maybe to others.

See, the thing is, Season Howe addressed her as "daughter." Not once, but twice. I know, it could be some sort of traditional witchy form of address, indicating love and respect, but . . .

No, really. That was what I tried to convince myself she meant. Figure of speech, right? Problem there is that the rest of Season's speech seemed pretty precise—not one for flowery speeches, that witch.

And there's more. If Season gave Mother Blessing her first rod, that implies, at the very least, some sort of teacher-pupil relationship. Which could also be a mother-daughter relationship.

If Season is Mother Blessing's mother, then what else hasn't Mother Blessing told me? Or Daniel—because I'm sure if he knew Season was his grandmother, he'd have said something. Apparent age, among witches, doesn't mean much, as Mother Blessing herself told me. Mother Blessing looks older than Daniel and Season, but none of them look anywhere near their actual ages. So Season could easily be older than Mother Blessing.

I had a lot of questions before, but now I have . . . well, A LOT a lot. Like why was she so willing to send me to Las Vegas after Season, knowing that I had just barely begun my magical training? Was she testing me somehow? Testing my willingness to fight, my courage, my hatred of Season? Or maybe testing Season's strength? And having my van moved—sure, she let me find out about it, introduced me to Edgar. But why didn't she tell me when she did it, or even ask permission? My van, after all. And the biggie that's been haunting me is this—I've wondered how Mother Blessing could have described the destruction of Slocumb so well, when supposedly she was already on her way into hiding, trying to protect her unborn children. But what if the answer is that it wasn't Season who destroyed Slocumb, but Mother Blessing? That's a big stretch, I know. But it's one answer to something that's been gnawing at me. And it goes back to the fact that Mother Blessing has been hiding things, lying to me.

I hate that. Hate lies, hate liars. I had grown to respect Mother Blessing—she's a real character, and a bit of a handful, but she was teaching me a lot, and I was willing to use what she taught to help her further her goal. Since it was the same as my own goal—revenge for Daniel's murder.

If she's been dishonest with me this whole time, though, that changes things. It doesn't change the fact that Season killed Daniel (although it adds, like, this whole layer of almost Shakespearean irony to it, doesn't it? Mother persuades son to kill his grandmother, but grandmother turns the tables . . .). What it changes are all the whys, and some of the whos, if not the whats.

It also changes my plans. I wanted to stay here, to learn as much as I could from Mother Blessing, to try to get close to her since she is my only link now to Daniel—not that she's the easiest person to get to know, since she will almost never actually talk about herself. But now . . .

. . . now, I think I need to get away from here. Fast.

To paraphrase old Willie S., there's something rotten, but it ain't in Denmark. It's right here in the Great Dismal. And I have this feeling that the longer I sit in "my" room, typing on this laptop, the rottener it's getting. I think it'd be best to get myself gone before MB comes out of her room looking for me.

Is it because I've been thinking about Josh and his noir movies that the phrase "you know too much" comes to mind? Because whenever there's someone in those movies who knows too much, the person who says it is always trying to kill them.

I think maybe I know too much.

Guess it's time to go.

More later.

K.

JEFF MARIOTTE has written more than forty-five novels, including the original supernatural thrillers *Cold Black Hearts*, *River Runs Red*, and *Missing White Girl*; the horror epic *The Slab*; and books set in the universes of *Buffy the Vampire Slayer*, *Angel*, *CSI*, *Supernatural*, *Dark Sun*, and others. Two of his novels have won the Scribe Award for Best Original Novel, presented by the International Association of Media Tie-In Writers. His nonfiction work includes the true crime book *Criminal Minds: Sociopaths, Serial Killers, and Other Deviants*, as well as official series companions to *Buffy the Vampire Slayer* and *Angel*. He is also the author of many comic books, including the original Western/horror series Desperadoes, some of which have been nominated for Stoker and International Horror Guild awards. Other comics work includes the horror series Fade to Black, the action-adventure series Garrison, the best-selling *Presidential Material: Barack Obama*, and the original graphic novel *Zombie Cop*. He is a member of the International Thriller Writers, the Western Writers of America, and the International Association of Media Tie-In Writers. With his wife, Maryelizabeth Hart, and partner, Terry Gilman, he co-owns Mysterious Galaxy, a bookstore specializing in science fiction, fantasy, mystery, and horror. He lives on the Flying M Ranch in the American southwest with his family and pets in a home filled with books, music, toys, and other examples of American pop culture. More information than you would ever want to know about him is at www.jeffmariotte.com.

Kerry knows too much. But has she learned
enough magic to keep herself alive? One thing's for sure:
she can run, but she can't hide. . . .

Don't miss the sequel,

Dark
Vengeance
VOL. 2

Kerry Profitt's diary, November 24

I was ready to run.

Not that I brought much with me to Mother Blessing's that I need to take away, but there are a few things—my old red-checked tennies, a couple of sweatshirts and some jeans I've grown attached to, my stash of cash, this laptop, BoBo the clown doll, and some of Daniel's journals—that I don't want to leave behind.

By now I know my way through the Swamp, so I'm not that concerned about provisions for the trip—no need to weigh myself down with energy bars or anything. But when I leave here this time, I'm never coming back. I don't want to forget anything that I might want later.

And, truth? I don't want to leave anything that Mother Blessing might be able to use to track me down.

But by the time I threw the few things I want to take into a duffel bag, Mother Blessing came out of her room and started wheeling around the house, slamming doors and cursing and shouting out—certainly for my benefit—things like "I can't believe what a liar that Season Howe is!"

I was hoping to get out of the house before she emerged from seclusion, so I'd be gone well before she knew I was missing. Because, let's face it, Thanksgiving hadn't exactly turned out like I'd planned. The groceries I had bought were still in my van—the turkey no doubt well thawed by now—at Edgar Brandvold's place, but Edgar had been murdered. I thought by Season Howe, since she seems to make a habit of killing people I know, including Daniel Blessing, Mother Blessing's son and the man I loved. But now everything I thought I knew about Mother Blessing and Season has been turned upside down, with the new information that Season is apparently Mother's mother. And, according to Season, there are other things Mother Blessing hasn't told me as well, which feed into certain questions I have run up against. Such as, which one was really the mega-destructo queen who trashed Slocumb, Virginia, three hundred years ago?

Confusion reigns. All I know for sure is that nothing is for sure. Maybe Mother Blessing killed Edgar to make me think Season had done it. Maybe Mother Blessing destroyed Slocumb and then sent her sons—Abraham and Daniel, both now deceased at Season's hands—after Season, to hide her own guilt.

Almost certainly Mother Blessing has been less than honest with me. And also almost certainly, she knows that since our confrontation with Season I am suspicious of her. The combination, it seems to me, is a dangerous one, which is why I really want to get gone.

But now she's banging around the house, and if I leave my room she'll see me. I'm trying to wait her out, hoping she'll give up and go to bed, and then I can scram.

The Great Dismal Swamp at night isn't exactly my favorite place. Dark, full of bugs and gators and snakes and the occasional bear. But right now, it beats the heck out of staying in this house an instant longer than I absolutely have to.

More later.
K.

Mother Blessing's door slammed again.

She'd been doing this for an hour—coming out of her room, rolling around the halls, the rubber wheels of her scooter squeaking on hardwood floors, then going back in. Slamming doors like an eight-year-old throwing a tantrum.

Except most eight-year-olds weren't potentially lethal.

Is she in for the night this time? Kerry wondered. *Or just for a couple of minutes?*

The answer could, literally, be that proverbial matter of life and death.

Gotta get out of here gotta get out of here gotta get out . . .

The door opened. Wheels squeaked. Barely breathing,

Kerry closed her laptop and listened. Mother Blessing had stopped shouting so much, but she was muttering something under her breath that Kerry couldn't make out. Panic gripped Kerry for a moment—the scooter was coming all the way down the hall to the guest room, the room in which Kerry had spent much of the autumn, learning magic at Mother Blessing's side. Given what had transpired earlier—Season Howe inform-ing Kerry, in front of Mother Blessing, that most of what she had been told about the mutual history of the two witches was wrong—Kerry couldn't help feeling that Mother Blessing would not be in a jovial mood when next they met.

Kerry had power. She knew that now. She had learned well, and magic seemed to come naturally to her.

But she was nowhere near Mother Blessing's level. If the old witch decided that it would be advantageous now to just take Kerry out, there would be little Kerry could do to dissuade her.

She held her breath for several seconds, but then the scoot-er's wheels squeaked again as Mother Blessing turned away from her door. Kerry heard the door to Mother Blessing's room open, and then slam shut again.

Is she working up her courage? Kerry thought. *Why? What kind of threat could I be to her?*

Sounds from Mother Blessing's room filtered down the hallway to her. They could have been the sounds of Mother Blessing preparing for bed—it was past ten now, her typical bedtime—but rain still hammered the roof, and it was hard to be sure.

Kerry waited another half hour. The minutes dragged by like days, weeks. Finally the noises from Mother Blessing's room died out.

Kerry was convinced that if she stayed, tomorrow would bring a confrontation with the old witch that she would probably not survive. She had successfully dodged it for tonight, probably because Mother Blessing herself was so weakened from the afternoon's magical battle with Season that she hadn't wanted to force the issue.

By morning Mother Blessing would have regained her strength. She would want to discuss the things Season had said—a discussion that would lead inexorably to Kerry's concerns that she had been lied to since arriving at the cabin in the Swamp earlier in the fall. If Kerry lived long enough, she would most likely accuse Mother Blessing of having lied to her own sons as well—of sending them off to kill a witch they didn't even know was their grandmother.

If Kerry was to get another day older, she had to leave tonight.

She had been ready for hours now, but she waited still longer. She wanted Mother Blessing to be deeply asleep. The old house's floors could creak when she walked across them, and the last thing she wanted was for Mother Blessing to wake up and find her on her way out. That would precipitate the very confrontation Kerry was trying to avoid.

Every minute was torture, every tick of the guest room wall clock agonizing. She almost took out her laptop to write some more in her journal, but then stopped herself. She wanted to be alert, aware, in case Mother Blessing woke up. Losing herself in her diaries was a distraction she couldn't afford. She couldn't even pace, for fear that her steps would wake the witch whose house she shared.

Midnight passed. *The witching hour,* she thought. Except for Mother Blessing, who, witch or no, almost always slept right through it.

But then, I guess I'm a witch too, now. Not as skilled and practiced as Mother Blessing or Season Howe. But if being a witch is defined by doing witchcraft, then I am one. So I can observe the witching hour all by my lonesome.

She waited, and let Mother Blessing sleep.

When the clock ticked over to twelve thirty, Kerry decided she had waited long enough. Her bag was already packed. She tied her long black hair back with a leather thong, pulled a coat from the closet, wrapped it around herself against the cold and rain she knew were waiting outside in the dark, and opened her door. Her room was at the end of a hallway, and she had to go past Mother Blessing's room to get out of the house. She stepped as lightly as she could manage, holding the duffel away from her body so it didn't rub against her jeans. In her other hand she carried boots, which she would only pull on when she was at the door.

She had almost made it when Mother Blessing's bedroom door opened, spilling light, and her scooter nosed out into the hall. Kerry's heart leapt into her throat as she spun around to see Mother Blessing glaring at her over her oxygen mask. The woman's breathing was labored, her voice muffled when she spoke.

"Where are y'all goin'?"

This was precisely what Kerry had hoped to avoid. She hadn't wanted a confrontation or a scene. She simply wanted to vanish, as she had from Northwestern University when she had decided that she wanted to come here, to the Swamp, to have Mother Blessing teach her magic so she could take revenge on Season Howe.

That worked out great, huh? she thought.

Now, facing Mother Blessing's glare, Kerry delivered the line she'd been practicing. "I'm . . . uh . . . going after Season," she said. "She can't be too far away yet."

Mother Blessing just stared, her breathing Darth Vader–esque through the mask.

"You've taught me a lot," Kerry went on. Her mind screamed at her to *shut up, already!* but her mouth didn't comply. "I think it's time to move on, though. Got to stay on Season's trail until I can kill her."

Mother Blessing stared. Finally she spoke again. "I don't think that's a good idea."

"Yeah, well, I kind of do," Kerry returned, defiance starting to rise in her. "So, thanks a lot and all, but I've got to get going."

"No."

Obviously conversation wasn't a good idea. Kerry dropped

the duffel, tugged on her boots, picked it up again. Another glance at Mother Blessing, who was rolling in her direction now, her mouth scowling behind the oxygen mask, and Kerry stepped out the door.

"No!" she heard Mother Blessing cry behind her.

Kerry slammed the door and ran through driving rain to the shallow-bottomed skiff Mother Blessing kept for traveling out of the Swamp. She hurled the duffel in, pushed it off the bank, climbed in, and shoved the oars into the oarlocks. As she started to row, she glanced back toward the house—which always looked like a tumbledown old trapper's cabin from the outside—and saw Mother Blessing silhouetted in the doorway, her arms raised in the air.

That, she thought, terrified, *is not good.*

But with strength that came from working hard around the Swamp for weeks, she dipped the oars into the murky water and pulled.

It was impossible to tell where the water ended and the trees began, and just as hard to know where the tops of the trees merged with the sky. Moonlight filtered through only in rare spots. Trees were a wall of black against black. The toads, crickets, night birds, the rare and piercing howl of a bobcat, were all but drowned out by the pounding rain and the occasional crack of thunder, adding to Kerry's confusion and disorientation.

At this moment, however, she was more concerned with steering the shallow boat between the trees and not grounding it than with direction. She needed to find her way through the honeycomb of canals and creeks to someplace where she could catch a ride far away from here, but it wouldn't do her any good to get away from Mother Blessing if she killed herself trying. Since she wasn't sure who had killed Edgar Brandvold, or why—and since she had told Mother Blessing that she'd left the minivan at his place when she arrived and found Edgar murdered—she didn't want to risk going back there. Mother Blessing had not been happy about her leaving, and if she were going to try to stop Kerry—or to send her simulacra to do that—the van would be the obvious place to start.

A flash of lightning momentarily illuminated a barricade of tree trunks right before her. Kerry put her oars to water and pulled backward, trying to brake herself, to lessen the impact of imminent collision. At what she figured was the last moment, she raised an oar and thrust it out before her to stave off the bank. She felt the oar hit the bank, felt the boat stop in the water just before it rammed.

But when she tried to lower the oar to the water again, something held it fast. She yanked at it, but to no avail. Whatever had her oar wasn't letting go—and, she realized, it was drawing her in toward the bank.

Simulacra? Kerry wondered. If she'd just snagged it on something, she would be able to free it, she was certain. She had a flashlight with her but hadn't bothered to use it, since it would have meant taking a hand off the oars. Now, though, she released the stuck oar and grabbed for the flashlight, at the top of her duffel bag. She drew it out and flicked it on.

Something had her oar, all right, but it wasn't one of Mother Blessing's manufactured men. It was a bald cypress root sticking out from the bank. It had wound itself three times around the end of the oar and was waving it like a magician with a wand.

Kerry knew the root could not have grabbed the oar like that without help. Mother Blessing was trying to stop her—and using the Swamp to do it!

While she watched, another root snaked toward her. She ducked away from its grasp. It came again, and she bashed it with the flashlight.

That wouldn't hold it for long. She clicked off the light and jammed it back into the duffel, zipping the bag closed to keep out the rain. With her remaining oar—no way would she be able to fight the tree for the other one, not while it had dozens of roots that might attack her—she pulled hard against the water, alternating sides of the skiff to keep on an even course.

She was only a few yards away from where she'd lost her oar when she felt something damp brush her face. *A spiderweb,* she thought, *or some low-hanging Spanish moss.* Either was possible here. She swiped at it with one hand—and it snaked around her wrist, pulling tighter as she tried to tug away.

Kerry screamed and yanked her arm. Whatever it was— she thought she felt leaves on it, like a vine of some kind—

wouldn't let go. She swung at it with the oar but couldn't break its grip. It started to lift her up out of the boat.

Panic threatened to overtake her as she struggled against the vine. Another one wrapped around her waist and tightened there, like a belt cinching up. Her free right hand dropped to her own belt, but the knife she wore sometimes in the Swamp wasn't there, and she remembered tossing it into the duffel when she'd packed.

When the next vine looped around her throat, she thought it was all over. It closed tightly on her, cutting off her airway. By now she was mostly out of the skiff, could feel with her feet that it was drifting away from her.

Which was when she remembered that she was a witch too.

A kind of calm settled over Kerry's racing mind. Mother Blessing was turning the Swamp against her through magic. But she wasn't the only magic-user around. She had taught Kerry quite a few tricks—but more important, she had taught her philosophies and systems. She may not have known a specific spell to free herself from living vines, but that didn't mean she was defenseless.

With her throat closed off and one hand out of commission, speaking the Old Tongue and making the correct gestures was tricky. But she managed to croak out the word *"Kalaksit!"* and curl the fingers of her free hand toward her palm while splaying the thumb out. White flame crackled at her fingertips. She felt herself relaxing even more, letting the now-familiar sensation wash over her—the thrill of power, the rush of magic. Raindrops sizzled against her fire. Aiming by the light the flickering flames provided, she pointed at the vine that encircled her throat and willed the fire into a narrow, straight blast. It cut the vine as keenly as a laser.

Next came the one around her waist, and then her arm. Kerry dropped back down to the skiff, but unbalanced, she went over backward, landing faceup in the shallow water. She allowed herself a bitter smile. It hardly mattered; she was already drenched from the rain. The flames at her fingertips died in the creek, but that was okay. She could always make more.

She climbed back into the skiff, found the remaining oar, and started to row.

Okay, then, she thought as she churned the water, driving the boat quickly up the creek. *Mother Blessing is definitely opposed to me leaving. Don't know yet if she's homicidal about it, but she's obviously serious.*

Kerry rowed and rowed. Her arms started to ache, her shoulders and back protesting from the effort. The rain gave up, and by the time light started to show itself, patches of silver and pink visible through the leafy ceiling to the east, she knew something was wrong. She had been making for the old Slocumb site—the blasted, cursed township Season and Mother Blessing had once shared—and she should have reached it within a few hours. Navigation had been difficult in the dark, but even so. . . .

More light filtered in through the trees and Kerry saw a bank that she recognized, with roots reaching through the bluff of clay and diving into the water, a big, pale mushroom sticking out of one like a dinner plate wedged halfway in. She had seen that bank at least an hour or two before, on one of the occasions when she'd taken out her flashlight to gauge her path. She was positive she hadn't been rowing in circles—the Swamp wasn't so well organized that one could even do that intentionally. Which could only mean that the Swamp itself was shifting, changing itself around in an effort to keep her here.

What if it isn't Mother Blessing? Kerry wondered as the icy hands of fear gripped her again. *What if it's Season—or the Swamp itself? What if it doesn't want me to leave? Will I ever get out then?*

But Kerry Profitt was the Bulldog, she reminded herself. It didn't matter who—or what—was trying to keep her here. The only thing that mattered was that she was determined to get out, and so she would. She drifted past the familiar bank. Now that the sun had come up, she knew which direction east was. Slocumb was to the east, and a highway ran alongside the Great Dismal in that direction. She would find an exit, at one spot or another.

Kerry had traveled maybe another half mile when the water started moving faster under her boat. It took her in the direction she wanted to go, so she let the current carry her, using the oar only to keep herself away from the banks. A family of feral pigs watched her race by from a bluff; crows and three snowy egrets took flight at her rapid approach.

Then the creek widened, and ahead she could see where it joined with a broader canal. By now she was completely lost—she was nowhere she had ever been before, or, more likely, the Swamp had never been configured in just this way before. She put the oar to water to help ease herself into the canal, but when her smaller tributary hit the larger one, the water there rushed faster than she had ever seen water move here. It was like a river's rapids, not like the near-stagnant swamp water she was used to. Her heart raced as she tried to steady the shallow skiff, but the little boat was no match for the sudden flow.

Water roared in her ears and splashed ahead of the skiff, and Kerry found herself spinning around and around, the oar useless to stop her. Then the tiny craft was hurled against a jagged bank, where it splintered. Kerry snatched up her duffel bag as the water rushed in, and hurled it up onto the bank. The water in the swamp was rarely deep, but things lived in it that she didn't want to encounter if she could help it—water moccasins and alligators foremost among them. Grabbing exposed roots, she pulled herself onto dry land, where she sat down hard and watched the boards that had once been the skiff separate and float away.

The waterways were the highways of the Swamp, Kerry knew. There were trails on land, but they were mostly animal paths, unsuited for anything as big and ungainly as a human being. Kerry was slender enough for most trails, but when they wound underneath spreading ferns and fallen trunks, they could be impassable even for her.

Still, it didn't look like she had much choice now. She headed vaguely east until she found a faint track and then followed it.

And still Mother Blessing wasn't done with her, she discovered. After maybe a mile or so, Kerry discovered that she was being followed. She heard the chuffing sound of a big cat first and froze in place. Slowly, carefully, she turned and looked back down her trail, and after a few minutes a bobcat showed itself, its strange golden eyes fixed on her. But the bobcat wasn't alone—a black bear parted the brush and stood beside the feline. Kerry knew that would never happen in nature—only Mother Blessing's intercession could have made those two creatures into allies.

Knowing that didn't make Kerry feel any better about it. Either one, bear or bobcat, could do a lot of damage if it attacked her. Both acting together, impossible as it was to imagine, could easily tear her to shreds.

She could defend herself, of course. But the idea of hurting either of those animals, forced against their own natures to cooperate in her destruction, was repellent to Kerry.

Fighting the tremor in her knees, the urge to run, she turned away slowly, showing them her back. She then continued down the trail she had found, heading into the morning sun, moving at a steady clip—not running, but not slow.

Behind her, she heard the animals keeping pace.

To panic, to run, would certainly bring them both charging down on her. This way they remained at bay, tracking without charging, while she tried to think of a way to reverse the spell that had enchanted them.

No such reversal came to mind. Kerry was exhausted. She hadn't slept since yesterday morning, Thanksgiving, which seemed a lifetime ago, and then the battle with Season, the effort of rowing all night—it was no wonder answers weren't coming to her as quickly as they might have.

Finally an idea occurred to her. The animals had been set on her trail by Mother Blessing, no doubt with malicious intent. They hadn't attacked her yet, but Kerry was convinced that they would when their instincts told them she was a threat or when she tried to run. She didn't know how she could alter the programming, but she was pretty sure she could change their target. She stopped, then spun around, facing them again. Speaking a couple of the magic words she had learned, gesturing with both hands, she pointed toward a nearby puddle and raised the water from it. With the water that now hovered in the air between herself and the animals, she sculpted the image of Mother Blessing—all three hundred pounds or more of her, complete with scooter, oxygen tanks, and beehive hairdo. She tried to look into the eyes of each animal, and she drove into their minds the concept that this person was their enemy, their mutual target. Finally she hurled the water sculpture at them. Bear and cat both flinched away, but it splashed against them, harmless but soaking.

When it was over, both creatures regarded Kerry almost casually, and then looked this way and that, up and down the path. They were no longer fixed on her, she believed. She waved her arms at them, and they backed away, turning and going back the way they had come.

Kerry didn't know how long Mother Blessing's spell would last—or how long her own would, for that matter. But if it held, and if these two unlikely companions found their way to Mother Blessing's cabin, the old witch was in for an unpleasant surprise.

The path twisted and turned, widening here, narrowing to almost nothingness there. Always it led east, which was where Kerry had decided salvation lay anyway So she stayed with it as best she could.

In another hour or so, she could hear the rush of cars on the highway. She struggled to place her weary feet. The duffel was so heavy she was regretting having brought it. The world no longer seemed to conspire against her—when vines snatched at her ankles or thorns tore at her sleeves, they were simply doing what vines and thorns naturally did. But she was almost ready to admit defeat anyway, not sure how long she could continue the hike. The sound of cars perked her up a little. But they were still at some distance, with plenty of thick swamp between her and them.

She drove herself on. When her mind started to wander, when she began to lose her focus, to fall asleep on her feet, she reminded herself of Mace Winston, whom Season had killed back in San Diego during the summer. That summer had changed everything for her—had taken a life that was moving in one direction, as surely as the creek that had carried her skiff, and spun it around just like the canal had done the little boat. Summer had introduced her to Daniel Blessing, three hundred years old and, as it turned out, the love of her life. She allowed the memory of his smile, kind and genuine, to fill her for a moment. It brought her a few seconds of peace, reminded her why she was doing all this. He was the handsomest man she'd ever seen—centuries old, sure, but witchcraft, she had learned, was the original Botox and didn't even involve needles or deadly germs.

But the summer had also brought Season Howe into her life, and Season had killed Mace, and later Daniel. Then, during the fall, when Kerry was in the Swamp learning from Daniel's mother, Season had apparently tracked down Rebecca in Santa Cruz, and Josh in Las Vegas. Josh hadn't survived the encounter. The only ones remaining from the summer house in La Jolla were herself, Rebecca, Brandy, and Scott.

Finally Season had shown up here, in the Great Dismal. Where it had all started, so many years before. Here she hadn't been able to defeat Mother Blessing and Kerry, but neither had they been able to triumph over her. It almost didn't matter— the things Season had said were enough to make Kerry rethink everything that had happened since August. She had been motivated by thoughts of revenge against Season ever since Daniel had died.

Now it wasn't so much revenge that spurred her on, although that was still a factor. Now——just since yesterday afternoon—what Kerry discovered she wanted most in the world was the truth. She wanted to know who had destroyed Slocumb. She wanted to understand the relationship between Season and Mother Blessing, wanted to know what Daniel and his brother Abraham had known about it.

That quest, instead of just simple revenge, kept her putting one foot before the other, ducking branches, dodging thorns. She tried to remain alert, worried that Mother Blessing would have turned the Swamp against her in ways she hadn't encountered yet. But her eyes grew bleary and her concentration flagged.

Until finally she topped a low rise and saw, at the bottom of a weed-choked slope, the highway she sought. Highway 17 ran north-south here, along the edge of the Great Dismal Swamp. It would take her away—away from Mother Blessing, away from Season Howe.

It was so beautiful, that strip of lined asphalt, that Kerry thought she would cry.

And from the *New York Times* bestselling authors
Nancy Holder and Debbie Viguié,
Look for:

Crusade

The ultimate battle.
The ultimate love.

The village of Cuevas, Spain
Team Salamanca: Jenn and Antonio,
Skye and Holgar, and Eriko and Jamie

Barely sunset, and death exploded all around Jenn Leitner.

It was a trap, she thought.

The sky crackled with flames; oily smoke choked the air and burned her lungs. Jenn struggled not to cough, fearing that the sound would expose her. On her elbows and knees, her dark auburn hair loose and falling into her eyes, she crawled from beneath the red-tiled roof of the medieval church as it collapsed in a crash of orange sparks. Fragments of tile, stone, and burning wood ricocheted toward the blood-colored moon, plummeting back down to the earth like bombs. She dug in her elbows and pushed forward with the toes of her boots, grunting as a large, fiery chunk of wood landed on her back with a sizzle. She fought to stay silent as the pain seared through her. Biting her lip hard, she tasted coppery blood as she rolled to extinguish the flames.

Next to her, Antonio de la Cruz hissed a warning. The scent of her blood would fill the night air, attracting the vampires they'd been sent to hunt—but who were hunting them instead. When Jenn was little, her grandmother had told her that sharks could smell a drop of blood in the water half a mile away. She hadn't gone in the ocean since. Cursed Ones could smell blood more than a mile away. With sharks you could choose to stay out of the water.

With Cursed Ones it was different. You couldn't leave the planet. You were trapped.

Like we are now.

Antonio studied her with his deep-set Spanish eyes. Jenn gave her head a shake to let him know she was all right; she could keep going. She had no time to search through her jacket for the garlic-infused salve that would block the odor of her blood. She prayed that the stench of the burning buildings—and burning bodies—would cloak the scent long enough to allow them to escape.

Past the church grounds the oak trees were on fire, acorns popping, leaves igniting like tattered tissue paper. Smoke filled the inky night sky, smothering the faint glow of the moon, but the hellish light from the fires illuminated Jenn's and Antonio's every move. Combine that with her bleeding lip, and they were two very easy targets for the savage monsters bent on massacring the village.

Antonio stopped suddenly and held up a warning hand. She watched him closely. Wisps of his wild dark hair escaped from his knitted cap; his full eyebrows were raised slightly, and his jaw was clenched. Like her he was dressed all in black—black sweater, black cargo pants, black knee protectors, and black leather boots—and now coated with ash. She could see the glint of the small ruby-studded cross that he wore in his left ear. A gift, he had said, when she'd asked about it. His face had darkened when he'd answered her, and she knew there was more to that story. So much of Antonio was a mystery to her, as intriguing as the sharp planes and hollows of his face.

He was focused, listening. All Jenn could hear were the flames and the terrorized, outraged cries of the villagers from the surrounding houses and office buildings. Her world became Antonio's face and Antonio's hand, blotched with soot, and she tensed her muscles so she'd be ready to move again when his hand dropped. She wished she could stop shaking. Wished she would stop bleeding and hurting. Wished someone else could do the rescuing, instead of them.

But somewhere in the darkness the Cursed Ones were watching. She imagined them staring at her, and could almost hear their cruel laughter dancing in the acrid air.

Three vampires and six hunters stalked one another through the steamy inferno. *If the other hunters are still alive. If they escaped the burning church.*

Don't think about that now. Don't think at all. Wait. Watch.

Cuevas, a small Spanish town a couple of hours from their home, had been terrorized by a group of vampires for weeks, and their mayor had begged for help. Jenn was one of a group of trained vampire hunters called the Salamancans, graduates of the Academia Sagrado Corazón Contra los Malditos—Sacred Heart Academy Against the Cursed Ones—at the centuries-old University of Salamanca. Father Juan, their master, had sent them to Cuevas to rid it of the Cursed Ones.

Instead the vampires were hunting the hunters, as if they

had known they were coming, as if they had lured them there. Jenn wondered how they'd known. Father Juan always sent the team out covertly. Was there a spy at the university? Had someone in Cuevas betrayed them?

Or is the Hunter's Manual right about all *vampires?*

Don't think.

Late that afternoon Jenn, Antonio, and the other hunters had parked in the woods and silently made their way to the church, where they waited, meditating or praying, and preparing for the battle ahead. The vampires appeared with the flat shadows of dusk, and in the literal blink of an eye—they moved faster than most people could see—they set fire to the stone ruins of the *castillo*, the brick-and-mortar shops of the nearby plaza, and the glass and steel of a handful of modern office buildings. Flower boxes lining the plaza, which had brimmed with pink and white geraniums, crackled like sparklers; windows shattered; car horns blared like Klaxons; and everywhere, everywhere, fires roared.

In their short two months' hunting together as a team, the Salamancans had fought greater numbers—once there had been as many as eleven—but those Cursed Ones had been newly converted. The younger the bloodsucker, the easier to defeat, as they would not have fully adapted to their new abilities . . . or their weaknesses.

Against older vampires, like the three lurking in the darkness, you could only hope they hadn't yet run up against a hunter. That they would have grown so used to slaughtering the helpless that they would underestimate those who knew how to fight back.

But the Cuevas C.O.'s had struck first, which meant they knew what the six hunters were capable of. By the time Jenn and the other Salamancans had smelled smoke, there had only been time to rouse Antonio from his meditations in the chapel behind the altar and crawl outside.

Now they were exposed and vulnerable. And—

Jenn blinked. Antonio was no longer beside her. Panic wrapped around her heart, and she froze, unsure of what to do. Directly in front of her an oak tree shuddered inside its thick coat of fire, and a huge limb snapped off, cascading into the dirt with a *fwom*.

He left me here, she thought. *Oh, God.*

Breathe, she reminded herself, but as she inhaled, smoke filled her lungs, and she pressed her hand over her mouth. Her balance gave way, and she collapsed onto the dirt. Jenn grunted back a hacking cough. The welt on her back burned like a bull's-eye; she was a prime target. And alone.

Where are you, Antonio? she silently demanded. *How could you leave me?*

Tears welled. Jenn gave her head a hard shake. She had to hustle. If she didn't move, she would die a horrible death. She had seen vampires kill people. But he wouldn't let that happen to her. Would he?

Don't think. Just move.

Jenn's fingernails dug into the dirt as she lifted herself up.

Commando-style she worked her way forward, scrambling to the left when another large oak branch cracked and fell toward her like a flaming spear. She had to get away from the collapsing buildings and the falling trees before she could think about going on the offensive.

There was a whisper of sound, a *shushshushshush*, and Jenn rolled farther to her left just as a vampire landed on his back beside her. His pale blue eyes were opened wide in a death mask, and his breath reeked of rotting blood. She thought he groaned a word, maybe a name.

Then all at once the vampire collapsed into dust and was scattered by the hot winds. *One down,* she thought, covering her mouth and nose to avoid inhaling any of the vampire's remains. The first time Jenn had seen that happen, she'd been unable to speak for over an hour. Now she couldn't help the triumphant smile that spread across her face.

Jenn struggled to her feet; Antonio stood a breath away, his eyes blazing, the stake that had killed the vampire still clenched in his hand. He towered over her, six feet to her five-five. As she reached out to touch his arm, a blood-curdling scream ripped through the night air, and she took off in its direction, expecting Antonio to do the same.

Instead his body hurtled past her, landing in a pile of burning branches and leaves.

"Antonio!" she screamed, then wheeled around in a fighter's stance, facing off against the vampire who had tossed him through the air like one might toss loose change onto a counter. The Cursed One was tall and bulky, grinning so that his fangs gleamed in the firelight. His face was covered in blood. Her stomach lurched, and she tried not to think about how many of the villagers were already dead.

Jenn swiftly grabbed a stake from the quiver on her belt, gripping it in her right hand, and ripped open a Velcro pocket with her left to retrieve a cross. She desperately wanted to look back at Antonio. She dared not.

The vampire sneered at her and snarled in a thick Leonese-Spanish accent, "*Pobrecita*, I can hear the frightened beating of your heart. Just like the rabbit in the trap."

He slashed her across the cheek with his talonlike nails before leaping back in a dizzying blur. Jenn felt the blood running hot and sticky down her cheek before she felt the sting.

Jenn circled him warily. *I'm a hunter,* she reminded herself, but the hand around her stake was shaking badly. Surely he could see it. If he attacked, there was a good chance she wouldn't be quick enough. The specialized training she had received at the academy had taught her how to anticipate a vampire's moves even when she couldn't see them. They moved so fast, the Cursed Ones. Father Juan said that they moved faster than man could sin. He said they could kill you and you would never know it had happened, but if you had been a brave and just person, the angels would tell you all about it, in song.

I'm not brave.

She took a deep breath and turned her head slightly to the side. Her best bet at tracking him was not to look directly at him. Movement was most effectively caught out of the corner of one's eyes. She had learned that at the academy, and it had saved her before. Maybe it would again.

But maybe not.

The vampire stayed visible, stalling, but more likely toying with her before he made his kill. Some vampires were matadors, drawing out the death dance like a ritual. For others the hunt was a means to an end—fresh human blood, pumped by a still-beating heart.

Movement in the shadows caught her eyes. Jenn fought not to react as one of the other hunters—*the* Hunter, Eriko Sakamoto—crept toward the vampire, her tiny frame belying her superior strength. Dressed in night hues like Jenn and Antonio, she wore a turtleneck, leather pants, and thick-soled boots that Velcroed halfway up her calves. Her short, gelled hair made her look like a tribal warrior. Fresh streaks of soot were smeared on her high, golden cheekbones.

The sound of the fires masked any noise from her approach. Eriko caught Jenn's eye, and Jenn began to edge to the right, placing the vampire between them.

"Hunters . . . *jóvenes* . . . you're nothing special after all," the Cursed One snarled.

"We're special enough to turn you to dust," Jenn growled, trying to hold the vampire's attention. She focused on his fangs instead of his eyes, so as not to be mesmerized by him. That was one of the first rules of survival—to resist the Cursed Ones' hypnotic gaze, designed to put their prey in thrall. "You'd better say your prayers. You're about to die."

The vampire scoffed, weaving closer, seemingly unaware that a hunter advanced behind him with her stake poised. The smell of Jenn's blood cloaked the subtler scent of unharmed human flesh.

"Prayer is for mortals," he said, "who must beg some deity to save them. And as we know, those prayers always go unanswered."

"Always?" Jenn asked, feeling the blood oozing down her cheek. The vampire stared at it as if he hadn't drunk in centuries.

"Always," he replied.

Eriko kept her distance, and Jenn had a terrible thought: *She's using me as bait.* Jenn began to back away, and the vampire made a show of taking a step toward her. Her hands were slick with sweat—from the heat, from her fear—and her grip on the stake began to slip. She worked her fingers around it. The vampire snickered.

Jenn took another step backward, her boot crunching down on something. Her stomach lurched as sparks flew upward. What if it was Antonio?

She couldn't stop herself from glancing down. It was only a branch. The vampire launched himself at her with a hiss.

"No!" Jenn shrieked, falling backward.

The vampire landed on top of her, his eyes filled with bloodlust. His fangs were long and curved; she flailed, forgetting all her training, every maneuver that could save her. His breath stank of fresh blood, and she heard herself whimper.

Antonio.

Then, suddenly, the Cursed One was gone. Jenn pulled herself into a crouch, aware that she'd lost her cross. Eriko had yanked the vampire to his feet and was on his back, legs wrapped around his waist. He batted at her as she laced her fingers underneath his chin, forcing back his head. He hissed and grabbed her ankles, trying to peel her off him.

"Jenn, stake him," Eriko shouted. "Now!"

Jenn blinked. She took two steps forward, and then she stopped for a fraction of an instant. Just stopped.

She could no longer see Eriko or the vampire. They were moving too fast for her to track. She lunged forward, stabbing at the air. There was no contact. She caught flashes, blurs, but not enough to give her a target. Through her exhaustion Jenn kept swinging, as her mind raced. If Eriko died, it would be on Jenn's head.

Then she saw them. The vampire had been forced to his knees, and Eriko stood behind him, her hands still laced beneath his chin. Jenn ran to stake him as Eriko flashed her a fierce smile and twisted off his head. His headless body held its shape; Eriko threw the head into the advancing flames. It was something Jenn could never have done; she didn't have Eriko's superhuman strength.

"At least someone's prayers were answered," Eriko said, panting, as the body disintegrated. She trotted toward a crumbling stone wall to their left, which marked the north end of the church's cemetery. "Let's keep moving."

Jenn looked back to where she had last seen Antonio, but he wasn't there. Another surge of panic washed over her as she raced toward the spot. He was simply *gone*. He wouldn't have just abandoned them, though; he couldn't have *left*.

"Antonio!" Jenn screamed. "Wait, Eriko. Antonio!"

"*Sí,*" he called. "*Sí*, Jenn."

Antonio pushed through the burning brush a few yards away, wisps of smoke curling from his charred clothes as he batted at them. His hands were blackened and peeling.

She ran to him and then stood hesitantly in front of him, frightened and ashamed of her doubts. "Are you okay?" she asked.

He nodded grimly. "I will be."

She began to shake. "I was worried. I thought . . ." She trailed off. It didn't matter what she had thought. All that mattered was that he was alive and there.

"You didn't think I would leave you?" Antonio questioned, his gaze intense as he reached out to cup her cheek with his hand. "I was coming to help you and Eriko." Then his soft expression flickered, and she saw his despair. He hid it well . . . though not well enough, at least for someone so focused on him as she was. The shadow in his eyes spoke of something he had refused to share with her—his deepest wound.

His darkest secret.

Tears stung her eyes. Jenn loved Antonio, and she wanted to trust him. But trust was something she'd left behind two years ago when she'd crossed the threshold of the university. She'd had to learn not to trust her eyes, her mind, or even her heart. Every time she forgot that, she nearly got herself killed.

"*Ay, no,*" Antonio whispered, gazing at her. "I would never leave you."

Antonio stroked her cheek with his thumb, and she closed her eyes, leaning into the touch. Calloused, velvet. When his lips brushed hers, she returned the kiss with a sob. She threw her arms around his neck and clung to him. His lips were soft and yielding against hers, and the taste of him mixed with the faint metallic flavor of the blood in her mouth.

Leaning against Antonio, she whimpered, wanting more. Then, suddenly, he *was* gone.

Jenn opened her eyes and saw Antonio hunched over a few feet away, eyes glowing and fangs protruding. Eriko strode up beside Jenn, a thick stake clasped in her hand. One throw and she could kill him.

"*Estoy bien,*" Antonio growled deep in his throat. He wiped something dark off of his lips and onto his black cargo pants.

Her blood.

"Eriko, I'm all right," he said in English.

His deep voice always made Jenn shiver, but with fear or desire she was never quite sure. Sometimes when they were kissing she would forget, just for a moment, all that kept them apart.

Antonio was a vampire.